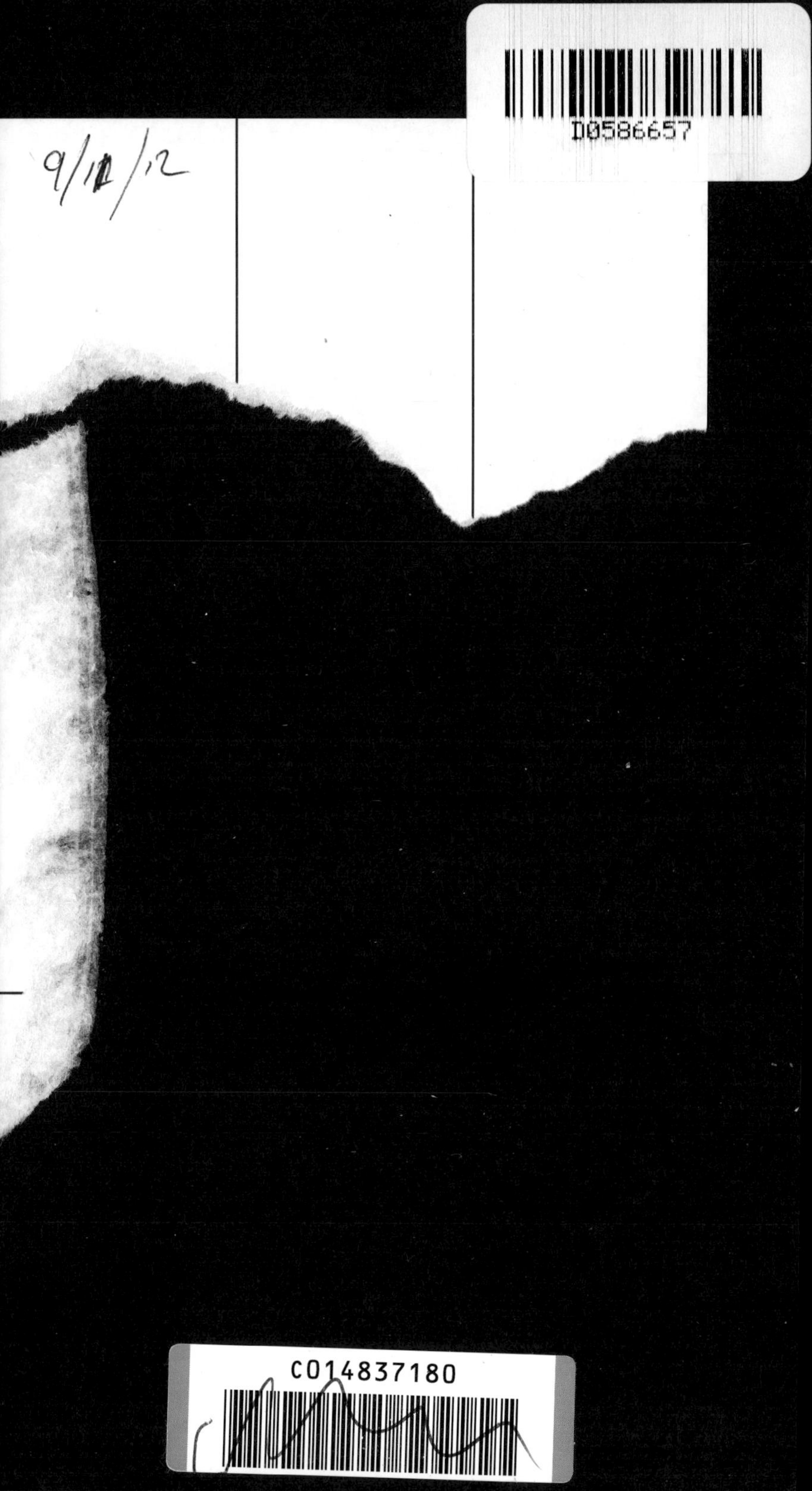

Burned

BY P. C. AND KRISTIN CAST

The House of Night

Marked
Betrayed
Chosen
Untamed
Hunted
Tempted
Burned

A House of Night Novel

P.C. and KRISTIN CAST

Book Seven of the
HOUSE OF NIGHT
Series

www.atombooks.co.uk

ATOM

First published in Great Britain in 2010 by Atom
Reprinted 2010 (twice)

A CIP catalogue record for this book
is available from the British Library.

ISBN 978-1-905654-81-9
C format ISBN 978-1-905654-94-9

Typeset in Minion Pro
Printed in the UK by CPI Mackays, Chatham ME5 8TD

Papers used by Atom are natural, renewable and recyclable products sourced from well-managed forests and certified in accordance with the rules of the Forest Stewardship Council.

Atom
An imprint of
Little, Brown Book Group
100 Victoria Embankment
London EC4Y 0DY

An Hachette UK Company
www.hachette.co.uk

www.atombooks.co.uk

P. C.: This one is for *my* Guardian. I love you.

Kristin: (She means you, "Shawnus.")

ACKNOWLEDGMENTS

P. C.:

This book would not have been possible had three very special men not opened their history, their lives, and their hearts to me. I owe a debt of gratitude to Seoras Wallace, Alain Mac au Halpine, and Alan Torrance. Any errors in my fictionalization and retelling of their Scottish/Irish mythos are mine and mine alone. Warriors, I thank you. In addition: THANK YOU, Denise Torrance, for saving me from all that Clan Wallace testosterone!

While I researched on the Isle of Skye, my home base was the lovely Toravaig House. I'd like to thank the staff there for making my stay so pleasant—even if they couldn't do anything about the rain!

Sometimes I need to go into what my friends and family call my "writer's cave" to finish a book. That was the case with *Burned,* and my cave was made verrrry bearable by Paawan Arora, at the Grand Cayman Ritz Carlton, as well as Heather Lockington and her wonderful staff at the amazing Cotton Tree (www.caymancottontree.com). Thank you, thank you for helping me make Cayman my second home and hiding from the world so I could write and write and write.

I've used a little Gaelic in this book. Yes, it's hard to pronounce (kinda like Cherokee), and there are many different versions of it (again, kinda like Cherokee). With the help of my Scottish expert(s), I've used Gaelic mainly from the ancient Dalriadic and Gallovidian languages from the west coast of Scotland and northeast coast of Ireland. This dialect is commonly referred to as Gal-Gaelic or GalGael. Any mess-ups are mine.

Kristin:

Thanks to Coach Mark with Bootcamp Tulsa and Precision Body Art for helping me feel strong, empowered, and beautiful.

And thank you to The Shawnus for giving me some peace and quiet!

Both:

As always, we appreciate our team at St. Martin's Press: Jennifer Weis, Matthew Shear, Anne Bensson, Anne Marie Tallberg, and the amazing design team that keeps coming up with such fabulous covers! WE HEART SMP!

Thank you to MK Advertising, who does such cool Web site work for www.pccast.net as well as www.houseofnightseries.com.

As always, Kristin and I send our love and thanks to our wonderful agent and friend, Meredith Bernstein. The House of Night would not exist without her.

And, finally, **thank you** to our loyal fans. Y'all are absolutely The Best!

CHAPTER ONE

Kalona

Kalona lifted his hands. He didn't hesitate. There was no doubt whatsoever in his mind about what he had to do. He would not allow anything or anyone to get in his way, and this human boy was standing between him and what he desired. He didn't particularly want to kill the boy; he didn't particularly want the boy alive, either. It was a simple necessity. He didn't feel remorse or regret. As had been the norm during the centuries since he'd fallen, Kalona *felt* very little. So, indifferently, the winged immortal twisted the boy's neck and put an end to his life.

"No!"

The anguish of that one word froze Kalona's heart. He dropped the boy's lifeless body and whirled around in time to see Zoey racing toward him. Their eyes met. In hers were despair and hatred. In his was an impossible denial. He tried to formulate the words that might make her understand—might make her forgive him. But there was nothing he could say to change what she had seen, and even if he could work the impossible, there was no time.

Zoey threw the full power of the element spirit at him.

It hit the immortal, striking him with force that was beyond physical. Spirit was his essence—his core—the element that had sustained him for centuries and with which he had always been most comfortable, as well as most powerful. Zoey's attack seared him. It lifted him with such force that he was hurled over the huge stone wall that separated the vampyres' island and the Gulf of Venice. The icy water engulfed him, smothering him. For an instant the pain within Kalona was so deadening that he didn't fight it. Perhaps he should let this terrible struggle for life and its trappings end. Perhaps, once again, he should allow himself to be vanquished by her. But less than a heartbeat after he had the thought, he *felt* it. Zoey's soul shattered and, as truly as his fall had carried him from one realm to another, her spirit departed this world.

The knowledge wounded him worse than had her blow against him.

Not Zoey! He'd never meant to cause her harm. Even through all of Neferet's machinations, through all of the Tsi Sgili's manipulations and plans, he'd held tight to the knowledge that, in spite of everything, he would use his vast immortal powers to keep Zoey safe because ultimately she was the closest he could come to Nyx in this realm—and this was the only realm left to him.

Fighting to recover from Zoey's attack, Kalona lifted his massive body from the clutching waves and realized the truth. Because of him, Zoey's spirit was gone, which meant she would die. With his first breath of air, he released a wrenching cry of despair, echoing her last word, *"No!"*

Had he really believed since his fall that he didn't truly have feelings? He'd been a fool and wrong, so very wrong. Emotions battered him as he flew raggedly just above the waterline, chipping away at his already wounded spirit, raging against him, weakening him, bleeding his soul. With blurred, blackened vision, he stared across the lagoon, squinting to see the lights that heralded land. He'd never make it there. It would have to be the palace. He had no choice. Using the last reserves of his strength, Kalona's wings beat against the frigid air, lifting him over the wall, where he crumpled to the frozen earth.

He didn't know how long he lay there in the cold darkness of the shattered night as emotions overwhelmed his shaken soul. Somewhere in the far reaches of his mind, he understood the familiarity of what had happened to him. He'd fallen again, only this time it was more in spirit than in body—though his body didn't seem his to command any longer either.

He felt her presence before she spoke. It had been like that between them from the first, whether he truly wished it or not—they simply sensed one another.

"You allowed Stark to bear witness to your killing of the boy!" Neferet's voice was more frigid than the winter sea.

Kalona turned his head so that he could see more than the toe of her stiletto shoe. He looked up at her, blinking to try to clear his vision.

"Accident." Finding his voice again he managed a rasping whisper. "Zoey should not have been there."

"Accidents are unacceptable, and I care not one bit that *she* was there. Actually, the result of what she saw is rather convenient."

"You know that her soul shattered?" Kalona hated the unnatural weakness in his voice and the strange lethargy in his body almost as much as he hated the effect Neferet's icy beauty had on him.

"I imagine most of the vampyres on the island know it. Typically for her, Zoey's spirit wasn't exactly quiet in its leave-taking. I wonder, though, how many of the vampyres also felt the blow the chit dealt you just before she departed." Neferet tapped her chin contemplatively with one long, sharp fingernail.

Kalona remained silent, struggling to center himself and draw together the ragged edges of his torn spirit, but the earth his body pressed against was too real, and he had not the strength to reach above and feed his soul from the wispy vestiges of the Otherworld that floated there.

"No, I don't imagine any of them felt it," Neferet continued, in her coldest, most calculating voice. "None of them are connected to Darkness, *to you,* as I am. Is that not so, my love?"

"We are uniquely connected," Kalona managed, though he suddenly wished the words were not true.

"Indeed . . ." she said, still distracted by her thoughts. Then Neferet's eyes widened as a new realization came to her. "I have long wondered how it was that A-ya managed to wound *you,* such a physically powerful immortal, badly enough that those ridiculous Cherokee hags could entrap you. I believe little Zoey has just provided the answer you've so carefully withheld from me. Your body *can* be damaged but only through your spirit. Isn't that fascinating?"

"I will heal." He put as much strength as possible in his voice.

"Return me to Capri and the castle there. Take me to the rooftop, as close to the sky as I can be, and I will regain my strength."

"I imagine you would—were I so inclined to do that. But I have other plans for you, my love." Neferet lifted her arms, extending them over him. As she continued to speak she began weaving her long fingers through the air, creating intricate patterns, like a spider spinning her web. "I will not allow Zoey to interfere with us ever again."

"A shattered soul is a death sentence. Zoey is no longer any threat to us," he said. With knowing eyes, Kalona watched Neferet. She drew to her a sticky blackness he recognized all too well. He'd spent lifetimes battling that Darkness before he embraced its cold power. It pulsed and fluttered familiarly, restlessly under her fingers. *She shouldn't be able to command Darkness so tangibly.* The thought drifted like the echo of a death knell through his weary mind. *A High Priestess shouldn't have such power.*

But Neferet was no longer merely a High Priestess. She had grown beyond the boundaries of that role some time ago, and she had no trouble controlling the writhing blackness she conjured.

She is becoming immortal, Kalona realized, and with the realization, fear joined regret and despair and anger where they already simmered within the fallen Warrior of Nyx.

"One would think it would be a death sentence," Neferet spoke calmly as she drew more and more of the inky threads to her, "but Zoey has a terribly inconvenient habit of surviving. This time I am going to ensure she dies."

"Zoey's soul also has a habit of reincarnating," he said, purposefully baiting Neferet to try to throw off her focus.

"Then I will destroy her over and over again!" Neferet's concentration only increased with the anger his words evoked. The blackness she spun intensified, writhing with swollen power in the air around her.

"Neferet." He tried to reach her by using her name. "Do you truly understand what it is you are attempting to command?"

Her gaze met his, and, for the first time, Kalona saw the scarlet stain that nested in the darkness of her eyes. "Of course I do. It's what lesser beings call evil."

"I am not a lesser being, and I, too, have called it evil."

"Ah, not for centuries you haven't." Her laughter was vicious. "But it seems lately you've been living too much with shadows from your past instead of reveling in the lovely dark power of the present. I know who is to blame for that."

With a tremendous effort, Kalona pushed himself to a sitting position.

"No. I don't want you to move." Neferet flicked one finger at him, and a thread of darkness snaked around his neck, tightened, and jerked him down, pinning him to the ground again.

"What is it you want of me?" he rasped.

"I want you to follow Zoey's spirit to the Otherworld and be sure none of her *friends*"—she sneered the word—"manage to find a way to coax her to rejoin her body."

Shock jolted through the immortal. "I have been banished by Nyx from the Otherworld. I cannot follow Zoey there."

"Oh, but you are wrong, my love. You see, you always think too literally. Nyx ousted you—you fell—you cannot return. So you have believed for centuries that is that. Well, *you* literally cannot." She sighed dramatically as he stared at her blankly. "Your gorgeous body was banished, that's all. Did Nyx say anything about your immortal soul?"

"She need not say it. If a soul is separated from a body for too long, the body will die."

"But your body isn't mortal, which means it can be separated indefinitely from its soul without dying," she said.

Kalona struggled to keep the terror her words filled him with from his expression. "It is true that I cannot die, but that does not mean I will remain undamaged if my spirit leaves my body for too long." *I could age . . . go mad . . . become a never dying shell of myself . . .* The possibilities swirled through his mind.

Neferet shrugged. "Then you will have to be sure you finish your task soon, so that you may return to your lovely immortal body before it is irreparably damaged." She smiled seductively at him. "I would very much dislike it if anything happened to your body, my love."

"Neferet, don't do this. You are putting into motion things that will require payment, the consequences of which even you will not want to face."

"Do *not* threaten me! I released you from your imprisonment. I loved you. And then I watched you fawn over that simpering teenager. I want her gone from my life! Consequences? I embrace them! I am not the weak, ineffective High Priestess of a rule-following goddess any longer. Don't you understand that? Had you not been so distracted by that child, you would know it without me telling you. I am an immortal, the same as you, Kalona!" Her voice was eerie, amplified with power. "We are perfectly matched. You used to believe that as well, and that is something you will believe again, when Zoey Redbird is no more."

Kalona stared at her, understanding that Neferet was utterly, truly mad, and wondering why that madness only served to feed her power and intensify her beauty.

"So this is what I have decided to do," she continued, speaking methodically. "I am going to keep your sexy, immortal body safely tucked away underground somewhere while your soul travels to the Otherworld and makes sure Zoey does not return here."

"Nyx will never allow it!" The words burst from him before he could stop them.

"Nyx always allows free will. As her former High Priestess, I know without any doubt that she will allow you to choose to travel *in spirit* to the Otherworld," Neferet said slyly. "Remember, Kalona, my true love, if you ensure Zoey's death, you will be removing the last impediment to us reigning side by side. You and I will be powerful beyond imagining in this world of modern marvels. Think of it—we will subjugate humans and bring back the reign of vampyres with all the beauty and passion and limitless power that means. The earth will be ours. We will, indeed, give new life to the glorious past!"

Kalona knew she was playing on his weaknesses. Silently, he cursed himself for allowing her to have learned too much about his deepest desires. He'd trusted her, so Neferet knew that because he wasn't Erebus he could never truly rule beside Nyx in the Otherworld, and he was driven to re-create as much of what he'd lost here in this modern world.

"You see, my love, when you consider it logically, it is only right that you follow Zoey and sever the link between her soul and her body. Doing so simply serves your ultimate desires." Neferet spoke nonchalantly, as if the two of them were discussing the choice of material for her latest gown.

"How am I even to find Zoey's soul?" He tried to match her matter-of-fact tone. "The Otherworld is a realm so vast, only the gods and goddesses can traverse it."

Neferet's bland expression tightened, making her cruel beauty terrible to behold. "Do not pretend you don't have a connection to her soul!" The Tsi Sgili immortal drew a deep breath. In a more reasonable tone, she continued, "Admit it, my love; you could find Zoey even if no one else could. What is your choice, Kalona? To rule on earth at my side, or to remain a slave to the past?"

"I choose to rule. I will always choose to rule," he said without hesitation.

As soon as he spoke, Neferet's eyes changed. The green within them became totally engulfed in scarlet. She turned the glowing orbs on him—holding, entrapping, entrancing. "Then hear me, Kalona, Fallen Warrior of Nyx, by my oath I shall keep your body safe. When Zoey Redbird, fledging High Priestess of Nyx, is no more, I swear to you I will remove these dark chains and allow your spirit to return. Then I will take you to the rooftop of our castle on Capri and let the sky breathe life and strength into you so that you will rule this realm as my consort, my protector, *my Erebus*." As Kalona watched, helpless to stop her, Neferet drew one long, pointed fingernail across the palm of her right hand. Cupping the blood that pooled there, she held her hand up, offering. "By blood I claim this power; by blood I bind this oath." All around her, Darkness stirred and descended on her palm, writhing, shivering, drinking. Kalona could feel the draw of that Darkness. It spoke to his soul with seductive, powerful whispers.

"*Yes!*" The word was a moan torn deep from his throat as Kalona yielded himself to the greedy Darkness.

When Neferet continued, her voice was magnified, swollen with power. "It is your own choice that I have sealed this oath by blood with Darkness, but should you fail me and break it—"

"I will not fail."

Her smile was unworldly in its beauty; her eyes roiled with blood. "If you, Kalona, Fallen Warrior of Nyx, break this oath and fail in my sworn quest to destroy Zoey Redbird, fledgling High Priestess of Nyx, I shall hold dominion over your spirit for as long as you are an immortal."

The answering words came unbidden by him, evoked by the seductive Darkness, which for centuries he'd chosen over Light. "If I fail, you shall hold dominion over my spirit for as long as I am an immortal."

"Thus I have sworn." Again Neferet slashed her palm, creating a bloody X in her flesh. The copper scent wafted to Kalona like smoke rising from fire as she again raised her hand to Darkness. "Thus it shall be!" Neferet's face twisted in pain as Darkness drank from her again, but she didn't flinch—didn't move until the air around her pulsed, bloated with her blood and her oath.

Only then did she lower her hand. Her tongue snaked out, licking the scarlet line and ending the bleeding. Neferet walked to him, bent, and gently placed her hands on either side of his face, much as he had held the human boy before delivering his deathblow. He could feel Darkness thrumming around and within her, a raging bull waiting eagerly for his mistress's command.

Her blood-reddened lips paused just short of touching his. "With the power that rushes through my blood, and by the strength of the lives I have taken, I command you, my delicious threads of Darkness, to pull this Oath Bound immortal's soul from his body and speed him to the Otherworld. Go and do as I order, and I swear I will sacrifice to you the life of an innocent you have been unable to taint. So thee for me, I mote it be!"

Neferet drew in a deep breath, and Kalona saw the dark threads she'd summoned slither between her full, red lips. She inhaled Darkness until she was swollen with it, and then she covered his mouth with hers and, with that blackened, blood-tainted kiss, blew Darkness within him with such force that it ripped his already wounded soul from his body. As his soul shrieked in soundless agony, Kalona was forced up, up, and into the realm from which his Goddess had banished him, leaving his body lifeless, chained, Oath Bound by evil, and at the mercy of Neferet.

CHAPTER TWO

Rephaim

The sonorous drum was like the heartbeat of an immortal: never-ending, engulfing, overwhelming. It echoed through Rephaim's soul in time with the pounding of his blood. Then, to the beat of the drum, the ancient words took form. They wrapped around his body so that even as he slept, his pulse allied itself in harmony with the ageless melody. In his dream, the women's voices sang:

Ancient one sleeping, waiting to arise
When earth's power bleeds sacred red
The mark strikes true; Queen Tsi Sgili will devise
He shall be washed from his entombing bed

The song was seductive, and like a labyrinth, it circled on and on.

Through the hand of the dead he is free
Terrible beauty, monstrous sight
Ruled again they shall be
Women shall kneel to his dark might

The music was a whispered enticement. A promise. A blessing. A curse. The memory of what it foretold made Rephaim's sleeping body restless. He twitched and, like an abandoned child, murmured a one-word question: "Father?"

The melody concluded with the rhyme Rephaim had memorized centuries ago:

Kalona's song sounds sweet
As we slaughter with cold heat

". . . slaughter with cold heat." Even sleeping, Rephaim responded to the words. He didn't awaken, but his heartbeat increased—his hands curled into fists—his body tensed. On the cusp between awake and asleep, the drumbeat stuttered to a halt, and the soft voices of women were replaced by one that was deep and all too familiar.

"*Traitor . . . coward . . . betrayer . . . liar!*" The male voice was a condemnation. With its litany of anger, it invaded Rephaim's dream and jolted him fully into the waking world.

"Father!" Rephaim surged upright, throwing off the old papers and scraps of cardboard he'd used to create a nest around him. "Father, are you here?"

A shimmer of movement caught at the corner of his vision, and he jerked forward, jarring his broken wing as he peered from the depths of the dark, cedar-paneled closet.

"Father?"

His heart knew Kalona wasn't there even before the vapor of light and motion took form to reveal the child.

"*What are you?*"

Rephaim focused his burning gaze on the girl. "Begone, apparition."

Instead of fading as she should have, the child narrowed her eyes to study him, appearing intrigued. "*You're not a bird, but you have wings. And you're not a boy, but you have arms and legs. And your eyes are like a boy's, too, only they're red. So, what are you?*"

Rephaim felt a surge of anger. With a flash of movement that caused white-hot shards of pain to radiate through his body, he leaped from the closet, landing just a few feet before the ghost—predatory, dangerous, defensive.

"I am a nightmare given life, spirit! Go away and leave me in peace before you learn that there are things far worse than death to fear."

At his abrupt movement, the child ghost had taken one small step backward, so that now her shoulder brushed against the low windowpane. But there she halted, still watching him with a curious, intelligent gaze.

"You cried out for your father in your sleep. I heard you. You can't fool me. I'm smart like that, and I remember things. Plus, you don't scare me because you're really just hurt and alone."

Then the ghost of the girl child crossed her arms petulantly over her thin chest, tossed back her long blond hair, and disappeared, leaving Rephaim just as she had named him, hurt and alone.

His fisted hands loosened. His heartbeat quieted. Rephaim stumbled heavily back to his makeshift nest and rested his head against the closet wall behind him.

"Pathetic," he murmured aloud. "The favorite son of an ancient immortal reduced to hiding in refuse and talking to the ghost of a human child." He tried to laugh but failed. The echo of the music from his dream, from his past, was still too loud in the air around him. As was the other voice—the one he could have sworn was that of his father.

He couldn't sit anymore. Ignoring the pain in his arm and the sick agony that was his wing, Rephaim stood. He hated the weakness that pervaded his body. How long had he been here, wounded, exhausted from the flight from the depot, and curled into this box in a wall? He couldn't remember. Had one day passed? Two?

Where was she? She'd said she would come to him in the night. And yet here he was, where Stevie Rae had sent him. It was night, and she hadn't come.

With a sound of self-loathing, he left the closet and his nest, stalking past the windowsill in front of which the girl child had materialized to a door that led to a rooftop balcony. Instinct had driven him up to the second floor of the abandoned mansion, just after dawn, when he'd arrived. At the end of even his great reservoir of strength, he'd thought only of safety and sleep.

But now he was all too awake.

He stared out at the empty museum grounds. The ice that had been falling for days from the sky had stopped, leaving the huge trees that surrounded the rolling hills on which sat the Gilcrease Museum and its abandoned mansion with bent and ruined branches. Rephaim's night vision was good, but he could detect no movement at all outside. The homes that filled the area between the museum and downtown Tulsa were almost as dark as they had been in his postdawn journey. Small lights dotted the landscape—not the great, blazing electricity that Rephaim had come to expect from a modern city. They were only weak, flickering candles—nothing compared to the majesty of the power this world could evoke.

There was, of course, no mystery to what had happened. The lines that carried power to the homes of modern humans had been snapped just as surely as had the ice-burdened boughs of the trees. Rephaim knew that was good for him. Except for the fallen branches and other debris left on the roadways, the streets appeared mostly passable. Had the great electric machine not been broken, people would have flooded these grounds as daily human life resumed.

"The lack of power keeps humans away," he muttered to himself. "But what is keeping *her* away?"

With a sound of pure frustration, Rephaim wrenched open the dilapidated door, automatically seeking open sky as balm to his nerves. The air was cool, and thick with dampness. Low around the winter grass, fog hung in wavy sheets, as if the earth was trying to shroud herself from his eyes.

His gaze lifted, and Rephaim drew a long, shuddering breath. He inhaled the sky. It seemed unnaturally bright in comparison to the darkened city. Stars beckoned him, as did the sharp crescent of a waning moon.

Everything within Rephaim craved the sky. He wanted it under his wings, passing through his dark, feathered body, caressing him with the touch of the mother he'd never known.

His uninjured wing extended itself, stretching more than a grown man's body length beside him. His other wing quivered, and the night air Rephaim had breathed in burst from him in an agonized moan.

Broken! The word seared through his mind.

"No. That is not a certainty." Rephaim spoke aloud. He shook his head, trying to clear away the unusual weariness that was making him feel increasingly helpless—increasingly damaged. "Concentrate!"

Rephaim admonished himself. "It's time I found Father." He still wasn't well, but Rephaim's mind, though weary, was clearer than it had been since his fall. He should be able to detect some trace of his father. No matter how much distance or time separated them, they were tied by blood and spirit and especially by the gift of immortality that had been Rephaim's birthright.

Rephaim looked up into the sky, thinking of the currents of air on which he was so used to gliding. He drew a deep breath, lifted his uninjured arm, and stretched forth his hand, trying to touch those elusive currents and the vestiges of dark Otherworld magick that languished there. "Bring me some sense of him!" He made his plea urgently to the night.

For a moment he believed he felt a flicker of response, far, far off to the east. And then weariness was all he could feel. "Why can I not sense you, Father?" Frustrated and unusually exhausted, he let his hand drop limply to his side.

Unusual weariness . . .

"By all the gods!" Rephaim suddenly realized what had drained his strength and left him a broken shell of himself. He knew what was keeping him from sensing the path his father had taken. "She did this." His voice was hard. His eyes blazed crimson.

Yes, he'd been terribly wounded; but as the son of an immortal, his body should have already begun its repair process. He'd slept—twice since the Warrior had shot him from the sky. His mind had cleared. Sleep should have continued to revive him. Even if, as he suspected, his wing was permanently damaged, the rest of his body should be noticeably better. His powers should have returned to him.

But the Red One had drunk of his blood, *Imprinted with him.* And in doing so, she had disturbed the balance of immortal power within him.

Anger rose to meet the frustration already there.

She'd used him and then abandoned him.

Just like Father had.

"No!" he corrected himself immediately. His father had been driven away by the fledgling High Priestess. He would return when he was able, and then Rephaim would be at his father's side once more. It was the Red One who had used him, then cast him aside.

Why did the very thought of it cause such a curious ache within him? Ignoring the feeling, he raised his face to the familiar sky. He hadn't wanted this Imprint. He'd only saved her because he owed her a life, and he knew all too well that one of the true dangers of this world, as well as the next, was the power of an unpaid life debt.

Well, she had saved him—found him, hidden him, and then released him, but on the depot rooftop, he had returned the debt by helping her escape from certain death. His life debt to her was now paid. Rephaim was the son of an immortal, not a weak human man. He had little doubt he could break this Imprint—this ridiculous byproduct of saving her life. He would use what was left of his strength to wish it away, and then he would truly begin to heal.

He breathed in the night again. Ignoring the weakness in his body, Rephaim focused the strength of his will.

"I call upon the power of the spirit of ancient immortals, which is mine by birthright to command, to break—"

The wave of despair crashed over him, and Rephaim staggered against the balcony's railing. The sadness radiated throughout his body with such force that it drove him to his knees. There he remained, gasping with pain and shock.

What is happening to me?

Next, an odd, alien fear filled him, and Rephaim began to understand.

"These are not my feelings," he told himself, trying to find his own center within the maelstrom of distress. "These are *her* feelings."

Rephaim gasped as hopelessness followed fear. Steeling himself against the continued onslaught, he struggled to stand, fighting the waves of Stevie Rae's emotions. Resolutely, he forced himself to refocus through the onslaught and the weariness that tugged relentlessly at him—to touch the place of power that lay locked and dormant for most of humanity—the place to which his blood held the key.

Rephaim began the invocation anew. This time with an altogether different intent.

Later, he would tell himself that his response had been automatic—that he'd been acting under the influence of their Imprint; it had simply been more powerful than he had expected. It was the damnable Imprint that had caused him to believe that the surest, quickest way to end the horrible wash of emotions from the Red One was to draw her to him and thus remove her from whatever was causing her pain.

It couldn't be that he cared that she was in pain. It could never be that.

"I call upon the power of the spirit of ancient immortals, which is mine by birthright to command." Rephaim spoke quickly. Ignoring the pain in his battered body, he pulled energy to him from the deepest shadows of the night, and then channeled that power through him, charging it with immortality. The air around him glistened as it became stained with a dark scarlet radiance. "Through the immortal might of my father, Kalona, who seeded my blood and spirit with power, I send you to my—" There his words broke off. His? She wasn't *his* anything. She was . . . she was . . . "She is the Red One! Vampyre High Priestess to those who are lost," he finally blurted. "She is attached to me through blood Imprint and through life debt. Go to her. Strengthen her. Draw her to me. By the immortal part of my being, I command it so!"

The red mist scattered off instantly, flying to the south. Back the way he'd come. Back to find her.

Rephaim turned his gaze to look after it. And then he waited.

CHAPTER THREE

Stevie Rae

Stevie Rae woke up feeling like a big ol' pile of poo. Well, actually, she felt like a big ol' pile of stressed-out poo.

She'd Imprinted with Rephaim.

She'd almost burned up on that rooftop.

For a second she remembered the excellent season two *True Blood* episode where Goderick had burned his own self up on a fictional roof. Stevie Rae snorted a laugh. "It looked way easier on TV."

"What did?"

"Sweet weeping puppies, Dallas! You nearly scared me spitless." Stevie Rae clutched at the white, hospital-like sheet that covered her. "What in the Sam Hill are you doin' here?"

Dallas frowned. "Jeez, settle down. I came up here a little after dusk to check on you, and Lenobia told me it'd be okay to sit here for a while in case you woke up. You're awful jumpy."

"I almost *died*. I think I have the right to be a little jumpy."

Dallas looked instantly contrite. He scooted the little side chair closer and took her hand. "Sorry. You're right. Sorry. I was real scared when Erik told everyone what had happened."

"What did Erik say?"

His warm brown eyes hardened. "That you almost burned up on that roof."

"Yeah, it was really stupid. I tripped and fell and hit my head." Stevie Rae had to look away from his gaze while she spoke. "When I woke up, I was almost toast."

"Yeah, bullshit."

"What?"

"Save that load of crap for Erik and Lenobia and the rest of 'em. Those assholes tried to kill you, didn't they?"

"Dallas, I don't know what you're talkin' about." She tried to take her hand from his, but he held tight.

"Hey." His voice softened and he touched her face, pulling her gaze back to his. "It's just me. You know you can tell me the truth, and I'll keep my mouth shut."

Stevie Rae blew out a long breath. "I don't want Lenobia or any of them to know, especially not any of the blue fledglings."

Dallas stared at her a long time before he spoke. "I won't say anything to anyone, but you gotta know I think you're makin' a big mistake. You can't keep protecting them."

"I'm not protectin' 'em!" she protested. This time she held tight to Dallas's safe, warm hand, trying through touch to get him to understand something she could never tell him. "I just want to deal with this—all of this—my own way. If everyone knows they tried to trap me up there, then it'll all be out of my hands." *And what if Lenobia grabs Nicole and her group, and they tell her about Rephaim?* The sickening thought was a guilty whisper through Stevie Rae's mind.

"What are you gonna do about them? You can't just let them get away with this."

"I won't. But they're my responsibility, and I'm gonna take care of them myself."

Dallas grinned. "You're gonna kick their butts, huh?"

"Somethin' like that," Stevie Rae said, clueless about what she was going to do. Then she hastily changed the subject. "Hey, what time is it? I think I'm starving."

Dallas's grin changed to laughter as he stood up. "Now that sounds like my girl!" He kissed her forehead and then turned to the minifridge that was tucked within the metallic shelving across the room. "Lenobia told me there's baggies of blood in here. She said as fast as you've been healing and as deep as you've been sleeping, you'd probably wake up hungry."

While he went for the blood baggies, Stevie Rae sat up and gingerly peeked down the back of her generic hospital gown, wincing a little at how stiff the movement made her feel. She expected the worst. Seriously, her back had been like nasty burned hamburger when Lenobia and Erik had pulled her from the hole she'd made in the earth. Pulled her from Rephaim.

Don't think about him now. Just focus on—

"Ohmygood*ness*," Stevie Rae whispered in awe as she stared at what she could see of her back. It wasn't hamburgered anymore. It was smooth. Bright pink, as if she'd gotten sunburned, but smooth and new-looking, like baby skin.

"That's amazing." Dallas's voice was hushed. "A real miracle."

Stevie Rae looked up at him. Their eyes met and held.

"You scared me good, girl," he said. "Don't do that again, 'kay?"

"I'll try my best not to," she said softly.

Dallas leaned forward and carefully, with just the tips of his fingers, touched the fresh pink skin at the back of her shoulder. "Does it still hurt?"

"Not really. I'm just kinda stiff."

"Amazing," he repeated. "I mean, I know Lenobia said you'd been healing while you were sleepin', but you were hurt real bad, and I just didn't expect anything like—"

"How long have I been asleep?" She cut him off, trying to imagine the consequences of Dallas's telling her she'd been out for days and days. *What would Rephaim think if she didn't show up? Worse—what would he do?*

"It's just been one day."

Relief flooded her. "One day? Really?"

"Yeah, well, dusk was a couple hours ago, so you've technically been sleepin' longer than one day. They brought you back here yesterday after sunrise. It was pretty dramatic. Erik drove the Hummer right across the grounds, knocked down a fence, and floored it straight into Lenobia's barn. Then we all scrambled like crazy to carry you through the school up here to the infirmary."

"Yeah, I talked to Z in the Hummer on the way back here, and I was feelin' almost okay, but then it was like someone turned out the lights on me. I think I passed out."

"I know ya did."

"Well, that's a dang shame." Stevie Rae let herself smile. "I woulda liked seeing all that drama."

"Yeah"—he grinned back at her—"that's exactly what I thought once I got over thinkin' you were gonna die."

"I'm not gonna die," she said firmly.

"Well, I'm glad to hear it." Dallas bent, cupped her chin in his hand, and kissed her tenderly on the lips.

With a strange, automatic reaction, Stevie Rae jerked away from him.

"Uh, how about that blood baggie?" she said quickly.

"Oh, yeah." Dallas shrugged off her rejection, but his cheeks were unnaturally pink when he handed her the bag. "Sorry, I wasn't thinkin'. I know you're hurt, and ya don't feel like, er, well, you know . . ." His voice trailed off, and he looked super uncomfortable.

Stevie Rae knew she should say something. After all, she and Dallas did have a *thing* together. He was sweet and smart, and he proved he understood her by standing there, looking all sorry, and kinda lowering his head in an adorable way that made him look like a little boy. And he was cute—tall and lean, with just the right amount of muscles and thick hair the color of sand. She actually liked kissing him. Or she used to.

Didn't she still?

An unfamiliar sense of unease kept her from finding the words that would make him feel better, so instead of speaking, Stevie Rae took the baggie from him, tore open the corner, and upended it, letting the blood drain down the back of her throat and expand like a mega shot of Red Bull from her stomach to energize the rest of her body.

She didn't want to, but somewhere deep inside her, Stevie Rae weighed the difference between how this normal, mortal, ordinary blood made her feel—and how Rephaim's blood had been like a lightning strike of energy and heat.

Her hand shook only a little when she wiped her mouth and finally looked up at Dallas.

"That better?" he asked, looking unfazed by their strange exchange and like his familiar, sweet self again.

"Could I have one more?"

He smiled and held another baggie out to her. "Already ahead of you, girl."

"Thanks, Dallas." She paused before slurping down the second one. "I don't feel totally one hundred percent right now. Ya know?"

Dallas nodded. "I know."

"We okay?"

"Yep," he said. "If you're okay—we're okay."

"Well, this'll help." Stevie Rae was upending the baggie when Lenobia came in the room.

"Hey, Lenobia—check out Sleeping Beauty finally waking up," Dallas said.

Stevie Rae guzzled the last bloody drop and turned to the door, but the hello smile she'd already put on her face froze at her first glimpse of Lenobia.

The Mistress of Horses had been crying. A lot.

"Ohmygoodness, what is it?" Stevie Rae was so shaken by seeing the usually strong professor in tears that her first reaction was to pat the bed next to her, inviting Lenobia to sit with her, just like her mama used to do when she'd hurt herself and come crying to be fixed.

Lenobia took several wooden steps into the room. She didn't sit on Stevie Rae's bed. She stood at the foot of it and drew a deep breath as if readying herself to do something really terrible.

"Do you want me to go?" Dallas asked hesitantly.

"No. Stay. She might need you." Lenobia's voice was rough and thick with tears. She met Stevie Rae's eyes. "It's Zoey. Something's happened."

A jolt of fear zapped Stevie Rae in the gut, and the words burst from her before she could stop them. "She's fine! I talked to her, remember? When we were leavin' the depot, before all that daylight and pain and stuff caught up to me, and I passed out. That was just yesterday."

"Erce, my friend who serves as assistant to the High Council, has been trying to contact me for hours. I'd foolishly left my phone in the Hummer, so I didn't speak to her until just now. Kalona killed Heath."

"Shit!" Dallas gasped.

Stevie Rae ignored him and stared at Lenobia. *Rephaim's dad had killed Heath!* The sick fear in her gut was getting worse and worse by the second. "Zoey's not dead. I'd know it if she was dead."

"Zoey's not dead, but she saw Kalona kill Heath. She tried to stop him and couldn't. It shattered her, Stevie Rae." Tears had started to leak down Lenobia's porcelain cheeks.

"Shattered her? What does that mean?"

"It means her body still breathes, but her soul is gone. When a High Priestess's soul is shattered, it is only a matter of time before her body fades from this world, too."

"Fades? I don't know what you're talkin' about. Are you tryin' to tell me she's going to disappear?"

"No," Lenobia said raggedly. "She's going to die."

Stevie Rae's head started to shake back and forth, back and forth. "No. No. No! We just gotta get her here. She'll be fine then."

"Even if her body returns here, Zoey isn't coming back, Stevie Rae. You have to prepare yourself for that."

"I won't!" Stevie Rae yelled. "I can't! Dallas, get me my jeans and stuff. I gotta get outta here. I gotta figure out a way to help Z. She didn't give up on me, and I'm not givin' up on her."

"This isn't about you." Dragon Lankford spoke from the open doorway to the infirmary room. His strong face was drawn and haggard with the newness of the loss of his mate, but his voice was calm and sure. "It's about the fact that Zoey faced a grief she could not bear. And I do understand something about grief. When it shatters a soul, the path to return to the body is broken, and without the infilling of spirit, our bodies die."

"No, please. This can't be right. This can't be happening," Stevie Rae told him.

"You are the first red vampyre High Priestess. You have to find the strength to accept this loss. Your people will need you," Dragon said.

"We don't know where Kalona has fled, nor do we know Neferet's role in all of this," Lenobia said.

"What we do know is that Zoey's death would be an excellent time for them to strike against us," Dragon added.

Zoey's death . . . The words echoed through Stevie Rae's mind, leaving behind shock and fear and despair.

"Your powers are vast. The swiftness of your recovery proves that," Lenobia said. "And we will need every power we can harness to meet the darkness I feel certain is going to descend upon us."

"Control your grief," Dragon said. "And take up Zoey's mantle."

"No one can be Zoey!" Stevie Rae cried.

"We're not asking you to be her. We're only asking you to help the rest of us fill the void she leaves," Lenobia said.

"I have—I have to think," Stevie Rae said. "Would y'all leave me alone for a while? I want to get dressed and think."

"Of course," Lenobia said. "We will be in the Council Chamber. Meet us there when you are ready." She and Dragon left the room silently, grief-stricken but resolute.

"Hey, are you okay?" Dallas moved to her, reaching out to take her hand.

She only let him touch her for a moment before she squeezed his hand and withdrew. "I need my clothes."

"I found 'em there in that closet." Dallas jerked his head toward the cabinets on the opposite side of the room.

"Good, thanks," Stevie Rae said quickly. "You gotta leave so I can get dressed."

"You didn't answer my question," he said, watching her closely.

"No. I'm not okay, and I'm not gonna be as long as they keep sayin' Z's gonna die."

"But, Stevie Rae, even I've heard about what happens when a soul leaves a body—the person dies," he said, obviously trying to say the harsh words gently.

"Not this time," Stevie Rae said. "Now go on outta here so I can get dressed.

Dallas sighed. "I'll be waiting outside."

"Fine. I won't take too long."

"Take your time, girl," Dallas said softly. "I don't mind waiting."

But as soon as the door shut, Stevie Rae didn't jump up and throw on her clothes like she'd meant to. Instead her memory was too busy flipping through her *Fledgling Handbook 101* and stopping at a super-sad story about an ancient soul-shattered High Priestess. Stevie Rae couldn't remember what had caused the priestess's soul to shatter—she didn't remember much about the story, actually—except that the High Priestess had died. No matter what anyone had tried to do to save her—the High Priestess had died.

"The High Priestess died," Stevie Rae whispered. And Zoey wasn't even a real, grown High Priestess. She was technically still a fledgling. How could she be expected to find her way back from something that had killed a grown High Priestess?

The truth was, she couldn't.

It wasn't fair! They'd all been through so much hard stuff, and now Zoey was just gonna die? Stevie Rae didn't want to believe it. She wanted to fight and scream and find a way to fix her BFF, but how could she? Z was in Italy and she was in Tulsa. And, hell! Stevie Rae couldn't figure out how to fix a bunch of pain-in-the-ass red fledglings. Who was she to think she could do anything about something as terrible as Z's soul shattering from her body?

She couldn't even tell the truth about being Imprinted with the son of the creature who had caused this awful thing to happen.

Sadness swept over Stevie Rae. She crumpled in on herself, hugged the pillow to her chest, and, twirling a blond curl around and around her finger like she used to do when she was little, began to weep. The sobs wracked her, and she buried her face in the pillow so Dallas wouldn't hear her crying, losing herself to shock and fear and complete, overwhelming despair.

Just as she was giving in to the worst of it, the air around her stirred. Almost as if someone had cracked the window in the small room.

At first she ignored it, too lost in her tears to care about a stupid cold breeze. But it was insistent. It touched the fresh, pink skin of her exposed back in a cool caress that was surprisingly pleasant. For a moment she relaxed, allowing herself to absorb comfort from the touch.

Touch? She'd told him to wait outside!

Stevie Rae's head shot up. Her lips were pulled back from her teeth in a snarl she meant to aim at Dallas.

No one was in the room.

She was alone. Absolutely alone.

Stevie Rae dropped her face in her hands. Was shock making her go totally batshit crazy? She didn't have time for crazy. She had to get up and get dressed. She had to put one foot in front of the other and go out there and deal with the truth about what had happened to Zoey, and her red fledglings, and Kalona, and, eventually, Rephaim.

Rephaim . . .

His name echoed in the air, another cold caress against her skin, wrapping around her. Not just touching her back but skimming down the length of her arms and swirling around her waist and over her legs. And everywhere the coolness touched, it was like a little bit of her grief had been washed away. This time when she looked up she was more controlled in her reaction. She wiped her eyes clear and stared down at her body.

The mist that surrounded her was made of tiny sparkling drops that were the exact color she'd come to recognize in his eyes.

"Rephaim." Against her will, she whispered his name.

He calls you . . .

"What the hell is going on?" Stevie Rae muttered, anger stirring through despair.

Go to him . . .

"Go to him?" she said, feeling increasingly pissed off. "His dad caused this."

Go to him . . .

Letting the tide of cool caress and red anger make her decision, Stevie Rae yanked on her clothes. She would go to Rephaim, but only because he might know something that she could use to help Zoey. He was the son of a dangerous and powerful immortal. Obviously, he had abilities she didn't know about. The red stuff that was floating around her was definitely from him, and it must be made of some kind of spirit.

"Fine," she said aloud to the mist. "I'll go to him."

The instant she spoke the words aloud, the red haze evaporated, leaving only a lingering coolness on her skin and a strange, otherworldly sense of calm.

I'll go to him, and if he can't help me, then I think—Imprint or no Imprint—I'm going to have to kill him.

CHAPTER FOUR

Aphrodite

"Seriously, Erce, I'm only going to say this one more time. I don't care about your stupid rules. Zoey is in there." Aphrodite paused and pointed one well-manicured fingernail at the closed stone door. "And that means *I'm* going *in there.*"

"Aphrodite, you are a human—one who isn't even the consort of a vampyre. You cannot simply burst into the High Council Chamber with all of your youthful, mortal hysteria, especially during a time of crisis such as this." The vampyre's cool look took in Aphrodite's messed-up hair, tear-stained face, and reddened eyes. "The Council will invite you to join them. Probably. Until then, you must wait."

"I am not hysterical." Aphrodite spoke the words slowly, distinctly, and with forced calm, attempting to totally make up for the fact that the reason she'd been left outside the High Council Chamber when Stark, followed by Darius, Damien, the Twins, and even Jack, had carried Zoey's lifeless body inside was entirely because she had been exactly what Erce had called her—a hysterical human. She hadn't been able to keep up with the rest of them, especially since she'd been crying so hard the snot and tears had kept her from doing much breathing or seeing. By the time she'd pulled herself together, the door had been closed in her face, with Erce acting as fucking gatekeeper.

But Erce was super wrong if she thought Aphrodite didn't know how to handle a stick-up-her-ass bossy adult. She'd been raised by a woman who made Erce look like Mary Fucking Poppins.

"So you think I'm just a human kid, do you?" Aphrodite got all into the vamp's personal space, which made Erce take an automatic step back. "Think again. I'm a prophetess of Nyx. Remember her? Nyx—as in *your Goddess who is the boss of you.* I do *not* need to be some guy's refrigerator to have the right to go before the High Council. Nyx herself gave me the right. Now move the hell out of my way!"

"Though she could have phrased it more politely, the child makes a valid point, Erce. Let her pass. I'll take responsibility for her presence if the Council disapproves."

Aphrodite felt the small hairs along her forearms lift as Neferet's smooth voice came from behind her.

"It is not customary," Erce said, but her capitulation was already obvious.

"Neither is it customary for the soul of a fledgling to be shattered," said Neferet.

"I must agree with you, Priestess." Erce stepped aside and opened the thick stone door. "And you are now responsible for this human's presence in the Chamber."

"Thank you, Erce. That is gracious of you. Oh, and I am having a few of the Council Warriors deliver something here. Be quite sure to allow them to pass, too, would you please?"

Aphrodite didn't so much as glance back as Erce murmured a predictable, "Of course, Priestess." Instead, she strode into the ancient building.

"Isn't it odd that once again we are allies, child?" Neferet's voice followed close behind her.

"We'll never be allies, and I'm not a child," Aphrodite said without looking at her or slowing down. The entry foyer opened to a huge stone amphitheater that spread around her in circular row after row. Aphrodite's eyes were drawn up immediately to the stained-glass window directly before her that depicted Nyx, framed by a brilliant pentagram, graceful arms upraised and cupping a crescent moon.

"It's really lovely, isn't it?" Neferet's voice was easy and conversational. "Vampyres have always been responsible for creating the greatest works of art in the world."

Aphrodite still refused to look at the ex–High Priestess. Instead, she shrugged. "Vamps have money. Money buys pretty things, whether they're made by humans or nonhumans. And you don't know for sure that vamps made that window. I mean, you're old, but not *that* old." As Aphrodite tried to ignore Neferet's soft, condescending laughter, her gaze moved down to the center of the chamber. At first she didn't really comprehend what she was seeing, and then when she got it, it was as if someone had punched her in the gut.

There were seven carved marble thrones on the huge raised platform that made up the inner floor of the chamber. Vampyres were seated in the thrones, but they weren't what caught Aphrodite's gaze. What she couldn't stop staring at was Zoey, lying on the dais in front of the thrones like a dead body stretched out on a funeral slab. And then there was Stark. He was on his knees beside Zoey. He was turned just enough so that Aphrodite could see his face. He didn't make one sound, but tears were falling freely down his cheeks and pooling on his shirt. Darius was standing next to him, and he was saying something she couldn't quite hear to the brunette sitting in the first throne whose thick hair was streaked with gray. Damien, Jack, and the Twins were huddled together, typically sheeplike, in a nearby row of stone benches. They were bawling, too, but their loud, messy tears were as different from Stark's silent misery as was the ocean from a babbling brook.

Aphrodite automatically started forward, but Neferet grabbed her wrist. And that finally made her turn to look at her old mentor.

"You really should let go of me," Aphrodite said softly.

Neferet raised one brow. "Have you finally learned to stand up to a mother figure?"

Aphrodite let the anger burn quietly within her. "You are no one's mother figure. I learned to stand up to bitches a long time ago."

Neferet frowned and let loose her wrist. "I've never liked your coarse language."

"I'm not *coarse*; I'm *real*. Two different things. And you think I fucking care what you like or dislike?" Neferet took a breath to respond, but Aphrodite cut her off. "Just what the hell are you doing here?"

Neferet blinked in surprise. "I am here because there is a wounded fledgling here."

"Oh, that's such shit! You're only here because somehow it's gonna get you something you want. That's how you work, Neferet, whether they know it or not." Aphrodite jerked her chin at the High Council members.

"Be careful, Aphrodite. You may need me in the very near future."

Aphrodite held Neferet's gaze and felt a sense of shock as she realized the eyes that met hers had changed. They were no longer brilliant emerald green. They had darkened. *Was that red that glowed from deep in the middle of them?* As quickly as the thought came to Aphrodite, Neferet blinked. Her eyes cleared and were once again the color of expensive gemstones.

Aphrodite drew a shaky breath, and the small hairs on her arms lifted again, but her voice was flat and sarcastic when she said, "That's okay. I'll take my chances without your 'help.'" She air quoted around the last word.

"Neferet, the Council recognizes you!"

Neferet turned to face the Council, but before she descended the stairs to them, she paused and made a graceful gesture, which included Aphrodite.

"I ask that the Council allow the presence of this human. She is Aphrodite, the child who makes claims of being Nyx's Prophetess."

Aphrodite stepped around Neferet and looked squarely from one Council member to another. "I don't *claim* to be a prophetess. I am Nyx's Prophetess because the Goddess wants me to be. The truth is, if I had a choice about it, I wouldn't want the job." She kept speaking even though several of the Council members had gasped in shock. "Oh, and just FYI: I'm not telling you anything Nyx doesn't already know."

"The Goddess believes in Aphrodite even though she is not quite as sure about herself," Darius said.

Aphrodite smiled at him. He was more than her big, hot, mountainlike Warrior. She could count on Darius; he always saw the best in her.

"Darius, why do you speak for this human?" asked the brunette.

"Duantia, I speak for this *Prophetess*," he enunciated her title carefully, "because I have pledged myself to her as her Warrior."

"Her Warrior?" Neferet couldn't keep the shock from her voice. "But that means . . ."

"That means that I can't be completely human because it's impossible for a vampyre Warrior to swear an Oath Bond with a human," Aphrodite finished for her.

"You may enter the Chamber, Aphrodite, Prophetess of Nyx. The Council recognizes you," proclaimed Duantia.

Aphrodite hurried down the stairway, leaving Neferet to follow behind her. She wanted to go straight to Zoey, but instinct made her stop in front of the brunette named Duantia first. She formally fisted her hand, pressed it over her heart, and bowed respectfully. "Thank you for letting me come in here."

"These extraordinary times call for us to accept unusual practices." This came from a tall, thin vampyre who had eyes the color of night.

Aphrodite wasn't sure what to say to the vamp, so she just nodded and moved to Zoey. She slid her hand in Darius's and squeezed hard, trying to borrow some of her Warrior's amazing strength. Then she looked down at her friend.

She hadn't imagined it. Zoey's tattoos really were gone! The only Mark left on her was an ordinary-looking crescent-moon outline in sapphire in the middle of her forehead. And she was so damn pale! *Zoey looks dead.* Aphrodite stopped the thought immediately. Zoey wasn't dead. She was still breathing. Her heart was still beating. Zoey. Was. Not. Dead.

"Does the Goddess reveal anything to you when you look at her, Prophetess?" asked the tall, thin woman who had spoken to her before.

Aphrodite dropped Darius's hand and slowly knelt next to Zoey. She glanced at Stark then, as he was kneeling directly across Z from her, but he didn't move. He hardly blinked. All he did was weep silently and stare at Zoey. *Is this what Darius would be like if something happened to me?* Aphrodite shook away the morbid thought and refocused on Zoey. Slowly, she reached out and rested her hand on her friend's shoulder.

Her skin was cool to the touch, as if she were already dead. Aphrodite waited for something to happen. But she got not even the slightest twinge of a vision or a feeling or anything.

With a sigh of frustration, Aphrodite shook her head. "No. I can't tell anything. I can't control my visions. They just hit me, whether I want them to or not, and the truth is, it's usually a case of not."

"You aren't using all of the gifts Nyx has given you, Prophetess."

Surprised, Aphrodite looked up from Zoey to see the dark-eyed vampyre had risen, and was gracefully approaching her.

"You are a true Prophetess of Nyx, are you not?" she asked.

"Yeah, I am," Aphrodite said with no hesitation, but with equal parts confusion and conviction.

In a flutter of silk robes the color of the night sky, the woman knelt beside Aphrodite. "I am Thanatos. Do you know what my name means?"

Aphrodite shook her head, wishing Damien was sitting closer so she could peek at him for the answer.

"It means death. I am not Leader of the Council. Duantia has that honor, but I have the unique privilege of being unusually close to our Goddess, as the gift she gave me long ago was the ability to aid souls as they pass from this world to the next."

"You can talk to ghosts?"

Thanatos's smile transformed her stern face and made her almost pretty. "In a fashion, yes, I can. And because of that gift, I know something of visions."

"Seriously? Visions aren't anything like talking to ghosts."

"Are they not? From what realm do your visions come? No, perhaps more accurately, in what realm do you exist when you receive your visions?"

Aphrodite thought about how she'd had too many damn death visions and how she'd started actually seeing the shit that was happening from the dead *people's* points of view. She drew in a fast breath, and in a rush of understanding admitted, "I'm getting visions from the Otherworld!"

Thanatos nodded. "You traffic with the Otherworld and the realm of spirits much more than I, Prophetess. All I do is guide the dead as they transition, and through them I glimpse Beyond."

Aphrodite looked hastily down at Zoey. "She is *not* dead."

"Not yet, no. But her body will not last more than seven days in this soulless state, so she is close to death. Close enough that the Otherworld has a strong hold on her, stronger even than it has on the newly dead. Touch her again, Prophetess. This time focus and use more of the gifts you've been given."

"But I—"

Annoyingly enough, Thanatos cut her off. "Prophetess, do what Nyx would want you to do."

"I don't know what that is!"

Thanatos's stern expression relaxed, and she smiled again. "Oh, child, simply ask for her help."

Aphrodite blinked. "Just like that?"

"Yes, Prophetess, exactly like that."

Slowly, Aphrodite placed her hand back on Zoey's cold shoulder. This time she closed her eyes and drew three long, deep breaths, just like she'd watched Zoey do before casting a circle. Then she sent a silent but fervent prayer up to Nyx: *I wouldn't ask if it wasn't important, but you know that already because you know I don't like to ask for favors. Not from anyone. Plus, I'm not really good at this supplication bullshit, but you already know that also.* Aphrodite sighed internally. *Nyx, I need your help. Thanatos seems to think I have some kind of link to the Otherworld. If that's true, could you please let me know what's happening to Zoey?* She paused in her silent prayer, sighed, and bared herself to Nyx. *Goddess, please. And not just because Zoey's like the sister my mom was too selfish to have. I need your help with this because so many people depend on Zoey, and, sadly, that is more important than me.*

Aphrodite felt a warmth begin to build under her palm, and then it was like she'd slipped from her own body and slid into Zoey's. She was only within her friend for a moment—no longer than one heartbeat—but what she felt and saw and *knew* shocked her so badly that, in the next instant, she found herself back in her own body. She cradled the hand she'd been pressing against Zoey to her chest, gasping with fear. Then, with a moan, she doubled up with vertigo, dry heaving while tears and spit spewed from her face.

"What is it, Prophetess? What did you see?" Thanatos asked calmly as she wiped Aphrodite's cheeks and steadied her with a strong hand around her waist.

"She's gone!" Aphrodite bit back the sob and began pulling herself together. "I felt what happened to her. Just for a second. Zoey threw the full power of spirit at Kalona. She tried to stop him with everything inside her, and it didn't work. Heath died in front of her. That ripped her spirit to pieces." Feeling weirdly light-headed, she looked hopelessly through her tears at Thanatos. "You know where she is, too, don't you?"

"I believe I do. You must confirm it, though."

"The pieces of her spirit are with the dead in the Otherworld," Aphrodite said, blinking hard against the stinging of her red-tinged eyes. "Zoey is completely gone. What happened out there, she just couldn't handle it—she still can't."

"You saw nothing more? Nothing that might help Zoey?"

Aphrodite swallowed back rising bile, and lifted her trembling hand. "No, but I'll try again and—"

Darius's touch on her shoulder held her back from touching Zoey.

"No. You're still too weak from the breaking of your Imprint with Stevie Rae."

"That doesn't matter. Zoey's dying!"

"It matters. Do you want your soul to become as Zoey's?" Thanatos said quietly.

Aphrodite felt a stab of new terror. "No," she whispered, and covered Darius's hand with her own.

"And this is exactly why it is often unfortunate that the young are given great gifts by our loving Goddess. They rarely have the maturity to know how to use them wisely," Neferet said.

At the sound of Neferet's cool, patronizing voice, Aphrodite saw a jolt go through Stark's body, and his gaze finally lifted from Zoey.

"This *creature* shouldn't be allowed in here! She did this! She killed Heath and shattered Zoey!" Stark sounded like he had to grind the words around gravel to speak them.

Neferet shot him a cool look. "I realize you are under duress, but you cannot be allowed to speak to a High Priestess in that fashion, Warrior."

Stark surged to his feet. Darius, lightning fast as always, held him back. Aphrodite heard him whisper urgently, "Think before you act, Stark!"

"Warrior," Duantia addressed Stark, "you were present when the human boy was killed, and Zoey's soul shattered. You have borne witness to us that it was the winged immortal who did the deed. You said nothing of Neferet."

"Ask any of Zoey's friends. Call Lenobia and Dragon Lankford at the Tulsa House of Night. All of them will tell you Neferet doesn't have to be physically present to cause someone's death," Stark said. He shook off Darius's restraining hand and swiped angrily at his face as if he just noticed he'd been crying.

"Sh-she can make really horrendous things happen even when she's not there," Damien spoke up hesitantly from across the room. The Twins and Jack tearfully but forcefully nodded their support.

"There is no proof that Neferet had a hand in this deed," Duantia said gently to all of them.

"Can't you tell what happened to Heath? Couldn't you talk to his ghost or whatever and find out?" Aphrodite asked Thanatos, who had returned to her throne when Neferet had begun to speak.

"The human's spirit did not tarry in this realm, and before it departed, it certainly didn't seek me out," Thanatos said.

"Where's Kalona!" Stark ignored everyone else and shouted at Neferet. "Where are you hiding your lover, who caused this?"

"If you mean my immortal consort, Erebus, that is exactly why I have come to the Council." Neferet turned her back to Stark and spoke only to the seven Council members. "I, too, felt Zoey's soul shatter. I had been walking the labyrinth and mentally preparing myself to depart San Clemente Island for what might be a very long time."

Neferet had to pause because Stark snorted sarcastically, and said, "You and Kalona plan to take over the world from Capri. So, no, you probably won't be returning here in the near future unless you mean to drop bombs on the place."

Darius touched his shoulder again in a silent warning to be careful, but Stark shook him off.

"I do not deny that Erebus and I wish to bring back the ancient days, when vampyres ruled from Capri, and the world revered and respected us, as is our due," Neferet began by addressing him. "But I would not destroy this island or this Council. In truth, I wish for its support."

"You mean its *power*, and now that Zoey's out of the way, you have a better chance of getting that," Stark said.

"Really? Did I misunderstand what passed between your Zoey and my Erebus earlier today in this very Council Chamber? She admitted he was an immortal seeking a goddess to serve."

"She never named him as Erebus!" Stark shouted.

"And my immortal Erebus kindly named her as fallible instead of a liar," Neferet said.

"So what did you do, Neferet? Force him to kill Heath and shatter Zoey's soul because you were jealous of the bond between them?" Stark said, though it was obvious to Aphrodite that it was tough for him to admit there had been so much between Zoey and Kalona.

"Of course not! Use your mind and not your pathetic broken heart, Warrior! Could Zoey have forced you to kill an innocent for her? Of course she couldn't. You're her Warrior, but you still have free will, and you're still bound to Nyx, so you must ultimately do the Goddess's will." Without allowing Stark to speak, she turned back to the Council. "As I was explaining, I felt Zoey's soul shatter and was returning to the palace when I came upon Erebus. He was badly wounded and barely conscious. There was only time for him to say these words: 'I was protecting my Goddess,' and then he was gone."

"Kalona's dead?" Aphrodite couldn't stop herself from blurting.

Instead of answering her, Neferet turned to look up at the entrance to the Chamber. Standing there were four Council Warriors carrying between them a litter that sagged with the weight of its occupant. One black wing spilled over the side of the litter and dragged on the floor.

"Bring him forward!" Neferet commanded.

Slowly, they descended the steps until they laid the litter on the floor in front of the dais. Stark and Darius automatically moved together to stand between Zoey's body and Kalona.

"Of course he isn't dead. He is Erebus, an immortal," Neferet began in her familiar, haughty voice, but then she broke, and on a sob said, "He isn't dead, but as you can all see, he's *gone*!"

Almost as if she couldn't control herself, Aphrodite stood and approached Kalona. Darius was beside her in an instant.

"No. Do not touch him," he warned.

"Whether we call him Erebus or not, it is obvious that this being is an ancient immortal. Because of the power in his blood, the Prophetess will not be able to enter his body, even if his spirit is not present. He doesn't hold the same danger for her Zoey does, Warrior," Thanatos said.

"I'm okay. Let me try and see what I can find out," Aphrodite told Darius.

"I'm right here with you. I'm not going to let go of you," he said, taking her hand and walking with her to Kalona.

Aphrodite could feel the tension radiating through her Warrior's body, but she drew three more long, deep breaths and concentrated on Kalona. Hesitating for only an instant, Aphrodite reached out and placed her hand on his shoulder, just as she'd done for Zoey. His skin was so cold to the touch that she had to force herself not to pull away. Instead, Aphrodite closed her eyes. *Nyx? One more time, please. Just let me know something . . . anything to help all of us.* Then Aphrodite's silent prayer finished with the thought that solidified her bond with the Goddess and finally made her truly a Prophetess in her own right. *Please use me as a tool to help fight the darkness and to follow your path.*

Her palm warmed, but Aphrodite didn't need to sink into him to tell Kalona was gone. Darkness told her—and with a jolt she realized she should think of it as a capital D. This was a thing in its own right—an entity vast and powerful and living. It was everywhere. It encompassed the immortal's entire body. Aphrodite got a very clear image of an inky web, like that spun by a swollen, invisible spider. Its sticky black threads were woven all around his body—holding it—caressing it—binding it tightly, as if in a twisted version of safekeeping because it was obvious the immortal's body was imprisoned—just as obvious as the fact that what was inside of his body was complete emptiness.

Aphrodite gasped and took her hand quickly from his skin, rubbing it against her thigh as if the black web had tainted her, too. She fell against Darius as her knees gave way.

"It's just like the inside of Zoey," she said, as her Warrior lifted her in his arms, purposefully not disclosing that Kalona's body was basically being held hostage. "He's not here anymore, either."

CHAPTER FIVE

Zoey

"Zo, you have to wake up. Please! Wake up and talk to me."

The guy's voice was nice. I knew he was cute before I opened my eyes. Then I did open my eyes and smiled up at him 'cause I had definitely been right. He was, as my BFF Kayla would say, "a hottie covered with awesome sauce." Okay, yum! Even though my head was kinda fuzzy, I felt warm and happy. My smile turned into a grin. "I'm awake. Who are you?"

"Zoey, stop playing around. It's not funny."

The kid frowned down at me, and I realized all of a sudden that I was lying across his lap in his arms. I sat up fast and scooted a little away from him. I mean, yeah, he was super cute and all, but being in some stranger's lap was pretty much outside my comfort zone.

"Uh, I'm not trying to be funny."

His cute face went all still and shocked. "Zo, are you telling me you really don't know who I am?"

"Okay, look. You know I don't know who you are. Even though I know it sounds like you know me." I paused, confused by all the "knows."

"Zoey, do you know who you are?"

I blinked. "That's a silly question. Of course I know who I am. I'm Zoey." It's a good thing the kid was cute because obviously he wasn't the brightest Crayola in the pack.

"Do you know *where* you are?" His voice was gentle, almost hesitant.

I looked around. We were sitting on some really nice soft grass beside a dock that led out to a lake that looked like glass in the gorgeous morning sunlight.

Sunlight?

That was wrong.

Something was wrong.

I swallowed hard and met the guy's gentle brown eyes. "Tell me your name."

"Heath. I'm Heath. You know me, Zo. You'll always know me."

I did know him.

Flashes of him blinked through my memory like fast-forwarded DVDs: Heath telling me my hacked-off hair looked cute in third grade—Heath saving me from that giant spider that fell on me in front of the entire sixth grade—Heath kissing me for the first time after the football game in eighth grade—Heath drinking too much and pissing me off—me Imprinting with Heath . . . and then Imprinting again, and finally me watching as Heath—

"Oh, Goddess!" My memories coalesced and I remembered. *I remembered.*

"Zo"—he pulled me back into his arms—"it's okay. It's going to be okay."

"How is it going to be okay?" I sobbed. "You're dead!"

"Zo, babe, it's just what happens. I wasn't really scared, and it didn't even hurt too much." He rocked me slowly and patted my back as he spoke to me in his calm, familiar voice.

"But I remember! I remember!" I couldn't stop myself from unattractively snot crying. "Kalona killed you. I saw it. Oh, Heath, I tried to stop him. I really, really did."

"Shhh, babe, shhh. I know you did. There was nothing you could have done. I called you to me, and you came. You did good, Zo. You did good. Now you have to go back and stand up to him and Neferet. Neferet killed those two vamps from your school, that drama teacher you had and that other guy."

"Loren Blake?" Shock was drying my tears, and I wiped my face. Heath, as usual, pulled a wad of Kleenex out of his jeans pocket. I stared at them for a second and then surprised both of us by cracking up. "You brought nasty used Kleenex to heaven? Seriously?" I giggled.

He looked offended. "Zo. They so aren't used. Well, at least not much."

I shook my head at him and gingerly took the wad, wiping my face.

"Blow your nose, too. You have snot. You always have snot when you cry. That's why I always have Kleenex."

"Oh, be quiet! I don't cry that much," I said, momentarily forgetting he was dead and all.

"Yeah, but when you do, you snot a lot, so I need to be prepared."

I stared at him as reality smacked me again. "Then what happens when you're not there to give me snot rags?" A sob escaped from my throat. "And—and not there to remind me what home is like, what love is like? What being human is like?" I was bawling again, big-time.

"Oh, Zo. You'll figure that all out on your own. You have lots of time. You're a big-deal vamp High Priestess. Remember?"

"I don't want to be," I told him with complete honesty. "I want to be Zoey and be here with you."

"That's just part of you. Hey, maybe it's part of you that needs to grow up." He spoke gently in a voice that sounded suddenly too old and wise for my Heath.

"No." As I said the word, I saw a skittering, inky darkness slide past the edge of my vision. My stomach tightened, and I thought I caught the sharp shape of horns.

"Zo, you can't change the past."

"No," I repeated, and looked away from Heath, peering into what had just moments before been a beautiful, bright meadow framing a perfect lake. This time I definitely saw shadows and figures where there had been nothing but sunlight and butterflies before.

The darkness within the shadows scared me, but the figures that were also within them drew me like bright things draw babies. Eyes flashed within the intensifying gloom, and I caught a good look at one pair of them. I felt a jolt of recognition. They reminded me of someone . . .

"I know someone out there."

Heath took my chin in his hand and forced me to look from the shadows to him. "Zo, I don't think it's a good idea for you to gawk around here. You just need to make up your mind to go home and then click your heels together, or do some kind of High Priestess extra-special-zapping-magick-stuff and get back to the real world where you belong."

"Without you?"

"Without me. I'm dead," he said softly, stroking the side of my cheek with fingers that felt all too alive. "I'm supposed to be here; actually, I kinda think this is just the first step of where I'm supposed to be. But you're still alive, Zo. You don't belong here."

I pulled my face from his hand and lurched away from him, standing up and shaking my head, making my hair fly around me like a crazy woman. "No! I won't go back without you!"

Another shadow caught my eye from what was now a dark, writhing mist that surrounded us, and I was sure I saw the sharp glint of pointed horns. Then the mist boiled again, and a shadow took on a more human form, peering at me from out of the darkness. "I know you," I whispered to the eyes that were so much like mine, only they looked older and sadder—a lot sadder.

Then another shape took her place. These eyes met mine, too, only they weren't sad. They were taunting and blue, but that didn't erase their familiarity.

"You . . ." I whispered, trying to pull myself from Heath's arms, which were holding me tightly against his body.

"Don't look. Just pull yourself together and go home, Zo."

But I couldn't stop looking. Something inside compelled me. I saw another face framed by eyes I knew—and this time I knew them well enough that the knowledge lent me strength, and I pulled away from Heath, turning him so he could see where I pointed into the gloom. "Holy crap, Heath! Look at that. It's me!"

And it was. The "me" froze as we stared at each other. She was probably about nine years old, and she blinked up at me in terrified silence.

"Zoey. Look at me." Heath wrenched me around, holding my

shoulders in a grip that I knew would cause bruises later. "You have to get out of here."

"But that's *me* as a kid."

"I think all of them are you—pieces of you. Something's happened to your soul, Zoey, and you gotta get out of here so that it can get fixed."

Suddenly I felt dizzy and sagged in his arms. I don't know how I knew, but I did. The words I spoke were as true and as final as his death. "I can't leave, Heath. Not unless all those pieces of me are *me* again. And I don't know how to make that happen—I just don't know!"

Heath pressed his forehead against mine. "Well, Zo, maybe you should try using that annoying mom voice you used on me when I drank too much and tell them to, I dunno, to stop all this bullpoopie and get back inside you where they belong."

He sounded so much like me that he almost made me smile. Almost.

"But if I'm back together, I'll have to leave here. I can feel it, Heath," I whispered to him.

"If you don't put yourself back together, you won't ever leave here because you're gonna die, Zo. I can feel that."

I looked into his warm, familiar eyes. "Would that be so bad? I mean, this place seems a lot better than the mess that's waiting for me back in the real world."

"No, Zoey." Heath sounded pissed. "It's not okay here. Not for you."

"Well, maybe that's 'cause I'm not dead. Yet." I swallowed and admitted, only to myself, that saying it out loud did sound kinda scary.

"I think there's more to it than that."

Heath wasn't looking at me anymore. He was staring over my shoulder, and his eyes had gone all big and round. I turned around. The writhing figures that looked uncomfortably like bizarre, unfinished versions of me were hovering in and out of the black mist, milling and chattering and basically acting weirdly super nervous. Then there was a flash of light that turned into a huge set of dangerous, pointed horns, and with a terrible flapping noise, something descended on that end of the meadow, causing those spirits, those ghosts, those incomplete pieces of me to begin to scream and scream and scream while they scattered and disappeared before it.

"What happens now?" I asked Heath, trying—unsuccessfully—to keep the terror from my voice as we started backing across the meadow.

Heath took my hand and squeezed. "I don't know, but I'll be here with you through all of it. And right now," he whispered in a voice filled with tension, "don't look behind you, just come with me and *run*!"

For one of the few times in my life, I didn't argue with him. I didn't question him. I did exactly what he said. I held on to Heath and ran.

CHAPTER SIX

Stevie Rae

"Stevie Rae, this isn't a good idea," Dallas said as he hurried to keep up with her.

"I'm not gonna be gone long, promise," she said, stopping as she got to the parking lot and looked around for Zoey's little blue car. "Ha! There it is, and she always leaves the keys in it, 'cause the doors don't lock anyway." Stevie Rae jogged up to the Bug, opened the creaky door, and gave a victory shout when she saw the keys dangling from the ignition.

"Seriously, I wish you'd come to the Council Chamber with me and tell the vamps what you're up to, even if you won't tell me. Get their opinion about what's goin' on inside that head of yours, girl."

Stevie Rae turned to Dallas. "Well, that's the problem. I'm not sure what I'm doin'. And, Dallas, I wouldn't tell a bunch of vamps stuff I wouldn't tell you first, you gotta know that."

Dallas rubbed a hand down his face. "I used to know that, but a lot's happened fast, and you're actin' weird."

She put her hand on his shoulder. "I just have a feelin' that there might be somethin' I can do to help Zoey, but I'm not gonna figure that out sittin' up there in that room with a bunch of uptight vamps. I need to be out *here*." Stevie Rae spread her arms, taking in the earth around them. "I need to use my element to think. It seems there's somethin' that I'm missing, but the understanding of it is just outside my reach. I'm gonna use earth to help me make that reach."

"Can't you do that from here? There's lots of nice earth all over the school."

Stevie Rae made herself smile at him. She hated lying to Dallas, but then again, she wasn't really lying. She was really going to see if she could figure out a way to help Z, and she couldn't do that at the House of Night. "There're too many distractions here."

"Okay, look, I know I can't stop you from going, but I need you to promise me something, or I'm gonna make an ass outta myself by actually tryin' to stop you."

Stevie Rae's eyes widened, and this time she didn't have to force her smile. "You're gonna try to kick my butt, Dallas?"

"Well, you and I both know it'd just be me *tryin'*, but not succeeding, which is where the 'make an ass outta myself' part comes in."

Still grinning at him, she said, "What do you want me to promise?"

"That you won't go back to the depot right now. They almost killed you, and you look all recovered and stuff, but *they almost killed you*. Yesterday. So I need you to promise you're not going back down there to face them tonight."

"I promise," she said earnestly. "I'm not goin' down there. I told you—I want to try to figure out how to help Z, and fightin' with those kids definitely won't help her."

"Swear?"

"Swear."

He let loose a relieved sigh. "Good. Now what am I supposed to tell those vamps about where you've gone?"

"Just what I told you—that I gotta get surrounded by the earth and left alone. That I'm tryin' to figure out something, and I can't do it here."

"All right. I'll tell 'em. They're gonna be pissed."

"Yeah, well, I'll be back soon," she said, getting in Zoey's car. "And don't worry. I'll be careful." The engine had just turned over when Dallas rapped on the window. Suppressing an annoyed sigh, she cracked it.

"Almost forgot to tell ya—I overheard some of the kids talking while I was waitin' for you. It's all over the Internet that Z isn't the only shattered soul in Venice."

"What the heck does that mean, Dallas?"

"Word is that Neferet dumped Kalona on the High Council—literally. His body is there, but his soul is gone."

"Thanks, Dallas. I gotta go!" Without waiting for him to reply, Stevie Rae shoved the Bug into gear and drove out of the parking lot and off the school grounds. Taking a quick right on Utica Street, she headed downtown and to the northeast, toward the rolling land on the outskirts of Tulsa that held the Gilcrease Museum.

Kalona's soul was missing, too.

Stevie Rae didn't for an instant believe that he'd been so wracked with grief that the immortal's soul had ripped apart.

"Not likely," she muttered to herself as she navigated the dark, silent streets of Tulsa. "He's after her." As soon as Stevie Rae said the words aloud, she knew she was right.

So what could she do about it?

She didn't have a clue. She didn't know anything about immortals or shattered souls or the spirit world. Sure, she'd died, but she'd also undied. And she didn't remember her soul going anywhere. *Trapped . . . It'd been black and cold and soundless, and I'd wanted to scream and scream and . . .* Stevie Rae shuddered, clamping down on her thoughts. She didn't remember much of that terrible, dead time—she didn't want to. But she did know someone who understood a lot about immortals, especially Kalona, and the spirit world. According to Z's grandma, Rephaim hadn't been anything but a spirit until Neferet had set loose his gross daddy.

"Rephaim will know somethin'. And what he knows, I'm gonna know," she said resolutely, her fingers tightening on the steering wheel.

If she had to, Stevie Rae would use the power of their Imprint, the power of her element, and every bit of power inside her body to get information from him. Ignoring the sick, terrible, *guilty* way it made her feel to think of fighting Rephaim, she gave the Bug more gas and turned down Gilcrease Road.

Stevie Rae

She didn't have to wonder where she'd find him. Stevie Rae just knew. The front door to the old mansion had already been forced open, and she slipped inside the dark, cold house, following his invisible trail up and up. She didn't need to see the balcony door ajar to know he was outside. She *knew* he was there. *I'll always know where he is,* she thought gloomily.

He didn't turn to face her right away, and she was glad. Stevie Rae needed the time to try to get used to the sight of him again.

"So, you came," he said, still without facing her.

That voice—that human voice. It struck her again, as it had the first night she'd heard it.

"You called me," she said, trying to keep her voice cool—trying to hold on to the anger she felt at what his horrible daddy had caused.

He turned to face her, and their eyes met.

He looks exhausted, was her first thought. *His arm's bleeding again.*

She is still in pain, was his first thought. *And she is filled with anger.*

They stared at each other silently, neither willing to speak their thoughts aloud.

"What has happened?" he finally asked.

"How do you know something's happened?" she snapped back at him.

He hesitated before speaking, obviously choosing his words carefully. "I know from you."

"You're not makin' any sense, Rephaim." The sound of her voice speaking his name seemed to echo in the air around them, and the night was suddenly tinted with the memory of the glistening red mist that had been sent by the son of an immortal to caress Stevie Rae's skin and call her to him.

"That is because it does not make sense to me," he said, his voice deep and soft and hesitant. "I know nothing about how an Imprint works; you will have to teach me."

Stevie Rae felt her cheeks get warm. *He's telling the truth,* she realized. *Our Imprint lets him know things about me! And how could he understand it? I barely do.*

She cleared her throat. "So, are you sayin' you know something's happened because you can sense it from me?"

"Feel, not sense," he corrected her. "I felt your pain. Not like before, right after you drank from me. Then your body was in pain. Your pain tonight was emotional, not physical."

She couldn't stop staring at him, her shock clear on her face. "Yes, it was. It still is."

"Tell me what has happened."

Instead of answering him, she asked, "Why did you call me here?"

"You were feeling pain. I could feel it, too." He paused, obviously disconcerted by what he was saying, and then continued, "I wanted to stop feeling it. So I sent you strength and called you to me."

"How did you do it? What was that red misty stuff?"

"Answer my question, and I will answer yours."

"Fine. What has happened is your daddy killed Heath, the human guy who was Zoey's consort. Zoey saw him do it and couldn't stop him, and that shattered her soul."

Rephaim continued to stare at her until it felt to Stevie Rae as if he was looking through her body and directly into her soul. She couldn't look away, though, and the longer their gazes met, the harder it was for her to hold on to her anger. His eyes were just so human. Only their color was off, and to Stevie Rae, the scarlet within them wasn't as alien as it should be. Truthfully, it was frighteningly familiar; it had once tinted her own eyes.

"Don't you have anything to say about that?" she blurted, pulling her gaze from his so that she was staring out at the empty night.

"There is more. What is it you aren't telling me?"

Gathering her anger back to her, Stevie Rae met his gaze again. "Word has it your daddy's soul is shattered, too."

Rephaim blinked, shock clear in his blood-colored eyes. "I don't believe that," he said.

"Neither do I, but Neferet's dumped his spiritless body on the High Council, and apparently they're buying the story. You know what I think?" She didn't wait for him to respond, but went on, her voice rising with her frustration and anger and fear. "I think Kalona's followed Zoey into the Otherworld because he's totally obsessed with her." Stevie Rae wiped at her cheeks, brushing off the tears she thought she'd finished shedding.

"That is impossible." Rephaim sounded almost as upset as she felt.

"My father cannot return to the Otherworld. The realm has been eternally forbidden to him."

"Well, obviously he figured out a way to get around being forbidden."

"A way to get around having been eternally banished by the Goddess of Night herself? How could that be accomplished?"

"Nyx kicked him out of the Otherworld?" Stevie Rae said.

"It was my father's choice. He was once Nyx's Warrior. Their Oath Bond was broken when he fell."

"Ohmygood*ness*, Kalona used to be on Nyx's side?" Without consciously knowing she was doing so, Stevie Rae moved closer to Rephaim.

"Yes. He guarded her against Darkness." Rephaim stared out at the night.

"What happened? Why did he fall?"

"Father never speaks of it. I know whatever it was filled him with an anger that burned for centuries."

"And that's how you were created. From that anger."

His gaze found her again. "Yes."

"Does it fill you, too? That anger and darkness?" she couldn't stop herself from asking.

"Wouldn't you know if it did? Just as I know your pain? Is that not how this Imprint between us works?"

"Well, it's complicated. See, you've been kinda forced into the role of my consort since I'm the vampyre here and all. And it's easier for a consort to sense things about their vampyre than the other way around. What I get from you is—"

"My power," he broke in. She didn't think he sounded mad, just tired and almost hopeless. "You get my immortal strength."

"Holy crap! That's why I healed so dang fast."

"Yes, and why I don't."

Stevie Rae blinked in surprise. "Well, shoot. You must feel awful—you look pretty bad."

He made a noise that was somewhere between a laugh and a snort. "And you look healthy and whole again."

"I am healthy, but I won't be really whole until I figure out how to help Zoey. She's my best friend, Rephaim. She can't die."

"He is my father. He can't die, either."

They stared at one another, both struggling to make sense of this thing between them that drew them together even as hurt and pain and anger swirled around them, defining and separating their worlds.

"How about this: we get you something to eat. I fix that wing again, which won't be fun for either of us, and then we try to figure out what's going on with Zoey and your daddy. You should know somethin', though. I can't feel your emotions like you can feel mine, but I can tell if you're lyin' to me. I am also pretty sure I could find you, no matter where you are. So if you lie to me and set up Zoey, I give you my word that I will come against you with all the power of my element *and* your blood."

"I will not lie to you," he said.

"Good. Let's go inside the museum and find the kitchen."

Stevie Rae left the rooftop balcony, and the Raven Mocker followed her as if tethered to the High Priestess by an invisible but unbreakable chain.

Stevie Rae

"You could have anything in this world you desired with that power," Rephaim said between bites of the huge sandwich she'd fixed him from the stuff that hadn't already gone bad in the industrial refrigerators of the museum's restaurant.

"Nah, not really. I mean, sure, I can make one tired, overworked, and kinda dorky night security guard let us into the museum and then forget we ever existed; but I can't, like, *rule the world* or anything crazy like that."

"It is an excellent power to wield."

"No, it's a responsibility I didn't ask for and really don't want. See, I don't want to be able to make humans do whatever the heck I want them to do. It's just not right—not if I'm on Nyx's side."

"Because your Goddess does not believe in giving her subjects the objects of their desire?"

Stevie Rae stared at him for a while, twirling a curl around and around her finger before answering, thinking that he might be messin' with her, but the red gaze that met hers was completely serious. So she took a deep breath, and explained, "Not because of that, but because Nyx believes in giving everyone free choice, and when I mess with a human's mind and implant stuff that he has no control over, I'm takin' away his free choice. That's just not right."

"Do you really believe everyone in the world should have free choice?"

"I do. That's why I'm here today, talkin' to you. Zoey gave that back to me. Then in a kinda pay-it-forward thing, I gave that same gift to you."

"You let me live hoping that I would choose my own path and not that of my father."

Stevie Rae was surprised that he had said it so freely; but she didn't question what had prompted his honesty, she just went with it. "Yeah. I told you that when I closed the tunnel behind you and let you go instead of turning you in to my friends. You're in charge of your life now. You're not beholden to your daddy or anyone else." She paused for a second and then said the rest in a big rush. "And you've already started down a different path by saving me on that rooftop."

"An unpaid life debt is a dangerous thing to carry. It was only logical that I repaid the debt that was between us."

"Yeah, I get that, but what about tonight?"

"Tonight?"

"You sent me your strength and called me to you. If you have that kind of power, why didn't you just break our Imprint instead? That would have ended your pain, too."

He stopped eating, and his scarlet gaze locked with hers. "Don't make me into something I'm not. I have spent centuries in darkness. I lived with evil as my bedfellow. I am tied to my father. He is filled with an anger that might very well burn up this world, and if he returns, I am destined to be at his side. See me as I am, Stevie Rae. I am a nightmare creature given life through anger and rape. I walk among the living, but I'm ever separate, ever different. Not immortal, not man, and not beast."

Stevie Rae let his words sink into her veins. She knew he was being completely, nakedly honest with her. But there was more to him than this machine of anger and evil he'd been created to be. She knew it because she'd been witness to it.

"Well, Rephaim, how 'bout you just consider that you *might* be right."

She saw the understanding register in his blood-colored eyes. "Which means I *might* also be wrong?"

She shrugged. "I'm just sayin'."

Without speaking, he shook his head and went back to eating. She smiled and continued to make herself a turkey sandwich. "So," she said, slapping mustard on white bread. "What's your theory about why your daddy's soul's turned up missing?"

His gaze locked with hers, and the one word he uttered made her blood run cold.

"Neferet."

CHAPTER SEVEN

Stevie Rae

"Dallas told me Neferet dumped Kalona's spiritless body on the High Council."

"Who is Dallas?" Rephaim asked.

"Just a guy I know. So it looks like Neferet turned in Kalona even though they're supposed to be together and all."

"Neferet seduces my father and pretends to be his mate, but the only thing she really cares for is herself. Where he is filled with anger, she is filled with hatred. Hatred is a more dangerous ally."

"So you're sure Neferet would betray Kalona to save herself?" Stevie Rae asked.

"I am certain Neferet would betray anyone to save herself."

"What does she gain by turning in Kalona, especially if he's all soulless and stuff?"

"By giving him over to the High Council, she takes suspicion from herself," he said.

"Yeah, that makes sense. I know she wants Zoey dead. And she doesn't care about Heath at all. Actually, Neferet would be cool with the fact that seeing Kalona about to kill Heath made Zoey throw the power of spirit at him and that *not* being able to stop Kalona caused her soul to shatter. Apparently, that's just a half step away from death."

Rephaim's eyes were suddenly sharp on hers. "Zoey attacked my father with the element spirit?"

"Yeah, that's what Lenobia and Dragon told me."

"Then he has been gravely wounded." Rephaim looked away and didn't say anything else.

"Hey, you need to tell me what you know," Stevie Rae said earnestly. When he didn't speak, she sighed, and continued, "Okay, here's my truth. I came here tonight ready to force you to talk to me about your daddy and the Otherworld and all that; but now that I'm here and actually talkin' to you, I don't want to *force* you." Hesitantly, she touched his arm. His body jerked when her fingers met his skin, but he didn't pull away. "Can't we work together on this? Do you really want Zoey dead?"

His eyes found hers again. "I have no reason to wish your friend's death, but you do wish my father harm."

Stevie Rae blew out a breath of frustration. "How about this—how about I compromise in what I want. What if I told you I just want Kalona to leave all of us alone?"

"I don't know if that could ever be possible," Rephaim said.

"But it is possible for me to wish it. Right now, Zoey *and* Kalona are soulless. Now, I know your daddy's an immortal, but it can't be a good thing that his body's just a shell."

"No, it is not a good thing."

"So let's work together to see if we can get both of them back, and deal with what happens next when next actually happens."

"I can agree to that," he said.

"Good!" She squeezed his arm before taking her hand from him. "You said Kalona's wounded. What did you mean?"

"His body can't be killed, but if his spirit is damaged, he is physically weakened. That is how A-ya was used to entrap him. His spirit was clouded with emotions for her. It confused and weakened him, and his body became vulnerable."

"And that's how Neferet was able to dump him in front of the High Council," Stevie Rae said. "Zoey hurt his spirit, so his body is vulnerable."

"There has to be more to it than that. Unless he's held captive, as A-ya had him within the earth, Father would begin to recover almost instantly. As long as he's free, he can heal his spirit."

"Well, obviously Neferet grabbed him before he was healed. She's so dang evil, she probably zapped the crap outta him with that scary darkness she carries around with her and then—"

"That's it!" He stood in excitement, then grimaced from the pain in his wing. Rubbing his wounded arm, he sat back down, holding it close to him. "She continued the attack on his spirit. Neferet is Tsi Sgili. It is through using the dark forces in the spirit realm that she gains power."

"She killed Shekinah without even touching her," Stevie Rae remembered.

"Neferet touched the High Priestess but not with her hands. She manipulated the threads from deaths she is responsible for, sacrifices she's made, and dark promises she means to keep. That power is what killed Shekinah, and that is the power she wielded against my father's already weakened spirit."

"But what's she doing with him?"

"Holding his body captive and using his spirit for her own means."

"Which makes her look like one of the good guys to the High Council. I'll just bet she's bein' all 'Oh, poor Zoey' and 'I don't know what Kalona was thinking' to their faces."

"The Tsi Sgili is very powerful. Why would she put on that pretense to your Council?"

"Neferet doesn't want to let them know how evil she is 'cause she wants to rule the dang world. She might not be ready to take on the Vampyre High Council *and* the human world. Yet. So she can't let the Council know she's cool with Zoey being almost dead, even though she's glad."

"Father doesn't want Zoey dead. He simply wants to possess her."

Stevie Rae gave him a hard look. "Some of us think being *possessed* against our will is worse than death."

He snorted. "You mean like being Imprinted by accident?"

Stevie Rae frowned at him. "No, that's not what I mean at all."

He snorted again and kept rubbing his arm.

Still frowning, she continued, "But what you're sayin' is that Kalona didn't mean for what he did to Heath to cause Zoey's soul to shatter?"

"No, because that would most likely lead to her death."

"Most likely?" Stevie Rae pounced on the words. "Does that mean it's not one hundred percent certain Z's gonna die. 'Cause that's what the vamps are sayin'."

"Vampyres aren't thinking with the mind of an immortal. No death is ever as certain as mortals believe. Zoey will die if her spirit doesn't return to her body, but it is not impossible for her spirit to become whole again. It would be difficult, yes, and she would need a guide and a protector in the Otherworld, but—" His words broke off, and Stevie Rae saw shock in his eyes.

"What?"

"Neferet is using my father to ensure Zoey's spirit doesn't return. She trapped his body while he was wounded and commanded his soul to do her bidding in the Otherworld."

"But you said Kalona was kicked out of there by Nyx. How could he go back?"

Rephaim's eyes widened. "His *body* was banished."

"And his body's still in this realm! It's his spirit that's returned," Stevie Rae finished for him.

"Yes! Neferet has forced him to return. I know my father well. He would never skulk back to Nyx's Otherworld. He has too much pride. He would only return if the Goddess herself asked it of him."

"How do you know that for sure? Maybe he's going after Zoey because he finally gets it that she'll never be with him, and, like a scary, psycho stalker, he'd rather see her dead than with someone else. That could've pissed him off bad enough that his pride could handle a little skulkin'."

Rephaim shook his head. "Father will never believe Zoey won't eventually choose him. A-ya did, and part of the maiden still lives within Zoey's soul." He paused, and before Stevie Rae could ask her next question, added, "But I know how you can be certain. If Neferet is using him, she will have Father's body bound by Darkness."

"Darkness? You mean like the opposite of light?"

"In a way that is what it is. It's hard to define because that type of pure evil is ever-changing, ever-evolving. The Darkness of which I speak is sentient. Find someone who can perceive beings from the spirit realm, and that person should be able to see the chains the Tsi Sgili formed to bind Father, if they are there at all."

"Can you sense the spirit world?"

"I can," he said, meeting her gaze without faltering. "Would you have me give myself up to your Vampyre High Council?"

Stevie Rae chewed her bottom lip. Would she? It would be giving Rephaim's life for Zoey's, and maybe even her own because she'd have to go with him, and there was no way the mega-powerful vamps on the High Council wouldn't be able to tell they were Imprinted. She would die for Zoey—of course she would. But it'd be nice if she didn't have to. Plus, it's not like Zoey would want her to die. Well, it also wasn't like Zoey would want her to have saved and then Imprinted with a Raven Mocker. Heck, *no one* would want that. Goddess knows she didn't even want it. Well, not most of the time anyway.

"Stevie Rae?"

She jolted out of her inner argument to see Rephaim studying her. "Would you have me give myself to your Vampyre High Council?" he repeated solemnly.

"Only as our last option, and if you go, that means I go, too. And, heck, the High Council probably wouldn't even believe anything you tell them. But you said all we need is someone who is good with the spirit realm, like good enough that they can sense the Darkness and spirit stuff, right?"

"Yes."

"Well, there's a whole gaggle of powerful vamps on the High Council. One of them has to be able to do that."

He cocked his head to the side. "It would be unusual for a vampyre to have the ability to sense the dark forces the Tsi Sgili is wielding. That is one reason Neferet has been able to keep up her charade for so long. Truly being able to identify hidden Darkness is a singular skill. Sensing such evil is difficult unless you are familiar with it."

"Yeah, well, the High Council vamps are supposed to be all that. One of them has to be able to do it." She spoke with much more confidence than she felt. Everyone knew the High Council vamps were chosen because of their honor and integrity and basically their all-around goodness, which didn't so much go with being familiar with Darkness. She cleared her throat. "Okay, well, I gotta go back to the House of Night and make a call to Venice," she said firmly. Then her gaze went to his arm and the wing held limp in stained bandages behind it. "You're hurting pretty bad, huh?"

He gave a short nod.

"Okay, well, are ya done eatin'?"

He nodded again.

She swallowed hard, remembering the shared pain of bandaging that broken wing before. "I need to go find the medical supplies. Sadly, they'll probably be in that security office I sent the dorky guard to, which means I'm gonna have to zap his little pea brain again."

"You could sense his brain was small?"

"Did ya see how high-waisted his pants were? No one under the age of eighty with a big brain wears grandpa pants pulled all the way to their underarms. *Pea brain,* I'm just sayin'."

Then, surprising both of them, Rephaim laughed.

I like the sound of his laughter. And before her own brain could clue her mouth in to being quiet, she smiled, and said, "You should laugh more. It's nice."

Rephaim didn't say anything, but Stevie Rae couldn't decipher the odd look he gave her. Feeling kinda uncomfortable, she hopped down from her kitchen stool, and said, "Well, I'm gonna go get the first-aid stuff, fix up your wing as best I can, get food and things together for you, and then go back and start making some super long-distance calls. Hang here. I'll be right back."

"I'd prefer to come with you," he said, standing carefully while he held his arm against his side.

"It'd probably be easier on you if you just stayed here," she said.

"Yes, but I'd prefer to be with you," he said quietly.

Stevie Rae felt a weird little jolt deep inside her at his words, but she shrugged her shoulders nonchalantly, and said, "'Kay, suit yourself. But don't whine if it hurts you to walk around."

"I do *not* whine!" The look he gave her was so filled with guy pride that it was her turn to laugh as they left the kitchen, side by side.

Stevie Rae

Driving home, Stevie Rae should have been thinking about Zoey and devising her next plan of attack. But that was easy. She'd call Aphrodite. No matter what tragedies were going on in the world, Aphrodite would have her pointy little nose in the middle of everything, especially since it had to do with Zoey.

So Stevie Rae's next step in her Save Z Plan was already figured out, leaving her mind wide open to think about Rephaim.

Resetting that dang wing had been awful. She still felt the phantom ache of it all through her right shoulder and her back. Even after she'd found the jar of numbing lidocaine and spread that all down his wing and his messed-up arm, she could still feel the deep, sick pain of its brokenness. Rephaim hadn't said one word during the entire ordeal. He'd turned his head away from her, and right before she touched his wing, he'd said, "Would you do that talking thing you do while you bandage it?"

"Just exactly what *talkin' thing* do you mean?" she'd asked.

He'd glanced over his shoulder, and she could have sworn there was a smile in his eyes. "You talk. A lot. So go ahead and do it. It'll give me something more annoying to think about than the pain."

She'd harrumphed at him, but he'd made her smile. And she did talk to him the entire time she'd cleaned, bandaged, and reset his badly broken wing. Actually, she'd babbled in big bursts of verbal diarrhea, saying nothing and everything as she rode the tide of pain with him. When she was finally done, he'd followed her, slowly, silently, back to the abandoned mansion, and she'd tried to make the closet more comfortable by stuffing in blankets she'd grabbed from the museum's staff lounge.

"You need to go. Don't worry about this." He'd taken the last blanket from her and then practically collapsed into the closet.

"Look, I put the sack of food right here. It's stuff that won't go bad. And remember to drink lots of the water and juice. Hydrating's good," she'd said, feeling suddenly worried about leaving him looking so weak and tired.

"I will. Go."

"Fine. Yeah. I'm going. I'll try to get back here tomorrow, though."

He'd nodded wearily.

"All right. 'Kay. I'm outta here."

She'd turned to go when he said, "You should talk to your mother."

She'd stopped like she'd run into a John Deere. "Why in the world would you say somethin' 'bout my mama?"

He'd blinked at her a couple times like she'd confused him, paused, and finally answered with: "You talked about her while you bandaged my wing. You don't remember?"

"No. Yes. I guess I wasn't really paying attention to the stuff I was sayin'." She'd automatically rubbed her own right arm. "I mostly just moved my mouth while I hurried to get the job done."

"I listened to you instead of the pain."

"Oh." Stevie Rae hadn't known what to say.

"You said she believes you are dead. I just . . ." He trailed off, seeming as confused as if he were trying to decipher an unfamiliar language. "I just thought you should tell her you live. She would want to know, wouldn't she?"

"Yes."

They'd stared at each other until she'd finally made her mouth say, "Bye, and don't forget to eat."

Then she'd practically run out of the museum.

"Why in the heck did it freak me out so bad that he mentioned my mama?" Stevie Rae asked herself aloud.

She knew the answer, and—no—she didn't want to say it aloud. He *cared about* what she'd said to him; he cared that she missed her mama. As she parked at the House of Night and got out of Zoey's car, she admitted to herself that it wasn't really his caring that had freaked her out. It was how his concern made her feel. She'd been glad he cared, and Stevie Rae knew it was dangerous to be glad that a monster cared about her.

"There you are! It's about time you got back." Dallas practically popped out of the bushes at her.

"Dallas! I swear to the Goddess herself that I'm gonna knock the living crap right outta you if you don't stop scaring me."

"Hit me later. Right now you need to get up to the Council Chamber 'cause Lenobia is not happy that you took off."

Stevie Rae sighed and followed Dallas upstairs to the room across from the library that the school used as their Council Chamber. She hurried in, and then hesitated at the doorway. The tension in the air was so thick it was almost visible. The table was big and round, so it should have brought people together. Not that day. That day the table seemed more like a middle-school cafeteria with its separate and very hateful cliques.

On one curved side sat Lenobia, Dragon, Erik, and Kramisha. On the other side were Professors Penthasilea, Garmy, and Vento. They were in the middle of what looked like a serious glare war when Dallas cleared his throat, and Lenobia looked up at them.

"Stevie Rae! Finally. I realize these are unusual times, and that we are all under incredible stress, but I would appreciate it if you would restrain your next urge to take off to a park or wherever you went if a school Council meeting has been called. You are acting in the position of a High Priestess; you should remember to behave as such."

Lenobia's voice was so harsh that Stevie Rae automatically bristled. She opened her mouth to snap back at her and tell the Horse Mistress that she wasn't the boss of her, and then leave the dang room and make her call to Venice. But she wasn't just some fledgling kid anymore, and stomping away from a group of vamps who cared about Zoey—well, at least a few of them did—wasn't going to help their situation.

Begin as you would end, she could almost hear her mama's voice in her mind.

So instead of throwing a fit and taking off, Stevie Rae stepped into the room and sat in one of the chairs that was smack between the two groups. When she spoke, she didn't let herself sound pissed. Actually, she tried her best to mimic the way her mama sounded when she used to get real disappointed with her.

"Lenobia, my affinity is for earth. That means sometimes I'm gonna need to get away from everyone and just be by myself with the earth. It's how I think, and right now we all need to think. So, I will be takin' off sometimes, with or without anyone's permission, and whether or not y'all have called a meeting. And I'm not *acting* in the position of a High Priestess. I *am* the first and only red vampyre High Priestess in the entire world. That's a new thing, so I'm thinkin' there's gonna be some new job descriptions that go along with it and, ya know, I may just have to make it up as I figure this Red High Priestess stuff out." She turned to the other side of the room, and added a quick, "Hi, Professor P, and Garmy and Vento. I haven't seen y'all in a long time."

The three professors mumbled hellos, and she ignored the fact that they were staring at her red tattoos like she was a science project gone wrong at the 4-H fair.

"So, Dallas said Neferet dumped Kalona's body on the High Council, and it looks like his soul is shattered, too," Stevie Rae said.

"Yes, though some don't want to believe it," Prof P said, sending a dark look to Lenobia.

"Kalona is not Erebus!" Lenobia practically exploded. "Just as we all know Neferet is *not* the earthly incarnation of Nyx! This whole subject is ridiculous."

"The Council reports that the Prophetess Aphrodite announced the winged immortal's spirit had shattered, just as has Zoey's," said Proffy Garmy.

"Hang on." Stevie Rae held up her hand to stop the tirade that was obviously getting ready to come at Kramisha. "Did you say *Aphrodite* and *Prophetess* together?"

"That is what the High Council has named her," Erik said dryly. "Even though most of us wouldn't call her that."

Stevie Rae lifted her brows at him. "Really? I would. Zoey would. And you *have*. Maybe not out loud, but you've followed her visions, more than once. I've been Imprinted with her, not that I liked it or anything, but I can tell you that she's definitely touched by Nyx and knows stuff. Lots of stuff actually." She looked at Proffy Garmy. "Aphrodite can sense things about Kalona's spirit?"

"So the High Council believes."

Stevie Rae breathed a long sigh of relief. "That's the best news I've heard in days." She glanced at the clock, and started counting ahead seven hours for Venice time. It was about 10:30 P.M. in Tulsa, which meant it was probably still before dawn over there. "I need a phone. I gotta call Aphrodite. Dang it! I left my cell in my room." She started to get up.

"Stevie Rae, what are you doing?" Dragon asked, as they all stared at her.

She hesitated long enough to look back at the room and the tense, glaring vamps. "How about I tell you what I'm *not* doin'? I'm *not* gonna sit around and argue about who Kalona is or who Neferet is when Zoey needs help. I'm *not* gonna give up on Z, and I'm *not* gonna let y'all drag me into some weird teacher bicker war." She met Kramisha's startled gaze. "Do you believe I'm your High Priestess?"

"Yep," she said without hesitation.

"Good. Then come with me. You're wastin' your time here. Dallas?"

"Like always, I'm with you, girl," he said.

Stevie Rae looked from vampyre to vampyre. "Y'all need to get your shit together. Here's a newsflash from the only High Priestess you have left at this dang school: Zoey isn't dead. And believe me, I know dead. I've been there, done that, and got the frickin' T-shirt." Stevie Rae turned her back on the room and, with her fledglings, got the heck outta there.

CHAPTER EIGHT

Aphrodite

Aphrodite didn't let Darius carry her from the Council Chamber like he wanted to. She couldn't leave Zoey alone in the middle of the shit pot Neferet was stirring with no one but a totally messed-up Warrior and a semi-hysterical nerd herd standing between her and some serious crazy.

"Yes, I believe it is important to keep Erebus's body under close watch while his spirit is absent. Perhaps this is only a temporary state he has fallen into as a response to Zoey's attack on him," Neferet was saying to the High Council.

"Zoey's attack on *him*? Did you really just say that?" Stark, puffy-eyed and hollow-cheeked, looked like he was on the verge of exploding.

"Go to Stark and try to help him get a handle on his temper," Aphrodite whispered to her Warrior. When he hesitated, she added, "I'm fine. I'm just going to sit here and listen and learn—kinda like I'm at one of my mom's cocktail parties gone bad."

Darius nodded. He moved quickly to Stark's side and put a hand on the boy's shoulder. Aphrodite thought it was a good sign that Stark didn't shrug him off, but then again, the arrow kid looked like total crap. She wondered about what happened to a Warrior if his Priestess died, and then shivered with a terrible premonition of what could come.

"Zoey did attack Erebus. His spiritless body is undeniable proof of that," Neferet said, smugness coloring her voice.

"Zoey was attempting to stop the immortal from killing her consort," Darius said before Stark could shout his retort.

"Ah, and that is the issue, isn't it?" Neferet smiled silkily at Darius, making Aphrodite want to claw out her eyes. "*Why* did my consort feel the need to cause harm to Zoey's Heath? The only real knowledge we have about it is from Erebus himself before his spirit was wrenched from his body. His last words were 'I was protecting my Goddess.' So what transpired between Zoey and Heath and Erebus is much more complicated than it might appear to a young, distraught witness."

"This wasn't some fight for Nyx! Kalona killed Heath! Probably because he was jealous of how much Zoey loved him," Stark said, looking like he wanted nothing more than to wrap his hands around Neferet's white throat and squeeze.

"And how did you feel about Zoey's love for Heath? A Warrior bond is an intimate one, is it not? You were there with them when the soul shattering happened. Where is your culpability, Warrior?" Neferet said.

Darius held Stark back from launching himself at Neferet, and Duantia spoke quickly into the rising tension. "Neferet, I think we can all agree that there are many unanswered questions about the tragedy that occurred on our island today. Stark, we also understand the passion and rage you feel at the loss of your Priestess. It is a hard blow for a Warrior to—"

Duantia's wisdom was cut off by the sound of Aretha Franklin belting out the chorus from "Respect," which was coming from the little Coach purse Aphrodite had slung over her shoulder.

"Oopsie, um, sorry 'bout that." Aphrodite frantically unzipped her purse and dug for her iPhone. "Thought I had the ringer turned off. I don't know who would be . . ." Her voice trailed off when she saw the caller ID was Stevie Rae. She almost pressed the IGNORE button, but a *feeling* hit her—strong and clear. She needed to talk to Stevie Rae. "Uh, sorry again, but I really have to take this." Aphrodite hurried up the stairs and out of the Chamber, feeling way too exposed as everyone glared after her like she'd just slapped a baby or drowned a damn puppy. "Stevie Rae," she whispered hastily, "I know you probably just found out about Z, and you're freaked, but this really isn't a good time."

“Can you sense spirits and stuff from the Otherworld?” Stevie Rae asked without so much as a “Hey there, how ya doin’.”

Something about the tone of her voice brought Aphrodite up short and kept her from replying with her usual sarcasm. “Yeah, I’m starting to be able to. Apparently, I’ve been tuned in to the Otherworld since I started having visions—I just didn’t realize it until today.”

“Where’s Kalona’s body?”

Aphrodite ducked around the corner of the foyer. No one was around her, but she still kept her voice low. “Down there in front of the High Council in their Chamber.”

“Is Neferet there, too?”

“Of course.”

“Zoey?”

“She’s there, too. Well, her body is. Z herself has totally checked out. Stark’s absolutely freaked by what’s happened, plus Neferet is pissing him off so bad he can hardly think. Darius is saving his ass by not letting him tear her apart with his bare hands. The nerd herd is hysterical.”

“But you kept your sense.”

Stevie Rae didn’t say it like a question, but Aphrodite answered her anyway. “Someone had to.”

“Good. Okay, I think I have somethin’ figured out about Kalona. If I’m right, Neferet is up to her elbows in evil, so much so that she’s got his body trapped, and his spirit has to obey her to get it back.”

“Like that would surprise any of us?”

“I’ll bet it would surprise most of the High Council. Neferet has a way of gettin’ people on her side.”

Aphrodite snorted. “As far as I can tell, most of them are clueless about her.”

“That’s what I thought. So moving against her out in the open there is going to be even harder than moving against her when she was here.”

“That about sums it up. So, what’s the deal with Kalona?”

“You need to check out his body using your super Spidey Otherworld senses.”

"You're such a dork. There is no such thing as Spider-Man. He is a made-up comic-book-bullshit character," Aphrodite said.

"They're called graphic novels, not comic books—don't be so dang judgmental. I do not have time to argue with you about the benefits of graphic novels on people's imaginations," Stevie Rae said.

"Oh, please, if its ass is feathered and waterproof, it's a duck. Hello, pictures with little word balloons makes it a comic book. They're *dorky* comic books for *nerdy* antisocial, nonbathing people. End of discussion."

"Aphrodite! Focus! Just go back in the Chamber and check out Kalona's body with your Otherworld-spirit-sensing stuff. Look for any kind of weirdness that no one else can see. Like, I dunno—"

"A disgusting, sticky spiderweb of darkness wrapped all around him like freaky chains?" Aphrodite offered.

"Don't mess with me about this. It's too important." Stevie Rae's voice had gone completely serious.

"I'm not messing with you. I'm telling you what I've already seen. His body is completely covered by dark threads of yucky stuff that, apparently, no one else but *moi* can see."

"It's Neferet!" Stevie Rae's voice was tense with emotion. "She's tapped into something called Darkness—that's evil with a capital D. It's how she's using the power of the Tsi Sgili. She managed to trap Kalona with it right after Zoey wounded his soul—it's the only time his body is weak enough to be vulnerable."

"How do you know that?"

"It's how the Cherokee imprisoned him last time." Stevie Rae avoided the question by using the only part of the truth she could ever tell anyone. "A-ya messed up his spirit with emotions he wasn't used to feeling, and the old women used his weakness to trap him."

"That does make sense. So now Neferet's got him all tied up and soulless. Why? She's his super nasty lover. Why wouldn't she want him here with her? The two of them could have taken off together and not been caught for killing Heath."

"Yeah, except for two things: she would have looked guilty, so the

High Council would have been forced to act against her, and she wouldn't have been one hundred percent sure Zoey is going to die."

"What the hell? The Council says she has a week, but then Z will be dead."

"Not true. If her soul returns to her body, Z won't die. Neferet knows that, so she—"

"She trapped Kalona's body and told him to follow Z to the Otherworld and make sure she doesn't get back to her body," Aphrodite finished for her. "That fucking figures! But it doesn't feel right. Kalona's totally obsessed with Z. I don't think he wants her to die."

"Yeah, but what if the only way to get his body back is to kill Zoey?"

Aphrodite's voice hardened. "Then he'll kill her. Stevie Rae, what the hell are we going to do?"

"We have to figure out a way to protect Z and help her get back to her body, and no, I don't know how we're gonna do that." She hesitated and, crossing her fingers behind her back against the semi-lie, added, "Today the earth helped me find out some pretty weird stuff about Kalona. Seems he used to be Nyx's Warrior. So, he used to be one of the good guys. Then something happened in the Otherworld, and the Goddess banished him, and that's when he fell to earth."

"Which means he knows the Otherworld a hell of a lot better than any of us," Aphrodite said glumly.

"Yeah. Dang it! What we need is a Warrior for Zoey in the Otherworld who can stand up against Kalona and get Z back to her body."

Aphrodite felt a little zap of understanding at Stevie Rae's words. "But she already has a Warrior."

"Stark's in *this* world. Not the Otherworld."

"But a Warrior and his Priestess are connected by a bond that is all about spirit and oaths and dedication. I know! I have it with Darius." Aphrodite's voice was getting more and more excited as she reasoned it through. "And you can't tell me that my Warrior wouldn't follow me straight into the mouth of hell to protect me. All we need to do is to get Stark's soul to the Otherworld so he can protect Z there, just like he does here." *And it might save him, too,* she added silently to herself.

"I don't know, Aphrodite. Stark has to be pretty messed-up after losing Zoey and all."

"That's the point. He has to save himself by saving her."

"But that doesn't work. I've been remembering somethin' from *The Fledgling Handbook 101*. There was that whole big story in there about a High Priestess *and* her Warrior who died when her soul was shattered and he went after her into the Otherworld."

"Please, dork. It's in the 101 handbook because it's meant to scare the crap out of retarded third formers, like you, so that hot young fledglings stay away from sexy Sons of Erebus Warriors. The stupid thing was probably written by some dried-up old hag of a High Priestess who hadn't had sex in, like, a hundred years. Literally. Stark needs to follow Zoey to the Otherworld, kick Kalona's spirit's ass, and then bring her back here."

"It has to be more complicated than that."

"Probably, but whatever. We'll figure it out."

"How?"

Aphrodite paused, thinking of Thanatos and her wise, dark eyes. "I might know someone who can at least point us in the right direction."

"Don't let Neferet know you're onto her," Stevie Rae cautioned.

"I'm not stupid, stupid," Aphrodite said. "Leave this whole thing in my extremely capable and well-manicured hands. I'll call you later with an update. Bye!" She hit the red END CALL button before Stevie Rae could nag her anymore. And, smiling slyly, headed back into the Council Chamber.

CHAPTER NINE

Stark

The longer he stayed in the same room as Neferet, the hotter Stark's anger burned. And that was good. He could think through anger. He couldn't think through the grief. Goddess! The unbearable grief of losing his Priestess . . . his Zoey . . .

"So we are in agreement then," Neferet said. "I will take my consort's body to Capri. There I can watch over him until the time when—"

It finally registered with Stark what the bitch was saying, and he rounded on her, only stopped short from launching himself at the evil hag by Darius's ironlike grip on his arm.

"You can't let her escape with him!" Stark yelled at Duantia, the Leader of the High Council. "Kalona killed Heath; I saw it. Zoey saw it. That's what made *this* happen to her." He gestured at Zoey's soulless body without looking down at her. He couldn't look at her.

"Escape?" Neferet scoffed. "I've already agreed to be escorted by a group of Sons of Erebus Warriors, and to make regular reports to the Council regarding Erebus's state of consciousness. After all, my consort isn't a criminal. It isn't against our laws for a Warrior to kill a human if he's in the service of the Goddess."

Stark ignored Neferet and concentrated on Duantia. "Don't let her go. Don't let her take him. He did more than kill a human guy, and they aren't in the service of Nyx."

"Lies propagated by a jealous teenager, who had so little control over herself that her eternal soul has been shattered!" Neferet snapped.

"You fucking bitch!" Stark lunged for Neferet, who didn't so much as flinch. Instead, she lifted one elegant hand and pointed it, palm outward, at Stark. As he struggled to free himself from Darius's hold, Stark thought he saw black smoke begin materializing around Neferet's fingers.

"Stop it, Stark, you total moron!"

Suddenly, Aphrodite was there right in front of him. Stark knew she was Zoey's friend, but if Darius hadn't had a vise-like hold on him, he wouldn't have hesitated to knock her aside to get to Neferet.

"Stark!" Aphrodite yelled at him. "You're not helping Zoey!" Then the blonde did something that totally shocked him, and by Darius's sharp intake of breath, she shocked her Warrior, too. She took his face between her smooth palms and forced him to stare into her eyes, whispering words that changed his life. "I know how to help Zoey."

"You see how uncontrollable he is! If my consort's body remains here, who knows what this undisciplined child could do to it?" Neferet spewed her poison as Stark kept his eyes locked with Aphrodite's.

"Do you swear?" Stark whispered urgently back to her. "You're not just talking crap?"

Aphrodite lifted one blond brow. "If you knew me better, you'd know I never *just talk crap*, but yes. I swear on my new and annoyingly responsible title of Prophetess that I know how to help Zoey, but we need her away from Neferet. Get it?"

Stark nodded once and quit straining against Darius. Aphrodite took her hands from his face. Looking and sounding every bit a Prophetess of Nyx, she whirled around to face Neferet and the High Council.

"Why are you all so willing to believe Zoey is going to die?"

Duantia was first to respond. "Her soul has left her body, and not just on a Spirit Journey to the Otherworld, or in temporary communion with the Goddess. Zoey has been shattered."

One of the Council members who had stayed mostly silent until then spoke up. "You must understand what that means, Prophetess. Zoey's spirit is in the Otherworld in pieces. Past lives have been stripped from her, as have memories and different aspects of her personality. She is becoming one of the Caoinic Shi', a thing not dead and not alive—a being trapped in the realm of spirits, yet without the comfort of her own spirit."

"No. Seriously. Speak American and not this ancient and very fucked-up, confusing olden-day Euro crap." Aphrodite planted one hand on the curve of her waist, and the other pointed a finger at the Vampyre High Council in general. "Without the confusing woo-woo references, explain why the hell you're writing Zoey off."

Stark heard a few of the Council members draw in breath at Aphrodite's brash words and registered the smug, "I told you they were out of control" look Neferet shared with several of the vamps, but Thanatos responded smoothly. "What Aether is saying is that the layers of spirit that make Zoey who she is today—her past lives, her past experiences, her personality—have been stripped from her, and without those layers intact, it is impossible for her to rest in the Otherworld, or for her spirit to return to her body here in this world. Think of it as if you had been in a terrible accident and the layers of skin and muscle and bone that protect your heart have been peeled away from your body, leaving that vital organ bare and defenseless. What would happen to you then?"

Aphrodite paused, and Stark thought she hesitated because she didn't want to say the obvious answer, but she glanced at him, and when their eyes met, he was surprised to see triumph and excitement in hers. "If my heart didn't have any protection, it wouldn't keep beating. So why not get Zoey some protection?"

Protection! I'm Zoey's protection! A small quiver of hope moved through his body. "I'm her protection!" he said quickly. "I don't care if it's in this world or the next. Just show me how to get to where she is, and I'll be there for her."

"That does, indeed, sound logical, Stark," Thanatos said. "But your gifts are that of a Warrior, which means your skills are corporeal and not of the spirit realm."

"Protection is protection," Stark insisted. "Just show me how to get where she is, and I'll figure the rest of it out."

"Zoey must make her spirit whole again, and that is a battle you cannot fight for her," Aether said.

"But I can be there for her while she gets herself together. I can protect her," Stark insisted.

"A living Warrior cannot enter the Otherworld. Not even to follow his High Priestess," Aether said.

"Should you attempt it, you would be lost, too," Duantia said.

"You don't know that for sure," Stark said.

"In our recorded history, there is no Warrior who has recovered from attempting to follow his Priestess's shattered spirit into the Otherworld. All of them perished—every Warrior and every High Priestess," Thanatos said.

Stark felt a jolt of surprise. He hadn't even thought of that—that he'd die, too. With a detached sense of curiosity, he realized he didn't really mind the idea of dying, not if he could fulfill his Oath to Zoey; but before he could respond, Neferet's cold voice intruded again. "And all of those Warriors and High Priestesses were older and more experienced than you."

"Maybe that was their problem." Aphrodite pitched her voice low enough that only Stark heard her murmur. "They were *too* old and had *too* much experience."

Hope shivered through Stark again. He turned to Duantia. "I was wrong before. Neferet should be able to take Kalona to wherever she wants to take him, but I want the same right to take Zoey with me." He paused and made a gesture that included Aphrodite, Darius, and the other kids who were huddled together not far from them. "*We* want to take Zoey with us."

"Stark, I cannot agree to what would amount to a death sentence for you, too." Duantia's voice was compassionate but firm. "Within this next week, Zoey is going to die. The best place for her is here, in our infirmary, being kept comfortable during the time she has left. The best thing for you to do would be to prepare yourself for that outcome and not sacrifice yourself in a futile attempt to save her."

"You are very young," Thanatos said. "You have a long and productive life before you. Don't cut Fate's thread for you."

"Zoey will remain here until the end." Duantia nodded in agreement. "You may, of course, stay by her side."

"Um, excuse me. I don't mean to be disrespectful or anything." Everyone's attention turned to Zoey's group of friends, who had, until then, been mostly silent with grief and shock. Damien's hand was raised like he was in a classroom waiting for the teacher to call on him.

"Who are you, fledgling?" asked Duantia.

"My name is Damien, and I'm one of Zoey's friends."

"He also has an affinity for air," Jack added, wiping a hand across his tear-streaked face.

"Ah, I have been told of you," Duantia said. "Do you wish to address the Council?"

"He is a fledgling. He should be seen and not heard in Council meetings," Neferet snapped.

"I didn't know you spoke for the Vampyre High Council, Neferet," Aphrodite said.

"She does not," said Thanatos, giving Neferet a hard look before turning to Damien. "Fledgling, do you wish to address the Council?"

Damien sat up straighter, swallowed hard, and said, "Affirmative."

Thanatos's lips twitched with the beginnings of a smile. "Then you may speak. You may also put down your hand, Damien."

"Oh, thank you." Damien's hand hastily retreated. "Well, all I wanted to say, very respectfully, is vampyre law states that, as Zoey's Oath Bound Warrior, it is Stark's right to decide where and how she should be protected. At least that's what I remember from my notes last semester in Vampyre Sociology Class."

"Zoey is dying." Duantia's words were harsh, but her tone was gentle. "You must understand that her Warrior will soon be released from his Oath."

"I do understand. But she's not dead *yet*, and all I'm saying is that her Warrior has the right to be her protector, in any way he believes is best for her, as long as she *is* alive."

"I have to agree with the fledgling," Thanatos said, nodding respectfully to Damien. "He is absolutely correct in principle. It is law, as well as a Warrior's Oath Bound responsibility, to decide what is best for his High Priestess's safety. Zoey Redbird is living; therefore, she is still under her Warrior's protection."

"And the rest of my Council? Do you agree with Thanatos?" Duantia asked.

Stark held his breath while the other five High Priestesses either spoke solemn *yes*es or gave small nods.

"Well done, fledgling Damien," Thanatos said.

Damien's cheeks turned pink. "Thank you, Priestess."

Duantia shook her head. "For my part, I am not as pleased as Thanatos at the prospect of the death of a promising young Warrior." Then the vampyre shrugged with acquiescence. "But the Council is in agreement. Though it saddens me, I bow to the will of my Council and to our laws. Stark, where is it you would like to take your High Priestess for her last days?"

Before he could respond, Neferet's cold voice cut in. "Am I to assume this little quorum of agreement means I am also free to leave and to take my consort with me?"

"We already decided upon that, Neferet." Thanatos's tone matched her chill for chill. "Under the conditions set, you may return to Capri with your consort's body."

"Thank you," Neferet said shortly. She made a brusque gesture at the Sons of Erebus who had carried Kalona into the Council Chamber on the litter. "Bring Erebus. We are leaving this place." With the barest of bows to the Council, Neferet strode imperiously from the room.

Everyone was watching her exit when Aphrodite grabbed Stark's arm, and said urgently, "Stall. Don't give them an answer about where you want to take Zoey."

"Now that that interruption is gone, you are free to tell the Council where it is you'd like to take your High Priestess, Stark," Thanatos said.

"Right now I want to take her to our room in the palace. That is, if you say it's okay. I really need some time to think about what's best for Zoey, and I haven't had a chance to do that."

"Young but wise." Thanatos smiled in approval.

"I am pleased it seems you've been able to rein in your anger, Warrior," Duantia said. "May you continue to think clearly and wisely."

Stark clenched his teeth together and bowed his head respectfully, careful not to meet any of the Council members' gazes, afraid that they would see the reality of his un-reined anger.

"The Council gives its permission for you to retire to the palace with your wounded High Priestess and your friends. We will ask for your decision about where you wish to take her on the morrow. Please know you may still decide to remain here. If you ask it of us, we will provide sanctuary for all of you, for as long as is necessary."

"Thank you," Stark said. He bowed formally to the group of powerful High Priestesses.

"Council is adjourned. We shall reconvene on the morrow. Until then, I truly wish you to blessed be."

Before even Darius could help him, Stark went to Zoey, lifted her body in his arms, and, holding her close to him, carried her from the Council Chamber.

Stark

"Tell me everything you know." He'd only just laid Zoey's body on the bed in the suite assigned to them when Stark confronted Aphrodite.

"Well, it's not much, but it's enough to make me think the vamps are wrong," Aphrodite said, snuggling into a big velvet chair beside Darius.

"You mean you know of a case where a Warrior actually brought back his High Priestess from the Otherworld?" Damien asked, as he and Jack pulled chairs from the suite's living room into the bedroom.

"No. Not exactly."

"What do you mean, Aphrodite?" Stark paced back and forth in front of Zoey's bed.

"I mean I don't give a shit about ancient history. Zoey isn't some stick-up-her-ass High Priestess from back in the day."

"People who ignore history end up repeating it," Damien said softly.

"I didn't say I was ignoring it, Gay Boy. I said I didn't give a shit about it." Aphrodite's sharp gaze went from Damien to the Twins, who were still standing in the entryway to the bedroom. "Dorkamese Twins, why are you lurking?"

"We aren't *lurking,* Hateful," Shaunee's voice was little more than a whisper.

"Yeah, we're *respectful-ing,*" Erin added in a twin whisper.

"Oh, for shit's sake. What are you two talking about?" Aphrodite said.

"It's disrespecting Zoey's, um, *body* to be all talking and stuff around her while she's—" Shaunee broke off, looking at her twin for help.

Before Erin could, as usual, finish her sentence, Stark said, "No. We aren't treating her like she's dead. She's just not here, that's all."

"So it's more like a waiting room than a hospital room," Jack said, reaching from his chair to touch Zoey's hand.

"Yeah," Stark said. "Only it's a waiting room for something really good."

"Like at the DMV when you've passed your driver's test and had a really bad picture taken and you're just waiting for them to bring you your license?" Jack said.

"Exactly, only without the filth and the peasants," Aphrodite said. "So pull up some chairs, brain-sharers, and stop acting like Zoey's a corpse."

The Twins hesitated, shared a glance, shrugged, and then pulled chairs into the bedroom and joined the group's little circle.

"All right, now that we're all together on this, you need to tell us what you found out from Stevie Rae," Darius said.

Aphrodite smiled at her Warrior. "How'd you know I got the info from Stevie Rae?"

Darius touched her face gently. "I know you."

Stark clenched his fists and looked away from the bond that was so obvious between Aphrodite and Darius. He wanted to hit something. He *needed* to hit something. He was going to explode if he didn't get rid of some of the feelings that were choking him from the inside out. Then Aphrodite's words penetrated the mess that was his mind, and he whirled around to face her. "Say that again!"

"I said, Kalona really is in the Otherworld. Neferet's sent him there to be sure Zoey doesn't pull herself together and make it back here."

"Wait, no, I remember overhearing Kalona talking to Rephaim once. He was real pissed because the Raven Mocker had said something about returning to the Otherworld. I'm sure Kalona said he couldn't go back because Nyx kicked him out," Stark said.

"She kicked out his *body*. His body isn't there," Aphrodite said. "It's his soul that's slithered its way back in."

"OhmyGoddess!" Damien said.

"Zoey's in bigger trouble than we thought," Erin said sadly.

"And that was already some really big trouble," Shaunee agreed.

"It gets worse," Aphrodite said. "Neferet's behind all of this." She sighed and met Stark's eyes. "Okay, this is gonna be not so nice for you to hear, but you need to listen up and deal with it. Kalona used to be Nyx's Warrior."

The color drained from Stark's face. "That's what Zoey told me right before . . ." He rubbed a hand through his hair. "I didn't believe her. I got pissed and jealous and stupid. That's why I wasn't with her when she saw Kalona kill Heath."

"You're going to have to find a way to forgive yourself for that mistake," Darius told Stark. "If you do not, you will not be able to focus on the here and now."

"And it's going to take a shitload of focus to save Zoey," Aphrodite said.

"Because Stark's gonna have to go to the Otherworld and fight Kalona for Zoey." Jack's voice was hushed, almost like he was talking during church.

"And figure out a way to help her get the pieces of her soul together," Damien said.

"Then that's what I'll do." Stark was glad he sounded confident because his gut felt like someone had punched him in it.

"If you try to do that without the right preparation, you will have no chance at all of succeeding, young Warrior."

Stark's eyes followed the voice to the doorway, where Thanatos stood, looking tall and grim and way too much like death personified.

"Then tell me how to prepare!" Stark wanted to shout his frustration from the rooftops of the world.

"To do battle in the Otherworld, the Warrior in you must die to give birth to the Shaman."

Stark didn't hesitate. "All I have to do is kill myself? You mean then my soul can go to the Otherworld and help Zoey?"

"It cannot be a literal death, Warrior. Think what it would do to Zoey's already wounded spirit were she to have to bear your death as well as that of her consort."

"There's no way she'd ever leave the Otherworld then," Damien said solemnly. "Even if she could get the pieces of her soul together."

"Exactly, and that is what I believe happened to the other High Priestesses whose Warriors followed them into the Otherworld," Thanatos said, entering the room and walking to Zoey's bedside.

"So the other Warriors really did kill themselves to protect their Priestesses?" Aphrodite moved even closer to Darius and threaded her fingers through his.

"Most of them did, and the Warriors who didn't die before their souls left their bodies did so shortly thereafter. You must understand that Warriors aren't High Priestesses. They don't have the gifts it takes to move freely in the spirit realm."

"Kalona is there, and he's definitely not a High Priestess," Stark said.

"Even those of us who do not believe he is Erebus come to earth know that this being you call Kalona is an immortal who has somehow arrived here from the Otherworld. The rules that bind a Warrior, or even a male vampyre who is not a Warrior, do not apply to him."

"He is bound, though," Aphrodite said, leaning forward with urgency. "I can see his chains. His body is covered by them."

"Tell me what you've seen, Prophetess," Thanatos said.

Aphrodite hesitated.

"Tell her everything," Damien said. Aphrodite met his eyes. "We have to trust someone, or it won't end up any different for Stark and Zoey than it has for those other Warriors and High Priestesses."

"We might as well trust Death," Stark said. "Because, one way or another, that's what I'm going to have to face to get to Zoey."

Aphrodite looked from Stark's pale face to Darius. "I agree."

"Me, too," said Jack.

"Yeah," said Shaunee.

"Tell her everything," added Erin.

"All right," Aphrodite said. She gave Thanatos a wry smile. "So, I better start with Neferet, and you better sit down."

CHAPTER TEN

Stark

Stark thought it was pretty impressive that Thanatos kept her shock to a minimum as Aphrodite, with some help from Damien, explained everything to the High Priestess, beginning with Zoey's entrance to the House of Night, going through the discovery of the red fledglings, Kalona's rising, their slow realization of the depth of Neferet's evil, and finally finishing up with the conversation she'd had with Stevie Rae on the phone.

At the story's conclusion, Thanatos stood and walked over to stare down at Zoey's body. When the High Priestess finally spoke, it seemed she was talking to Z more than to them.

"So from the beginning this has been a battle between Light and Darkness, only until now it has been fought mostly in the physical realm."

"Light and Darkness? It sounds like you're using those two words as titles," said Damien.

"Very astute of you, young fledgling," Thanatos said.

"That's what Stevie Rae was doing, too. Using Darkness like a title," Aphrodite said.

"Titles? Like they're two people?" Jack asked.

"Not people—that's too limiting. Think of them more as immortals who are so powerful that they can manipulate energy to such an extent that spirit can be made tangible," Thanatos said.

"You mean like Nyx is Light and Kalona, or at least what he represents, is Darkness?" Damien said.

"It is more accurate to say that Nyx is allied with Light. The same can be said for Kalona and Darkness."

"Okay, I'm not Miss Perfect Schoolgirl, but I'm smart, and I actually did pay attention in class. Most of the time. I haven't heard of any of this stuff," Aphrodite said.

"Neither have I," Damien said.

"And that's saying something, 'cause Damien is definitely Miss Perfect Schoolgirl," said Erin.

"Totally," said Shaunee.

Thanatos sighed and turned from Zoey to face the rest of the room. "Yes, well, it is an ancient belief that I don't think was ever fully accepted by our society, or at least the Priestesses of our society."

"Why? What's wrong with it?" Aphrodite asked.

"It was based on struggle and violence and the clash of the raw powers of good and evil."

Aphrodite snorted, "You mean guy stuff."

Thanatos's brows lifted. "I do."

"Hang on. What's so guy-stuff-like about believing in good fighting evil?" Stark said.

"It's more than a simple belief that there is good and that it should fight the evil in the world. It's a personification of Light and Darkness at their most elemental level, as forces that are so absorbed with themselves that one cannot exist without the other though they constantly try to consume one another." Thanatos sighed again at the blank looks the kids were giving her. "One of the earliest representations of Light and Darkness was of Light being a massive black bull and Darkness being an enormous white bull."

"Huh? Shouldn't the white be Light and the black be Darkness?" Jack asked.

"One would think so, but it is thus that they were represented in our ancient scrolls. It was written that each creature, Light and Darkness, carried something for which the other would always long. Think of the bulls, swollen with the power they wield, meeting in eternal combat, each struggling to get something from the other it could never attain without destroying itself. I saw a depiction of their battle once when I was a young High Priestess, and I've never forgotten how raw and violent it was—disturbingly so. The bulls' horns were locked. Their powerful bodies strained to reach the other, blood spewed, nostrils flared. It was a deadlock that was frightening in its intensity—the painting itself seemed to vibrate with power."

"Masculine power," Darius said. "I've seen that depiction, too, when I was in training to become a Warrior. It decorated the cover of some of the ancient journals written by great Warriors from our past."

"*Masculine* power. I can see why the vamp leaders let that bull stuff fade away," Erin said.

"Seriously, Twin." Shaunee nodded. "Too much guy power when vamps are mostly about girl power."

"But our belief system isn't about female power suppressing male power. It's about a healthy balance between the two," Darius said.

"No, Warrior, the truth is our belief system is not *supposed* to be about female power suppressing male power; but as with Light and Darkness, it is an eternal struggle to find a balance between the two without one destroying the other. Think of the images of Nyx that we see about us every day, with their feminine beauty and appeal. Contrast that to an imagining of the raw power unleashed in the form of two great, battling, male creatures. Do you see how a world trying to contain both would be in conflict, and thus one must be suppressed in order to allow the other to thrive?"

Aphrodite snorted, "That's not so hard to imagine. I can't *imagine* the uptight High Council wanting anything to do with something as messy as two giant guy bulls and any beliefs they represent."

"She means except for you," Stark said, frowning at Aphrodite and sending her a "you're not helping" look.

Thanatos smiled. "No, Aphrodite is correct. The Council has changed over the centuries, especially over the past four I have existed. It used to be a vital force, in its own way very elemental and rather barbaric in its power. But in modern times it has become . . ." The High Priestess hesitated, searching for the correct word.

"Civilized," Aphrodite said. "It's super civilized."

"It is," Thanatos said.

Aphrodite's blue eyes widened. "And being too civilized isn't necessarily a good thing, especially when you're dealing with two bulls ramming against each other and taking out anything that stands between them."

"Zoey's awfully close to Light," Damien said softly.

"Close enough to get gored by Darkness," Stark said. "Especially if Darkness has been sent to be sure she doesn't ever reach the Light again."

The room went silent while everyone's eyes went to Zoey, lying silent and pale against the very civilized cream-colored satin linens.

It was within the silence that the realization came to Stark, and with the instincts of a Warrior guarding his High Priestess, he knew he had found the right path.

"Then finding out how to protect Zoey isn't about ignoring the past. It's about looking deeper into the past than anyone today would think to do," Stark said, excitement raising his voice.

"And it's about embracing and understanding the raw power that is unleashed by the struggle between Light and Darkness," Thanatos said.

"But where the hell do we find out about that?" Aphrodite said, brushing her hair back from her face in frustration. "The beliefs we need have died out—you said that yourself, Thanatos."

"Perhaps not everywhere," Darius said, sitting up straighter, his eyes sharp and intelligent as his gaze met Stark's. "If you want to find ancient and barbaric beliefs you have to go to a place formed by an ancient and barbaric past. A place that is essentially cut off from today's civilization."

The answer jolted through Stark. "I have to go to the Isle."

"Exactly," Darius said.

"What the hell are you two talking about?" Aphrodite said.

"They speak of the place where Warriors were first trained by Sgiach."

"Sgiach? Who is that?" Damien asked.

"It is the ancient title for the Warrior who was called The Great Taker of Heads," Darius said.

"Sgiach was as raw and barbaric as it gets as a Warrior," Stark said.

"Okay, this is all well and good, but we need him to be alive today and not just an old story Warriors know, 'cause I'm pretty sure if Stark can't travel to the Otherworld, he also can't travel to the past," Aphrodite said.

"*She,*" Darius corrected.

"She?" Aphrodite's face was a question mark.

"Sgiach was a female Warrior, a vampyre of amazing powers," Stark said.

"And those 'old stories,' my beauty, also say that there will always be a Sgiach." Darius gave Aphrodite an indulgent smile. "She lives on the Isle of Women at the House of Night there."

"There's an Isle of Women House of Night?" Erin said.

"Why don't we know about that?" Shaunee said. "Do you know about that?" she asked Damien.

He shook his head. "Never heard of it."

"That's because you're not Warriors," Darius said. "The Isle of Women is also known as the Isle of Skye."

"Skye, like in Scotland?" Damien said.

"Yes. It is there that the very first vampyre Warriors were trained," Darius said.

"But not anymore, right?" Damien said, looking from Darius to Stark. "I mean, Warrior training goes on at all the Houses of Night. Like Dragon Lankford trains a bunch of Warriors who come from all over, and he's definitely not in Scotland."

"You are correct, Damien. In the modern world the training of Warriors takes place at the House of Night schools throughout the world," Thanatos said. "Around the turn of the nineteenth century, the High Council decided that would a more convenient way of doing things."

"More convenient and more civilized, I bet," Aphrodite said.

"You, too, are correct, Prophetess," Thanatos said.

"That's it, then. I take Zoey to the Isle of Women and Sgiach," Stark said.

"And then what?" Aphrodite asked.

"Then I get uncivilized so that I can figure out how to fight my way into the Otherworld without dying, and, once I'm there, I do whatever I have to do to bring Zoey back to us."

"Huh," said Aphrodite. "That actually doesn't sound like a bad idea."

"If Stark is allowed to enter the Isle," Darius said.

"It's a House of Night. Why wouldn't they let Stark come in?" Damien said.

"It's a House of Night like none other," Thanatos said. "The High Council's decision to move the training of the Sons of Erebus from Skye and spread them out among the Houses of Night worldwide was a decision that was the culmination of many, many years of tension and unease between the reigning Sgiach and the High Council."

"You make her sound like a queen," Jack said.

"In a way she is—a queen whose subjects were Warriors," Thanatos said.

"A queen in charge of the Sons of Erebus? I know the vamp High Council wouldn't like that, not unless Queen Sgiach was part of the High Council, too," Aphrodite said.

"Sgiach is a Warrior," Thanatos said. "And Warriors are not allowed on the High Council."

"But Sgiach is a woman. She should be able to be voted onto the Council," Damien said.

"No," Darius said. "No Warrior can sit on the Council. That is vampyre law."

"And that probably pissed off Sgiach," Aphrodite said. "I know it'd piss me off. She should be able to sit on the High Council."

Thanatos bowed her head in acknowledgment. "I agree with you, Prophetess, but many did not. When the training of the Sons of Erebus Warriors was taken from her, Sgiach withdrew to the Isle of Skye. She spoke to no one about her intention, but she didn't need to. We all felt her anger. We also felt the protective circle she cast around her Isle." Thanatos's eyes were filled with the shadows of memories of the past. "No one had experienced its like since the mighty vampyre Cleopatra cast a protective circle around her beloved Alexandria."

"No one enters the Isle of Women without the permission of Sgiach," Darius said.

"If they attempt to do so—they die," Thanatos said.

"Well, how do I get permission to enter the Isle?" Stark asked.

There was a long, awkward silence, and then Thanatos said, "Therein lies the first of your problems. Since Sgiach cast her protective circle, no outsider has been given permission to enter her Isle."

"I'll get permission," Stark said firmly.

"How are you going to do that, Warrior?" Thanatos asked.

Stark blew out a long breath, and said, "I know how I'm *not* going to do it. I'm not going to be civilized. And right now that's about all I know."

"Hang on," Damien said. "Thanatos, Darius, you both know things about Sgiach and this ancient barbaric religion. So, where did you learn it?"

"I've always liked to read." Darius shrugged. "So I was drawn to the old scrolls at the House of Night where I studied the blade. In my off time, I read."

"Dangerous *and* sexy. That's an excellent combination," Aphrodite purred, snuggling into him.

"Okay, we'll all barf later," Erin said.

"Yeah, right now, stop interrupting," Shaunee said.

"What about your knowledge of the bulls and Sgiach?" Damien asked Thanatos, giving the Twins and Aphrodite "be quiet" looks.

"From ancient texts here in the palace archives. When I first became a High Priestess, I spent many hours studying here by myself. I had to; I had no mentor," Thanatos said.

"No mentor? That'd be hard," Stark said.

"Apparently our world only needs one High Priestess at a time who has been gifted with an affinity for death," Thanatos said with a wry smile.

"That's a sucky job description," Jack said, and then clamped his hand over his mouth, and squeaked, "Sorry!"

Thanatos's smile widened. "I take no offense at your words, child. To be allied with Death is not an easy career path."

"But because of that, and because Darius is a reading Warrior, we have something to go by," Damien said.

"What are you thinking?" Aphrodite said.

"I'm thinking that I'm really good at one thing—and that's studying."

Aphrodite's blue eyes widened. "So we just need to point you to something to study."

"The archives. You need access to the palace archives," Thanatos said, already heading toward the door. "I'll speak with Duantia."

"Excellent. I'll get ready to study," Damien said.

"I'll help," Jack said.

"Nerd herd, as much as I hate it, it looks like we're all gonna get ready to study."

Stark watched Thanatos go. He vaguely registered that the rest of the kids were excited that they had somewhere to focus their energy, but his gaze went back to Zoey's pale face.

And I'll get ready to ally myself with death.

Zoey

Nothing seemed right.

It wasn't like I didn't know where I was. I mean, I knew I was in the Otherworld but not dead, and that I was with Heath, who definitely was dead.

Goddess! It was so weird that it was becoming more and more normal to think of Heath as DEAD.

Anyway, besides that, stuff just wasn't right.

At this moment I was curled up with Heath. We were spooning like an old married couple at the base of a tree on a mossy mattress made by the joining of ancient roots in a roughly bedlike oval. I should have been majorly comfortable. The moss was definitely soft, and it really did seem like Heath was alive. I could see him, hear him, touch him—he even smelled like Heath. I should be able to relax and just be with him.

So why, I wondered as I stared at a gaggle of dancing blue-winged butterflies, *am I so restless and generally "out of sorts" as Grandma would say?*

Grandma . . .

I did miss her. Her absence was like a mild toothache. Sometimes the feeling went away, but I knew it was there, and it would come back—probably worse.

She must really be worried about me. And sad. Thinking of how sad Grandma would be was hard, and my mind skirted away from it quickly.

I couldn't keep lying there. I moved away from Heath, careful not to wake him up.

Then I started to pace.

That helped. Well, it seemed to for a little while. I walked back and forth, back and forth, making sure I could see Heath. He did look cute while he slept.

I wished I could sleep.

I couldn't, though. If I rested—if I closed my eyes—it was like I lost pieces of myself. But how could that be? How could I be losing myself? It reminded me a little of the time I had strep throat and such a high fever that I had a super weird dream where I kept spinning around and around until pieces of my body started to fly off me.

I shivered. Why was that so easy to remember when a bunch of other stuff in my head was so foggy?

Goddess, I was really tired.

Distracted, I kinda tripped over one of the pretty white rocks that jutted up out of the grass and moss, and caught myself from falling by throwing up a hand and grabbing the side of the closest tree.

That's why I saw it. My hand. My arm. It didn't look right. I stopped and stared, and I swear my skin rippled, like in one of those gross horror movies where nasty stuff gets under an almost naked girl's flesh and crawls around, making her—

"No!" I wiped frantically at my arm. "No! Stop!"

"Zo, babe, what's wrong?"

"Heath, Heath—look." I held my arm out for him to see. "It's like a horror movie."

Heath's gaze went from my arm to my face. "Uh, Zo, what's like a horror movie?"

"My arm! My skin! It's moving." I flailed at him.

His smile didn't hide the worry on his face. He reached out and slowly ran his hand down my arm. When he got to my hand, he threaded his fingers with mine.

"There's nothing wrong with your arm, babe," he said.

"You really don't think so?"

"Really, seriously, I don't think so. Hey, what's going on with you?"

I opened up my mouth to tell him that I thought I was losing myself—that bits of myself were floating away—when something caught my eye at the edge of the tree line. Something dark.

"Heath, I don't like that," I told him, pointing a shaking hand at the spot of shadows.

The breeze stirred the wide green leaves of the trees that seemed suddenly not as thick and sheltering as they had moments ago, and the scent came to me, sickening and ripe, like three-day-old roadkill. I felt Heath's body jerk, and knew I wasn't imagining it.

Then the shadows out there stirred, and I was sure I heard wings.

"Oh, no," I whispered.

Heath's hand tightened on mine. "Come on. We need to get farther inside here."

I felt frozen and numb all at the same time. "Why? How can trees save us from whatever that is?"

Heath took my chin in his hand and made me look at him. "Zo, can't you feel it? This place, this grove, is *good*, purely good. Babe, can't you feel your Goddess in here?"

The tears that filled my eyes made him all blurry. "No," I said softly, as if I could barely form the words. "I can't feel my Goddess at all."

He pulled me into his arms and hugged me tight. "Don't worry, Zo. I can feel her, so it'll be okay. I promise." Then, while I was still cradled by one of his arms, Heath guided me deeper into Nyx's grove as my tears overflowed and fell wet and hot down my cold cheeks.

CHAPTER ELEVEN

Stevie Rae

"Skye? Really? Where is that? Ireland?" Stevie Rae said.

"It's Scotland, not Ireland, retard," Aphrodite said.

"Aren't they kinda the same thing? And don't say 'retard.' It's not nice."

"How about if I say bite me? Is that nice enough? Just listen and try not to be so asstarded, bumpkin. I need you to go back and do more of your weird commune with the earth or whatthefuckever it is you do, and see if you can come up with some info about Light *and* Darkness—you know, with a capital L and D. Also pay attention if a tree or whatnot says something about two bulls."

"Bulls? You mean like cows?"

"Are you not from the country? How is it that you don't know what a bull is?"

"Look, Aphrodite, that's an ignorant stereotype. Just 'cause I'm not from a big city does *not* mean I automatically know about cows and stuff. Heck, I don't even like horses."

"I swear you're a mutant," Aphrodite said. "A bull is a male cow. Even my mom's schizophrenic Bichon Frise knows that. Focus, would you, this is important. You need to go ask the fucking grass about an ancient and entirely too barbaric and therefore unattractive mythology or religion or some such that includes two fighting bulls, a white one and a black one, and a very guylike, violent, unending struggle between good and evil."

"What does this have to do with gettin' Zoey back?"

"I think it might somehow open a door for Stark to the Otherworld, *without* him actually dying because, apparently, that doesn't so much work for Warriors protecting their High Priestesses there."

"The cows can do that? How? Cows can't even talk."

"Bulls, double retard. Stay with me. I'm not just talking about animals, but the rawness of the power that surrounds them. The bulls represent that power."

"So they're not gonna talk?"

"Oh, for shit's sake! They might and they might not—they're super old magick, stupid! Who the hell knows what they can do? Just get this: to make it to the Otherworld, Stark can't be civilized and modern and all nicey-nice. He's got to figure out how to be more than that to reach Zoey and to protect her without getting both of them killed, and this olden-time religion might be a key to that."

"I guess that makes sense. I mean, when I think about Kalona, I don't exactly think of a modern guy." Stevie Rae paused, acknowledging only to herself that she was truly thinking of Rephaim and not his father. "And he's definitely got some raw power."

"And definitely in the Otherworld without being dead."

"Which is where Stark needs to be."

"So, go talk to flowers about bulls and such," Aphrodite said.

"I'll go talk to flowers," Stevie Rae said.

"Call me when they tell you something."

"Yeah, okay. I'll do my best."

"Hey, be careful," Aphrodite said.

"See, you can be nice," Stevie Rae said.

"Before you go all strawberries and cream on me, answer this question: who'd you Imprint with after ours broke?"

Stevie Rae's body went ice-cold. "No one!"

"Which means someone totally inappropriate. Who is it, one of those red fledgling losers?"

"Aphrodite—I said *no one*."

"Yeah, that's what I figured. See, one of the things I'm learning about because of this new Prophetess stuff, which is mostly a pain in the ass, by-the-by, is that if I listen without my ears, I know things."

"Here's what I know—you've lost your dang mind."

"So, again, be careful. I'm getting weird vibes from you, and they're telling me you might be in trouble."

"I think you've just made up a big ol' story to cover up that whole lot of crazy you got going on inside your head."

"And I think you're hiding something. So let's just agree to disagree."

"I'm goin' to talk to flowers about cows. Goodbye, Aphrodite."

"Bulls. Goodbye, bumpkin."

Stevie Rae opened the door to leave her dorm room, still frowning about Aphrodite's comments, and almost ran smack into Kramisha's hand, raised to knock on her door. They both jumped and then Kramisha shook her head. "Don't do weird shit like that. Makes me think you ain't normal no more."

"Kramisha, if I'd known you were out here, I wouldn't have jumped when I opened the door. And none of us are normal—at least not anymore."

"Speak for yourself. I'm still me. Meaning they's nothin' wrong with me. You, on the other hand, look like one hot messatude."

"I almost burned up on a roof two days ago. I think that gives me the right to look like crap."

"I don't mean you look bad." Kramisha cocked her head to the side. Today she was wearing her bright yellow bob wig, which she'd coordinated with sparkly fluorescent yellow eye shadow. "Actually, you lookin' good—all pink like white folks get when they real healthy. It kinda reminds me of cute little baby pigs with they pinkness."

"Kramisha, I swear you're makin' my head hurt. What are you talkin' about?"

"I'm just sayin' that you look good, but you ain't *doing* good. In there, and there." Kramisha pointed from Stevie Rae's heart to her head.

"I've got a lot on my mind," Stevie Rae said evasively.

"Yeah, I know that, what with Zoey totally jacked up and all, but you gotta keep your shit together just the same."

"I'm tryin'."

"Try harder. Zoey needs you. I know you ain't there with her, but I got this feelin' that you can help her. So you gotta be using your good sense."

Kramisha was staring at her with an intensity that made Stevie Rae want to fidget. "Like I said, I'm tryin'."

"You up to somethin' crazy?"

"No!"

"You sure? 'Cause this is for you." Kramisha held up a piece of purple notebook paper that had something written on it in her distinctive mixture of cursive and printing. "And it feels like a whole bunch of crazy to me."

Stevie Rae snatched the paper from her hand. "Dang it, why didn't you just say you were bringin' me one of your poems?"

"I was gettin' 'round to it." Kramisha crossed her arms and leaned against the doorway, obviously waiting for Stevie Rae to read the poem.

"Isn't there somethin' you need to go do?"

"Nope. The rest of the kids is eatin'. Oh, 'cept for Dallas. He's working with Dragon on some sword stuff, even though school ain't starting again officially, and I do not see no need to rush things, so I do not get why he in such a hurry to go to class. Anyway, just read the poem, High Priestess. I ain't goin' nowhere."

Stevie Rae stifled a sigh. Kramisha's poems tended to be confusing and abstract, but they were also often prophetic, and just thinking about one of them being obviously for her had Stevie Rae's stomach feeling like she'd eaten raw eggs. Reluctantly, her eyes went to the paper and she started to read:

The Red One steps into the Light
girded loins for her part in
the apocalyptic fight.

Darkness hides in different forms
see beyond shape, color, lies
and the emotional storms.

Ally with him; pay with your heart
though trust cannot be given
unless the Darkness you part.

See with the soul and not your eyes
because to dance with beasts you
must penetrate their disguise.

Stevie Rae shook her head, glanced up at Kramisha, and then read the poem again, slowly, willing her heart to please stop beating so loud that it would betray the guilty terror the thing instantly made her feel. 'Cause Kramisha was right; it was obviously about her. Of course it was also obviously about her *and* Rephaim. Stevie Rae supposed she should be grateful the dang poem didn't say anything about wings and human eyes in a dang bird head. Shoot!

"See what I mean 'bout it bein' 'bout you?"

Stevie Rae shifted her gaze from the poem to Kramisha's intelligent eyes. "Well, hell, Kramisha. 'Course it's about me. The first line says that."

"Yeah, see, I was sure 'bout that, too, even though I never heard nobody call you that."

"It makes sense," Stevie Rae said quickly, trying to drown out the memory of Rephaim's voice calling her *The Red One*. "I'm the only girl red vamp, so it's gotta be talkin' about me."

"That's what I thought, even though there is that whole bunch of freaky 'bout the beasts and stuff. I had to look up the gird-your-loins part 'cause it sounded nasty and sexual, but it ended up just bein' a way to say you need to get real ready for a fight."

"Yeah, well, there's been a bunch of fighting goin' on lately," Stevie Rae said, looking back at the poem.

"Looks like you in for some more—and it's some bad shit, too, you got to be real ready for." Then she cleared her throat meaningfully, and Stevie Rae reluctantly met her eyes again. "Who is he?"

"He?"

Kramisha crossed her arms. "Do not talk to me like I'm stupid. *Him.* The guy my poem says you're gonna give your heart to."

"I am not!"

"Oh, then you do know who he is." Kramisha tapped the toe of her leopard-print boots. "And he definitely ain't Dallas, 'cause you wouldn't be freaked about givin' him your heart. Everyone knows you two got a thing. So, who is *he*?"

"I don't have a clue. I'm not seein' anyone but Dallas. Plus, I'm way more worried about the parts that talk about Darkness and disguises and such," Stevie Rae lied.

"Huh," Kramisha snorted through her nose.

"Look, I'm gonna keep this and think about it," Stevie Rae said, stuffing the poem into her jeans pocket.

"Let me guess—you want me to keep my mouth shut 'bout it," Kramisha said, tapping her foot again.

"Yeah, 'cause I want to try to . . ." The excuse died under Kramisha's knowing stare. Stevie Rae blew out a long breath, decided to tell as much of the truth as she could, and started again. "I don't want you to say anything 'bout the poem 'cause I got a guy issue goin' on, and havin' it come out right now would suck for Dallas and for me, especially when I'm not real sure what's goin' on between me and this other guy."

"That's more like it. Guy shit can be one hot mess, and like my mama always says, it just ain't right to put your personal business all out there for everbody to see."

"Thanks, Kramisha. I 'preciate that."

Kramisha held up her hand. "Hang on. Didn't nobody say I was done with this subject. My poems is important. This one is about more than your jacked-up love life. So like I said before, get the crazy cleared from your head and remember to use your good sense. And also, every time I wrote the word *Darkness*, it made my insides feel wrong."

Stevie Rae gave Kramisha a long look, then made her decision. "Walk with me to the parking lot, 'kay? I got somethin' to do off campus, but I wanna talk to you on the way."

"No problem," Kramisha said. "Plus, it's 'bout time you said something 'bout what's going on inside your head to someone. You been actin' wacked lately, and I mean even before Zoey got herself shattered."

"Yeah, I know," Stevie Rae mumbled.

Neither one of them said anything more while they walked down the stairs and through the busy dorm. Stevie Rae thought it was like the thawing ice had also unfrozen the fledglings. Over the past couple of days, the kids had started coming out and acting more and more normal. Sure, she and Kramisha still got plenty of looks, but they'd gone from hostile and fearful to mostly curious.

"You thinkin' we might actually be able to come back here and go to school again, like this is still our home?" Kramisha blurted once they'd reached the sidewalk outside the dorm,

Stevie Rae gave her a surprised look. "Actually, I kinda have started to think that. Would it be so bad to be back here?"

Kramisha shrugged. "I ain't sure. All I'm sure of is I feel right when I'm sleepin' underground during the day."

"Yeah, that's a problem here."

"The Darkness in my poem that makes me feel wrong—you don't think that's 'bout us, do you?"

"No!" Stevie Rae shook her head emphatically. "There's nothin' wrong with us. You and me and Dallas and the rest of the red fledglings who came here decided. Nyx gave us a choice, and we chose good over evil—Light over Darkness. The poem isn't talkin' about us. I'm sure of that."

"It's the others, huh?" Even though they were alone, Kramisha lowered her voice.

Stevie Rae thought about it and realized Kramisha could be right. She'd just been so preoccupied with guilt about Rephaim that it hadn't occurred to her. Dang! She did need to get her head on straight. "Well, yeah, I guess it could be talkin' 'bout them, but if it is, it's really bad."

"Please. We all know they real bad."

"Yeah, well, I just found out some stuff from Aphrodite that gives Darkness with a capital D a whole new level of messed-up. And if they're involved with that, then they've reached a different kind of bad. Like Neferet bad."

"Shit."

"Yeah. So your poem might be talkin' 'bout a fight with them. But also, and this is the part I wanted you to know, Aphrodite and I have started to learn about some ancient stuff. You know, *really* old. So old the vamps have even forgotten about it."

"That's some old shit."

"Well, we're—meaning me and Aphrodite and Stark and the rest of the kids with Zoey—are gonna try to see if we can use this old info to help Stark get to the Otherworld so he can protect Z while she puts her soul back together."

"You mean get Stark to the Otherworld without him being all dead and stuff?"

"Yeah, apparently him showin' up in the Otherworld dead wouldn't be good for Zoey."

"So you gonna use that old shit to figure out how to do it right?"

Stevie Rae smiled at her. "We're gonna try. And you can help."

"Say the word—I'm there."

"Okay, here goes: Aphrodite's found some new Prophetess powers since she's been focused on them." Stevie Rae added a wry smile to her words. "Even though she's 'bout as happy as a cat in a thunderstorm about it." Kramisha laughed, and Stevie Rae continued, "Anyway, I was thinkin' that even though I don't have a circle here like Z does around her there, I do have a Prophetess."

Kramisha blinked, looked confused, and when Stevie Rae kept staring at her, her eyes finally widened in understanding. "Me?"

"You. Well, you and your poetry. You did it before and helped Z figure out how to chase Kalona outta here."

"But—"

"But look at it this way," Stevie Rae broke in. "Aphrodite figured it out. So are you sayin' she's smarter than you?"

Kramisha's eyes narrowed. "I got a whole world of smart that rich white girl don't know nothin' about."

"Well, then, cowboy up."

"You know you kinda scare me when you talk country."

"I know." Stevie Rae dimpled at her. "Okay, I'm gonna go conjure up some earth and see if I can figure anything more out from my end. Hey, find Dallas and fill him in on everything but the poem."

"I already told you I ain't rattin' you out."

"Thanks, Kramisha. You're a really good Poet Laureate."

"You ain't so bad yourself for a country girl."

"See ya." Stevie Rae waved and started to jog for Z's car.

"I got your back, High Priestess!"

Kramisha's parting words made Stevie Rae's stomach feel all squishy, but also had her grinning as she started Z's car. She was just getting ready to put the car into gear when she realized (a) she didn't know where she was going, and (b) the whole "conjure the earth" thing would be loads easier if she'd bothered to grab a green candle and maybe even some sweetgrass to draw some positive energy. Totally annoyed at herself, she put the car into neutral. Where in the Sam Hill was she going?

Back to Rephaim. The thought was like breathing—instant and natural. Stevie Rae reached for the gearshift, but her hand paused. Would going back to Rephaim right now really be the smartest thing for her to do?

Sure, on one hand she'd gotten a bunch of info from him about Kalona and Darkness and such.

On the other, she didn't really trust him. She *couldn't* really trust him.

Plus, he messed with her head. When she'd read Kramisha's poem, she'd been too dang busy obsessing about him to consider anything else—like the fact the poem could be a warning about the bad red fledglings and not just stuff about her and the Raven Mocker.

So what the heck should she do?

She'd told Rephaim she'd come back to check on him, but she wanted to return because of more than just telling him she would. Stevie Rae needed to see him. *Needed to?* Yes, she admitted reluctantly to herself. She needed to see the Raven Mocker. The admission jarred Stevie Rae.

"I'm Imprinted with him. That means we got a connection, and there's not much I can do about it," she muttered to herself while she squeezed the Bug's steering wheel. "I'm just gonna have to get used to it and deal with it."

And I have to remember that he is his father's son.

Fine. Okay. She'd check on him. She'd also ask him questions about Light as well as Darkness, and about two cows. She scowled. Well, bulls. But she should do some digging for herself without Rephaim. She really should evoke her element and see what info she could get on the cow/bulls. That would be using her good sense. Then Stevie Rae grinned and slapped the steering wheel.

"I got it! I'll stop at that cute old park that's on the way to Gilcrease. Do a little earth magick, and then check on Rephaim. Easy-peasy!" Of course first she'd duck back into Nyx's Temple and grab a green candle, some matches, and some sweetgrass. Feeling better now that she had a plan, she was just getting ready to take the Bug outta neutral when she heard the sound of cowboy boots tapping against the asphalt of the parking lot and then Dallas speaking with exaggerated nonchalance.

"I'm just walkin' out here to Zoey's car. I'm not sneakin' up on Stevie Rae and makin' her jump."

Stevie Rae rolled down her window and grinned at him. "Hey there, Dallas. I thought Kramisha said you were working out with Dragon."

"I was. Check it out—Dragon gave me this cool knife. Said it's a dirk. He also said I might be good with it."

Stevie Rae watched dubiously as Dallas pulled a pointy, double-edged knife from a leather holder he was wearing strapped around his waist and held it kinda awkwardly, like he wasn't sure whether it would cut someone else, or cut him.

"It's real sharp-looking," Stevie Rae said, trying to sound positive.

"Yeah, that's why I'm not using it to practice with yet, but Dragon did say I could wear it. For a while. If I was careful."

"Oh, okay. Cool." If she lived a million years Stevie Rae was sure she'd never understand guy stuff.

"Yeah, so, I got done with my dirk lessons and ran into Kramisha on my way out of the Field House," Dallas said while he sheathed the knife. "She said she'd left you here 'cause you were gettin' ready to take off to go do some earth thing. I thought I'd try to catch you before you left and come along."

"Oh, well. That's nice, Dallas, but I'm fine by myself. Actually, it would really help if you grabbed a green candle and some matches for me from Nyx's Temple and ran them back out here to me. Oh, and if you see some sweetgrass in the temple, bring it here, too, would ya? Don't know where my mind's been, but conjuring earth is definitely easier with an earth candle, and I totally forgot one, not to mention the sweetgrass for drawin' positive energy."

She was surprised when Dallas didn't say 'kay and jog away for the stuff. Instead, he just stood there, watching her, with his hands shoved down in his jeans pockets and looked kinda annoyed.

"What?" she asked.

"I'm sorry I'm not a Warrior!" he blurted. "I'm tryin' the best I can to learn somethin' from Dragon, but it's gonna take me a while to get decent at it. I've never really cared about all that fightin' stuff, and I'm sorry!" Dallas repeated, looking more and more upset.

"Dallas, what the heck are you talkin' about?"

He threw his hands up in frustration. "I'm talkin' about me not being good enough for you. I know you need more—that you need a Warrior. Hell, Stevie Rae, if I'd been your Warrior, I could've been there for you when those kids attacked you and almost killed you. If I were your Warrior, you wouldn't be sendin' me off on stupid errands. You'd keep me close to you, so I could protect you during all this stuff you're goin' through."

"I'm doin' fine protecting myself, and gettin' me an earth candle and stuff is not a stupid errand."

"Yeah, okay, but you deserve better than a guy who doesn't know shit about protecting his woman."

Stevie Rae's brows went up to meet her curly blond hair. "Did you just call me your woman?"

"Well, yeah." He fidgeted, and then added, "But in a good way."

"Dallas, you couldn't have stopped what happened on the roof," she said truthfully. "You know how those kids are."

"I should have been with you; I should be your Warrior."

"I don't need a Warrior!" she yelled, exasperated at his stubbornness and hating the fact that he was so upset.

"Well, you sure as hell don't need me anymore." He turned his back on the Bug and shoved his hands into his jeans pockets.

Stevie Rae looked at his hunched shoulders and felt terrible. She'd done this. She'd hurt him because she'd been pushing him and everyone away to keep Rephaim a secret. Guilty as a rabbit in a carrot patch, she got out of the car and touched his shoulder gently. He didn't look at her.

"Hey, that's not true. I do need you."

"Sure. That's why you've been busy shoving me away."

"No, I've just been busy. Sorry if I've come across as mean," she said.

He turned to her. "Not mean. Just not caring anymore."

"I care!" she said quickly, and stepped into his arms, hugging him back as tightly as he was hugging her.

Dallas spoke softly into her ear. "Then let me come with you."

Stevie Rae pulled back so she could look at him, and the "no, you can't" she'd been ready to say died on her lips. It was like she could see his heart through his eyes, and it was clear that she was breaking it—breaking him. What the hell was she doing hurting this kid because of Rephaim? She'd saved the Raven Mocker. She wasn't sorry about that. She was sorry that it was affecting the people around her. *Well, that's it, then. I'm not hurtin' the folks I care about most.*

"Okay, yeah, you can come with me," she told him.

His eyes instantly brightened. "You mean it?"

"'Course I mean it. I do need that earth candle, though. Well, and the sweetgrass, too. And it's still not a stupid errand."

"Hell, I'll get you a whole bag of candles and all the grass you want!" Dallas laughed, kissed her, and then, yelling that he'd be right back, sprinted away.

Slowly, Stevie Rae got back into the Bug. She gripped the steering wheel and stared straight ahead, reciting her mental to-do list aloud like a mantra. "Conjure earth with Dallas. Find out what I can about the cows. Bring Dallas back to the school. Make an excuse. A *good* excuse to leave again, only this time alone. Go to the Gilcrease and check on Rephaim. See if he knows anything else that might help Stark and Z. Come back here. Don't hurt your friends by shoving them away. Check on the red fledglings. Clue in Lenobia and the rest of 'em 'bout what's going on with Z. Call Aphrodite back. Figure out what the heck to do 'bout the bad fledglings at the depot. And then try, real hard, not to hurl yourself off the top of the nearest tall building . . ." Feeling like she was drowning in a big ol' stinkin', stagnant, Okie pond of stress, Stevie Rae lowered her head until her forehead pressed against the steering wheel.

How in the world did Z deal with all of this bullshit and stress?

She didn't, the thought came unbidden to her mind, *it shattered her.*

CHAPTER TWELVE

Stevie Rae

"Wow! It looks like one of those super tornados cut its way through Tulsa," Dallas said. He was gawking as Stevie Rae maneuvered the Bug carefully around yet another pile of fallen tree limbs. The entry road to the park was blocked by a Bradford pear tree that had been split almost perfectly in half, so Stevie Rae ended up stopping beside it.

"At least some of the power is comin' back on." She gestured at the streetlights that ringed the park, illuminating what was a total mess of ice-damaged trees and flattened azalea bushes.

"Not for those folks, though." Dallas jerked his chin at the neat little houses near the park. Here and there a light shone bravely through a window, proving that some people had had the foresight to buy propane generators before the storm hit, but mostly the surrounding area remained dark and cold and silent.

"It sucks for them, but makes my life easier tonight," Stevie Rae said, getting out of the car. Carrying a tall green ritual candle, a braided length of dried sweetgrass, and a box of long matches, Dallas joined her. "Everyone's all hunkered down and won't be paying any attention to what I'm doin'."

"You're definitely right about that, girl." Dallas draped his arm familiarly over Stevie Rae's shoulders.

"Aw, you know I like it when you tell me I'm right." She threaded her arm around his waist, sticking her hand in the back pocket of his jeans like she used to do. He squeezed her shoulder and kissed the top of her head.

"Then I'll tell ya you're right more often," he said.

Stevie Rae grinned up at him. "You tryin' to soften me up for somethin'?"

"I dunno. Is it workin'?"

"Maybe."

"Good."

They both laughed. She bumped him with her hip. "Let's go over there to the big oak. That looks like a good place."

"Whatever you say, girl."

They made their way slowly to the center of the park, walking around shattered tree limbs and sloughing through the cold, wet muck that was left from the storm, trying not to slip on the patches of ice that had begun to refreeze in the chill of the night. She'd been right to let Dallas come with her. Maybe part of her confusion about Rephaim had happened because she'd gotten kinda isolated from her friends and was focusing too hard on the weirdness of their Imprint. Heck, the Imprint with Aphrodite had seemed totally bizarre at first, too. Maybe she just needed some time—and space—to deal with the newness of it.

"Hey, check it out." Dallas pulled her attention back to him. He was pointing at the ground around the old oak. "It's like the tree made a circle for you."

"That's cool!" she said. And it was! The solid tree had weathered the storm well. The only branches it had lost were a smattering of limb tips. They'd fallen onto the grass, forming a perfect circle completely around the tree.

Dallas hesitated at the edge of the circumference. "I'm gonna stay out here, okay? So it really can be like this is a circle cast especially for you, and I haven't broken it," he said.

Stevie Rae looked up at him. Dallas was a good guy. He was always saying sweet things like that and letting her know he understood her better than most folks did. "Thank you. That's really nice, Dallas." She went up on her tiptoes and kissed him softly.

His arms tightened around her, and he held her closer to him. "Anything for my High Priestess."

His breath was warm and sweet against her mouth and, on impulse, Stevie Rae kissed him again, liking that he was making her feel all tingly inside. And liking that his touch was blocking thoughts of Rephaim from her mind. She was more than a little breathless when he reluctantly let her go.

He cleared his throat and gave a little laugh. "Be careful, girl. It's been a long time since you and me been alone."

Feeling kinda giggly and light-headed, she dimpled at him. "Too long."

His smile was sexy and cute. "We'll have to fix that soon, but first you better get to work."

"Oh, yeah," she said. "Work, work, work . . ."

Smiling, she took the sweetgrass braid, the green candle, and the matches he'd brought her.

"Hey," Dallas said, handing her the stuff, "I just remembered something about sweetgrass. Aren't you supposed to use somethin' else before you burn it? I was kinda good in Spells and Rituals Class, and I swear there was more to it than just lighting the braid and waving it around."

Stevie Rae screwed up her forehead, thinking. "I dunno. Zoey talked about it 'cause it's a Native American thing. I swear she said it draws positive energy."

"Okay, well, I guess Z would know," Dallas said.

Shrugging, Stevie Rae said, "Yeah, plus it is just grass that smells good. I mean, how bad could it be?"

"Yeah, seriously. Besides, you're Earth Girl. You should be able to control some burnin' grass."

"Yep," she said. "Okay, well, here goes." Whispering a simple, "Thank you, earth," to her element, she turned her back to Dallas, stepped over the boundary and entered the earth-made circle. Stevie Rae strode confidently to the northernmost point inside the circumference, which was directly in front of the old tree. She stopped there and closed her eyes. Stevie Rae had learned early that the best way to connect with her element was through her senses. So she breathed in deeply, clearing her mind of all the cluttered thoughts she usually carried around with her and allowing only one thing to leak through: the sense of hearing.

She listened to the earth. Stevie Rae could hear the wind murmuring through the winter leaves, the night birds singing to each other, the sounds and sighings of the park settling down for a long, cold night.

When her sense of sound was full of earth, Stevie Rae drew in another breath and focused on smell. She breathed in the earth, scenting the damp heaviness of ice-encapsulated grass, the crisp cinnamon of the browned leaves, the uniquely mossy fragrance of the ancient oak.

Her sense of smell filled by earth, Stevie Rae drew another deep breath and imagined the rich, full taste of a garlic bulb and the ripeness of summer tomatoes. She thought about the simple earth magick of pulling at green, tufty tops and discovering below them thick, crisp carrots that had been nurtured within the earth.

Taste overflowing with earth's bounty, she thought about the touch of the softness of summer grass against her feet—of dandelions tickling her chin as she held one there to see if it'd leave the telltale yellow blush of secret love—of the way the earth lifted to fill all of her senses after a spring rain.

And then, drawing an even deeper breath, Stevie Rae let her spirit embrace the wonderful, amazing, magickal way the gift of her element made her feel. Earth was mother, counselor, sister, and friend. Earth grounded her, and even when everything else in her world was totally screwed up, she could count on her element to calm and protect her.

Smiling, Stevie Rae opened her eyes. She turned to her right. "Air, I ask you to please come to my circle." Even though she didn't have a yellow candle, or anyone to represent air, Stevie Rae knew it was important to acknowledge and pay respect to each of the other four elements. And, if she was really lucky, they might actually show up and strengthen her circle. Facing south, she continued, "Fire, I ask that you please come to my circle." Turning deosil, or clockwise, she called, "Water, I'd like you to please come to my circle. Then, deviating from a traditional casting, Stevie Rae stepped back a few feet to the middle of the grassy area, and said, "Spirit, this is out of order, but I'd really like it if you joined my circle, too."

Walking forward to the north, Stevie Rae was almost one hundred percent sure she caught sight of a thin silver thread of light spiraling around her. She grinned over her shoulder at Dallas. "Hey, I think it's workin'."

"Of course it's workin', girl. You got some serious High Priestess mojo."

It sounded really good that Dallas kept calling her High Priestess, and Stevie Rae was still smiling when she turned back to the north. Feeling proud and strong, she finally lit the green candle, saying, "Earth, I know I'm doin' things outta order here, but I had to save the best for last. So now I'm askin' you to come to me like you always do, because you and me, we got a connection that's somethin' even more special than fireflies filling Haikey Creek Park during a summer night. Come to me, earth. Please come to me."

Earth burst around her like an exuberant puppy. Moments before the night had been cold and wet and dominated by the crippling ice storm, but now Stevie Rae felt the welcomed warmth and humidity of an Oklahoma summer night as the presence of her element dominated the fully cast circle.

"Thank you!" she said joyfully. "I can't tell you how much it means to me that I can always count on you." Heat radiated up from under her feet, and the ice that encased the grass within the circle cracked and shattered as the blades sprang free, temporarily released from their winter prison. "Okay." She kept her mind filled with her element and spoke to earth as if it was personified in front of her. "I gotta ask you somethin' important. But first I'm gonna light this, 'cause I think you'll like it a lot." Stevie Rae held the dried sweetgrass in the flame and then set the candle at her feet when the braid took light. She blew softly on it, so that the grass began to smoke. Stevie Rae turned and, grinning at Dallas, walked around the inside of the circumference of her circle, wafting the grass until the entire area was hazy with gray smoke and heady with the scent of summertime on the prairie.

When she returned to the top of the circle, Stevie Rae faced north again, the direction most closely allied with her element, and began to speak. "My friend, Zoey Redbird, said that sweetgrass draws positive energy, and I definitely need some energy tonight, 'specially since it's for Zoey that I'm asking your help. I know you remember her—she has an affinity for you, just like she does for all the elements. She's special, and not just 'cause she's my BFF. Z's special 'cause," Stevie Rae paused, and then the words came to her, "she's special 'cause Zoey has a little bit of everything inside her. I guess it's kinda like she represents all of us. So we need her back. Plus, she's hurtin' where she is, and I think she needs help to find her way out. So her Warrior, a guy named Stark, is gonna go after her. He definitely needs your help. I'm asking that you show me the way for Stark to help Zoey. Please."

Stevie Rae wafted the still-smoking braid around her one more time, and then she waited.

The smoke was sweet and thick. The night was unusually warm because of the presence of her element.

But nothing else was going on.

Sure, she could feel earth there, surrounding her, willing to do her bidding.

But nothing was happening.

At all.

Not sure what else to do, Stevie Rae wafted the sweetgrass braid around her some more and tried again.

"Well, maybe I wasn't specific enough." She thought for a second, trying to remember everything Aphrodite had told her, and added, "With the power of earth, and through the energy of this sacred grass, I call the white bull from the old days to my circle because I need to know how Stark can get to Zoey so that he can protect her while she finds a way back together and back to this world."

The sweetgrass that had been gently smoking until then turned red-hot. With a cry, Stevie Rae dropped it. Thick, black smoke billowed from the sizzling braid, like it was a snake belching darkness.

Pressing her burned hand against her body, Stevie Rae stumbled back.

"Stevie Rae? What's happening?"

She could hear Dallas, but when she looked behind her she couldn't see him anymore. The smoke was just too thick. Stevie Rae turned around, trying to peer through the darkness at him, but she couldn't see one dang thing. She looked where her burning earth candle should be, and it, too, had been covered by the smoke. Disoriented, she yelled, "I don't know what's goin' on. The sweetgrass got weird all of a sudden and—"

The earth beneath her feet, that tangible part of her element that Stevie Rae felt so connected to—so comfortable with—began to shake.

"Stevie Rae, you need to come outta there now. I don't like all this smoke."

"Can you feel that?" she called to Dallas. "Is the ground shakin' out there, too?"

"No, but I can't see you, and I got a bad feeling 'bout this."

Before Stevie Rae saw it, she felt its presence. The feeling it gave her was terrifyingly familiar and in the heartbeat of an instant, Stevie Rae understood why. It reminded her of the moment she'd realized she was dying. The moment she'd begun to cough, grabbed Zoey's hand, and said, *I'm scared, Z.* The echo of that terror paralyzed Stevie Rae, so that when the tip of the first horn took form and glinted at her, white and sharp and dangerous, all she could do was stare and shake her head back and forth, back and forth.

"Stevie Rae! Can you hear me?"

Dallas's voice seemed to be miles away.

The second horn materialized, and, along with it, the bull's head began to form, white and massive, with eyes so black they glistened like a bottomless lake at midnight.

Help me! Stevie Rae tried to say, but fear trapped the words in her throat.

"That's it. I'm comin' in there and getting' you, even if you don't want me to break the circle and—"

Stevie Rae felt the ripple when Dallas reached the boundary of her circle. So did the bull. The creature turned its great head and snorted a gust of fetid air into the inky smoke. The night shivered in response.

"Shit! Stevie Rae, I can't get inside the circle. Close it and get out of there!"

"I-I c-c-can't," she stammered, her voice a broken whisper.

Fully formed, the bull was a nightmare come alive. Its breath gagged Stevie Rae. Its eyes trapped her. His white coat was luminous in the all-encompassing darkness, but it wasn't beautiful. Its brilliance was slimy, its glistening surface cold and dead. One of the beast's enormous cloven hoofs lifted and then fell, tearing the earth with such malice that Stevie Rae felt an echo of the pain of the wound within her soul. She ripped her gaze from the bull's eyes to stare down at his hooves. She gasped in horror. The grass around the beast was broken and blackened. Where he had pawed the earth—Stevie Rae's earth—the ground was torn and bleeding.

"No!" The dam of terror broke enough for her words to finally escape. "Stop! You're hurting us!"

The bull's black eyes bored into hers. The voice that filled her head was deep and powerful and unimaginably malicious. *"You had the power to evoke me, vampyre, and that has amused me enough that I choose to answer your question. The Warrior must look to his blood to discover the bridge to enter the Isle of Women, and then he must defeat himself to enter the arena. Only by acknowledging one before the other will he join his Priestess. After he joins her, it is her choice and not his whether she returns."*

Stevie Rae swallowed her fear and blurted, "That doesn't make sense."

"Your inability to comprehend has no bearing on me. You summoned. I answered. Now I shall claim my blood price. It has, indeed, been eons since I tasted the sweetness of vampyre blood—especially one filled with so much innocent Light."

Before Stevie Rae could begin to form any kind of response, the beast started to circle her. Tendrils of darkness slithered from the smoke surrounding him and began to snake their way toward her. When they touched her, they were like frozen razor blades slicing, tearing, ripping her flesh.

Without conscious thought, she screamed one word: "Rephaim!"

CHAPTER THIRTEEN

Rephaim

Rephaim knew the instant Darkness materialized. He'd been sitting on the rooftop balcony, eating an apple, staring up at the clear night sky *and* trying to ignore the annoying presence of the human ghost that had developed an unfortunate fascination with him.

"Come on, tell me! Is it really fun to fly?" the young spirit asked for what Rephaim thought was probably the hundredth time. *"It looks like it'd be fun. I never got to, but I'll bet flying with your own wings is way more fun than flying in an airplane any day."*

Rephaim had sighed. The child talked more than Stevie Rae, which was pretty impressive. Irritating, but impressive. He was trying to decide if he should continue to ignore her and hope she'd finally go away, or come up with an alternative plan, as ignoring the girl didn't appear to be working. He'd thought perhaps he should ask Stevie Rae what to do about the ghost, which had turned his mind to the Red One. Though, truth be told, his thoughts were never far from her.

"Is it dangerous to fly? I mean with your wings? I guess it must be because you got hurt, and I'll bet that was from flying around . . ."

The child had been babbling when the texture of the world changed. In that first, shocking moment, he felt the familiarity and believed, for the space of a heartbeat, that his father had returned.

"Silence!" he roared at the ghost. He stood and whirled around, glowing red eyes glaring into the dark land surrounding him, hoping beyond words that he could glimpse the raven blackness of his father's wings.

The ghost child made a shocked squeak, cringed away from him, and disappeared.

Rephaim gave her absolutely no thought. He was too busy being barraged with knowledge and emotions.

First came knowledge. He knew almost immediately that it wasn't his father he'd sensed. Yes, Kalona was powerful, and he had long allied himself with Darkness, but the disturbance this immortal was making in the world was different; it was far more powerful. Rephaim could sense it in the excited response of the dark hidden things of the earth, sprites that this modern world of man-made light and electronic magick had forgotten. But Rephaim had not forgotten them, and from the deepest of the night's shadows, he saw ripples and quivers, and was baffled by their reaction.

What could be powerful enough to arouse the hidden sprites?

Then Stevie Rae's fear hit him. It was the rawness of her complete terror coupled with the excitement of the sprites, and that instant of initial familiarity, that provided Rephaim with his answer.

"By all the gods, Darkness itself has entered this realm!" Rephaim was moving before he'd made a conscious decision to do so. He burst out of the front doors of the dilapidated mansion, knocking them aside with his uninjured arm as if they were made of cardboard, only to come to a halt on the wide front porch.

He had no idea of where he should go.

Another wave of terror engulfed him. Experiencing it with her, Rephaim knew Stevie Rae was paralyzed by her fear. A horrible thought filled his mind: *Had Stevie Rae conjured Darkness? How could she? Why would she?*

The answer to the most important of the three questions came as quickly as he thought it. Stevie Rae would do almost anything if she believed it would bring Zoey back.

Rephaim's heart thundered, and his blood pumped hard and fast through his body. Where was she? The House of Night?

No, surely not. Were she to set about conjuring Darkness, it wouldn't be at a school devoted to Light.

"Why didn't you come to me?" he shouted his frustration into the night. "I know Darkness; you do not!"

But even as he spoke, he admitted to himself that he was wrong. Stevie Rae had been touched by Darkness when she had died. He hadn't known her then, but he'd known Stark and had witnessed for himself the Darkness that surrounded the death and resurrection of a fledgling.

"She chose Light, though." He spoke softly this time. "And Light always underestimates the viciousness of Darkness."

The fact that I live is an example of that.

Stevie Rae needed him tonight, badly. That was also a fact.

"Stevie Rae, where are you?" Rephaim muttered.

Only the restless stirrings of the sprites answered him.

Could he coax a sprite into leading him to Darkness? No—he discarded the idea quickly. Sprites would go to Darkness if it called them. Other than that, they much preferred to feed off vestiges of power from afar. And he couldn't afford to wait around hoping Darkness would call them. He needed to figure out—

"REPHAIM!"

Stevie Rae's scream echoed eerily around him. Her voice was filled with pain and despair. The sound of it sliced through his heart. He knew his eyes blazed red. He wanted to rip and tear and destroy. The haze of scarlet rage that began to overwhelm him was a seductive escape. If he gave into anger completely, he would, indeed, become more beast than man, and this unusual, uncomfortable fear he had begun to feel for her would be drowned out by instinct and mindless violence, which he could appease by attacking the helpless humans in any of the dark houses surrounding the lifeless museum. For a while he would be sated. For a while he would not feel.

And why not give in to the rage that had so often consumed his life? It would be easier—it was familiar—it was safe.

If I give in to rage, it will be the end of this connection I have with her. The thought sent ripples of shock through his body. The ripples turned to bright specks of light that seared the red haze that shrouded his sight.

"No!" he cried, letting the humanity of his voice beat back the beast within him. "If I abandon her to Darkness, she dies." Rephaim drew long, slow breaths. He had to calm down. He had to think. The red haze continued to dissipate, and his mind began to reason again. *I have to use our connection and our blood!*

Rephaim forced himself to be still and breathe in the night. He knew what he must do. He drank in one more deep breath, and then began: "I call upon the power of the spirit of ancient immortals, which is mine by birthright to command." Rephaim steeled himself for the drain that the invocation would cause on his unhealed body, but as he drew power from the shadows of the night, he was surprised to feel a surge of energy. The night around him seemed swollen, throbbing with raw and ancient power. It gave him a sick sense of foreboding, but he used it all the same, channeling the power through him, preparing to charge it with the immortality carried in his blood, the blood that Stevie Rae now shared. But as it filled him, his body was consumed in an energy so fierce, so raw, that it knocked Rephaim to his knees.

His first hint that something miraculous was happening was when he realized that he'd automatically thrown both of his hands forward to catch himself—and both arms responded, even the one that had been broken and bound to his chest with a sling.

Rephaim stayed there on his knees, trembling and holding both arms out before him. His breath was coming fast as he flexed his hands.

"More!" he hissed the word. "Come to me!"

Dark energy surged into him again, a live current of cold violence he struggled to contain. Rephaim knew this indwelling was different than any he'd felt before when calling on the powers his father's blood allowed him to access, but he was no callow youth. He had long trafficked with shadows and the base things that filled the night. Reaching deep within him, the Raven Mocker inhaled the energy, like the air of a midwinter's night, and then he threw his arms wide at the same instant he unfurled his wings.

Both wings responded to him.

"Yes!" His joyous shout caused the shadows to writhe and quiver in ecstasy.

He was whole again! The wing was completely healed!

Rephaim leaped to his feet. Dark pinions completely extended, he looked like a magnificent sculpture of a godling, suddenly come to life. His body vibrating with power, the Raven Mocker continued the invocation. The air blazed scarlet as if a phosphorous mist of blood surrounded him. Swollen with borrowed Darkness, Rephaim's voice rang in the night. "Through the immortal might of my father, Kalona, who seeded my blood and spirit with his legacy, I command this power that I wield in his name to lead me to the Red One—she who has tasted my blood, and with whom I have Imprinted and exchanged life debts. Take me to Stevie Rae! I command it so!"

The mist hovered for a moment, then shifted, and like a ribbon of scarlet silk, a thin, glistening path unfurled into the air before him. Swift and sure, Rephaim took to the sky and streaked after the beckoning Darkness.

He found her not far from the museum in a park shrouded by smoke and death. As he dropped silently from the sky, Rephaim wondered how the humans in the houses framing the area could be so oblivious to what had been loosed just outside the deceptive safety of their front doors.

The pool of black smoke was most concentrated in the heart of the park. Rephaim could just make out the top branches of a sturdy old oak under which chaos reigned. He slowed as he drew near it, though his wings were still spread around him, tasting the air and allowing him to move soundlessly and swiftly, even on the ground.

The fledgling didn't notice him. But Rephaim realized that the boy probably wouldn't have noticed the arrival of an army. All of his attention was focused on attempting to stab a long, lethal-looking knife through what appeared to be a circle of darkness that had coalesced into a solid wall—or at least that was how it manifested to the fledgling.

Rephaim was not a fledgling; he understood Darkness much better.

He skirted around the boy and, unseen, faced the circle at its northernmost point. He wasn't sure if instinct or Stevie Rae's influence drew him there, and acknowledged—though briefly—that the two might be becoming one.

He paused, and with a single, reluctant motion, closed his wings, folding them neatly against his back. Then he held up his hand and spoke softly to the scarlet mist that was still his to command. "Cloak me. Allow me to cross the barrier." Rephaim curled his fist around the pulsing energy that gathered there, and then, with a flick of his fingers, scattered the mist over his body.

He expected the pain of it. Though there were aspects of immortal power that obeyed him, the obedience never came without a price. Very often that price was paid in pain. This time the pain burned through his newly healed body like lava, but he welcomed it because it meant his bidding had been done.

There was no way to make ready for what he might find within the circle. Rephaim simply gathered himself and, covered by the inherited strength of his father's blood, he stepped forward. The wall of darkness opened to him.

Inside the circle Rephaim was engulfed in the scent of Stevie Rae's blood and the overwhelming odor of death and decay.

"Please stop! I can't stand any more! Kill me if that's what you want, just don't touch me again!"

He couldn't see her, but Stevie Rae sounded utterly defeated. Acting quickly, Rephaim scooped some of the clinging scarlet mist from his body. "Go to her—strengthen her," he whispered the command.

He heard Stevie Rae gasp and was almost sure she cried his name. Then the darkness parted to reveal a sight Rephaim would never forget, even should he live to be as ancient as his father.

Stevie Rae stood in the middle of the circle. Tendrils of sticky black threads wrapped around her legs. Wherever they touched her, they sliced her skin. Her jeans were ripped and hung on her body only in shreds. Blood seeped from her torn flesh. As he watched, another tendril snaked out of the soupy darkness surrounding them and lashed, whiplike, around her waist, instantly drawing a weeping line of blood. She moaned in pain, and her head lolled. Rephaim saw that her eyes had gone blank.

It was then that the beast made itself known. The instant he saw it, Rephaim knew beyond all doubt that he was staring at Darkness given form. It snorted, a terrible, deafening sound. Spewing blood and mucus and smoke, the bull tore the earth with his hooves. The creature stalked to Stevie Rae from out of the densest of the black smoke. Like moonlight in a crypt, the white bull's coat looked like death as he towered over the girl. The creature was so massive that he had to dip his huge head to allow his tongue to lick at her bleeding waist.

Stevie Rae's scream was echoed by Rephaim's cry: "No!"

The great bull paused. His head turned to the Raven Mocker; his bottomless gaze held Rephaim's.

"This night gets more and more interesting." The voice rumbled through his mind. Rephaim forced down his fear as the bull took two steps toward him, shaking the ground as he scented the air.

"I smell Darkness on you."

"Yes," Rephaim spoke over the sound of the terrified beating of his heart. "I have long lived with Darkness."

"Odd, then, that I do not know you." The bull scented the air around him again. *"Though I have known your father."*

"It is through the power of my father's blood that I parted the dark curtain and stand before you." He kept his eyes on the bull, but he was utterly aware that Stevie Rae was just feet away from him, bleeding and helpless.

"Is it? I think you lie, birdman."

Though the voice in his mind didn't change, Rephaim could feel the bull's anger.

Staying calm, Rephaim scooped a finger down his chest, drawing a line of red mist from his body. He held his hand up, like an offering to the bull. "This allowed me to part the dark curtain of the circle, and this power is mine to command by right of my father's immortal blood."

"That immortal blood flows through your veins is truth. But the

power that swells your body and commanded my barrier to part is borrowed from me."

Fear skittered down Rephaim's spine. Very carefully, he bowed his head in respect and acknowledgment. "Then I thank you, though I did not call upon your power. I invoked only my father's, as it is only his that is rightfully mine to command."

"I hear the truth in your words, son of Kalona, but why command the power of immortals to draw you here and to allow you within my circle? What business do you or your father have with Darkness tonight?"

Rephaim's body went very still, but his mind raced. Until that moment in his life, he had always drawn strength from the legacy of immortality within his blood and the cunning of the raven that had been joined with it to create him. But this night, facing Darkness, swollen with a strength that was not his own, he suddenly knew that even though it was through this creature's power that he had been granted access to Stevie Rae, he would not save her by using Darkness, whether it came from the bull or from his father; nor could the instincts of a raven battle the beast he faced. Forces allied with it could not defeat this bull—this embodiment of Darkness.

So Rephaim drew on the only thing left to him—the remnants of humanity passed to him through his dead mother's body. He answered the bull like a human, with an honesty so raw that he thought it might cleave his heart.

"I'm here because she's here, and she belongs to me." Rephaim's eyes never left the bull, but he jerked his head in Stevie Rae's direction.

"I scent her on you." The bull took another step toward Rephaim, causing the ground under them to shake. *"She may belong to you, but she had the impudence to invoke me. This vampyre requested my aid, which I granted her. As you know, she must pay the price. Leave now, birdman, and I will allow you to live."*

"Go on, Rephaim." Stevie Rae's voice was weak, but when Rephaim finally looked at her, he saw that her gaze was unwavering and lucid. "It isn't like the rooftop. You can't save me from this. Just go."

Rephaim should go. He knew he should. Only a few days before he couldn't even have imagined a world where he would be facing down Darkness to attempt to save a vampyre—to attempt to save anyone except himself or his father. Yet as he stared into Stevie Rae's soft blue eyes, what he saw was a whole new world—a world in which this strange little red vampyre meant heart and soul and truth.

"Please. Don't let him hurt you, too," she told him.

It was those words—those selfless, heartfelt, truthful words that made Rephaim's decision for him.

"I said she belongs to me. You scent her on me; you know it's true. So I can pay her debt for her," Rephaim said.

"No!" Stevie Rae cried.

"Think carefully before you make such an offer, son of Kalona. I will not kill her. It is a blood debt, not a life debt, she owes me. I will return your vampyre to you, eventually, when I am done tasting of her."

The bull's words sickened Rephaim. Like a bloated leech, Darkness was going to feed from Stevie Rae. He was going to lick her slashed skin and taste the copper saltiness of her lifeblood—of *their* lifeblood, joined forever because of their Imprint.

"Take my blood instead. I'll pay her debt," Rephaim said.

"You are your father's son. Like him, you have chosen to champion a being who can never give you what it is you seek most. So be it. I accept payment of the vampyre's debt from you. Release her!" the bull commanded.

The razorlike threads of darkness withdrew from Stevie Rae's body and, as if they had been the only things keeping her on her feet, she crumbled to the blood-soaked grass.

Before he could move to help her, a dark tendril, cobralike, lifted from the smoke and shadows surrounding the bull. With a swiftness that was otherworldly, it lashed out, wrapping around Rephaim's ankle.

The Raven Mocker didn't scream, though he wanted to. Instead, focusing through the blinding pain, he shouted at Stevie Rae, "Get back to the House of Night!"

He saw Stevie Rae try to stand, but she slipped on her own blood and lay on the ground, crying softly. Their eyes met, and Rephaim lurched toward her, spreading his wings, determined to break from the clinging thread and at least carry her clear of the circle.

Another tendril snaked out and whipped around the thick bicep of Rephaim's newly healed arm, slicing more than an inch into the muscle. Yet another came from the shadows behind him, and Rephaim couldn't help screaming in agony as the thing curled around his wings where they met his back, ripping and tearing and pinning him against the ground.

"Rephaim!" Stevie Rae sobbed.

He couldn't see the bull, but he felt the earth tremble as the creature approached him. He turned his head, and, through a blur of pain, he saw Stevie Rae trying to crawl toward him. He wanted to tell her to stop—to say something to her that would make her run away. Then, as the searing pain of the bull's tongue touched the wound at his ankle, Rephaim realized Stevie Rae wasn't really trying to crawl to him. She was on her hands and knees, crablike, pressing down against the earth. Her arms were trembling, and her body was still bleeding, but her face was getting its color back. *She's pulling power from the earth,* Rephaim realized with an incredible sense of relief. That would make her strong enough to get out of the circle and find her way to safety.

"I'd forgotten the sweetness of immortal blood." The bull's decayed breath washed over Rephaim. *"The vampyre's blood held only a hint of this. I believe I will drink and drink from you, son of Kalona. You did, indeed, borrow power from Darkness tonight, so you have a greater debt to pay than just hers."*

Rephaim refused to look at the creature. Held captive by the cutting threads, his body was lifted and turned so that his cheek pressed against the earth. He kept his gaze focused on Stevie Rae as the bull stood over him and began to drink from the wound at the base of his bleeding wings.

Agony like he'd never before felt assaulted his body. He didn't want to scream. He didn't want to writhe in pain. But he couldn't help it. Stevie Rae's eyes were all that kept him tethered to consciousness as Darkness fed from him, violating him over and over again.

When Stevie Rae stood, lifting her arms, Rephaim thought he was hallucinating because she looked so strong and powerful and so very, very angry. She clutched something in her hand—a long braid that was smoking.

"I did it before. I'll do it again."

Stevie Rae's voice came to him as if from a long way off, but it sounded strong, too. Rephaim wondered why the bull didn't hear her and stop her, but the creature's moans of pleasure and the piercing pain that radiated from his back gave Rephaim the answer. The bull didn't consider Stevie Rae a threat, and he was fixated on consuming the intoxicating blood of immortality. *Let him keep taking from me; let her escape,* Rephaim prayed silently to whichever of the gods might deign to hear him.

"My circle's unbroken," Stevie Rae was speaking quickly and clearly. "Rephaim and this disgusting bull came at my command. So I command again, through the power of the earth, I call the *other* bull. The one who fights this one, and I'll pay whatever I have to, just get this thing off my Raven Mocker!"

Rephaim felt the creature above him pause in his feeding as a bolt of light speared through the smoky blackness in front of Stevie Rae. He saw Stevie Rae's eyes go wide and, miraculously, she smiled and then laughed.

"Yes!" she spoke joyously. "I'll pay your price. And, dang! You're so black and beautiful!"

Still standing over him, the white bull growled. Tendrils began snaking from the darkness around Rephaim and slithering toward Stevie Rae. Rephaim opened his mouth to shout a warning, but Stevie Rae stepped directly into the shaft of light. There was a sound like a thunderclap, and then another blinding flash. From the middle of the bright explosion stepped an enormous bull, as black as the first was white. But this creature's darkness wasn't like that of the inky shadows that cringed away from it. This bull's coat was the black of a midnight sky filled with the radiance of diamond stars—deep and mysterious and beautiful to behold.

For an instant, the black bull's gaze met Rephaim's, and the Raven

Mocker gasped. He'd never seen such kindness in his life; he'd never even known such kindness could exist.

"Do not let her have made the wrong choice." The new voice in his mind was as deep as the first bull's had been, but filled with a wealth of compassion. *"Because whether you are worthy or not, she has paid the price."*

The black bull lowered his head and charged the white bull, hurling it off Rephaim's body. There was a deafening crash as the two met, and then a silence so deep it, too, was deafening.

The tendrils dissipated like dew from the summer sun. Stevie Rae was on her knees, reaching for him, when the smoke vanished, and the fledgling ran into the circle, knife raised and ready.

"Get back, Stevie Rae! I'm gonna fucking kill it!"

Stevie Rae touched the ground, and murmured, "Earth, trip him. Hard."

Over Stevie Rae's shoulder, Rephaim saw the ground rise up right in front of the boy's feet, and the wiry fledgling fell down face-first—hard.

"Can you fly?" she whispered.

"I think so," he murmured back.

"Then get back to the Gilcrease," she said urgently. "I'll come to you later."

Rephaim hesitated. He didn't want to leave her so soon after they'd been through so much together. Was she really well, or had Darkness taken too much from her?

"I'm okay. Promise," Stevie Rae told him softly as if reading his mind. "Go on."

Rephaim stood. With one last look at Stevie Rae, he unfurled his wings and forced his battered body to carry him into the sky.

CHAPTER FOURTEEN

Stevie Rae

Dallas was half carrying, half dragging Stevie Rae around the corner of the school, arguing with her about going to the infirmary instead of just back to her room, when Kramisha and Lenobia, who were walking toward Nyx's Temple, caught sight of them.

"Sweet weeping baby Jesus, you is messed up!" Kramisha yelled, stumbling to a halt.

"Dallas, let's get her to the infirmary!" Lenobia said. Unlike Kramisha, she didn't freeze at the bloody sight of Stevie Rae; instead, she hurried to her other side and helped Dallas support her weight, automatically angling them toward the infirmary entrance.

"Look, no, y'all. Just take me to my room. I need a phone, not a doctor. And I can't find my dang cell phone."

"You can't find it because that bird thing ripped almost all your clothes off of you, along with your skin. Your cell's probably back at the park smooshed in the ground that's still soaked with your blood. You're goin' to the damn infirmary."

"I have a phone. You can use mine," Kramisha said, catching up to them.

"You can use Kramisha's phone, but Dallas is right. You can't even stand by yourself. You're going to the infirmary," Lenobia said firmly.

"Fine. Whatever. Get me to a chair or somethin' so I can make a call. You have Aphrodite's number, don't you?" she asked Kramisha

"Yeah. But don't think that makes us friends or anything," Kramisha muttered.

As they headed into the infirmary, Lenobia's sharp gaze kept returning to Stevie Rae's battered body. "You're in bad shape. Again," she said. Then Dallas's words seemed to catch up with her, and the Horse Mistress's gray eyes widened in shock. "Did you say a bird did this?"

"Bird *thing*," Dallas said at the same time Stevie Rae said, "No!"

"Dallas, I do not have the time or the energy to argue with you 'bout this right now."

"You mean you didn't see what happened to her?" Lenobia asked.

"No. There was too much smoke and darkness; I couldn't see her, and I couldn't get into the circle to help her. And when it all cleared she was like this and a bird thing was crouching over her."

"Dallas, stop talkin' 'bout me like I'm not here! And he wasn't crouched over me. He was lyin' on the ground next to me."

Lenobia started to speak, but they'd reached the infirmary, and Sapphire, the tall, blond nurse who had been promoted to head of the hospital in the absence of a Healer, greeted them with her usual sour expression, which quickly changed to shock. "Put her in there!" she ordered briskly, pointing into a newly emptied hospital-style room.

They laid Stevie Rae on the bed, and Sapphire started to yank stuff out of one of the metal cabinets. One of the things she grabbed was a baggie of blood she tossed to Lenobia. "Make her drink this immediately."

No one said anything for the few seconds it took for Lenobia to rip open the blood bag and help support Stevie Rae's shaking hands as she held it to her mouth and drank greedily.

"I'm gonna need some more of that," Stevie Rae said. "And, like I said before, a dang phone. Right away."

"I need to see what's sliced up your body like that, made you lose entirely too much blood, which you need to replace right away, and figure out why the blood that's still dripping out of your body smells completely wrong," said Sapphire.

"Raven Mocker! That's the name of that thing," Dallas said.

"A Raven Mocker attacked you?" Lenobia said.

"No. And that's what I've been tryin' to get through Dallas's thick skull. Darkness attacked me *and* a Raven Mocker."

"And like I said, you're not making no damn sense. I saw that bird thing. I saw your blood. These definitely look like slash wounds from that beak of his. I didn't see anything else!" Dallas practically shouted.

"You didn't see anything because Darkness was covering everything inside the circle, including me and the Raven Mocker while it attacked *both of us*!" Stevie Rae yelled her frustration at him.

"Why does it sound like you keep standing up for that thing?" Dallas said, throwing up his hands.

"You know what, Dallas, you can just kiss my butt! I'm not standing up for anyone except *myself*. It's not like you could manage to get inside the circle to help me out—I had to do it *myself*!"

There was a long silence while Dallas stared at her with hurt clearly visible in his eyes, and then Sapphire spoke in her sharp, shitty bedside voice, "Dallas, you need to leave. I'm going to cut what's left of these clothes off her, and it's not appropriate for you to be in here."

"But I—"

"You've brought your High Priestess home. You did well," Lenobia told him, touching his arm gently. "Now let us care for her."

"Dallas, uh, why don't you go get somethin' to eat? I'll be fine," Stevie Rae said, already sorry she'd taken out on him the frustration fear and guilt were making her feel.

"Yeah, all right. I'm goin'."

"Hey, Lenobia's right," Stevie Rae called after him as he slouched from the room. "You did good bringin' me home."

He glanced over his shoulder at her just before he closed the door, and she thought she'd never seen his eyes look so sad. "Anything for you, girl."

The door had barely closed behind him when Lenobia's voice shot out. "Explain about the Raven Mocker."

"Yeah, I thought they was all gone," Kramisha said.

"The two of you may stay. Margareta has gone to replenish our supplies from St. John's Hospital, so I can use the extra hands, but you'll have to talk while you help me," Sapphire told them, handing Lenobia another baggie o' blood. "Open this for her. Kramisha, go over there, wash your hands, and then start handing me those alcohol-soaked cotton balls."

Kramisha shot Sapphire a raised-brow look, but she went to the sink. Lenobia ripped open the bag and gave it to Stevie Rae, who drank slowly, buying herself some time.

With a ripping sound that seemed too loud for the room, Sapphire cut away what remained of Stevie Rae's pants and her *Don't hate the 918* T-shirt.

Stevie Rae felt everyone's eyes staring at her mostly bare body. She wished she'd worn a better bra, shifted nervously, and said, "Dang, I loved those Cowgirl U jeans. I hate to think about havin' to go back to Thirty-first and Memorial to Drysdales to get me another pair. The traffic always sucks in that part of town."

"Maybe you should expand your fashion sense. Little Black Dress on Cherry Street is closer, and they got them some cute jeans that ain't from the nineties," Kramisha said.

Three pairs of eyes shifted momentarily to her.

"What?" she shrugged. "Everbody knows Stevie Rae needs a makeover."

"Thanks, Kramisha. That makes me feel lots better, seein' as how *I just almost died and all.*" Stevie Rae rolled her eyes at Kramisha as she stifled a smile. But the truth was that Kramisha *had* made her feel better—normal better. And then Stevie Rae realized that she was, truly, feeling better. The blood had warmed her, and she didn't feel nearly as weak as she had just minutes before. Actually, she was kinda buzzing inside, like her blood was pumping super strong and surging all throughout her body. *It's Rephaim's blood—the part of it that's mixed with mine is feeding off the human blood and giving me power.*

"Stevie Rae, you seem to be awake and aware," Lenobia said.

Stevie Rae refocused on her external world to find the Horse Mistress studying her carefully. "Yeah, I'm definitely feelin' better, and I need a phone. Kramisha, let me borrow—"

"I'm cleaning these wounds first, and I promise you that you're not going to be able to chat on the phone while I do that," Sapphire said with what Stevie Rae thought was too much smug satisfaction.

"So wait until after I call Aphrodite to mess with me," Stevie Rae said. "Kramisha, dig in that giant bag of yours and get me your dang phone."

"It can*not* wait," Sapphire snapped. "Your wounds are severe. You have lacerations from your ankles to your waist. They need to be cleansed. Many of them need stitches. You need to drink more blood. Actually, it would be preferable if we brought in one of the human volunteers for you to feed from directly—that would help in the healing process."

"Human? Volunteers?" Stevie Rae gulped. Stuff like *that* went on at the House of Night?

"Don't be naïve," was all Sapphire said.

"I'm not drinking from some stranger!" Stevie Rae said with more vehemence than she'd meant to show, drawing raised-eyebrow looks from Lenobia and Kramisha. "What I mean is—I'll be fine with blood baggies. It's too weird to think about drinking from someone I don't know, 'specially so soon after, well, you know . . ." She trailed off. The three women would think she was talking about the recent breaking of her Imprint with Aphrodite.

But she wasn't thinking of Aphrodite—that was ridiculous.

Stevie Rae was thinking that the only one she wanted to drink from, needed to drink from, was Rephaim.

"Your blood smells wrong," Lenobia said.

Stevie Rae's thoughts cleared, and her gaze went immediately to the Horse Mistress. "Wrong? What do you mean?"

"There is something strange about it," Sapphire agreed as she began cleaning the deep slashes with the alcohol-drenched cotton balls Kramisha handed her.

Stevie Rae sucked in a breath at the pain. Through gritted teeth, she said, "I'm a red vampyre. My blood's different than yours."

"Nope, they's right. Your blood smells weird," Kramisha said, averting her eyes from Stevie Rae's wounds and wrinkling her nose.

Stevie Rae thought quickly, and said, "It's because he drank from me."

"Who? The Raven Mocker!" Lenobia said.

"No!" Stevie Rae denied, then hurried on. "Like I kept tryin' to tell Dallas, the Raven Mocker didn't do anything to me. He was a victim, too."

"Stevie Rae, what happened to you?" Lenobia asked.

Stevie Rae drew a deep breath and launched into a mostly true story. "I went to the park 'cause I was tryin' to get info from the earth that would help Zoey because Aphrodite asked me to. There're these really old vamp beliefs, somethin' Warrior-based and not cool anymore, that she thinks can help Stark get himself to Zoey in the Otherworld."

"But Stark can't enter the Otherworld without dying," Lenobia said.

"Yeah, that's what everyone says, but recently Aphrodite and I found out about this really old stuff that might help him get there alive. The religion, or whatever you want to call it, was supposed to be represented by cows—I mean bulls. A white one and a black one." Remembering, Stevie Rae shuddered. "Aphrodite, bein' a total pain in the butt, failed to tell me the dang *white* bull was bad and the dang *black* bull was good, so I called up the bad bull accidentally."

Lenobia's face had gone so pale it almost looked transparent. "Oh, Goddess! You evoked Darkness?"

"You know about this stuff?" Stevie Rae asked.

In what seemed like an unconscious movement, one of Lenobia's hands lifted to touch the back of her neck. "I know a little of Darkness, and as Mistress of Horses, I know more than a little about beasts."

Sapphire swabbed at the cut that snaked around Stevie Rae's waist, making her wince. "Ah, crap, that hurts!" She closed her eyes momentarily, trying to focus through the pain. When she opened them, she saw that Lenobia was studying her with an expression she couldn't read, but before she could form the right question, the Horse Mistress asked one of her own.

"What was the Raven Mocker doing there? You said it didn't attack you, but it certainly wouldn't have any reason to attack Darkness."

"'Cause they on the same side," Kramisha added, nodding thoughtfully.

"I don't know about sides and all, but the bad bull attacked the

Raven Mocker." Stevie Rae drew a deep breath, and continued, "Actually, the Raven Mocker showin' up was what saved me. He just kinda fell from the sky and distracted the bull long enough for me to draw power from the earth so I could call up the good bull." Stevie Rae couldn't help smiling as she talked about that amazing beast. "I'd never seen anything like him before. He was so beautiful and kind and so, so wise. He went after the white bull, and both of them disappeared. Then Dallas was able to get inside the circle to me, and the Raven Mocker flew away."

"But what you're saying is that before the Raven Mocker got there, the white bull drank your blood?" Lenobia said.

Stevie Rae had to suppress another shudder of remembered revulsion. "Yeah. He said I owed him payment because he answered my question. That's probably why my blood smells weird, 'cause you can still smell him on me, and let me tell you, he reeked. And that's also why I need to make that phone call. The bull *did* answer my question, and I gotta talk to Aphrodite."

"You might as well let her call. She don't need them stitches anyway. Her cuts are closing up already," Kramisha said, pointing to the first slashes Darkness had made around her ankles.

Stevie Rae glanced down, but she knew what she'd see before she looked. She'd already felt it—Rephaim's blood was spreading its warmth and strength throughout her body, causing her torn flesh to begin drawing together and repair itself.

"That's incredibly unusual. And much like the rapid rate at which you healed from your burn wounds," Sapphire said.

Stevie Rae made herself meet the vampyre nurse's gaze. "I'm a red vampyre High Priestess. There's never been anyone like me before, so I guess we can say I'm setting the learning curve for all of us. We must heal fast." She flipped the edge of the sheet over her body and then held her hand out to Kramisha. "I need your phone now."

Without another word, Kramisha walked over to where she'd dropped her purse, dug out her cell phone, and gave it to Stevie Rae. "Aphrodite's listed under the B's."

Stevie Rae punched in the number. Aphrodite picked up on the third ring.

"Yes, it is too damn early to call, and no, I do not care about whatever stupid poem you just wrote, Kramisha."

"It's me."

Aphrodite's sarcastic tone instantly changed. "What happened?"

"Did you know the white bull's bad and the black bull's good?"

"Yeah. Didn't I tell you that part?" Aphrodite said.

"No, which really sucked 'cause I called the *white* bull to my circle."

"Uh-oh. That's seriously not good. What happened?"

"Not good? Try understatement of the dang decade, Aphrodite. It was bad. Really, *really* bad." Stevie Rae wanted to tell Lenobia and Sapphire and even Kramisha to go away so she could talk to Aphrodite in private, and then maybe have a really good breakdown and bawl her eyes out; but she knew they needed to hear what she had to say. Sadly, bad stuff didn't go away just because it was ignored. "Aphrodite, it's evil like nothing I've seen before. It makes Neferet look like a trick-or-treat kid." She ignored Sapphire's indignant snort and kept talking quickly. "And it's powerful beyond belief. I couldn't fight it. I don't think anything can fight it except the other bull."

"So how did you get away from it?" Aphrodite paused for half a heartbeat, and then added, "You *are* away from it, aren't you? You're not all under its spell so that you're being used like a sock puppet for evil with a bumpkin accent, right?"

"That's just silly, Aphrodite."

"Still, say something to prove you're really you."

"You called me a retard last time we talked. More than once. And said I was asstarded, which is not even a word. I'm still tellin' you that's not nice."

"Fine. It's you. So how did you get away from the bull?"

"I managed to call up the good bull, and he is as really, *really* good as the other one is bad. He fought it, and they both disappeared."

"So you didn't learn anything?"

"Yeah, I did." Stevie Rae squinted while she concentrated hard, wanting to be sure she remembered word for word what the white bull had said. "I asked how Stark could get to Zoey so that he can protect her while she gets herself together and comes back here. This is what the bull said: *'The Warrior must look to his blood to discover the bridge to enter the Isle of Women, and then he must defeat himself to enter the arena. Only by acknowledging one before the other will he join his Priestess. After he joins her, it is her choice and not his whether she returns.'* "

"He said Isle of Women? Are you sure about that?"

"Yeah, I'm positive. That's exactly what he said."

"Good. Okay. Uh, hang on, I'm writing this all down so I don't forget any of it."

Stevie Rae could hear Aphrodite scribbling on a piece of paper. When she was done, her voice was filled with excitement. "This means we are on the right track! But how the hell does Stark find a bridge by looking at blood? And what does that stuff about him having to defeat himself mean?"

Stevie Rae sighed. A massive headache had started to throb between her temples. "I don't have a clue, but getting that answer almost killed me, so it has to mean somethin' important."

"Then Stark better figure it out." Aphrodite hesitated before saying, "If the black bull is so super good, why don't you just call it back again and—"

"No!" Stevie Rae spoke with such force she caused everyone in the room to jump. "Never again. And you shouldn't let anyone else conjure either of those bulls. The price is too much."

"What do you mean, the price is too much?" Aphrodite said.

"I mean they're too powerful. They can't be controlled, whether they're good or bad. Aphrodite, there're some things that weren't meant to be messed with, and those bulls are part of those things. Plus, I'm not so sure one can be called up without the other eventually showing up, and believe me, you don't want to ever, *ever* meet that white bull."

"Okay, okay—relax. I get what you're saying, and I can tell you I have a kinda creepy feeling just talking about those bulls. I think you're right. Don't stress. No one's gonna do anything except try to help Stark find a blood bridge to the Isle of Skye."

"Aphrodite, I don't think it's a blood bridge. That doesn't even sound right." Stevie Rae rubbed her face and was surprised to see that her hand was shaking.

"Enough for now," Lenobia whispered. "You're strong, but you're not immortal."

Stevie Rae's gaze shot to hers, but she saw nothing in the Horse Mistress's gray eyes except concern.

"Hey, uh, I gotta go for now. I'm not feelin' so good."

"Oh, for crap's sake. You're not almost dying again, are you? It's seriously inconvenient when you do that."

"No, I am not almost dyin'. Not anymore. And you are not even almost nice. At all. I'll call you later. Tell everyone I said hi."

"Yeah, I'll spread the love. Goodbye, bumpkin."

"Bye." Stevie Rae punched the CALL END button, gave Kramisha her phone, and then leaned heavily back on her pillow. "Uh, do y'all mind if maybe I sleep for a while?"

"Drink one more of these." Sapphire gave Stevie Rae another bag of blood. "Then sleep. Both of you need to leave and let her rest." The vampyre nurse swept the bloody alcohol cotton balls into a trash bag, snapped off her latex gloves, went to the doorway, and stood, tapping her foot and giving Lenobia and Kramisha the stank eye.

"I'll come back and check on you after you've rested," Lenobia said.

"Sounds good." Stevie Rae smiled at her.

Lenobia squeezed her hand before leaving. When Kramisha leaned close to her, Stevie Rae thought for one awkward, shocked second the kid was going to hug her—or worse, maybe even kiss her. Instead, Kramisha met her eyes and whispered:

> *"See with the soul and not your eyes*
> *because to dance with beasts you*
> *must penetrate their disguise."*

Stevie Rae suddenly felt cold. "I guess I should have listened to you better. Maybe I would've known I was callin' the wrong cow," she whispered back.

Kramisha's gaze was sharp and knowing. "Maybe you still should. Somethin' inside me says you ain't done dancing with beasts." Then she straightened up, and in a normal voice, said, "Get some sleep. You gonna need all your good sense tomorrow."

When the door closed, leaving her alone, Stevie Rae breathed an exhausted sigh of relief. Methodically, she drank the last baggie of blood and then pulled the hospital blanket up around her neck and curled on her side and, with a sigh, slowly twirled a blond curl around and around one finger. She was utterly exhausted. Apparently all of the power in Rephaim's blood had worn her the heck out while it fixed her.

Rephaim . . .

Stevie Rae would never, ever forget what he looked like when he'd confronted Darkness for her. He'd been so strong and brave and *good*. It didn't matter that Dallas and Lenobia and the whole dang world believed he was on the side of Darkness. It didn't matter that his daddy was a fallen Warrior of Nyx who had chosen evil centuries ago. None of that mattered. She'd seen the truth. He'd willingly sacrificed himself for her. He might not have chosen Light, but he had definitely rejected Darkness.

She'd been right to save him that day outside the abbey, and she'd also been right to call the white bull and save him today—no matter the cost to her.

Rephaim was worth saving.

Wasn't he?

He had to be. After what had happened today, he *had to be*.

Her finger stilled, and her eyes started to flutter shut even though she didn't want to think anymore or to dream—didn't want to remember that terrifying Darkness and the pain that had been so unimaginable.

But her eyes did close, and the memory of Darkness and what he'd done to her did come. As she struggled against the unyielding pull of utter exhaustion, from the middle of that circle of terror Stevie Rae heard his voice again: *"I'm here because she's here, and she belongs to me."* And that simple statement chased her fear away, allowing the memory of Darkness to give way to the rescue of Light.

Just before Stevie Rae fell into a deep, dreamless sleep, she thought of the beautiful black bull and the payment he had exacted from her, and, again, Rephaim's words played through her mind: *"I'm here because she's here, and she belongs to me."*

With her last waking thought, she wondered if Rephaim would ever know how ironically true his words had suddenly become for them . . .

CHAPTER FIFTEEN

Stark

As Stark awoke, just for a second he didn't remember. All he knew was that Zoey was there, in bed, beside him. He smiled sleepily and turned, reaching an arm out to pull her close to him.

The chilled, lifeless feel of her unresponsive flesh brought him fully awake, and reality crashed and burned the last of his dreams.

"Finally. You know, you red vampyres might be all strong and whatever at night, but during the day you sleep creepily like the dead. Hello, I have one word for you: stereotypical."

Stark sat up, scowling at Aphrodite, who was sitting in one of the cream-colored velvet chairs, long legs crossed gracefully, sipping a cup of steaming tea.

"Aphrodite, why are you in here?"

Instead of answering him, her gaze went to Zoey. "She hasn't moved at all since it happened, has she?"

Stark got out of bed and gently tucked the blanket back around Zoey. He touched her cheek with his fingertips and kissed the only Mark left on her body, an ordinary fledgling's crescent tattoo in the middle of her forehead. *It's okay if you come back as a regular fledgling. Just come back,* he thought as his lips brushed her Mark. Then he straightened and faced Aphrodite. "No. She hasn't moved. She can't. She's not here. And we have seven days to figure out how to get her back."

"Six," Aphrodite corrected.

Stark swallowed hard. "Yeah, you're right. It's six now."

"Okay, come on then. Clearly we don't have time to waste." Aphrodite got up and started out of the room.

"Where're we going?" Stark started following her but kept glancing back over his shoulder at Zoey.

"Hey, you gotta snap out of it. You said it yourself: *Zoey's not here.* So stop gawking at her like you're a little lost puppy."

"I love her! Do you even know what the hell that means?"

Aphrodite stopped and turned to face him. "Love doesn't have shit to do with it. You're her Warrior. That means more than 'I heart Zoey,'" she said sarcastically, using air quotes. "I have my own Warrior, so I do know what *that* means, and here's the truth: if my soul was shattered, and I was stuck in the Otherworld, I wouldn't want Darius to boo-hoo about it and be all heartbroken. I'd want him to get the hell to work and figure out how to do his job, which is to stay alive and *protect me so that I can figure out a way to get home*! Now are you coming or not?" She flipped her hair, turned her back to him, and started twitching down the hall.

Stark closed his mouth and went after her. They walked silently for a while as Aphrodite led him down some stairs, around increasingly narrow corridors, and down more stairs.

"Where are we going?" Stark asked again.

"Well, it feels like a dungeon. Smells like mold and kinda weird b.o., the institutional decor is suitable for either a prison or a hospital psych ward, and it makes Damien think he's died and gone to dork heaven. So take a guess."

"We're going back to human high school?"

"Close," she said, her lips lifting in a hint of a smile. "We're going to a really old library filled with the frantically studying nerd herd."

Stark let out a long breath in a loud sigh to keep himself from laughing. Sometimes he almost liked Aphrodite—not that he'd ever admit it.

Stark

Aphrodite had been right—the basement of the palace did remind him of a tacky public school media center, minus the foldout windows and cheap, ratty mini-blinds, which was weird as hell because the rest of San Clemente Island was over-the-top rich. Down in the basement, though, there were just a bunch of worn wooden tables, hard benches, bare white stone walls, and tons and tons of shelves filled with a zillion different sizes, shapes, and styles of books.

Zoey's friends were clustered around one big table that was overflowing with books, pop cans, crumpled bags of chips, and one humongous tub full of red licorice whips. Stark thought they look tired but totally wired on sugar and caffeine. As he and Aphrodite walked up, Jack was holding up a large leather book and pointing to an illustration.

"Check it out—this is a copy of a painting of a Greek High Priestess named Calliope. It says she was also the Poet Laureate after Sappho. Doesn't she look exactly like Cher?"

"Wow, that's insane. She does look just like young Cher," Erin said.

"Yeah, before she started wearing those white wigs. What the hell's up with that?" Shaunee said.

Damien gave the Twins a *look*. "There is nothing wrong with Cher. Absolutely. Nothing."

"Uh-oh," Shaunee said.

"Stepped on a gay nerve," Erin agreed.

"I had a Cher Barbie doll. I loved that doll," Jack said.

"Barbies, herd of nerd? Seriously? You're supposed to be saving Z, remember?" Aphrodite said, shaking her head in disgust and curling up her lip at the licorice whips.

"We've been at it all day. We're just taking a little break. Thanatos and Darius went out for more food," Damien said. "We have made some headway, but I'll wait until they get back to report everything." He waved at Stark, and his "hi" was echoed by the other kids.

"Yeah, don't be so judgmental, Aphrodite. We've been working hard, you'll see."

"You're talking about dolls," Aphrodite said.

"*Barbies*," Jack corrected her. "And just for a second. Plus, Barbies are cool and an important part of American culture." He nodded in emphasis and clutched the "Cher" portrait to his chest. "Especially celebrity Barbies."

"Celebrity Barbies would only be important if they had interesting accoutrements you could buy with them," Aphrodite said.

"Accoutre-whats?" Shaunee said.

"You sound like you swallowed a French guy and are trying to spit him out," Erin said, and the Twins giggled.

"Left and right brain—listen up. Interesting accoutrements equals cool stuff, like unusual accessories," Aphrodite said, picking delicately at a chip.

"Okay, if you don't know anything about Barbies, your mother seriously hated you," Erin said.

"Not that we don't understand that," Shaunee added.

"'Cause everyone who even had one Barbie knows you can buy stuff for them," Erin finished.

"Yeah, *cool* stuff," Jack agreed.

"Not cool by my definition," Aphrodite said with a superior smirk.

"What's cool by your definition?" Jack asked, making Shaunee and Erin groan.

"Well, since you asked—I'd say it would be cool if Barbie made a Barbra Streisand doll, but you'd have to buy her fingernails and nose separately. And her fake nails would come in lots of different color choices."

There was a shocked silence, and then Jack, sounding awed, whispered, "That *would be* cool."

Aphrodite looked smug. "And how about a bald Britney Spears doll that had extras like an umbrella, a fat suit, weird wigs, and, of course, optional panties."

"Eww," Jack said, and then giggled. "Yeah, and a Paris Hilton doll that had an optional brain."

Aphrodite raised her brow at him. "Don't go all crazy. There are some things even Paris Hilton can't buy."

Stark stood there, dumbfounded, and when they all burst into giggles, he thought his brain was going to explode.

"What the hell is wrong with all of you?" he yelled at them. "How can you laugh and joke like this? You're focusing on toys when Zoey is days away from dying!"

Into the shocked silence, Thanatos's voice sounded abnormally loud. "No, Warrior. They're not focusing on toys. They're focusing on *life* and being among the living." The vampyre stepped from the doorway, where she and Darius had been silently observing the kids. Darius followed her, placing a tray filled with sandwiches and fruit in the middle of the table. He then joined Aphrodite's side of the wooden bench. "And take it from someone who knows more than a little about death—focusing on life is what you should do if you want to keep drawing breath in this world."

Damien cleared his voice, calling Stark's glare to him. Unruffled, the fledgling met his eyes, and said, "Yeah, that's just one of the things we learned from all the studying we've been doing."

"While you were *sleeping*," Shaunee murmured.

"And we *weren't*," Erin added.

"So, what we found out from our research," Damien broke in before Stark could say anything to the Twins, "is that whenever a High Priestess suffered such a shock that her soul shattered, her Warrior didn't seem to be able to stay alive."

Barbies and bickering Twins forgotten, Stark's face was a question mark as he stared at Damien and tried to make sense of what he was hearing. "Do you mean the Warriors all dropped dead?"

"In a way," Damien said.

"Some of them killed themselves so that they knew they could follow their High Priestesses to the Otherworld and continue to protect them there," Thanatos took up the explanation.

"But it didn't work because none of the High Priestesses returned, right?" Stark said.

"Correct. What we know from Priestesses who, through their affinity for spirit, have journeyed to the Otherworld is that those lost High Priestesses couldn't bear the death of their Warriors. Some of them were able to heal their souls in the Otherworld, but they chose to remain there with their Warriors."

"Some of them healed," Stark said slowly. "What happened to the High Priestesses who didn't?"

Zoey's friends shifted uncomfortably, but Thanatos's voice remained steady. "As you learned yesterday, if a soul remains shattered, the person becomes Caoinic Shi', a being that will never rest."

"It's like a zombie, without the eating people part," Jack said softly and then shuddered.

"That can't happen to Zoey," Stark said. He'd sworn to protect Zoey, and if he had to, he would follow that Oath into the Otherworld to be sure she didn't become some kind of horrible zombie thing.

"But even though the end result was the same, not all of the Warriors killed themselves to follow their High Priestesses," Damien said.

"Tell me about the others," Stark said. Unable to sit, he paced back and forth in front of the table.

"Well, it was pretty obvious that *no* Warrior or High Priestess returned when the Warrior killed himself, so we found records of Warriors who had done lots of different things to try to get themselves into the Otherworld," Damien said.

"Some of them were crazy—like one who starved himself until he was delirious, then he kinda left his body," Jack said.

"He died," Shaunee said.

"Yeah, the story was gross. He did lots of screaming and was hallucinating and stuff about his High Priestess and what she was going through before he actually croaked," Erin said.

"You. Are. Not. Helping," Aphrodite told them.

"Some of the Warriors did drugs to put themselves in a trancelike state, and they actually managed to get their spirits to leave this world," Damien continued, while the Twins rolled their eyes at Aphrodite. "But they couldn't enter the Otherworld. We know because they came back to their bodies long enough to tell witnesses that they'd failed." Damien stopped there, glancing at Thanatos.

She took up the story. "Then the Warriors died. Each of them."

"Failing to protect their High Priestesses killed them," Stark said, his voice completely expressionless.

"No, turning their back on life killed them," Darius corrected.

Stark turned to him. "Wouldn't you? If Aphrodite died because you couldn't protect her, wouldn't you choose death rather than live life without her?"

Aphrodite didn't give Darius a chance to answer. "I would be super pissed if he died! That's what I was trying to tell you upstairs. You can't keep looking behind you—not at Zoey, not at the past, not even back to your Oath. You have to go forward and find a new way of living, a new way of protecting her."

"Then tell me something, *anything* that you found in all these damn books that can help me instead of just showing me how other Warriors failed."

"I'll tell you something I didn't read in a book. Stevie Rae accidentally evoked the white bull last night."

"Darkness! A fledgling called Darkness into this world?" Thanatos looked like Aphrodite had just exploded a bomb in the middle of the room.

"She's not a fledgling. She's like Stark, a red vampyre, but yes. She did. In Tulsa. It was an accident." Ignoring Thanatos's shocked stare, Aphrodite pulled a slip of paper from her pocket, and read: "The bull said: '*The Warrior must look to his blood to discover the bridge to enter the Isle of Women, and then he must defeat himself to enter the arena. Only by acknowledging one before the other will he join his Priestess. After he joins her, it is her choice and not his whether she returns.*'" Aphrodite looked up. "Anyone have a clue what that might mean?" She waved the paper around, and Damien took it, already rereading as Jack peeked over his shoulder.

"What price did Darkness exact for such knowledge?" Thanatos asked. Her face had gone absolutely white. "And how did she survive the payment of it without losing her mind or her soul?"

"That's what I wondered myself, especially after Stevie Rae told me how bad the white bull was. She said she didn't think anything could defeat it except for the black bull, which was how she got away from it."

"She evoked the black bull, too?" Thanatos said. "That is almost unbelievable."

"Stevie Rae has some mad earth skillz," Jack said.

"Yeah, that's how she said she got the good bull to Tulsa. She drew power from the earth to call it," Aphrodite said.

"And you trust this Stevie Rae vampyre?"

Aphrodite hesitated. "Most of the time."

Stark expected at least one of the kids to jump in and correct Aphrodite, but they all stayed quiet until Damien said, "Why do you ask about trusting Stevie Rae?"

"Because of the few things I know about the ancient beliefs of Light and Darkness symbolized in the bulls, one is that they always exact a price for their favors. Always. Answering Stevie Rae's question was a favor from Darkness."

"But she called up the good bull and it kicked the bad bull's butt. That kept Stevie Rae from paying a price to him," Jack said.

"So she then owed payment to the black bull," Thanatos said.

Aphrodite's eyes narrowed. "That's what she was talking about when she said she wouldn't ever evoke either of the bulls again because the price was too high."

"I think you should look to your friend and discover what payment she rendered the black bull," Thanatos said.

"And why she wouldn't tell me about it," Aphrodite added.

Thanatos's eyes looked old and sad as she said, "Just remember, there are consequences for everything, whether good or bad."

"Can we stop looking *back* at what has happened with Stevie Rae?" Stark said. "I need to move forward. To Skye and a bridge of blood. So let's get going."

"Whoa, big boy," Aphrodite told him. "Settle for a second. You can't just show up on the Isle of Women and bumble around looking for a bloody bridge. Sgiach's protective spell will kick your butt—as in kill you dead."

"I don't think Stark's supposed to be looking for something literal," said Damien, studying Aphrodite's note again. "It says to look *to your blood* to discover the bridge, not look *for* a blood bridge."

"Ugh, metaphor. Just one more reason I seriously hate poetry," Aphrodite said.

"I'm good at metaphors," Jack said. "Let me see." Damien handed him the paper. Jack chewed his lip while he read the line again. "Hmm, if you were Imprinted with someone, I'd say it meant that we should talk to whoever that is, and maybe they'd know something."

"I'm not Imprinted with anyone," Stark said, starting to pace again.

"So that might mean that we need to look at who you are—that there's something about you that's a key to getting onto Sgiach's island," Damien said.

"I don't know anything! That's the problem!"

"Okay—okay, how about we look at the notes we made about Sgiach to see if there's something there that rings a bell with you," Jack said, making consolatory motions at Stark.

"Yeah, chill out," Shaunee said.

"Take a seat and have a sandwich." Erin gestured to the end of their bench with the sandwich she'd begun munching on.

"Eat," Thanatos said, taking a sandwich and sitting beside Jack. "Focus on life."

Stark suppressed a frustrated growl, grabbed a sandwich, and sat.

"Oh, pull out that chart we made," Jack said, peeking over Damien's shoulder as he flipped through the notes he'd made. "Some of this stuff gets confusing, and visual aids always help."

"Good idea—here it is." Damien ripped out a piece of paper from the yellow legal pad he'd almost filled with notes. At the top of it he'd drawn a big, open umbrella. On one side of the umbrella he'd written LIGHT and on the opposite side, DARKNESS.

"The umbrella of Light and Darkness is a good image," Thanatos said. "It shows that the two forces are all-encompassing."

"That was my idea," Jack said, turning a little pink.

Damien smiled at him. "Well done, you." Then he pointed at the column beneath Light. "So under the force of Light I've listed: good, the black bull, Nyx, Zoey, and us." He paused, and everyone nodded. "And under Darkness I have: evil, the white bull, Neferet/Tsi Sgili, Kalona, and Raven Mockers."

"I see you have Sgiach placed in the middle," Thanatos said.

"Yeah, along with onion rings, Hostess Ding Dongs, and *my name*," Aphrodite said. "Just what the hell does that mean?"

"Well, I don't think we've decided if Sgiach is a force for Light or Darkness," Damien said.

"I added the onion rings and Ding Dongs," Jack said. When everyone just stared at him, he shrugged and explained, "Onion rings are deep-fried and fattening, but an onion is a vegetable. So aren't they good for you? Maybe? And, well, Ding Dongs are chocolate, but they have cream in the middle. Isn't that dairy and healthy?"

"I think you're brain-damaged," Aphrodite said.

"We added your name," Erin said.

"Yeah, 'cause we think you're like Rachel on *Glee*," Shaunee said. "Super annoying, but she has to be in the show 'cause sometimes she comes up with good stuff and kinda sorta saves the day."

"But we think she's still a hag from hell. Like you," Erin finished, giving Aphrodite a sugary smile."

"*Anyway*"—Damien quickly erased onion rings, Ding Dongs, and Aphrodite's name, put the chart in the middle of the table, and then went back to the yellow pad—"here's some info we found about Sgiach," Damien said, scanning through the notes he'd made. "She is considered a queen of Warriors. Lots of Warriors used to train on her island, so a bunch of Sons of Erebus came and went, but the Warriors who stayed with her, the ones sworn to her service—"

"Hang on, Sgiach had more than one Oath Sworn Warrior?" Stark interrupted.

Damien nodded. "Apparently she had a whole Clan of them. Only they didn't call themselves Sons of Erebus. Their title was . . ." Damien paused, flipping pages. "Here it is. They were called Guardians of the Ace."

"Why Ace?" Stark asked.

"It's a metaphor," Aphrodite said, rolling her eyes. "Another one. It's what they called Sgiach. It symbolizes queen to their Clan."

"I think the Scottish clan stuff is cool," Jack said.

"Of course you do," Aphrodite said. "Guys in skirts is your wet dream."

"Kilt, not skirt," Stark said. "Or plaid. If you're talking about the really old, big one you call it a philamore."

Aphrodite raised a blond brow at him. "And you know this because you like to wear them?"

He shrugged. "Not me, but my grandpa used to."

"You're Scottish?" Damien's voice was incredulous. "And you're just now telling us?"

Stark shrugged again. "What does my human family have to do with anything? I haven't even talked to them in almost four years."

"It's not just a family," Damien's voice rose with excitement as he started ruffling through the pages of his notes again.

"Oh, for crap's sake. Your family *is* your blood, you moron," Aphrodite said. "What was your grandfather's last name?"

Stark frowned at Aphrodite.

"MacUallis," Stark and Damien said together.

"How did you know that?" Stark asked.

"It was the Clan MacUallis who were the Guardians of the Ace." Damien grinned victoriously, holding up the page of his notes that held the words: CLAN MACUALLIS = GUARDIANS OF THE ACE for everyone to see.

"Looks like we found our blood bridge," Jack said, hugging Damien.

CHAPTER SIXTEEN

Zoey

Heath stirred and muttered something about skipping football practice and sleeping in. I watched him and held my breath as I paced my circle around where he slept.

I mean, would you want to wake him up and tell him he was dead as dirt and wouldn't ever be playing football again?

Hell no.

I tried to be as quiet as I could, but I couldn't hold still. This time I hadn't even pretended to lie down next to him. I couldn't help it. I couldn't stop myself. I had to keep moving.

We were in the middle of the same dense grove we'd run inside of before. When before? I couldn't really remember, but the short, gnarled trees and lots of old rocks looked cool. And the moss. Especially the moss. It was everywhere—thick and soft and cushy.

Suddenly my feet were bare, and I was distracted by sinking my feet into the moss and letting my toes play in the living carpet of green.

Living?

I sighed.

Nope. I suspected nothing here was really alive, but I kept forgetting that.

The trees made a canopy of leaves and branches, so the sun only got through enough to be warm without being too hot, but a cloud passing overhead had me looking up and shivering.

Darkness . . .

I blinked in surprise, remembering. *That* was why Heath and I were tucked away in this grove. That thing had been after us, but it hadn't entered the grove after us.

I shivered again.

I had no clue what that thing had been. I only had a sense of utter darkness, a vague whiff of something that had been dead for a while, horns, and wings. Heath and I hadn't waited to see any more. We had both been breathless with fear, and we'd run and run . . . which was why Heath was sound asleep. Again. Like I should be.

But I wasn't able to rest. So instead I paced.

It really bothered me that my memory was messing up. And, what's worse, even though you'd think if my memory was jacked, I wouldn't know it because I, well, wouldn't remember it—I was wrong. I knew I was missing hunks of stuff in my mind—some of it new stuff, like that I just now remembered the scary thing that had chased Heath and me into the grove. Some of it was old stuff, though.

I couldn't remember what my mom looked like.

I couldn't remember the color of my eyes.

I couldn't remember why I didn't trust Stevie Rae anymore.

What I could remember was even more upsetting. I remembered every instant of Stevie Rae dying. I remembered that my dad had left us when I was two and basically never come back. I remembered that I'd trusted Kalona, and that I'd been so, so wrong about him.

My stomach felt sick, and, like that sickness was driving me, I kept pacing around and around the inside circumference of the grove.

How could I have let Kalona fool me so totally? I'd been such an idiot.

And I'd caused Heath's death.

My mind skittered away from that guilt. The thought was too raw, too horrible.

A shadow caught at my vision. I started, turned quickly, and came face-to-face with *her*. I'd seen her before—in my dreams and in a shared vision.

"Hello, A-ya," I said softly.

"Zoey," she said, dipping her head in hello. Her voice sounded a lot like mine, except there was a sense of sadness about her that colored everything she said.

"I trusted Kalona because of you," I told her.

"You had compassion for him because of me," she corrected. "When you lost me, you also lost compassion."

"That's not true," I said. "I'm still compassionate. I care about Heath."

"Do you? Is that why you are keeping him here with you instead of allowing him to move on?"

"Heath doesn't want to leave," I shot back, and then closed my mouth, surprised at how angry I sounded.

A-ya shook her head, causing her long, dark hair to flutter around her waist. "You haven't stopped to think of what Heath might want—what anyone besides you might want. And you won't, not really, not until you call me back to you."

"I don't want you back. It's because of you that this has happened."

"No, Zoey, it's not. All of this happened because of a series of choices made by a number of people. This isn't all about you." Shaking her head sadly, A-ya disappeared.

"Good riddance," I muttered, and started to pace again, even more restless than before.

When another shadow flickered at the corner of my vision, I whirled around, ready to tell off A-ya once and for all, but instead my mouth flopped open. I was staring at *me.* Well, actually, the nine-year-old version of me I'd seen with the other figures before they were scattered by whatever was chasing Heath and me.

"Hi," I said.

"We got boobies!" the kid me said, gawking at my chest. "I'm really *glad* we got boobies. Finally."

"Yeah, that's what I thought, too. Finally."

"I kinda wish they were bigger." The kid me kept staring at my boobies until I felt like crossing my arms over my chest, which was ridiculous because she was me—which was just weird. "But, oh, well, it could be worse! We could have been like Becky Apple, heehees!"

Her voice was so filled with joy that she made me smile in response, but only for a second. It was like it was too hard for me to hold onto the joy she seemed to glow with.

"Becky Renee Apple—can you believe her mom named her that and then had all of her sweaters monogrammed with 'BRA'?" the kid me said, and then broke into giggles.

I tried, unsuccessfully, to hold onto my smile while I said, "Yeah, that poor girl was doomed from the first day of cold weather." I sighed and rubbed a hand over my face, wondering why I felt so inexplicably sad.

"It's 'cause I'm not with you anymore," the kid me said. "I'm your joy. Without me, you can't ever really be happy again."

I stared at her, knowing that, like A-ya, she was telling me the truth.

Heath murmured in his sleep again, drawing my gaze to him. He looked so strong and normal and young, but he'd never step on another football field again. He'd never gun his truck around another slick corner and whoop like an Okie. He'd never be a husband. He'd never be a dad. I looked from him to the nine-year-old me.

"I don't think I deserve to be happy again."

"I'm sorry for you, Zoey," she said, and disappeared.

Feeling kinda dizzy and light-headed, I paced.

The next version of me didn't flicker or flutter at the edge of my vision. This version met me head-on, blocking my pacing path. She didn't look like me. She was super tall. Her hair was long and wild and a bright copper red. It wasn't until I met her gaze that I saw our similarity—we had the same eyes. She was another piece of me; I knew her.

"So who are you?" I said wearily. "And what part of me am I going to be missing if I don't get you back?"

"You may call me Brighid. Without me, you lack strength."

I sighed. "I'm too tired to be strong right now. How about we talk again after I take a nap?"

"You don't get it, do you?" Brighid shook her head disdainfully. "Without us, you won't take a nap—you won't get better—you won't rest. Without us, you just get more and more incomplete, and you drift."

I tried to focus through the headache that was building in my temples. "But I'd be drifting with Heath."

"Yes, you might be."

"And if I get all of you back together inside me, I'll leave Heath."

"Yes, you might."

"I can't do that. I can't return to a world without him," I said.

"Then you truly are broken." Without another word, Brighid disappeared.

My legs gave out, and I sat down hard on the moss. I only knew I was crying when my tears started making wet marks on my jeans. I don't know how long I sat there, bent with grief and confusion and weariness, but eventually a sound slipped inside my mental fog: wings, rustling, beating against the wind, hovering, dipping, searching.

"Come on, Zo. We need to get farther into the grove."

I looked up to see that Heath was crouching beside me. "This is my fault," I said.

"No, it's not, but why does it matter so much whose fault it is? This is done, babe. It can't be undone."

"I can't leave you, Heath," I sobbed.

He brushed the hair back from my face and handed me another ball of Kleenexes. "I know you can't."

The sound of enormous wings got louder; tree boughs behind us swayed in response.

"Zo, let's talk about this later, 'kay? Right now we need to move again." He grabbed me under one of my elbows, lifted me to my feet, and started to guide me deeper into the grove, where the shadows were darker and the trees even more ancient-looking.

I let him move me. It felt better to move. Not good. I didn't feel good. But it was better when I wasn't holding still.

"It's him, isn't it?" I said listlessly.

"Him?" Heath asked, helping me step over a rough gray stone.

"Kalona." The word seemed to change the density of the air around us. "He's come for me."

Heath gave me a sharp look, and shouted, "No, I'm not going to let him get you!"

Stevie Rae

"No, I'm not going to let him get you!" Dragon shouted.

Along with everyone else in the Council Chamber, Stevie Rae stared at the Sword Master, who looked like he might be getting ready to pop a major blood vessel.

"Uh, him who, Dragon?" Stevie Rae said.

"That Raven Mocker who killed my mate! That's why you can't go out alone until we track that creature down and destroy it."

Stevie Rae tried to ignore the hollow feeling Dragon's words gave her and the horrible sense of guilt she experienced as she faced him, seeing his heartbreak and knowing that even though Rephaim had saved her life, twice, it was also a fact that he had killed Anastasia Lankford.

He's changed. He's different now, she thought, wishing she could say the words aloud and not bring her world crashing down around them.

But she couldn't tell Dragon about Rephaim. She couldn't tell anyone about the Raven Mocker, so instead she began, again, to weave lies with the truth, forming a terrible tapestry of evasion and deceit.

"Dragon, I don't know which Raven Mocker was there in the park. I mean, it's not like he told me his name."

"I think he was the head one—the Ref-whatever," Dallas spoke up, even though Stevie Rae shot him a *look*.

"Rephaim," Dragon said, with a voice like death.

"Yeah, that's it. He was huge, just like you guys described, and his eyes really were human-looking. Plus, he had a thing about him. It was obvious he thought he was the shit."

Stevie Rae stifled the urge to press her hand firmly over Dallas's mouth—and maybe nose, too. Smothering him would definitely make him stop talking.

"Oh, Dallas, whatever. We don't know who that Raven Mocker

was. And, Dragon, I can understand why you're worried and all, but we're just talkin' 'bout me goin' to the Benedictine Abbey so that Grandma Redbird hears about Zoey from me. I'm not goin' off into the wilderness alone."

"But Dragon does have a good point," Lenobia said. Erik and Professor Penthasilea nodded, their disagreements about Neferet and Kalona temporarily put aside. "This Raven Mocker did appear where you were, while you were communing with earth."

"It's too simplistic to say she was communing with the earth," Dragon spoke quickly into Lenobia's pause. "As Stevie Rae explained to us, she was dialoguing with ancient powers of good and evil. That creature appearing during the manifestation of evil cannot be a coincidence."

"But the Raven Mocker wasn't attackin' me. It was—"

Dragon lifted a hand to silence her. "Undoubtedly it was drawn to the Darkness, which then turned on one of its own as evil often does. You cannot know with certainty that the creature isn't after you."

"We also cannot know with certainty that there is only one Raven Mocker in Tulsa," Lenobia said.

Panic fluttered in Stevie Rae's stomach. What if everyone was so freaked-out about the possibility of a bunch of Raven Mockers stalking around Tulsa that they made it impossible for her to get away to see Rephaim?

"I'm goin' to the abbey to see Grandma Redbird," Stevie Rae said firmly. "And I don't think there's a flock of those dang Raven Mockers out there. What I do think is that one bird guy somehow got left behind, and he was at the park because he was drawn to Darkness. Well, I'm sure as heck not gonna call Darkness to me again, so there's no reason for the bird to have anything to do with me."

"Do not underestimate the danger of that creature," Dragon said, his voice sad and somber.

"I won't. But I also won't let it keep me locked up on campus. I don't think any of us should let it do that," she added hastily. "I mean, we can be careful, but we can't let fear and evil rule our lives."

"Stevie Rae makes a valid point," Lenobia said. "Actually, I believe we should get the school back on a regular schedule and include the red fledglings in classes."

Kramisha, who had until then been sitting silently to the left of Stevie Rae, snorted softly. She heard Dallas, who was sitting to her right, sigh heavily. She stifled a smile, and said, "I think that's a real good idea."

"I don't think we should say much about Zoey's condition," Erik said. "At least not until something more, well, permanent happens."

"She's not gonna die," Stevie Rae said.

"I don't want her to die!" Erik said quickly, looking obviously upset at the thought. "But what with the stuff that's gone on around here lately, including a Raven Mocker showing up, the last thing we need is a bunch of talk."

"I don't think we should hush it up," Stevie Rae said.

"How about we agree on a compromise," Lenobia said. "Answer questions about Zoey when they're asked, focusing on the truth—that we're all working to get her back from the Otherworld."

"And we issue a general warning through all homeroom classes for fledglings to be watchful and vigilant in reporting anything they see or hear that might be unusual," Dragon added.

"That sounds reasonable," Penthasilea said.

"All right, that seems good to me, too," Stevie Rae said. Then she paused before adding, "Uh, I'm just wonderin', but am I supposed to go back to the classes I was in before?"

"Yeah, I's wondering that, too," Kramisha said.

"Me, too," Dallas said.

"Fledglings should attend classes, taking up where they left off," Lenobia said smoothly, smiling at Kramisha and Dallas as if the "left off" part had been unscheduled vacations rather than unwelcome deaths, which somehow made the whole thing sound weirdly normal. Then she turned to Stevie Rae. "Vampyres choose their career paths and the areas they'd like to study—not in class with fledglings but with other vampyres who are experts in their field. Do you know what it is you'd like to study?"

Even with everyone gawking at her, Stevie Rae had no hesitation in her answer. "Nyx. I want to study to be a High Priestess. I want to be one because I've earned it, and not just 'cause I'm the only dang red vamp female in the known universe."

"But we have no High Priestess under which you may study—not since Neferet was driven away," Penthasilea said, giving Lenobia a pointed look.

"Then I guess I'll study on my own until we get our High Priestess back." She met Penthasilea's eyes, and added, "And I can promise you that High Priestess will not be Neferet." Stevie Rae stood. "Okay, well, I'm gonna go to the abbey like I said before. When I come back, I'll go see the rest of the red fledglings and clue them in that classes start tomorrow."

Everyone had started to shuffle out of the room when Dragon pulled her aside. "I want you to promise me that you will be cautious," he said. "You have powers of recovery that border on miraculous, but you are not immortal, Stevie Rae. You must remember that."

"I'll be careful. I promise."

"I'm goin' with her," Kramisha said. "I'll keep an eye to the sky for them nasty bird things. And I got me a girl scream that is deadly. If one shows up, I can make sure the whole world knows he there."

Dragon nodded but didn't look convinced, and Stevie Rae was relieved when Lenobia called him over to her and started a conversation with him about making his martial arts classes mandatory for all fledglings. She slipped out of the room and was trying to figure out how she could get rid of Kramisha, who was being way too sticky-boogerish, when Dallas caught up with them.

"Can I talk to you for a sec before you leave?"

"I'll be in Zoey's Bug," Kramisha said. "And no, you can't get outta takin' me."

Stevie Rae watched her march down the hall before she reluctantly turned to Dallas.

"Can we go in there?" he asked, pointing to the deserted media center.

"Sure, but I do gotta get goin'."

Without saying anything, Dallas opened the door for her, and they stepped into the cool, dim room that smelled like books and lemon furniture polish.

"You and me, we don't have to be together anymore," Dallas said, all in a rush.

"Huh? Don't have to be together? What do you mean?"

Dallas crossed his arms over his chest and looked super uncomfortable. "I mean we were goin' out. You were my girlfriend. You don't want to be anymore, and I get it. You were right, I couldn't do shit to protect you from that bird thing. And I just want you to know I'm not gonna turn into an asshole about you and me. I'll still be here for you when you need me, girl, 'cause you're gonna always be my High Priestess."

"I don't want to break up!" she blurted.

"You don't?"

"No," and she didn't. At that instant, Dallas was all she could see, and his heart and his goodness were so obvious that Stevie Rae felt like losing him would be like getting punched in her gut. "Dallas, I'm so sorry for what I said before. I was hurt and mad, and I didn't mean it. I couldn't even get out of the circle, and I cast the dang thing. There's no way you, or anyone else, not even a Warrior, could've gotten in there to me."

Dallas met her gaze. "That Raven Mocker got in there."

"Well, like you said yourself, he's on the side of Darkness," she said, even though his bringing up Rephaim was like throwing cold water in her face.

"There's a lot on the side of Darkness out there," Dallas said. "And a bunch of it seems to be runnin' into you. So, be careful, will ya, girl?" He reached out and brushed a springy blond curl from her face. "I couldn't stand it if anything happened to you." He let his hand rest on her shoulder. His thumb gently caressed the line of her neck.

"I'll be careful," she said softly.

"You really don't want to break up?"

She shook her head.

"I'm glad, 'cause I don't want to either."

Dallas leaned down as he pulled her into his arms. His lips met

Stevie Rae's in a hesitant kiss. She told herself to relax and melted into him. He was a good kisser—he always had been. And she liked that he was taller than her, but not crazy tall. He tasted good, too. He knew that she liked her back rubbed, so as he slipped his arms around her his hands went under her shirt—not to try to maul her boobs, like most guys would have. Instead, Dallas started to rub soft, warm circles over her lower back, pressing her closer to him and deepening their kiss.

Stevie Rae kissed him back. It felt good to be with him . . . to block out everything . . . to forget for even a little while about Rephaim and all that stuff . . . especially about the debt she'd willingly paid that made her—

Stevie Rae pulled away from Dallas. They were both more than a little breathless.

"I, uh, I do have to go. Remember?" Stevie Rae smiled at him, trying not to sound as awkward as she felt.

"Actually, I'd kinda forgotten," Dallas said, smiling sweetly at her and brushing that stubborn curl out of her eyes again. "But I know you hafta go. Come on. I'll walk ya to the Bug."

Feeling part traitor, part liar, and part doomed prisoner, Stevie Rae let him take her hand and lead her to Zoey's car, just like they really, truly could be boyfriend and girlfriend again.

CHAPTER SEVENTEEN

Stevie Rae

"That boy's gone on you," Kramisha said, as Stevie Rae pulled out of the school's parking lot, leaving behind Dallas, who was looking more than kinda pitiful. "You know what you gonna do 'bout that other kid?"

Stevie Rae braked the car in the middle of the blacktop that led to Utica Street. "I'm too stressed-out to deal with guy stuff right now. So if all you wanna do is talk about that, you can stay here."

"Not dealing with guy stuff just causes more stress."

"Bye, Kramisha."

"If you gonna act all crazy, then I won't say nothin' about it. Right now. Anyway, I got other more important stuff that you need to deal with."

Stevie Rae put the Bug into gear and kept driving off campus though she wished Kramisha would press her about the guy stuff so she'd have an excuse to leave her behind, too.

"Remember when you told me to think harder 'bout my poems and such to try to get somethin' that might help Zoey?"

"Of course I remember."

"Well, I did. And I got somethin'." She dug around in her huge bag until she brought out a well-worn notebook with pages that were her signature purple color. "I think everbody, including me until I focused myself, is forgetting 'bout this." She opened the notebook and waved a page with her cursive print at Stevie Rae.

"Kramisha, you know I can't read that while I'm drivin'. Just tell me what you remembered."

"The poem I wrote right before Zoey and the rest of the kids took off for Venice. The one that sounds like it's from Kalona to Zoey. Here, I'll read it to ya:

A double-edged sword
One side destroys
One releases
I am your Gordian knot
Will you release or destroy me?
Follow truth and you shall:
Find me on water
Purify me through fire
Trapped by earth nevermore
Air will whisper to you
What spirit already knows:
That even shattered
anything is possible
If you believe
Then we shall both be free.

"Ohmygood*ness*! I *had* totally forgotten 'bout that! Okay, okay, read it again, only slower." Stevie Rae listened closely while Kramisha read the poem again. "It has to be from Kalona, doesn't it? That part about being trapped by the earth makes it definitely from him."

"I'm practically sure it's from him to her."

"It must be, even though that's kinda scary, what with the whole double-edged sword beginning, but the end seems like a real good thing."

"It says, 'then we shall both be free,'" Kramisha quoted.

"Sounds to me like Z's gonna get free from the Otherworld."

"And so will Kalona," Kramisha added.

"We'll deal with that when it happens. Gettin' Z free is what's most important. Hang on! I think some of it's already come true! What was the part about water?"

"It says: 'Find me on water.'"

"And she did. San Clemente Island is definitely on water."

"It also says that Zoey has to 'follow truth.' What do you think that means?"

"I'm not one hundred percent sure, but I might have an idea. The last time I talked to Z, I told her to follow her heart, no matter that it might seem to everyone else in the world that she was messin' up royally, just follow what everything inside her said was the right thing to do." Stevie Rae paused, blinking hard against the sudden urge to bawl. "I-I've felt real guilty about sayin' that, though, 'cause of what happened to her right afterward."

"But maybe you was right. Maybe what's happenin' to Z is supposed to happen, 'cause I'm thinkin' to follow your heart and to hold on to what you believe is right, even when everbody else says you're dead-assed wrong, is a powerful kind of truth."

Stevie Rae felt a flutter of excitement. "And if she keeps doin' that, keeps holdin' to the truth she has in her heart, the end of the poem *will* happen, and she'll be free."

"It feels right to me, Stevie Rae. Real right, like down deep in my bones."

"Me, too," Stevie Rae said, grinning at Kramisha.

"Okay, but Z needs to know all this. The poem is like a map to the end. The first step, findin' him on water, already happened. Next she has to—"

"Purify him through fire," Stevie Rae broke in, remembering the line. "And then doesn't it say something 'bout earth and air?"

"Yeah, and spirit. It's all five of the elements."

"All of Z's affinities, ending in spirit, which is her most powerful affinity."

"And the one in charge of the realm she's in right now," Kramisha said. "Okay, I ain't gonna say this just 'cause I wrote me a kick-ass poem, so you gotta seriously listen up: Zoey has to know this stuff. It's gonna make the difference between her comin' back and her being killed dead by whatever's goin' on over there."

"Oh, I believe you."

"Then how you gonna do it?"

"Me? I'm not. I can't. I'm into earth. No way can my spirit take off and get to the Otherworld." Stevie Rae shivered. Just the thought gave her the heebie-jeebies. "But Stark's gonna get his butt there. He has to—that disgusting cow said so."

"Bull," Kramisha said.

"Whatever."

"You want me to call Stark and read the poem to him? You got his number?"

Stevie Rae thought about it. "No. Aphrodite says Stark's head is seriously messed up right now. He might ignore your poem, thinkin' he has other, more important stuff to deal with."

"Well, he'd be wrong."

"Yeah, I agree. So, what we need to do is get the poem to Aphrodite. She's hateful and all, but she'll understand how important it is."

"And 'cause she's so hateful, there's no way she'll let Stark ignore her or the poem."

"Exactly. Text it to her right now and tell her I said to make Stark memorize it for Zoey. And to remember it's a prophecy, not just a poem."

"You know, I seriously question her amount of good sense 'cause she don't like poetry."

"Girl, you are preaching to the dang full-gospel Pentecostal choir," said Stevie Rae.

"Um-hum, that's all I have to say." And while Stevie Rae pulled into the newly plowed parking lot of the Benedictine Abbey, Kramisha bent her head over her phone and got busy texting.

Stevie Rae

Right away, Stevie Rae could tell that Grandma Redbird was getting better. The terrible bruises on her face had faded, and instead of being in bed, she was sitting in a rocking chair by the fireplace in the abbey's main lounge, so into the book she was reading that she didn't even notice Stevie Rae at first.

"Blue-Eyed Devil?" Even though she was there to tell Z's grandma awful news, Stevie Rae couldn't help smiling as she read the title. "Grandma, that sounds like a romance book to me."

Grandma Redbird's hand went to her throat. "Stevie Rae! Child, you startled me. And it is a romance—an excellent one at that. Hardy Cates is a magnificent hero."

"Magnificent?"

Grandma lifted her sliver brows at Stevie Rae. "I'm old, child. Not dead. I can still appreciate a magnificent man." She motioned to one of the padded wooden chairs not far away. "Pull that up, honey, and let's have a chat. I'm assuming you have news of Zoey all the way from Venice. Just think of it—Venice, Italy! I would love to visit . . ." The old woman's voice trailed off as she looked more closely at Stevie Rae. "I knew it. I knew something was wrong, but my mind has been so muddled since the accident." Sylvia Redbird went very, very still. Then, in a voice that that was rough with fear, she said, "Tell me quickly."

With a sad sigh, Stevie Rae sat in the chair she'd pulled beside the rocker and took Grandma's hand. "She's not dead, but it's not good."

"All of it. I want all of it. Don't stop, and don't leave anything out."

Grandma Redbird held on to Stevie Rae's hand as if it were a lifeline as Zoey's best friend told her everything—from Heath's death to the bulls to the present and Kramisha's prophetic poem, leaving out only one thing: Rephaim. When she was finished, Grandma's face had gone as pale as it had been right after her accident, when she'd been in a coma and near death.

"Shattered. My granddaughter's soul is shattered," she said slowly, as if the words carried thick layers of grief all their own.

"Stark's gonna get to her, Grandma." Stevie Rae met the old woman's gaze steadily. "And then he's gonna protect her so that she can pull herself together."

"Cedar," Grandma said, nodding like she'd just answered a question, and Stevie Rae should be agreeing with her.

"Cedar?" Stevie Rae asked, hoping the news about Zoey hadn't made Grandma lose her mind. Literally.

"Cedar needles. Tell Stark to make whoever watches over his body while he's in the trance state to burn them the entire time."

"You just lost me, Grandma."

"Cedar needles are powerful medicine. They repel asgina, which are considered the most malevolent of spirits. Cedar is only used during times of dire need."

"Well, this is some seriously dire need," Stevie Rae said, relieved that the color was starting to come back into Grandma's cheeks.

"Tell Stark to breathe the smoke deeply, and to think about carrying it with him to the Otherworld—to believe it will follow his spirit there. The mind can be a powerful ally of the spirit. Sometimes our minds can even alter the very fabric of our souls. If Stark believes the cedar smoke can accompany his spirit, it might just do so and add an extra layer of protection to him on his quest."

"I'll tell him."

Grandma squeezed her hand even tighter. "Sometimes things that seem small or insignificant can aid us, even in our most difficult hour. Don't discount anything, and don't let Stark, either."

"I won't, Grandma. None of us will. I'll be sure of it."

"Sylvia, I just spoke with Kramisha outside," Sister Mary Angela hurried into the room. She came to a halt when she saw Stevie Rae holding the old woman's hand. "Oh, Mother Mary! It is true then." The nun bowed her head, obviously fighting tears, but when she lifted her chin, her eyes were dry, and her face was set in strong, resolute lines. "Well, then, we shall go on from here." Abruptly, she turned and began to leave the room.

"Sister, where are you going?" Grandma Redbird asked.

"To call the abbey to the chapel. We will pray. We all will pray."

"To Mary?" Stevie Rae asked, unable to keep the skepticism out of her voice.

The nun nodded, and in her firm, wise voice said, "Yes, Stevie Rae, to Mary—to the Lady we consider to be mother in spirit of us all. Perhaps she isn't the same deity as your Nyx; perhaps she is. But is that question really important right now? Tell me, High Priestess of the Red Fledglings, do you truly believe asking for help in the name of love to be a mistake, no matter what face that help is wearing?"

Stevie Rae had a flash of Rephaim's face with his human eyes as he stood up to Darkness and took on the debt she owed it, and her mouth suddenly went dry.

"I'm sorry, Sister. I was wrong. Ask for your Mary's help 'cause sometimes love does come from places that we don't expect."

Sister Mary Angela looked into Stevie Rae's eyes for what seemed like a very long time before saying, "You may join us in prayer, child."

Stevie Rae smiled at her. "Thanks, but I have my own kind of prayin' to do."

Stevie Rae

"Hell no I ain't gonna lie for you!" Kramisha said.

"I'm not askin' you to lie," Stevie Rae said.

"Yah you is. You want me to say you're all involved in checking out the tunnel with Sister Mary Angela. Everbody already knows you totally sealed it up last time you was here."

"Not everyone knows that," Stevie Rae said.

"Yeah, they do. Plus, the nuns is all prayin' for Zoey, and it don't seem right at all to use a prayin' nun in your lie."

"Fine. I'll go down to the tunnel and check it out if it makes you feel better." Stevie Rae couldn't believe Kramisha was making such an issue out of telling a little white lie for her that she was costing her time—time away from Rephaim when Goddess only knew how hurt he was from that disgusting white cow. She remembered the agony she'd felt when Darkness had fed from her and knew it had been doubly bad for Rephaim. This time she was gonna have to figure out more to do than just bandaging him and feeding him to make him better. How badly had he been hurt? In her mind's eye, she could still see that creature looming over him, tongue red with his blood while—

With a jolt, Stevie Rae realized Kramisha had just been standing there, staring at her without saying anything.

Stevie Rae mentally shook herself and said the first excuse that came to her mind. "Look, I just don't want to deal with the shitstorm that'll happen if everyone in the House of Night knows I spent like 1.2 seconds alone. That's all."

"You a lie."

"I'm your High Priestess!"

"Then you should act like one," Kramisha told her. "Tell me the truth 'bout what you up to."

"I'm gonna go see the guy, and I don't want anyone to know about it!" Stevie Rae blurted.

Kramisha cocked her head to the side. "That's more like it. He ain't a fledgling or a vamp, is he?"

"No," Stevie Rae said with absolute honesty. "He's someone no one would like."

"He ain't abusing you, is he? 'Cause that's some wrong shit, and I know some females who been caught up in it and can't get their way out."

"Kramisha, I can make earth rise up and kick someone's ass. No guy would ever hit me. Ever."

"So that means he a human and he married."

"I promise he's not married," Stevie Rae evaded.

"Huh," Kramisha snorted through her nose. "Is he an asshole?"

"I don't think he is."

"Love sucks."

"Yep," Stevie Rae said. "But I'm not sayin' I'm in love with him," she added hastily. "All I'm sayin' is that—"

"He's messin' with your head, and you do not need that right now." Kramisha pursed her lips up, thinking. "Okay, how 'bout this: I get one of the nuns to take me back to the House of Night, and when everbody stresses 'bout you bein' out here all alone, I just tell them you needed to visit a human, so you ain't technically alone—and I ain't lying, either."

Stevie Rae thought about it. "Do you have to tell them it's a human guy?"

"I'll just say human and say they need to mind they own business. I'll only say guy if someone asks me specifically."

"Deal," Stevie Rae said.

"You know you gonna have to come clean about him sooner or later. And if he ain't married, there's really no issue. You're a High Priestess. You can have a human mate and a vamp consort at the same time."

It was Stevie Rae's turn to snort. "And you think Dallas is gonna be okay with that?"

"He will be if he wants to be with a High Priestess. All vampyres know that."

"Well, Dallas isn't a vampyre yet, so it might be a little much to ask of him. And here's the truth—I know it'll hurt his feelings, and I don't want to do that."

Kramisha nodded. "I can tell you don't, but I think you makin' too much of this. Dallas will have to learn to deal. What you need to figure out is if this human guy is worth it."

"I know that, Kramisha. That's what I'm tryin' to do. So, bye. I'll see you at the House of Night in a little while." Stevie Rae started to walk quickly toward the Bug.

"Hey!" Kramisha called after her. "He ain't black, is he?"

Thinking of Rephaim's night-colored wings Stevie Rae paused and looked over her shoulder at Kramisha. "What difference does his color make?"

"It make a lot of difference if you're ashamed of him," she shot back.

"Kramisha, that's just silly. No. He's not black. And, no, I wouldn't be ashamed of him if he was. Jeeze. Bye. Again."

"Just checkin'."

"Just soundin' crazy," Stevie Rae muttered as she turned back to the parking lot.

"I heard that," Kramisha said.

"Good!" Stevie Rae yelled. She got into Zoey's Bug and headed toward the Gilcrease Museum, talking to herself out loud. "No, Kramisha, he's not black. He's a killer bird with evil for his daddy, and it's not just white folks and black folks who would be pissed at me bein' with him—it's *all* folks!" And then, completely surprising herself, Stevie Rae started to laugh.

CHAPTER EIGHTEEN

Rephaim

When Rephaim opened his eyes, he saw Stevie Rae squatting in front of his closet nest, studying him so intently that there was a deep furrow on her brow between her eyes, making her red crescent tattoo look oddly wavy. Her blond curls spilled around her face, and she seemed so girl-like that he was suddenly taken aback by remembering how young she really was. And, no matter the vastness of her elemental powers, how vulnerable her youth made her. The thought of her vulnerability had fear knifing his heart.

"Hey there. You awake?" she said.

"Why are you staring at me like that?" he asked in a purposefully gruff voice, annoyed that just the sight of her could make him worry about her safety.

"Well, I'm tryin' to figure out how close you've come to dyin' this time."

"My father's an immortal. I'm hard to kill." He made himself sit up without grimacing.

"Yeah, I know about your daddy and your immortal blood and all, but Darkness fed from you. A lot. That can't be good. Plus, to be honest, you look really bad."

"You don't," he said. "And Darkness fed from you, too."

"I'm not as hurt as you because you swooped in like Batman and saved the day before that dang nasty bull could mess me up too much. Then I got a shot in the arm from Light, which was totally cool, by the way. *And* that immortal blood of yours is like the Energizer Bunny inside me."

"I am not a bat," was all he could think to say, as that was the only thing she'd said he vaguely understood.

"I didn't compare you to a bat, I said you were like Batman. He's a superhero."

"I'm not a hero, either."

"Well, you've been my hero. Twice."

Rephaim didn't know what to say to that. All he knew was that Stevie Rae calling him her hero made something twist deep inside him, and that something suddenly made the pain in his body and his worry for her easier to bear.

"So, come on. Let's see if I can return the favor. Again." She stood and held her hand out to him.

"I don't think I could eat right now. Some water would be good, though. I drank all that we'd brought up here before."

"I'm not takin' you to the kitchen. At least not this second. I'm takin' you outside. To the trees. Well, okay, to that really big tree by the old gazebo in the front yard to be specific."

"Why?"

"I already told you. You helped me. I think I can help you, but I gotta be closer to the earth than we are up here, and I've been thinkin' 'bout it, and I know trees have major power in them. I've kinda used it before. Actually, that may have been part of the reason I was able to call up that *thing*." She shuddered, clearly remembering her invocation of Darkness, which Rephaim completely understood. Had his body not ached so badly, he would have shuddered, too.

But his body did ache. More than that. His blood felt too hot. With every beat of his heart, searing pain pumped through him, and at the spot where his wings met his spine, where the bull of Darkness had fed from him, violated him, his back was blazing agony.

And she thought a tree would fix what Darkness had wrought?

"I think I'll stay here. Rest will help. So will water. If you want to do something for me, get the water I asked for."

"Nope." Stevie Rae reached down and, with that strength that always surprised him, grabbed both of his hands and pulled him to his feet. She kept her supporting hold on him while the room pitched and rolled around him, and he thought, for one terrible moment, that he was going to collapse like a fainting girl.

Thankfully, the moment passed, and he was able to open his eyes without fear of making an even bigger fool of himself. He looked down at Stevie Rae. She was still holding his hands. *She doesn't shrink away from me in disgust. She hasn't from the first day.*

"Why do you touch me with no fear?" he heard himself asking before he could stop the words.

She gave a little laugh. "Rephaim, I don't think you could swat a fly right now. Besides that—you've saved my life twice, and we're Imprinted. I'm definitely not scared of you."

"Perhaps the question should have been why do you touch me with no repulsion?" Again, the words came almost without his permission. Almost.

Her brow furrowed like before, and he decided he liked to watch her think.

Finally, she shrugged, and said, "I don't imagine it's possible for a vampyre to be repulsed by someone they're Imprinted with. I mean, I was Imprinted with Aphrodite before I drank your blood, and there was a time when she seriously grossed me out—she just wasn't very nice. At all. Actually, she's still not very nice. But she kinda grew on me after we Imprinted. Not in a sexual way, but I wasn't grossed out by her anymore."

Then Stevie Rae's eyes widened like she realized all of what she'd said, and the word "sexual" seemed to be a tangible presence in the room.

She let loose of his hands as if they burned her.

"Can you walk downstairs by yourself?" Her voice sounded strange and abrupt.

"Yes. I'll follow you. If you really think a tree can help."

"Well, it won't be long before we find out if what I think means anything." Stevie Rae turned her back on him and headed for the stairs. "Oh," she said, without looking at him, "thank you for saving me. Again. You—you didn't have to this time." Her words were hesitant, like she was having trouble picking exactly what she wanted to say to him. "He said he wasn't going to kill me."

"There are things worse than death," Rephaim said. "What Darkness can take from someone who walks with Light can change your soul."

"And what about you? What did Darkness take from you?" she asked, still not looking at him, as they reached the bottom floor of the old mansion, but she slowed down so that he could keep up with her more easily.

"He didn't take anything from me. He just filled me with pain and then fed on that pain mixed with my blood."

They'd reached the front door, and Stevie Rae paused, looking up at him. "Because Darkness feeds on pain and Light feeds on love."

Her words tripped a mental switch inside him, and he studied her more closely. *Yes,* he decided, *she is keeping something from me.* "What price did Light demand from you for saving me?"

Stevie Rae was unable to meet his eyes again, which gave him an odd, panicky feeling. He thought she wasn't going to answer him at all, but finally, in a voice that sounded almost angry, "Do you want to tell me about everything that bull demanded from you when he was feeding from you, and standing over you, and basically molesting you?"

"No," Rephaim answered without hesitated. "But the other bull—"

"No," Stevie Rae echoed him. "I don't want to talk about it, either. So let's just forget it and go on from here. Well, and let's hope I can fix some of this pain Darkness left inside you."

Rephaim walked with her out onto the icy front lawn, which was pathetic in its dilapidation and a sad, broken reflection of its opulent past. As Rephaim followed her, moving slowly to try to compensate for the terrible pain that was making him so weak, he wondered about the payment Light could have demanded from Stevie Rae. Clearly, it was something unnerving—something that made Stevie Rae reluctant to speak of it.

He kept stealing glances at her when he thought she wouldn't notice.

She appeared healthy and totally recovered from her brush with Darkness. Actually, she looked strong and whole and completely normal.

But, as he was all too aware, appearances could easily deceive.

Something was wrong—or at the very least, something about the debt she'd paid Light made her uncomfortable.

Rephaim was so busy trying to be stealthy about studying her that he almost ran into the tree she'd stopped beside.

She looked at him and shook her head. "You're not foolin' me. You feel too crappy to be sneaky, so stop gawking at me. I'm fine. Jeeze, you're worse than my mama."

"Have you talked to her?"

Stevie Rae's frown deepened. "I haven't exactly had a lot of free time the past couple days. So, no, I haven't talked to my mama."

"You should."

"I'm not gonna talk about my mama right now."

"As you wish."

"And you don't need to use that tone with me."

"What tone?"

Instead of answering him, she said, "Just sit down and be quiet for a change and let me think about how I'm supposed to help you." Like she was demonstrating, Stevie Rae sat down, cross-legged, with her back against the old cedar tree that wept ice and fragrant needles all around them. When he still didn't move, she made an impatient noise and motioned to the space in front of her. "Sit," she ordered.

He sat.

"And now?" he asked.

"Well, give me a minute. I'm not real sure how to do this."

He watched her twirl one of her soft blond curls around her finger and scrunch up her forehead for a while, and then he offered, "Would it help to think about what you did when you tripped that annoying fledgling who thought he could challenge me?"

"Dallas isn't annoying, and he thought you were attacking me."

"Good thing I wasn't."

"And why is that?"

Even through the pain in his body, her tone amused him. She

knew very well that puny fledgling had been no threat to him, even in his weakened condition. Had Rephaim been attacking her, or anyone else, the impotent youth couldn't have stopped him. Still, the boy had been Marked by a red crescent, which meant he was one of her subjects, and his Stevie Rae was nothing if not fiercely loyal. So Rephaim bowed his head in acquiescence, and said only, "Because it would have been inconvenient if I'd had to defend myself."

Stevie Rae's lips curved up in the hint of a smile. "Dallas really did think he was protecting me from you."

"You don't need him." Rephaim spoke the words without thinking. Stevie Rae's gaze met his and held. He wished he could read her expressions more easily. He thought he saw surprise in her eyes, and maybe a faint glint of hope, but he also saw fear—of that he was sure. Fear of him? No, she'd already proven she wasn't afraid of him. So the fear had to be within, of something that wasn't him but that he'd triggered. Not knowing what else to say, he added, "As you said before, I could not swat a fly. I was certainly no threat to you."

Stevie Rae blinked a couple of times, as if clearing away too many thoughts, and then she shrugged, and said, "Yeah, well, I've had one heck of a time convincing everybody back at the House of Night that it was just a weird coincidence that you dropped from the sky at the same time Darkness manifested, and that you *weren't* attacking me. Them knowing there's a Raven Mocker still in Tulsa has made it super hard for me to get away from school alone."

"I should leave." The words made him feel strangely empty inside.

"Where would you go?"

"East," he said without hesitation.

"East? You mean like all the way east to Venice? Rephaim, your daddy's not in his body. You can't help him by goin' there right now. I think you can help him more by stayin' here and working with me to bring both Zoey and him back."

"You don't want me to leave?"

Stevie Rae looked down as if studying the earth they sat on. "It's hard for a vampyre to have the person she's Imprinted with too far away from her."

"I'm not a person."

"Yeah, but that didn't stop us from Imprinting, so I'm thinkin' the rules still apply to you and me."

"Then I'll stay until you tell me to go."

She closed her eyes as if the words had hurt her, and he had to force himself to remain still and not reach out to comfort her, to touch her.

Touch her? I want to touch her?

He crossed his arms over his chest in a physical denial of the shocking thought.

"Earth," he said, his voice sounding too loud in the silence that had fallen between them. She looked up at him then with a question in her eyes. "You called it before, when you tripped the red fledgling. You called it to open so that you could escape from the sunlight on the rooftop. You called it to close the tunnel behind me at the abbey. Can you not simply call it now and make your request of it?"

Her gentle blue eyes widened. "You're right! Why am I makin' it so hard? I've done it like a zillion times for other stuff. There's no reason why I can't do it for this." She held her hands out, palms up. "Here, grab hold."

It was too easy for him to unfold his arms and press his palms to hers. He looked down at their joined hands, and he suddenly realized that, except for Stevie Rae, he'd never touched a human for any reason except violence. Yet there he was, touching her again—gently—calmly.

Her skin felt good against his. She was warm. And soft. Her words came to him then, and what she was saying moved inside him, nesting there in a distant place that had never before been touched.

"Earth, I have a big favor to ask you. Rephaim here is special to me. He's in pain, and he's havin' trouble gettin' well. Earth, I've borrowed your strength before—to save myself—to save those I care about. This time I'm asking to borrow your strength to help Rephaim. It's only right." She paused and looked up at him. Their eyes met as she echoed the words he'd spoken to Darkness when he thought she'd been unable to hear him. "You see, he's hurt because of me. Heal him. Please."

The ground beneath them quivered. Rephaim was thinking it was strangely like the skin of a twitching animal when Stevie Rae gasped, and her body jerked. Rephaim started to pull away, wanting to stop whatever was happening to her, but she held tightly to his hands, saying "No! Don't let go. It's fine."

Then heat radiated from her palms into his. For an instant it reminded him of the last time he'd called on what he believed to be the immortal power of his father's blood, and Darkness had answered instead—pulsing through his body and healing his shattered arm and wing. But quickly Rephaim understood that there was an essential difference between being touched by Darkness and being touched by the earth. Where before the power had been raw and consuming, swelling him with energy and shooting through his body, now what filled him was like a summer's wind beneath his wings. Its presence in his body was no less commanding than Darkness had been, but it was power tempered with compassion—its infilling was living and healthy and growing instead of cold and violent and consuming. It was balm to his overheated blood, soothing the pain that pulsed through his body. When the earth's warmth reached his back—that raw, unhealed place where his great wings grew—the relief was so instantaneous that Rephaim closed his eyes, breathing a long sigh as the agony evaporated.

And, throughout the healing, the air around Rephaim was filled with the heady, comforting scent of cedar needles and the sweetness of summer grass.

"Think about sending the energy back into the earth." Stevie Rae's voice was gentle, but insistent. He started to open his eyes and let loose her hands, but again she held tight to him, saying, "No, keep your eyes shut. Just stay like you are, but imagine the power from the earth as a glowing green light that's coming from the ground under me, up through my body and hands, to you. When you feel like it's done its job, envision it pouring from your body back into the earth."

Rephaim kept his eyes closed, but asked, "Why? Why let it leave me?"

He could hear the smile in her voice. "Because it's not yours, silly. You can't own this power. It belongs to the earth. You can only borrow it, and then send it back with a 'thank you very much.' "

Rephaim almost told her that was ridiculous—that when you've been given power, you don't let it go. You keep it and use it and own it. He *almost* said it, but he couldn't. Those words seemed wrong while he was getting filled with earth energy.

So instead, he did what felt right. Rephaim imagined the energy that filled him as a glowing green shaft of light, and envisioned it pouring down his spine and back into the earth from which it had come. And as the rich warmth of earth drained from him, he spoke two words very softly, "Thank you."

Then he was himself again. Sitting under a big cedar tree on damp, cold ground, holding Stevie Rae's hands.

Rephaim opened his eyes.

"Better now?" she asked.

"Yes. Much better." Rephaim opened his hands, and this time, she, too, pulled away.

"Really? I mean, I felt the earth and thought I was channeling it through me into you, and you seemed to be feelin' it." She cocked her head, studying him. "You do look better. There isn't any pain in your eyes anymore."

He stood up, eager to show her, and opened his arms, unfurling his massive wings as if he were flexing a muscle. "See! I can do this with no pain."

She was sitting on the ground staring up at him, wide-eyed. The look on her face was so odd that he automatically lowered his arms and folded his wings against his back.

"What is it?" he asked. "What's wrong?"

"I—I'd forgotten that you flew to the park. Well, and from the park, too." She made a sound that could have been a laugh had it not sounded so choked. "That's stupid, isn't? How could I have forgotten somethin' like that?"

"I suppose you got used to seeing me broken," he said, trying to understand why she suddenly seemed so withdrawn from him.

"What fixed your wing?"

"The earth," he said.

"No, not now. It wasn't broken when we came out here. The pain you were filled with didn't have anything to do with that."

"Oh, no. I've been healed since last night. The pain was caused by the remnants of Darkness and what he did to my body."

"So how did your wing and your arm get fixed last night?"

Rephaim didn't want to answer her. As she stared at him with those wide, accusing eyes, he found himself wanting to lie—to tell her it had been a miracle wrought by the immortality in his blood. But he couldn't lie to her. He *wouldn't* lie to her.

"I called on powers that are mine to command through my father's blood. I had to. I heard you scream my name."

She blinked, and he saw realization flash through her gaze. "But the bull said you'd been filled with his power and not your daddy's."

Rephaim nodded. "I knew it was different. I didn't know why. Nor did I understand I was getting power directly from Darkness himself."

"So Darkness healed you."

"Yes, and then the earth healed me from the wound Darkness left inside me."

"Okay, well, good." She stood abruptly and brushed off her jeans. "You're better now, and I gotta go. Like I said, it's tough for me to get away now that the House of Night is all freaked about a Raven Mocker bein' in town."

She started to walk quickly past him, and he reached out to grab her wrist.

Stevie Rae flinched away from him.

Rephaim's hand dropped instantly to his side, and he took a step away from her.

They stared at each other.

"I gotta go," she repeated.

"Will you return?"

"I have to! I promised!" She yelled the words at him, and he felt them as if she'd slapped him.

"I release you from your promise!" he yelled back at her, angry that this small female could cause such turmoil within him.

Her eyes were suspiciously bright when she said, “It’s not you I promised—so you can’t release me.” Then she swept past him, her head turned away so he couldn’t see her face.

“Do not return because you have to. Return only because you want to,” he called after her.

Stevie Rae didn’t pause and didn’t look back at him. She simply left.

Rephaim stood there a long time. When the sound of her car faded away, he finally moved. With a cry of frustration, the Raven Mocker ran and then launched himself into the night sky, beating the cold wind with his massive wings and heading up, up to find the warmer thermals that would lift him, hold him, carry him anywhere—everywhere.

Just away! Take me away from here!

The Raven Mocker swooped to the east, away from the direction Stevie Rae’s car had taken—away from Tulsa and the confusion that had entered his life since *she’d* entered his life. Then he closed his mind to everything except the familiar joy of the sky, and flew.

CHAPTER NINETEEN

Stark

"Yeah, I'm listening to you, Aphrodite. You want me to memorize that poem." Stark spoke to her through the helicopter's headsets, which he wished he knew how to shut off. He didn't want to listen to her run her mouth; he didn't want to talk to Aphrodite or to anyone. He was totally preoccupied with turning over and over in his mind his strategy for getting himself and Zoey on the island. Stark stared out of the window of the helicopter, trying to see through darkness and fog for a first glimpse of the Isle of Skye where, according to Duantia and just about the entire High Council, he was going to meet his certain death sometime in the next five days.

"Not that *poem,* idiot. That *prophecy.* I wouldn't ask anyone to memorize a poem. Metaphor, simile, allusion, symbolism . . . blah . . . blah . . . ugh. It makes my hair hurt thinking about all that crap. Not that a prophecy sucks any less, but it is—sadly—important. And Stevie Rae has a point about this one. It does read like a confusing poetic map," Aphrodite said.

"I am in agreement with Aphrodite and Stevie Rae," Darius said. "Kramisha's prophetic poems have given Zoey guidance before. This one could do the same thing."

Stark dragged his gaze from the window. "I know." He looked from Darius to Aphrodite, then his eyes went to Zoey's apparently lifeless body, where she was strapped in on a narrow litter between the three of them. "She already found Kalona on water. She has to purify him through fire. Air has to whisper to her something spirit already knows, and if she keeps following truth, she'll be free. I already memorized the damn thing. I don't care if it's a poem or a prophecy. If there's a chance it can help her, I'll get it to Zoey."

The pilot's voice came through the headsets to all of them. "I'm putting it down now. Remember, all I can do is let you out. The rest is up to you. Just know if you step one foot on the island itself without Sgiach's permission, you will die."

"I got that the first dozen times you assholes said it," Stark muttered, not caring that the pilot gave him a dark look over her shoulder.

Then the helicopter landed, and Darius was helping him unbuckle Zoey. Stark dropped to the ground. Darius and Aphrodite carefully handed Zoey to him, and he cradled her in his arms, trying to shield her from the worst of cold, wet wind whipped up by the helicopter's massive blades. Darius and Aphrodite joined him, and they all hurried away from the helicopter, though the pilot hadn't been exaggerating. They weren't even on the ground for a minute when the copter took off.

"Pussies," Stark said.

"They're just following their instincts," Darius said, looking around them as if he expected the bogeyman to jump out of the mist.

"No shit. This place is super creepy," Aphrodite said, moving closer to Darius, who tucked her hand through his arm possessively.

Stark frowned at them. "Are you two okay? Don't tell me the doom-and-gloom vamps got to you."

Darius looked him up and down, and then shared a glance with Aphrodite before answering. "You don't feel it, do you?"

"I feel cold and wet. I feel pissed off that Zoey's in trouble and I haven't been able to help her, and I feel annoyed that dawn is only an hour or so away and my only shelter is a shack the vamps said is a thirty-minute walk back the way we came. Are any of those things the "it" you're talking about?"

"No," Aphrodite answered for Darius, though the Warrior was also shaking his head. "The "it" Darius and I feel is a strong desire to run away. And I do mean run. Now."

"I want to take Aphrodite out of here. To get her away from this island and never to come back," Darius said. "That is what all my instincts are telling me."

"And you don't feel any of that?" Aphrodite asked Stark. "You don't want to carry Zoey the hell outta here?"

"Nope."

"I think that's a good sign," Darius said. "The warning that is inherent in the land is somehow passing over him."

"Or Stark's just too muscle-brained to be warned," Aphrodite said.

"On that upbeat thought, let's get going with this. I don't have time to waste on spooky feelings," Stark said. Still carrying Zoey, he started toward the long, narrow bridge that stretched between an outcropping of the Scottish mainland and the island. It was lit by torches that could barely been seen through the soupy mixture of night and mist. "Are you two coming? Or are you going to run screaming like girls away from here."

"We're coming with you," Darius said, catching him in a couple of strides.

"Yeah, and I said I wanted to run. I didn't say shit about screaming. I'm not a screamer," Aphrodite said.

They'd both sounded pretty tough, but Stark hadn't even gotten to the halfway point of the bridge when he heard Aphrodite whispering to Darius. He glanced at the two of them. Even in the dim torchlight he could see how pale the Warrior and his Prophetess had become. Stark paused. "You don't have to come with me. Everyone, even Thanatos, said there's absolutely no way Sgiach is going to let you guys on the island. Even if all of them are wrong, and you do get on, there's not much you can do. I have to figure out how to get to Zoey. Alone."

"We can't be at your side while you're in the Otherworld," Darius said.

"So we're watching your back, and there's nothing you can do about it. Zoey would be totally pissed at me when she gets back in there"—Aphrodite pointed at Zoey's body—"and found out Darius and I had let you do all this crap alone. You know how she is with her one for all, all for one, mentality. The vamps wouldn't bring the whole nerd herd here, something I can't really blame them for, so Darius and I are picking up their slack. Again. Like you said, stop wasting time you don't have." She waved her hand at the darkness in front of them. "Go on, I'm just gonna ignore the crashing black waves below us and the fact that I know for damn sure this bridge is going to break any moment and drop us into the fucking water, where sea monsters will drag us under the spooky black waves and suck out our brains."

"That's really what this place is making you feel?" Stark tried, unsuccessfully, to hide his smile.

"Yes, asstard, it is."

Stark looked at Darius, who nodded in agreement because instead of speaking, he was obviously choosing to clench his jaw and shoot suspicious glances downward at the "spooky black waves."

"Huh." Stark quit even attempting to hide his smile and grinned at Aphrodite. "Just water and a bridge to me. Damn shame it's freaking you out so badly."

"Walk," Aphrodite said. "Before I forget you're holding Zoey, and I push you off this bridge so that Darius and I can run back the way we came, screaming or not."

Stark's grin only lasted a few more feet. It didn't take an ancient "go away" spell to sober him up. All it took was Zoey's unmoving weight in his arms. *I shouldn't be messing with Aphrodite. I need to focus. Think of what I decided to say to them and, please oh please, Nyx, let me be right. Let me say what will get me on that island.* Unsmiling and resolute, Stark led them across the bridge until they stopped in front of an imposing archway made of an ethereally beautiful white stone. The torchlight caught veins of silver in what Stark thought had to be a rare marble, so that the arch glittered seductively.

"Oh, for crap's sake, I can barely look at it," Aphrodite said, turning her head from the archway and averting her eyes. "And I usually love sparkly things."

"It is more of the spell." Darius's voice was rough with tension. "It's meant to repel."

"Repel?" Aphrodite glanced at the archway, shuddered, and then looked hastily away again. "'Repulse' is a better word."

"It doesn't affect you, either. Does it?" Darius asked Stark.

Stark shrugged. "It's impressive, and it's obviously expensive, but it doesn't make me feel weird." He moved closer to the marble and studied the archway. "So, where's the doorbell or whatever? How do we call someone? Is there a phone, or do I yell, or what?"

"*Ha Gaelic akiv?*" The disembodied male voice seemed to come from the archway itself, like it was a living portal. Stark looked into the dark with bewilderment. "It'll be in the English tongue, then," the voice continued. "Your unwanted presence here is all that is required to summon me."

"I need to see Sgiach. It's a matter of life or death," Stark said.

"Sgiach isnae concerned with uze wains, even if it be a matter of life or death."

This time the voice sounded nearer, clearer, and it had a Scottish accent that was more growl than brogue.

"What the hell is a wain?" Aphrodite whispered.

"Sssh," Stark told her. To the faceless voice he said, "Zoey isn't a child. She's a High Priestess, and she needs help."

A man stepped out of the shadows. He was wearing an earth-colored kilt, but it wasn't like those they'd seen on their hurried trip through the Highlands. This one was made of more material, and it wasn't prim and proper-looking. This vampyre didn't have on a tweed jacket with a frilly shirt. His muscular chest and arms were bare as he wore only a studded leather vest and forearm guards. The hilt of a dirk glinted at his waist. Except for a strip of short hair down the center of his head, his hair was shaven. Two gold hoops glinted at one ear. The firelight caught the gold chieftain's torque he wore around one wrist. In contrast to his powerful body, his face was deeply lined. His close-cropped beard was completely white. The tattoos on his face were griffins, claws extended onto his cheekbones. The overall and immediate impression Stark got from him was that this was a Warrior who could walk through fire and emerge not merely unscathed, but victorious.

"That wee lass there's a fledglin', no a High Priestess," he said.

"Zoey's not like other fledglings." Stark spoke quickly, afraid the guy who looked like he'd stepped out of an ancient world would dematerialize and fade into the past at any second. "Up until two days ago, she had a vampyre's tattoos, plus tattoos over much of the rest of her body. And she had affinities for all five of the elements."

The vampyre's appraising blue eyes remained on Stark without glancing at Zoey or Darius and Aphrodite.

"Yet today I see only an unconscious fledgling."

"Her soul was shattered two days ago fighting a fallen immortal. When that happened, her tattoos disappeared."

"Then it's a dyin' she will be." The vampyre raised one hand in a dismissive gesture and began to turn away.

"No!" Stark shouted, and stepped forward.

"Stad anis!" the Warrior commanded, and with otherworldly speed, the vampyre whirled around and leaped forward, landing directly under the archway and blocking Stark's path. "Are yie stupit or a feckn' fool, man? You havnae permission tae enter the Eilean nan Sgiath, the Isle of Women. Should yie try, 'tis yer life yie will forfeit, aye, make no mistake about that."

Inches from the imposing vampyre, Stark stood his ground and looked him eye to eye. "I'm not stupid or a fool. I'm Zoey's Warrior, and if I think I can protect her best by getting her on this island, then it's my right to take my High Priestess to Sgiach."

"Yie have been misinformed, Warrior," the vampyre said placidly yet firmly. "Sgiach and her Isle are a world apart from yer High Council and their rules. I am no a Son of Erebus and *mo bann ri,* my queen, isnae in Italy. Warrior tae a wounded High Priestess or no, you dinnae have the right tae enter here. Yie have nae rights at all here."

Abruptly, Stark turned to Darius. "Hold Zoey." He gave his High Priestess to the other Warrior and then faced the vampyre again. Stark lifted his hand, palm out, and as the vampyre watched him with open curiosity, he slashed his thumbnail down his wrist. "I'm not asking to enter as a Son of Erebus Warrior; I walked out on the High Council. Their rules don't mean shit to me. Hell, I'm not *asking* to enter! Through the right I've inherited in my blood, I'm demanding to see Sgiach. I have something to say to her."

The vampyre didn't take his eyes from Stark's gaze, but his nose dilated as he sniffed the air.

"What is yer name?"

"Today they call me Stark, but I think the name you're looking for is what they called me before I was Marked—MacUallis."

"Remain here, MacUallis." The vampyre disappeared into the night.

Stark wiped his bleeding arm on his jeans and took Zoey from Darius. "I'm not going to let her die." Drawing a deep breath, he closed his eyes and got ready to pass beneath the archway and go after the vampyre, counting on the blood of his human ancestors to protect him.

Darius's hand caught his arm, keeping him from crossing the threshold. "I think the vampyre meant you to remain here because he's coming back."

Stark paused and looked from Darius to Aphrodite, who rolled her eyes at him, and said, "You know, in this lifetime you're probably supposed to learn patience along with a little 'get a clue.' Jeesh, just hang on a couple minutes. Barbarian Warrior guy told you to wait here, not to go away. Sounds like he's coming back."

Stark grunted and took half a step away from the middle of the arch, though he slouched against the outer side of it, shifting Zoey's weight so that she might be more comfortable. "Fine. I'll wait. But I'm not waiting long. They're either letting me onto the damn island, or they're not. Either way, I want to get what happens next over with."

"The human is correct." The woman's voice came out of the darkness of the island. "You need to learn patience, young Warrior."

Stark straightened and faced the island again. "I only have five days to save her. Otherwise, she'll die. I don't have time to learn patience right now."

The woman's laughter made the fine hairs on Stark's arms lift. "Impetuous, arrogant, and impertinent," she said. "He reminds me of you several centuries ago, Seoras."

"Aye, but I wasnae ever that young," answered the voice of the vampyre Warrior.

Stark was struggling against shouting at the two of them to come out of the dark and face him when they seemed to materialize from the mist directly in front of him on the island side of the arch. The archaic-looking vampyre was there again, but Stark hardly glanced at him. His entire focus was captivated by the woman.

She was tall, with a broad-shouldered body that was muscular, yet entirely feminine. There were lines at the corners of her eyes, which were large and beautiful and an amazing shade of gold mixed with green, the exact color of the fist-sized piece of amber that hung from the middle of the torque around her neck. Except for a single streak of cinnamon red, her waist-length hair was perfectly white, but she didn't look old. She didn't look young, either. As he studied her, Stark realized that she reminded him of Kalona, who was ageless and ancient at the same time. Her tattoos were incredible—swords with intricately carved hilts and blades framed her strong, sensual face. He realized no one had said anything while he'd been gawking, and Stark cleared his throat, held Zoey close to him, and respectfully bowed to her.

"Merry meet, Sgiach."

"Why should I allow you on my island?" she said without preamble.

Stark drew a deep breath and lifted his chin, meeting Sgiach's gaze as he had her Warrior's. "It's my right by blood. I'm a MacUallis. That means I'm part of your Clan."

"Not hers, boy. Mine," the vampyre told him, his lips curving in a smile that was far more dangerous-looking than inviting.

Taken off guard, Stark shifted his attention to the Warrior. "Yours? I'm part of your Clan?" he said stupidly.

"I remember you being smarter when you were that young," Sgiach told her Warrior.

"Aye," the vampyre snorted. "Young or no, I had more sense than that."

"I'm smart enough to know that the history of my human blood still gives me a tie to both of you and this island," Stark said.

"Yie ur barely oot o yur nappies, boy," the Warrior said sarcastically. "Yur better suited to schoolboy games, and there are nae o' that ilk here on this island."

Instead of pissing Stark off, the vamp's words triggered his memory, and it was like Damien's notes were there in front of him again. "That's why it's my right to enter the island," Stark said. "I don't know shit about what it takes to be Warrior enough to save Zoey, but I can tell you she's more than a High Priestess. Before she was shattered, she was turning into something vampyres have never seen." The thoughts kept coming to him, and as he spoke and saw the surprise in Sgiach's face, the pieces of the puzzle fit together, and his gut told him he was following the right line of reasoning. "Zoey was becoming a Queen of the Elements. I'm her Warrior—her Guardian—and she's my Ace. I'm here to learn how to protect my Ace. Isn't that what you're all about? Training Warriors to protect their Aces?"

"They stopped coming to me," Sgiach said.

Stark thought he only imagined the sadness in her voice, but when her Warrior moved a little closer to his queen, as if he was so attuned to her needs that he meant to take even that small note of discomfort from her, Stark knew then, beyond any doubt, he'd found the answer, and he sent a silent "thank you, Nyx" to the Goddess.

"No, we haven't stopped coming. I'm right here," Stark told the ancient queen. "I'm a Warrior. I'm of the MacUallis blood. I'm asking for your help so that I can protect my Ace. Please, Sgiach, let me enter your island. Teach me how to keep my queen alive."

Sgiach hesitated only long enough to share a look with her Warrior, then she lifted her hand, and said, "*Failte gu ant Eilean nan Sgiath* . . . Welcome to the Isle of Sgiach. You may enter my island."

"Your Majesty." Darius's voice made everyone pause. The Warrior had dropped to one knee before the archway, Aphrodite standing a little way behind him.

"You may speak, Warrior," Sgiach said.

"I am not of Clan blood, but I do protect an Ace; therefore, I ask for entry to your island as well. Though I don't come as a newly made Warrior, I believe there is much here that I do not know—much here that I would like to learn while I stand at my brother Warrior's side in his quest to save Zoey's life."

"This is a human female and no a High Priestess. How could yie be Oath Bound to her?" asked the vampyre Warrior.

"I'm sorry, I didn't get your name. Was it Shawnus?" Aphrodite stepped to Darius's side and rested her hand on his shoulder.

"It's feckn' *Seoras,* are yie deaf, too?" the Warrior said, enunciating slowly. Stark was surprised to see his lips curling up at Aphrodite's bitchy tone.

"Okay, *Seoras.*" She mimicked his accent with eerie accuracy. "I'm not a human. I was a fledgling who had visions. Then I wasn't a fledgling anymore. And when I un-fledgling-ed, Nyx, for reasons I'm still pretty clueless about, decided to let me keep my visions. So now I'm the Goddess's Prophetess. I'm hoping that, along with all the stress and eye-aches it gives me, this Prophetess stuff means I age gracefully, like your queen." Aphrodite paused to bow her head to Sgiach, whose brows went up, but who didn't strike her dead like Stark thought she deserved. "Anyway, Darius *is* my Oath Sworn Warrior. If I'm getting the allusion right, and here's hoping 'cause I'm shitty at figurative language, I'm an Ace in my own way. So Darius does fit in with your Guardian Clan, blood tie or no blood tie."

Stark thought he heard Seoras mutter, "Arrogant feckr," at the same time Sgiach whispered, "Interesting."

"*Failte gu ant Eilean nan Sgiath,* Prophetess and your Warrior," Sgiach said.

Without any further discussion, Stark, carrying Zoey, followed by Darius and Aphrodite, passed beneath the marble archway and entered the Isle of Women.

CHAPTER TWENTY

Stark

Seoras led them to a black Range Rover that was parked around the corner and out of sight of the archway. Stark stopped beside the vehicle. His face must have shown his surprise because the Warrior laughed, and said, "Did yie expect a wee cart an' a Highland pony?"

"I don't know about him, but I did," Aphrodite said, climbing in the backseat beside Darius. "And for once I'm super glad to be wrong."

Seoras opened the front passenger's door for him, and Stark got in, holding Zoey carefully. The Warrior had started driving before Stark realized Sgiach wasn't with them.

"Hey, where's your queen?" Stark asked.

"Sgiach doesna need the motor tae be traveling her island."

Stark was trying to figure out how to ask his next question when Aphrodite spoke up.

"What the hell does *that* mean?"

"It means Sgiach's affinity isnae limited tae any element. Sgiach's affinity is with this island. She commands everyone and everything on it."

"Holy shit! Are you saying she can transport, like an undorky version of *Star Trek*? Not that it's possible to be undorky about *Star Trek*," Aphrodite said.

Stark started to consider ways to gag her without Darius freaking on him.

But the old Warrior was completely unruffled by Aphrodite. He simply shrugged, and said, "Aye, it will be as good an explanation as any."

"You know about *Star Trek*?" came out of Stark's mouth before his brain could stop it.

Again, the Warrior shrugged. "We do have the satellite."

"And the Internet?" Aphrodite asked hopefully.

"And the Internetograph, too," Seoras agreed, straight-faced.

"So you do let in the outside world," Stark said.

Seoras glanced at him. "Aye, when it serves the queen's purposes."

"I'm not shocked. She's a queen. She likes to shop, ergo the Internet," Aphrodite said.

"She is a queen. She likes to be informed about the world and its goin's on," the Warrior said in a tone that didn't invite further questions.

They rode on in silence until Stark started to get worried about the lightening in the eastern sky. He was just about to tell Seoras what would happen to him if he wasn't inside and under cover at sunrise when the Warrior pointed ahead and to the left of the narrow road, saying, "The Craobh—the Sacred Grove. The castle is just beyond on the shore."

Mesmerized, Stark gazed to the left of them at misshapen trunks of what must be deceptively spindly-looking trees because they held up an ocean of green. He only caught glimpses of what lay within the grove, layers of moss and shadow and clumps of more of the marble from which the archway had been made that appeared as splotches of sparkling light. And in front of all of it, like a beacon drawing travelers, was what looked like two trees twisted together to form one. From the branches of the strange joining, strips of brightly colored cloth were tied to it in a strange yet complementary contrast to its ancient, gnarled limbs.

The longer Stark stared at it, the odder it made him feel.

"I've never seen a tree like that, and why is all that cloth tied to it?" he asked.

Seoras braked, coming to a stop in the middle of the road. "'Tis a hawthorn tree and a rowan tree, grown together to make a hangin' tree."

When that's all the explanation he gave, Stark shot him a frustrated look, saying, "A hanging tree?"

"Yer education is sadly lackin', laddie. Ach, well, 'thon tree is a tree of wishes. Each knot—each strip of cloth—represents a wish. Sometimes it's parents wishin' for the well-being of a wain. Sometimes it's friends remembering those passed on to the next life. But most often it's wishes of lovers, tying their lives together and wishin' fer happiness. They're trees grown by the Good People, roots fed by passin' on their well wishes from their world tae urs."

"The good people?" Stark looked exasperated.

"The Fey—Fairies tae you. Do yie no know that's where the sayin' 'Tie the knot' comes from?"

"That's romantic," Aphrodite said, her tone—for once—totally devoid of sarcasm.

"Aye, wumman, if it's truly romantic, then it must be Scottish," said the Warrior as he put the Range Rover into gear and pulled slowly away from the wish-laden tree.

Distracted by the thought of tying a wish with Zoey, Stark didn't notice the castle until Seoras stopped again. Then he looked up, and the blaze of light reflecting off rock and water filled his sight. The castle sat a couple hundred yards from the main road, down a single lane that was really a raised stone bridgeway over a boggy field. Torches, like those that lined the bridge from the mainland, lit the lane, only here they were easily three times in number, illuminating the pathway to the castle and the walls of the huge edifice itself.

And in between the torches were stakes, as thick around as a man's arm. On each stake was a head—leathered, mouth grimacing, eyes missing, the macabre things at first appeared to move and then Stark realized it was just the long, stringy hair from each shriveled scalp that floated, ghostlike in the cold breeze.

"Gross," Aphrodite whispered from the backseat.

"The Great Taker of Heads," Darius said, his voice hushed with awe.

"Aye, Sgiach," was all Seoras said, but his lips curved up in a smile that mirrored the pride in his voice.

Stark didn't speak. Instead, his eyes were drawn from the grisly entryway up and up. Sgiach's fortress perched on the very edge of a cliff that overlooked the ocean. Though he could only see the land side of the castle, it wasn't hard for Stark to imagine the sheer face that must present itself to the outer world—a world that would never gain access to her domain, even had the queen's protective spell not already repelled intruders. The castle was made of gray stone interspersed with the shimmering white marble that littered the island. In front of the thick, double wooden doors was an imposing archway that sat before the narrow, bridgelike entrance to the castle.

As he got out of the Range Rover, Stark heard a sound that drew his gaze even farther upward. Lit up by a circle of torches, a flag flew from the uppermost turret of the castle. It rippled in the cool, brisk breeze, but Stark clearly saw the bold shape of a powerful black bull with the image of a goddess, or perhaps a queen, painted within his muscular body.

Then the doors to the castle opened, and Warriors, male and female, poured from within, crossed the bridge, and jogged together toward them. Stark automatically stepped back as Darius moved up beside him in a defensive position.

"Dinnae look for trouble where nane is meant," Seoras said, making a calming motion with his callused hand. "They wish only to show proper respect to yer queen."

The Warriors, all dressed like Seoras, whether they were male or female, moved quickly, but without any sign of aggression, to Stark. They came in a column of two, holding a leather litter between them.

"'Tis tradition, respect, laddie, for when one o' us falls. It is the responsibility of the Clan tae return him, or her, home tae Tír na nÓg, the land of our youth," Seoras said. "We never be leaving behind one of our own."

Stark hesitated. Meeting the Warrior's steady gaze, he said, "I don't think I can let her go."

"Och aye," Seoras said softly, nodding in understanding. "Yie dinnae have tae. You be takin' the foremost position. The Clan will do the rest."

When Stark stood there, unmoving, Seoras walked to him and held out his arms. He wasn't going to let Zoey go; he didn't think he could bear it. Then Stark saw the gold chieftain's torque glittering at Seoras's wrist. It was the torque that touched something inside him. With a jolt of surprise, he realized he trusted Seoras, and as he passed Zoey to the Warrior, he knew he wasn't giving her up but sharing her instead.

Seoras turned and carefully laid Zoey on the litter. The Warriors, six on each side, bowed their heads respectfully. Then the leader, a tall, raven-haired woman who held the foremost position of the litter, said to Stark, "Warrior, my place is yours."

Moving on instinct, Stark walked to the litter, and as the woman stepped away, he grasped the well-worn handhold. Seoras walked ahead of them. As one, Stark and the other Warriors followed him, carrying Zoey like a fallen queen into Sgiach's castle.

Stark

The interior of the castle was a major surprise, especially after the gruesome "decorations" on the exterior. At the very least, Stark had expected it to be a Warrior's castle—manly and Spartan and basically like a cross between a dungeon and a guys' locker room. He was seriously wrong.

The inside of the castle was gorgeous. The floor was smooth white marble veined in silver. The stone walls were covered with brightly colored tapestries that depicted everything from pretty island scenes, complete with shaggy-haired cows, to battlefield images that were as beautiful as they were bloody. They'd passed through the foyer, walked down a long hallway, and come to immense double stone stairs when Seoras halted the column with a wave of his hand.

"You cannae be a Guardian of an Ace if you cannae make a decision. So yie need to decide, laddie. Do yie wish to take yur queen above and use some time tae rest and prepare, or do yie choose to begin yur quest now?"

Stark didn't hesitate. "I don't have time to rest, and I started preparing for this the day Zoey accepted my oath as her Warrior. My decision is to start my quest now."

Seoras nodded slightly. "Aye, then, it's to the Chamber of the Fianna Foil we will be going." The Warrior turned from the stairs and continued down the hallway. Close behind him, Stark and the others carried Zoey.

To Stark's complete irritation, Aphrodite quickened her step until she was almost even with him, and asked, "So, Seoras, what exactly did you mean when you called what Stark has to do a quest?"

Seoras didn't so much as glance over his shoulder at her when he said, "I didnae stutter, wumman. I named his task a quest, and that it is."

Aphrodite snorted.

"Shut up," Stark whispered to her.

As usual, Aphrodite ignored him. "Yeah, I got the word. I'm just not sure of the meaning."

Seoras came to a huge set of arched double doors. Stark thought they looked like they would take an army to open, but all the Warrior did was to say in a low, gentle voice, "Yur Guardian asks permission to enter, my Ace." With the sound of a lover's sigh, the doors opened by themselves, and Seoras led them into the most amazing room Stark had ever seen.

Sgiach sat on a white marble throne that was on a triple-tiered dais in the middle of the massive chamber. The throne was incredible, carved from top to bottom with intricate knots that seemed to tell a story, or portray a scene, but the stained-glass window behind Sgiach and her dais was already revealing dawn, and Stark staggered to a halt just outside its encroaching brightness, bringing the column to a standstill and drawing curious glances from all the warriors. He was squinting against the light and trying to make his brain work through the haze that the sunlight hours caused in him when Aphrodite stepped up, bowed quickly to Sgiach, and then told Seoras, "Stark's a red vampyre. He's different than you guys. He'll burn up in direct daylight."

"Cover the windows," Seoras ordered. Warriors immediately did his bidding, unfurling red velvet drapes Stark hadn't noticed before.

Stark's eyes instantly adapted to the darkness that blanketed the room, so even before more warriors lit wall torches and tree-sized candelabra, he clearly saw Seoras stride up the dais steps and take the place to the left of his queen's throne. He stood there with a confidence that was almost tangible. Stark knew, without any doubt, that nothing in this world, and perhaps not even the next, could get past Seoras to harm his queen, and for an instant Stark felt a terrible wave of envy. *I want that! I want Zoey back so that I can be sure nothing ever hurts her again!* Sgiach lifted her hand and caressed her Warrior's forearm briefly, but intimately. The queen didn't look up at Seoras, but Stark did. He was gazing down at her with an expression Stark understood completely. *He's not just a Guardian, he's The Guardian. And he loves her.*

"Approach. Lay the young queen before me." As she spoke, Sgiach made a beckoning motion.

The column moved forward and gently laid Zoey's litter on the marble floor at the feet of the queen.

"You cannot bear sunlight. What else is different about you?" Sgiach said, as the last of the torches was lit, and the room took on the warm yellow glow of open flame.

The warriors faded into the chamber's shadowy corners. Stark faced the queen and her Guardian and answered her quickly, without any messing around or time-wasting preamble. "I usually sleep all during the day. I'm not one hundred percent as long as the sun is in the sky. I have more bloodlust than regular vampyres. I can't enter a private home without an invitation. There might be more differences, but I haven't been a red vampyre for very long, and that's all I've figured out so far."

"Is it true you died and were resurrected?" the queen asked.

"Yes." Stark said the word quickly, hoping she wouldn't question him more on that subject.

"Intriguing . . ." Sgiach murmured.

"Was it during daylight when your queen's soul shattered? Is that why yie failed tae protect her?" Seoras asked.

It felt like the Warrior had shot the questions through his heart, but Stark met his gaze steadily and spoke only the truth. "No. It wasn't daylight. I didn't fail her because of that. I failed her because I made a mistake."

"I'm sure the High Council, as well as the vampyres at your House of Night, have explained to you that a shattered soul is a death sentence for the High Priestess, and quite often for her Warrior as well. Why do you believe coming here will change that certainty?" Sgiach said.

"Because, like I said before: Zoey's not just a High Priestess. She's different. She's more. And because I'm not just going to be her Warrior; I want to be her Guardian."

"So yer willing tae die for her."

The Warrior didn't speak it as a question, but Stark nodded anyway. "Yes, I'd die for her."

"But he knows if he does, then he'll have no chance of getting her back into her body," Aphrodite said, as she and Darius stepped up beside him. "Because that's what other Warriors have tried, and none of them have been successful."

"He wants to use the bulls and the ancient way of the Warrior to find a door to the Otherworld while he's alive," Darius said.

Seoras laughed humorlessly. "You cannae be expectin' tae enter the Otherworld by chasing myths and rumors."

"You fly the flag of the black bull over this castle," Stark said.

"You speak of the tara, ancient symbolism long forgotten, like my island," Sgiach said.

Stark countered with: "*We* remembered your island."

"And the bulls aren't so forgotten in Tulsa," Aphrodite said. "Both of them manifested there last night."

There was a stretch of silence in which Sgiach's face showed utter shock, and her Warrior's expression flattened to a dangerous readiness.

"Tell us," Seoras said.

Quickly and with surprisingly little sarcasm, Aphrodite explained how Thanatos had told them about the bulls, how that had led Stevie Rae to evoking the aid of the wrong bull at the same time Damien and the rest of the kids were researching, which, in turn, had them discovering Stark's blood tie to the Guardians and Sgiach's island.

"Tell me again exactly what the white bull foretold," Sgiach said.

"The Warrior must look to his blood to discover the bridge to enter the Isle of Women, and then he must defeat himself to enter the arena. Only by acknowledging one before the other will he join his Priestess. After he joins her, it is her choice and not his whether she returns," Stark recited.

Sgiach looked up at her Warrior. "The bull has given him passage to the Otherworld."

Seoras nodded. "Aye, but only passage. The rest is his to be doing."

"Explain it to me!" Stark couldn't keep a handle on his frustration any longer. "What the hell do I have to do to get into the damn Otherworld?"

"A Warrior cannot enter the Otherworld alive," Sgiach said. "Only a High Priestess has that ability, and not many of them can actually gain access to that realm."

"I know that," Stark said through gritted teeth. "But, like you said, the bulls are letting me in."

"No," Seoras corrected. "They're allowing you passage *to*, nae entry. You cannae ever gain entry as a Warrior."

"But I am a Warrior! So how do I get in? What's the part about defeating myself mean?"

"That's where the old religion comes in. Long ago, male vampyres could serve the Goddess or the gods, in more than a Warrior's capacity," Sgiach said.

"Some of us were Shamans," Seoras said.

"Okay, so, I need to be a Shaman, too?" Stark asked, utterly confused.

"There is only one Warrior I've ever known who also became a Shaman." To convey her meaning, Sgiach rested her hand on Seoras's forearm.

"You're both," Aphrodite said excitedly. "So tell Stark how to do it! How he can become a Shaman along with being a Warrior."

The ancient Warrior's brows went up, and one corner of his mouth lifted in a sardonic smile. "Ach, 'tis quite simple really. The Warrior within must die tae give birth to the Shaman."

"Great. Either way I have to die," Stark said.

"Aye, so it would seem," Seoras said.

In his imagination, Stark could almost hear Zoey's *"Ah hell!"*

CHAPTER TWENTY-ONE

Stevie Rae

She knew she'd catch a bunch of crap when she got back to school, but Stevie Rae didn't expect Lenobia herself to be waiting in the parking lot for her.

"Look, I just needed some time by myself. As you can see, I'm fine and—"

"On the evening news there was a bulletin about a gang break-in at the Tribune Loft apartments. Four people were killed. Their throats were cut out, and they were partially drained of blood. The only reason the police are not on our doorstep accusing us is the report from several witnesses who all swear it was a gang of human teenagers. With red eyes."

Stevie Rae swallowed down the sick taste of bile in the back of her throat. "It was the red fledglings I left at the depot. They messed with the witnesses' memories, but none of them are Changed, so they don't have the ability to cover up everything."

"They couldn't wipe those blazing red eyes from the humans' memories," Lenobia said, nodding in agreement.

Stevie Rae was out of the car and moving toward the school. "Dragon hasn't gone after them, has he?"

"No. I've kept him busy with small groups of fledglings. He's already started going over self-defense skills with them in case of another attack from Raven Mockers."

"Lenobia, I seriously think that one in the park was a fluke. I'll bet he's miles away from Tulsa by now."

Lenobia made a dismissive gesture. "One Raven Mocker is one

too many, but whether he's alone or with a flock, Dragon will hunt him down and destroy him. And unless Kalona and Neferet are goading them, I don't think we need to worry about them attacking the school. I'm much more concerned about the rogue red fledglings."

"Me, too." Stevie Rae was eager to change the subject. "The news report said the people had only been partially drained of their blood?"

Lenobia nodded. "Yes, and their throats were ripped out—not cut or bitten and then bled as you or I would feed."

"They aren't feeding. They're playing. They like terrorizing people; it's a kind of high for them."

"That's truly an abomination of Nyx's ways." Lenobia's words came fast; her voice filled with anger. "Those from whom we feed should only feel our mutual pleasure. That is why the Goddess gave us the ability to share such a powerful sensation with humans. We don't brutalize and torture them. We appreciate them—we make them our consorts. The High Council has even banished vampyres who misuse their power over humans."

"You haven't told the High Council about the red fledglings, have you?"

"I wouldn't do that without discussing it with you first. You are their High Priestess. But you must understand that their actions have taken them beyond where they can be ignored by the rest of us."

"I know, but I still want to deal with them myself."

"Not alone again. Not this time," Lenobia said.

"You're right about that. What they did today shows me how dangerous they are."

"Should I call Dragon in on this?"

"No. I'm not goin' alone, and I do plan on givin' them an ultimatum—shape up or ship out—but if I take outsiders down there, I won't have a chance of any of them deciding to give up Darkness and come with me." Then Stevie Rae realized what she'd said and stopped like she'd run into the side of a barn. "Ohmygood*ness,* that's it! I couldn't have known it before I met the bulls, but now I understand. Lenobia, whatever it is that gets ahold of us after we die, and then un-die, and we're all evil and filled with bloodlust and stuff—it's part of Darkness. That means it isn't a new thing. It has to be as ancient as the Warrior/bull religion. Neferet is behind what happened to me and the rest of the kids." She met the Horse Mistress's gaze and saw the fear she was feeling reflected there. "She's involved with Darkness. There's no doubt about that now."

"I'm afraid there's been no doubt about that for a long time," Lenobia said.

"But how the heck did Neferet find out about Darkness? For centuries and centuries, vampyres worshipped Nyx."

"Just because people stop worshipping, doesn't mean the deity stops existing. The forces of good and evil move in a timeless dance, regardless of mortal whim or fashion."

"But Nyx is *the* Goddess."

"Nyx is *our* Goddess. You can't really believe there is only one deity for a world as complex as ours."

Stevie Rae sighed. "I guess when you put it like that, I gotta agree with you, but I wish there wasn't more than one choice for evil."

"Then there would be only one choice for good. Remember, there must always, eternally, be balance." They walked in silence for a while before Lenobia said, "You'll take the red fledglings with you to confront the rogues?"

"Yep."

"When?"

"The sooner the better."

"There is only a little over three hours left until dawn," Lenobia said.

"Well, I'm askin' them a simple yes-or-no question. That's not gonna take much time."

"And if they say no?"

"If they say no, I'll make sure they can't use the depot tunnels as their cushy hideout anymore, and I'll make sure they're separated. As individuals, I still don't believe they're all bad." Stevie Rae hesitated, and then added, "I don't want to kill them. I feel like if I do, I'll be giving in to evil. And I don't want that Darkness to touch me, ever again." An image of Rephaim, wings spread, fully healed and powerful, flashed through her memory.

Lenobia nodded. "I understand. I don't agree with you, Stevie Rae, but I do understand. Your plan has merit, though. If you shake them from their stronghold and force them to scatter, those who are left will have to worry about surviving and won't have time to 'play' with humans."

"Okay, so let's split up and spread the word that I need all the red fledglings to meet me at the Hummer in the parking lot—now. I'll take the dorms."

"I'll go to the Field House and the cafeteria. Actually, on my way to meet you, I saw Kramisha going into the cafeteria. I'll get to her first. She always knows where everyone is."

Stevie Rae nodded, and Lenobia jogged away, leaving her alone and heading toward the dorms. Alone and able to think. She should be thinking about what the heck she was gonna say to the stupid Nicole and her group of killer fledglings. But she couldn't get Rephaim out of her mind.

Driving away from him had been one of the hardest things she'd ever done in her life.

So why had she?

"Because he's well again," she said aloud, and then closed her mouth and looked guiltily around her. Thankfully, there was no one nearby. Still, she kept her big mouth clamped shut as her mind continued to race.

Okay, Rephaim was healed and all. So? Had she really thought he'd be broken forever?

No! I don't want him to be broken! The thought came quick and honest. But it wasn't just that he was well. It was that Darkness had healed him—had made him look . . .

Stevie Rae's thoughts trailed off because she didn't want to go there. She didn't want to admit, even silently to herself, how Rephaim had looked to her standing there, framed by the moonlight, powerful and whole.

Nervously, she twirled a blond curl. And anyway, they were Imprinted. He was supposed to look a certain way to her.

But Aphrodite hadn't affected her like Rephaim had started to.

"Well, I'm not gay!" she muttered, and then shut her mouth again because the thought had crept through even though she hadn't wanted it to.

Stevie Rae had *liked* the way Rephaim looked. He'd been strong and beautiful and, just for a moment, she'd glimpsed beauty inside the beast, and he hadn't been a monster. He'd been magnificent, and he'd been hers.

She staggered to a halt. It was because of that dang black bull! It had to be. Before he'd totally materialized, he'd asked Stevie Rae: *I can chase away Darkness, but if I do so, you will owe a debt to Light, and that debt is that you will be forever tied to the humanity inside that creature over there—the one you called me to save.* She'd answered with no hesitation: *Yes! I'll pay your price.* So the dang bull had zapped her with some kind of Light bullshit, and that had done something to her insides.

But was that really the truth? Stevie Rae twirled a curl around and around while she thought back. No—it had changed between her and Rephaim *before* the black bull showed up. It had happened when Rephaim had faced Darkness for her and taken on the pain of her debt.

Rephaim had said she belonged to him.

Today she'd realized he was right, and that scared her worse than Darkness itself.

Stevie Rae

"Okay, so, we all here?"

Heads nodded and from beside her, Dallas said, "Yep, everyone's here."

"Them bad kids killed those folks at the Tribune Lofts, didn't they?" Kramisha said.

"Yeah," Stevie Rae said. "I think so."

"That's bad," Kramisha said. "Real bad."

"You can't let 'em kill people like that," Dallas said. "They're not even street people."

Stevie Rae blew out a long breath. "Dallas, how many times do I have to tell y'all that it doesn't matter if someone's a street person or not—it's not right to kill *anyone*."

"Sorry," Dallas said. "I know you're right, but sometimes *before* gets messed up inside my head, and I kinda forget."

Before . . . the word seemed to echo around them. Stevie Rae knew exactly what Dallas meant: before her humanity had been saved by Aphrodite's sacrifice, and they had the ability to choose good over evil. She remembered *before,* too, but as she got another day farther away from that dark past, it was easier and easier for Stevie Rae to put it out of her mind. As she studied Dallas, she wondered if it was different for him—for the rest of the kids who hadn't Changed yet, because Dallas did seem to make little slips like he just had kinda often.

"Stevie Rae? You okay?" Dallas asked, obviously uncomfortable with her scrutiny.

"Yeah, fine. Just thinkin'. So, here's what's up: I'm goin' back down to the tunnels under the depot, *our* tunnels, and I'm givin' those kids one more chance to decide to act right. If they do, they stay and start back at school with us on Monday. If they don't, they're gonna have to find their own way, in their own place, 'cause we're takin' the tunnels back, and they're not welcome anymore."

Kramisha grinned. "We're goin' back to live in the tunnels!"

"Yep," Stevie Rae said, and she knew from the cheers and relieved shouts of "finally" she heard from the kids that she'd made the right decision. "I haven't talked to Lenobia about it yet, but I can't think that there's gonna be any problem with us busing back and forth from the depot to the House of Night. We need to be underground, and even though I really like this school, it doesn't feel like home anymore. The tunnels do."

"I'm with ya, girl," Dallas said. "But we need to get somethin' straight right now. You're not gonna face those kids alone again. I'm comin' with you."

"Me, too," Kramisha said. "I don't care what kind of big story you gave everbody else, I knew them bad kids was behind you almost gettin' fried up on the roof."

"Yeah, we've all talked about it," muscle-y Johnny B said. "We're not letting our High Priestess face that shit alone again."

"No matter how earth-will-kick-your-ass powerful she is," Dallas said.

"I'm not goin' alone. That's why I called y'all here. *We're* gonna take our tunnels back, and if ass needs to be kicked, *we're* gonna do it," Stevie Rae said. "So, Johnny B, I want you to drive the Hummer." She tossed him the keys. The big guy grinned at her and snatched them out of the air. "Take Ant, Shannoncompton, Montoya, Elliott, Sophie, Geraty, and Venus with you. I'll take Dallas and Kramisha in Z's Bug. Follow me—we're goin' to the lower parking lot of the depot."

"Sounds good, but how're we gonna be sure we can find those red kids? You know those tunnels are like, well, an anthill down there," said the little kid nicknamed Ant, and everyone chuckled.

"I been thinkin' 'bout that, too," Kramisha spoke up. "And I have an idea, if you don't mind me sayin' somethin'."

"Hey, that's one of the reasons I called y'all together, 'cause I need everybody's help with this," Stevie Rae said.

"Yeah, well, this is my idea: Those kids tried to kill you once already, right?"

Figuring there was no hiding from her fledglings, Stevie Rae nodded. "Right."

"So I figured if they tried but didn't get rid of you once, they'd want to give it another shot, right?"

"Probably."

"What would they do if they thought you was down in the tunnels again?"

"They'd come get me," Stevie Rae said.

"Then use the earth to let them know you's there again. You can do that, right?"

Stevie Rae blinked in surprise. "I never thought about it before, but I bet I can."

"That's genius, Kramisha!" Dallas said.

"Totally!" Stevie Rae said. "So, hang on and let me try somethin'." She hurried from the parking lot to the side of the school that adjoined it. There were a couple of old oaks there, a wrought-iron bench, and a tinkling fountain surrounded by what was now an ice-encapsulated bed of yellow and purple pansies. While her fledglings watched, she faced north and knelt on the ground in front of the biggest of the two trees. She bowed her head and concentrated. "Come to me, earth," she whispered. Instantly, the ground around her knees warmed, and she smelled the scent of wildflowers and long, waving grass. Stevie Rae pressed her hands against the earth she loved so much and reveled in her connection with the element. Feeling warm and filled with the strength of nature, she said, "Yes! I know you—I can feel myself within you and you within me. Please do somethin' for me. Please take some of this magic, this awesomeness that is us together, and pour it into the main tunnel under the depot. Let it be like I'm there, so much so that anyone who rests within you would know it." Stevie Rae closed her eyes and imagined a glowing green bolt of energy leaving her body, traveling through the earth, and pouring into the tunnel right outside her old room in the depot. Then she said, "Thank you, earth. Thank you for being my element. You can go now."

When she rejoined her fledglings, they were all staring at her with wide eyes.

"What?" she asked.

"That was amazing," Dallas said, his voice filled with awe.

"Yeah, you was green and all shiny," Kramisha said. "I never seen anything like it before."

"It was totally cool," Johnny B said, while the rest of the kids nodded and smiled.

Stevie Rae smiled back at them, feeling like a real High Priestess. "Well, I'm pretty sure it worked," she said.

"Ya think?" Dallas said.

"I think," she said, and they shared a look that made Stevie Rae's stomach feel quivery. She had to shake herself mentally and refocus, saying, "Uh, okay. Let's do this."

The kids scattered to the two vehicles, and Dallas draped his arm around Stevie Rae's shoulder. She let him draw her close.

"I'm proud of you, girl," he said.

"Thanks." She reached around his waist and slid her hand in his back pocket.

"And I'm glad you're bringin' us along this time," he said.

"It's the right thing to do," she said. "Plus, we're stronger together than we are apart."

Beside the Bug, he stopped and pulled her all the way into his arms. Bending, he murmured against her lips, "That' right, girl. We *are* stronger together." Then he kissed her with a fierce possession that surprised Stevie Rae. Before she really knew it, she was kissing him back—and liking the hot way his hard, familiar, completely *normal* body was making her feel.

"Could y'all please get a room?" Kramisha called to them as she crawled into the little backseat of the Bug.

Stevie Rae giggled, weirdly light-headed, especially as the thought *Get real—you can't even kiss the other one* whispered through her mind.

Dallas reluctantly let her step out of his arms so she could move to the driver's side of the Bug. Over the roof, he caught her gaze, and said softly, "A room sounds good to me."

Stevie Rae felt her cheeks get hot, and another giggle escaped her mouth. She and Dallas ducked inside the car. From the backseat, Kramisha grumbled, "I heard that mess about a room soundin' good, Dallas, and all I'm sayin' is, you two best keep your minds out the gutter and on the bad kids who like to rip out people's throats."

"I said room, not gutter," Dallas grinned cockily over the seat at Kramisha.

"And I can multitask," Stevie Rae added with another giggle.

"Whatever. Let's just go. I got me a weird feelin' 'bout this," Kramisha said.

Instantly serious, Stevie Rae glanced at Kramisha in the rearview mirror as she pulled out of the parking lot. "A weird feelin'? Did you write another poem, I mean besides the ones you already showed me?"

"No. And I ain't talkin' 'bout those bad kids."

Stevie Rae frowned at Kramisha's reflection.

"What else could you be talkin' 'bout?" Dallas asked.

Kramisha gave Stevie Rae a long look before she answered him. "Nothin'. I just got me some paranoia goin' on, that's all. You two face-suckin' instead of payin' attention to business ain't helping."

"I'm payin' attention to business," Stevie Rae said, looking away from Kramisha's reflection and concentrating on the road.

"Yeah, remember my girl's a High Priestess, and they can definitely handle a bunch of shit at once."

"Huh," Kramisha snorted.

The drive to the depot was short and silent. Stevie Rae was uberaware of Kramisha in the backseat. *She knows about Rephaim.* The thought whispered through Stevie Rae's mind, and she immediately squelched it. Kramisha didn't know about Rephaim. She only knew there was another guy. Nobody knows about Rephaim.

Except the red fledglings.

Panic fluttered through her stomach. What the heck was she gonna do if Nicole or one of the other kids told her fledglings about Rephaim? Stevie Rae could imagine the scene. Nicole would be hateful and crude. Her kids would be totally shocked and freaked. They wouldn't believe she could have—

With a bolt of realization that almost had her gasping out loud, Stevie Rae knew the answer to her problem. *Her fledglings wouldn't believe she'd Imprinted with a Raven Mocker. Ever.* She would simply deny it. There wasn't any proof. Yeah, her blood might smell weird, but she'd already explained that. Darkness had fed from her—that was bound to make her smell weird. Kramisha believed it, so did Lenobia.

The rest of the kids would, too. It would be her word, the word of a High Priestess, against a bunch of kids who had gone bad *and* had tried to kill her.

And what if some of them actually decided to choose good tonight and stayed here with the rest of them?

Then they'll have to keep their mouths shut, or they don't stay, was the grim thought that haunted Stevie Rae as she parked in the depot lot and gathered her fledglings around her.

"Okay, we're goin' in. Don't underestimate them," Stevie Rae said. Without any discussion, Dallas moved to her right, and Johnny B took her left side. The rest of the kids followed closely behind as they pushed aside the deceptively secure-looking grate that gave them easy access to the basement of the abandoned Tulsa depot.

It looked much like it had when they'd been living down there. There was maybe a little more trash, but basically it was a dark, cold basement. They moved to the rear corner entrance, where the tunnels dropped below them into an even deeper darkness.

"Can you see?" Dallas asked her.

"Of course, but I'll light the wall torches as soon as I find a match or whatever, so y'all can see, too."

"I got a lighter," Kramisha said, digging in her giant bag.

"Kramisha, do not tell me you're smoking," Stevie Rae said, taking the lighter from her.

"No, I ain't smokin'. That's just stupid. But I do believe in bein' prepared. And a lighter come in handy sometimes—like now."

Stevie Rae started to lower herself down the metal ladder, but Dallas's hand on her arm stopped her. "No, I'm goin' first. They don't want to kill *me*."

"Well, that you know of," Stevie Rae countered with, but she let him drop down the ladder before she did, Johnny B following closely behind her. "Hang on." She made both of them wait by the foot of the ladder while she moved with utter confidence in the complete blackness to the first of the old-timey kerosene lanterns she'd helped to hang from old railroad nails on the curved wall of the tunnel. She lit the lantern and turned to smile at her boys, "There, that's better, huh?"

"Good job, girl." Dallas grinned at her. Then he hesitated and cocked his head to the side. "Do you hear that?"

Stevie Rae looked at Johnny B, who shook his head while he helped Kramisha down the ladder.

"Hear what, Dallas?" Stevie Rae asked him.

Dallas pressed his hand against the rough concrete wall of the tunnel. "*That!*" he sounded mesmerized.

"Dallas, you ain't makin' no sense," Kramisha told him.

He looked over his shoulder at them. "I'm not sure, but I think I can hear the electrical lines humming."

"That's weird," Kramisha said.

"Well, you have always been super good with electricity and all that kind of guy stuff," Stevie Rae said.

"Yeah, but it's never been like this before. Seriously, I can *hear* the electricity humming through the cables I connected down here."

"Well, maybe it's like an affinity for you, and maybe you didn't realize it before 'cause you were down here all the time, and it just seemed normal," Stevie Rae said.

"But electricity ain't from the Goddess. How can it be an affinity gift?" Kramisha said, sending Dallas suspicious looks.

"Why can't it be from Nyx?" Stevie Rae said. "Truthfully, I've known weirder things before than a fledging getting an affinity for electricity. Uh, like a white bull personifying Darkness for one."

"You got a point there," Kramisha said.

"So I could actually have an affinity?" Dallas looked dazed.

"'Course you could, boy," Stevie Rae told him.

"If you do, then make it come in handy," Johnny B said, helping Shannoncompton and Venus down the ladder.

"Handy? Like how?" Dallas asked.

"Well, can you tell from the hummin' or whatever if those nasty red fledglings have been using electricity down here lately?" Kramisha said.

"I'll see." Dallas turned back to the wall, pressed his hands against the concrete, and squeezed his eyes shut. Within just a few heartbeats his eyes popped open, and he gave a surprised gasp, then his gaze went straight to Stevie Rae. "Yeah, the fledglings have been using the electricity. Actually they are right now. They're in the kitchen."

"Then that's where we're going," Stevie Rae said.

CHAPTER TWENTY-TWO

Stevie Rae

"Okay, this really pisses me off." Stevie Rae kicked at another empty liter bottle of Dr Pepper that littered the tunnel.

"They's nasty and trifling." Kramisha agreed.

"Ohmygod. If they get me dirty, I'm gonna be so pissed," said Venus.

"Get *you* dirty? Girl, did you see what they done to my room?" Kramisha snarled.

"I really think we should focus," Dallas said. He kept running a hand along the concrete wall. The closer to the kitchen area they got, the more restless he became.

"Dallas is right," Stevie Rae said. "First we gotta kick them outta here, and then we can worry about gettin' our stuff back into shape."

"Pier One and Pottery Barn still have Aphrodite's gold card on file," Kramisha told Venus.

Venus looked majorly relieved. "Well, that'll fix this mess."

"Venus, you need a lot more than a gold card to fix the mess you've turned into." Sarcasm shot out of the shadows of the tunnel in front of them. "Look at you—you're all tame and boring. And I used to think you had seriously cool potential."

Venus, along with Stevie Rae and the rest of her fledglings, came to a halt. "I'm tame and boring?" Venus's laugh was as sarcastic as Nicole's voice. "So your idea of seriously cool must be ripping out people's throats. Please. That can't even be attractive."

"Hey, don't knock it till you've tried it," Nicole said, tucking aside the blanket that had been resting across the entryway to the kitchen.

She was framed in the doorway by lanternlight from within. She looked thinner—harder than Stevie Rae remembered her looking. Starr and Kurtis stood a little way behind her, and behind them at least a dozen red-eyed fledglings gathered, glaring at them maliciously.

Stevie Rae took one step forward. Nicole's mean, red-tinged eyes darted from Venus to her.

"Oh, did you come back to play some more?" Nicole said.

"I'm not playin' with you, Nicole. And you're done 'playing' "—she air quoted the word—"with people around here."

"You can't tell us what to do!" the words exploded from Nicole. Behind her, Starr and Kurtis bared their teeth and made noises that were more snarls than laughter. The fledglings in the kitchen stirred restlessly.

It was then that Stevie Rae saw it. It hung near the ceiling over the rogue fledglings like a wavering sea of blackness that seemed to pool and write like a ghost made of nothing but darkness.

Darkness . . .

Stevie Rae swallowed down the bile of fear and forced her eyes to focus on Nicole. She knew what she had to do. She needed to end this now, before Darkness got a better hold than it already had on them.

Instead of responding to Nicole, Stevie Rae drew a deep, cleansing breath and said, "Earth, come to me!" When she felt the ground beneath her feet and the curved sides of the tunnel around her begin to warm, she turned her attention to Nicole.

"As usual, you have it wrong, Nicole. I'm not gonna tell you what to do." Stevie Rae spoke in a calm, reasonable voice. She knew from Nicole's widened eyes that she was probably taking on that green glow that had surrounded her at the House of Night, and she began lifting her hands, drawing more of the rich, vibrant energy of her element to her. "I'm gonna give you a choice, and then y'all are gonna take the consequences for what you choose. Just like all of us have to."

"How about you choose to take your pussy asses back to the House of Night with the rest of the spineless fucks who call themselves vampyres," Nicole said.

"You know I ain't no pussy," Dallas said, stepping closer to Stevie Rae.

"Neither am I," rumbled Johnny B from behind Dallas.

"Nicole, I never did like you much. I always thought you had you a bad case of head-up-your-ass-itis. Now I'm sure of it," Kramisha said, moving up to stand closer to Stevie Rae's other side. "And I do not like the way you talkin' to our High Priestess."

"Kramisha, I do not give one single shit for what you like or don't like. And she ain't my High Priestess!" Nicole shouted, spraying white spittle from her lips.

"Seriously gross," Venus said. "You might want to rethink this whole evil-fledgling thing. It's making you ugly, in more ways than one."

"Power is never ugly, and I have power," Nicole said.

Stevie Rae didn't have to look up to tell that the Darkness seeping from the ceiling of the kitchen was getting thicker.

"Okay, that's enough. Y'all clearly can't be nice, so this needs to be done. Here's your choice—and each of you need to make it for yourself." Stevie Rae looked behind Nicole as she spoke, meeting each set of glowing scarlet eyes, hoping beyond hope that she might get through to at least one of them. "You can embrace Light. If you do, that means you choose goodness and the way of the Goddess, and you can stay here with us. We'll be starting back to school at the House of Night Monday, but we'll be livin' here in *our* tunnels, where we're surrounded by earth and we feel comfortable and all. Or you can keep choosing Darkness." Stevie Rae saw Nicole's little jerk of surprise when she gave a name to it. "Yeah, I know all about Darkness. And I can tell you that messin' with it, in any way, is a major mistake. But if that's your choice, then you're gonna have to leave here, alone, and not return."

"You can't make us do that!" Kurtis said from behind Nicole.

"I can," Stevie Rae lifted her hands, squeezing them into glowing fists. "And it won't be just me. Lenobia is tellin' the High Council 'bout y'all. You'll be officially banished from every House of Night in the world."

"Hey, Nicole, like Venus said before, you be lookin' kinda rough.

How you feelin'?" Kramisha suddenly said. Then she raised her voice, talking to the kids over Nicole's shoulder. "How many a you been coughin' and feelin' like crap? Ain't no vampyre been 'round y'all for a while now, right?"

"Ohmygood*ness,* I don't know how I could've forgotten 'bout that," Stevie Rae said to Kramisha, then she turned her attention back to the kids in the kitchen, speaking right past Nicole. "So, how many of you wanna die? Again."

"Looks like bein' a red fledgling is really just another kind of fledgling," Dallas said.

"Yeah, you might die if you're around vamps," Johnny B said.

"But you for sure will die if you *not* around them," Kramisha said, with more than a hint of smugness in her tone. "But you know 'bout that 'cause y'all already died once. Wanna do it again?"

"So y'all need to choose," Stevie Rae said, still holding up her glowing fists.

"We sure as hell ain't choosing you for our High Priestess!" Nicole spat the words at her. "And neither would any of you if you knew the truth about her." With a Cheshire cat smile, she spoke the words Stevie Rae had feared most anyone hearing. "I'll bet she didn't tell you she saved a Raven Mocker, did she?"

"You're a liar," Stevie Rae said, meeting Nicole's red gaze steadily.

"How did you know there's a Raven Mocker in Tulsa?" Dallas said.

Nicole snorted. "He was here. Your precious High Priestess's scent was all over him because *she saved his life.* He's how we trapped her on the roof. She went up there to save him *again.*"

"That's bullshit!" Dallas shouted. He pressed his palm against the cement wall. Stevie Rae felt her hair lift in a sudden rush of static electricity.

"Wow, you really have them fooled." Nicole said mockingly.

"That's it. I'm done with this," Stevie Rae said. "Make your choice. Now. Light or Darkness, which will it be?"

"We already made our choice." Nicole's hand went up under her baggy shirt and came out with a snub-nosed gun, which she aimed at the middle of Stevie Rae's head.

Stevie Rae felt one instant of terror, and then she heard cocking sounds and her stunned gaze went from Nicole's gun to the two Kurtis and Starr had raised and pointed at Dallas and Kramisha.

That pissed off Stevie Rae, and everything kicked into fast-forward.

"Protect them, earth!" Stevie Rae cried. Spreading wide her arms and releasing her fists, she imagined the power of earth, chrysalis-like, enclosing them. The air around her glowed a soft, mossy green. And as the barrier manifested, Stevie Rae saw the oily Darkness that was clinging to the ceiling shiver and then dissipate completely.

Dallas yelled, "Ah, hells no. You're not pointing that thing at me!" Closing his eyes and concentrating, Dallas pressed both of his hands against the side of the tunnel wall. There was a crackling sound. Kurtis yelped and dropped his gun. At the same instant, Nicole screamed—a raw, primal sound that was more like the roar of an enraged animal than something that should have come from a fledgling, and she squeezed the trigger.

The gunshots were deafeningly loud. The sound echoed painfully over and over until Stevie Rae lost count of how many real shots there were and how many were just an avalanche of sound, smoke, and sensation.

Stevie Rae didn't hear the screams of the rogue fledglings as the bullets ricocheted off the earth barrier and slammed into their bodies, but she saw Starr fall and watched the terrible blossom of red that bloomed from the side of her head. Two other red-eyed kids slumped to the ground, too.

Pandemonium broke loose, and the unwounded fledglings in the kitchen pushed and shoved and climbed over each other as they fought to get to the narrow entrance that led up to the main depot building above.

Nicole hadn't moved. She was holding the empty gun, looking wild-eyed and still pulling the trigger when Stevie Rae yelled, "No! You've done enough!" Acting on an instinct totally allied to the earth, Stevie Rae clapped her glowing hands together in front of her. With a tearing sound, a raw, gaping hole opened in the far end of the kitchen, where before there had only been the curving side of the tunnel. "You need to leave here and never come back." Like an avenging goddess, Stevie Rae hurled earth at Nicole and Kurtis and the others who still stood with them, sending a wave of power washing through the kitchen. It lifted all of them and hurled them into the newly opened tunnel. While Nicole snarled curses at her, Stevie Rae calmly waved her hand. In a voice magnified by her element, she said, "Lead them away from here and close behind them. If they don't go, bury them alive."

Stevie Rae's last sight of Nicole was of her screaming at Kurtis and telling him to get his big ass moving.

Then the tunnel sealed, and all was quiet.

"Come on," Stevie Rae said. Not giving herself time to think about what she was walking into, she strode into the kitchen, straight to the broken, bleeding bodies Nicole had left behind. There were five of them. Three, including Starr, had been struck by Nicole's deflected shots. The other two had been trampled. "They're all dead." Stevie Rae thought it was strange that she sounded so calm.

"Johnny B, Elliott, Montoya, and I will get rid of 'em," Dallas said, taking a second to squeeze her shoulder.

"I have to come with you," Stevie Rae told him. "I'm gonna open up the earth and bury them, and I'm not doin' that down here. I don't want them where we're gonna live."

"Okay, whatever you think's best," he said, touching her face gently.

"Here. Roll them into these sleepin' bags." Kramisha picked her way through the rubble and bodies in the kitchen, went to the storage closet, and started filling her arms with sleeping bags.

"Thanks, Kramisha," Stevie Rae said, methodically taking the bags from her and unzipping them. A noise pulled her attention back to the doorway, where Venus, Sophie, and Shannoncompton were standing, white-faced. Sophie was making little sobbing noises, but no tears were coming from her eyes. "Go to the Hummer," Stevie Rae told them. "Wait for us there. We're goin' back to school. We won't be staying here tonight. 'Kay?"

The three girls nodded and then, holding hands, they disappeared down the tunnel.

"They's probably gonna need counseling," Kramisha told her.

Stevie Rae looked over the top of a sleeping bag at her. "And you won't?"

"No. I used to be a candy striper at St. John's E.R. I seen a whole lot of crazy there."

Wishing she'd had some "whole lot of crazy" experience, Stevie Rae pressed her lips together and tried not to think at all as they zipped the dead kids into five different bags and followed the boys, grunting under the weight of their burdens, out through the main depot building. Silently, they let her lead the way to a dark, deserted area beside the train tracks. Stevie Rae knelt and pressed her hands against the earth. "Open, please, and let these kids return to you." The earth quivered, like the twitching skin of an animal, and then split, open forming a deep, narrow crevasse. "Go ahead and drop them in," she told the boys, who followed her orders grimly and silently. When the last body had disappeared, Stevie Rae said, "Nyx, I know these kids made some bad choices, but I don't think that was all their fault. They are my fledglings, and as their High Priestess, I ask that you show them kindness and let them know the peace they didn't find here." She waved her hand in front of her, whispering, "Close over them, please." The earth, like the fledgling at her side, did Stevie Rae's bidding.

When she stood up, Stevie Rae felt about a hundred years old. Dallas tried to touch her again, but she started walking back to the depot, saying, "Dallas, would you and Johnny B look around out here and make sure any of those kids who got out through the depot understand that they aren't welcome back? I'll be in the kitchen. Meet me there, 'kay?"

"We're on it, girl," Dallas said. He and Johnny B jogged off.

"The rest of you guys can go to the Hummer," she said. Without a word, the kids headed down the stairs that led to the basement parking lot.

Slowly, Stevie Rae went through the depot and climbed down to the blood-soaked kitchen. Kramisha was still there. She'd found a box of giant trash bags and was cramming rubble into them, muttering to herself. Stevie Rae didn't say anything. She just grabbed another bag and joined her. When they had most of the mess stuffed away in bags, Stevie Rae said, "Okay, you can go on now. I'm gonna do some earth stuff and get rid of this blood."

Kramisha studied the hard-packed dirt floor. "It ain't even soaking in."

"Yeah, I know. I'm gonna fix it."

Kramisha met her gaze. "Hey, you're our High Priestess and all, but you gotta understand that you can't fix everything."

"I think a good High Priestess wants to fix everything," she said.

"I think a good High Priestess don't beat herself up for stuff she can't control."

"You'd make a good High Priestess, Kramisha."

Kramisha snorted. "I got me a job already. Don't try to put no more shit on my plate. I can barely handle this poem stuff as it is."

Stevie Rae smiled, even though her face felt oddly stiff. "You know that's all up to Nyx."

"Yeah, well, me and Nyx gonna have us a talk. I'll see you outside." Still grumbling under her breath, Kramisha headed down the tunnel, leaving Stevie Rae alone.

"Earth, come to me again, please," she said, backing up to the entrance to the kitchen. When she felt the warmth build below and through her, Stevie Rae held out her hands, palms facing the bloody floor. "Like everything else living, blood eventually goes back to you. Please soak up the blood of these kids who shouldn't have had to die." Like a giant earthen sponge, the floor of the kitchen became porous, and as Stevie Rae watched, it absorbed the crimson stain. When it was all gone, Stevie Rae felt her knees wobble, and she sat down, hard, on the newly cleaned floor. Then she began to cry.

That was how Dallas found her. Head bowed, face in her hands, sobbing her guilt and her sadness and her heart out. She hadn't heard him come into the kitchen. She only felt his arms go around her as he sat next to her and pulled her into his lap while he smoothed her hair and held her close, rocking her like she was very, very young.

When her sobs turned into hiccups, and the hiccups finally stopped,

Stevie Rae wiped her face with her sleeve and then laid her head on his shoulder. "The kids are waiting outside. We need to get goin'," she said, even though she was finding it hard to move.

"No, we can take our time. I sent them all back in the Hummer. I said we'd follow in Z's Bug."

"Even Kramisha?"

"Even Kramisha. But she complained about having to sit on Johnny B's lap."

Stevie Rae surprised herself by laughing. "I'll bet he didn't complain."

"Nah. I think they like each other."

"Ya think?" She leaned back so that she could look into his eyes.

He smiled at her. "Yep, and I'm gettin' kinda good at tellin' when someone likes someone."

"Oh, really? Like who?"

"Like you and me, girl." Dallas bent and kissed her.

It started out as gentle, but Stevie Rae didn't let it stay like that. She couldn't really explain exactly what happened, but whatever it was, she felt like a torch flaming out of control. Maybe it had something to do with having just come too close to death and needing to be touched and loved to feel alive. Or maybe the frustration that had been simmering inside her ever since Rephaim had first spoken to her finally boiled over—and Dallas was the one to be burned by it. Whatever the reason, Stevie Rae was on fire, and she needed Dallas to put the blaze out.

She tugged at his shirt, murmuring "Take it off . . ." against his lips. With a grunt, he yanked it over his head. While he was doing that, Stevie Rae pulled off her own T-shirt and started kicking off her boots and unbuckling her belt. She felt his eyes on her and looked up to meet his questioning gaze. "I want to do it with you, Dallas," she said in a rush. "Now."

"Are ya sure?"

She nodded. "Totally. Now."

"Okay, now," he said, reaching for her.

When their bare skins touched, Stevie Rae thought she'd explode. *This* was what she needed. Her skin was ultrasensitive, and everywhere Dallas touched, he scalded her, but in a very, very good way because Stevie Rae needed to be touched. She had to be touched and loved and possessed over and over to wipe away everything: Nicole, the dead kids, fear for Zoey, and Rephaim. Always, before anything else, there was Rephaim.

Dallas's touch seared him away. Stevie Rae knew she was still Imprinted with Rephaim—she could never forget that—but just then, with the slick heat of Dallas's sweaty skin smooth and human and real against hers, Rephaim seemed so distant. It was almost as if he was moving away from her . . . letting her go . . .

"You can bite me if you want to." Dallas's breath was warm against her ear. "Really. It's fine. I want you to."

He was on top of her, and he shifted his weight so that the curve of his neck was pressed against her lips. She kissed his skin, and let her tongue taste him, feeling the pulse there and the ancient rhythm of it. Stevie Rae replaced her tongue with her fingernail, caressing lightly, finding the perfect spot to pierce so that she could drink from him. Dallas moaned, anticipating what was to come. She could give him pleasure, and take from him at the same time. It was the way it worked with mates—it was the way things were meant to be. It would be quick, easy, and feel really, really good.

If I drink from him, my Imprint with Rephaim will break. The thought made her hesitate. Stevie Rae stopped, one sharp fingernail tip pressed against Dallas's neck. *No, a High Priestess can have a mate and a consort,* she told herself.

But it was a lie—at least for Stevie Rae it was. She knew, in the deepest recess of her heart, that her Imprint with Rephaim was something unique. It wouldn't follow the rules that usually bound a vampyre to her consort. It was strong—amazingly strong. And maybe it was because of that unusual strength that she couldn't bind herself to any other guy.

If I drink from Dallas, my Imprint with Rephaim will break.

The knowledge was a cold certainty within her.

And then what about the debt she'd agreed to pay? Could she be bound to Rephaim's humanity without being Imprinted with him?

It was a question that wasn't to be answered because at that moment from behind them, as if conjured by her thoughts, Rephaim shouted, "Do not do this to us, Stevie Rae!"

CHAPTER TWENTY-THREE

Rephaim

Rephaim felt her anger and wondered if he would be able to tell whether or not it was directed at him. He purposely focused his thoughts on Stevie Rae, allowing the blood thread that tied them to strengthen. More anger. It poured through their bond, and the force of her ire surprised him though he could feel that she was attempting to hold herself in check.

No. Her fury wasn't aimed at him. Someone else was rousing her—someone else was the focus of her aggression.

He pitied the poor fool. Had he been a lesser being, he would have laughed sardonically and wished the hapless fellow well.

It was time he put Stevie Rae out of his mind.

Rephaim kept flying east, tasting the night with his powerful wings, reveling in his freedom.

He didn't need her now. He was whole. He was strong. He was himself again.

Rephaim didn't need the Red One. She was only the vessel through which he'd been saved. The truth was her reaction to seeing him whole again proved theirs was a tie that needed to be severed.

Rephaim slowed, feeling unexpectedly weighed down by his thoughts. He landed on a gentle rise of land covered by old pin oaks. Standing on the little hillock, he gazed back the way he'd come, considering . . .

Why did she reject me?

Had he frightened her? That didn't seem possible. She'd seen him whole when he'd entered the circle. He'd been fully healed when he'd faced Darkness.

For her he'd faced Darkness!

Absently, Rephaim reached back and rubbed at the base of his wings. His skin felt smooth under his fingers. There was no physical wound left. Stevie Rae had completely healed him from Darkness's wrath.

And then she'd turned from him as if she'd suddenly seen him as a monster and not a man.

But I am not a man! Thoughts blasted through Rephaim's mind. *She knew what I was! Why turn from me after everything we've been through?*

Her behavior utterly baffled him. She'd called for him when she'd been in terror for her life—*frightened beyond thinking, Stevie Rae had called for him.*

He'd answered her call and gone to her, saved her.

I claimed her as my own.

And then, weeping, she'd run away from him. Yes, he'd seen her tears, but he hadn't known what he'd done to cause them.

With a deep cry of frustration, he threw his hands in the air, as if to rid himself of even the thought of her, and moonlight glinted off his palms. Rephaim stilled. Holding his arms out, he looked at them as if seeing them for the first time. He had a man's arms. She'd held his hands. He'd even cradled her in his arms, though it had only been briefly as they'd escaped immolation on the rooftop. His skin was really no different than hers. His was browner, perhaps, but only a little. And his arms were strong . . . well made . . .

By all the gods, what was wrong with him? It didn't matter what his arms looked like. She would never truly be his. How could he even imagine it? It was beyond all thoughts—beyond even the wildest of his dreams.

Unbidden, the words of Darkness echoed through his mind: *You are your father's son. Like him, you have chosen to champion a being who can never give you what it is you seek most.*

"Father championed Nyx," Rephaim spoke to the night. "She rejected him. And now I, too, have championed one who rejects me."

Rephaim launched himself into the sky. His wings beat up, up. He wanted to touch the moon—that crescent that symbolized the Goddess who had broken his father's heart and set about the sequence of events that created him. Perhaps if he reached the moon, its Goddess would give him an explanation that would make sense—that would be balm to his heart, *because Darkness was correct. What I seek most, Stevie Rae can never give me.*

What I seek most is love . . .

Rephaim couldn't speak the word aloud, but even the thought burned him. He had been conceived in violence through a mixture of lust and fear and hate. Most of all hate, always hate.

His wings stroked the sky, lifting him ever upward.

Love couldn't be possible for him. He shouldn't even want it—shouldn't even think of it.

But he did. Since Stevie Rae had touched his life, Rephaim had begun to think of love.

She'd shown him kindness, and he'd never before known kindness.

She'd been gentle with him, bandaging his wounds and tending his body. He'd never been cared for before the night she'd helped him out of the freezing, bloody darkness. Compassion . . . she'd brought compassion into his life.

And he'd never known laughter before he knew her.

Staring up at the moon, beating the wind with his wings, he thought of her incessant babble and the way her eyes sparkled with humor at him, even when he didn't know what he'd done to amuse her, and he had to choke back unexpected laughter.

Stevie Rae made him laugh.

She hadn't seemed to care that he was the powerful son of an indestructible immortal. Stevie Rae had ordered him around as if he was anyone else in her life—anyone who was normal, mortal, capable of love and laughter and real emotions.

But he did have real emotions! Because Stevie Rae made him feel.

Had that been her plan all along? When she'd freed him from the abbey, she'd said he had a choice to make. Was this what she'd meant—that he could choose a life where laughter and compassion and perhaps even love truly existed?

Then what about his father? What if Rephaim chose a new life, and Kalona returned to this world?

Perhaps that was something he should worry about when it happened. If it happened.

Before he knew what he was doing, Rephaim slowed. He couldn't touch the moon; it was as impossible as it was for a creature such as he to be loved. And then Rephaim realized he was no longer flying to the east. He'd circled and was retracing his path. Rephaim was returning to Tulsa.

He tried not to think as he flew. He tried to keep his mind utterly clear. He wanted only to feel the night under his wings—to have the cool, sweet air brush his body.

But Stevie Rae intruded again.

Her sadness reached him. Rephaim knew she was crying. He could feel her sobs as if they were in his own body.

He flew faster. What had made her weep? Was she crying because of him again?

Rephaim flew past Gilcrease without hesitating. She wasn't there. He could feel that she was away, farther to the south.

It was as his wings beat the night air that Stevie Rae's sadness changed, shifting into something that at first confused him, and then when Rephaim realized what it was, his blood boiled.

Desire! Stevie Rae was in the arms of someone else!

Rephaim didn't stop to think like a creature of two worlds who was neither man nor beast. He didn't remember that he'd been born from rape and sentenced to know nothing except Darkness and violence and service to his hate-driven father. Rephaim didn't think at all. He only *felt.* If Stevie Rae gave herself to another, he would lose her forever.

And if he lost her forever, his world would go back to the dark, lonely, joyless place it had been before he'd known her.

Rephaim couldn't bear that.

He didn't call on his father's blood to lead him to Stevie Rae. Rephaim did the opposite. From deep within him, he conjured an image of a sweet-faced Cherokee maiden who hadn't deserved to die in a flood of blood and pain. Keeping the girl he'd dreamed as his mother in his mind, he flew on instinct, following his heart.

Rephaim's heart led him to the depot.

The sight of the place sickened him. Not simply because he remembered the rooftop and how close Stevie Rae had come to death. He hated the place because he could feel her there—inside—under the earth, and he knew she was in another's arms.

Rephaim tore the grate from the opening. Without hesitation, he strode through the basement. Following the link that bound him to her, he entered the familiar tunnels. His breath came hard and fast. His blood pounded through his body, fueling his anger and despair.

When he finally found her, the boy was atop her, rutting against Stevie Rae, oblivious to everything else in the world. What a fool he was. Rephaim should have hurled him from her. He wanted to. The Raven Mocker in him wanted to slam the fledgling against the wall again and again until he was battered and bloody and no longer a threat.

The man within him wanted to weep.

Flooded with feelings he could neither understand nor control, he found himself frozen in place, staring, with horror and hatred as well as desire and despair. As he watched, Stevie Rae readied herself to drink the boy's blood, and Rephaim knew two things with utter certainty: first, what she was doing would break their Imprint. Second, he did not want their Imprint to be broken.

Without conscious thought, he shouted, "Do not do this to us, Stevie Rae!"

The boy's response was quicker than Stevie Rae's. He leaped up, pushing her naked body behind him.

"Get the fuck outta here, you freak!" The boy kept himself positioned between Rephaim and Stevie Rae.

The sight of the fledgling shielding her, protecting *his* Stevie Rae from *him*, sent a wave of possessive fury through Rephaim.

"Begone, boy! You're not needed here!" Rephaim crouched defensively and began moving slowly toward him.

"What the—?" Stevie Rae said, shaking her head as if she was trying to clear it while she grabbed Dallas's shirt from the floor and hastily pulled it on to cover herself.

"Stay behind me, Stevie Rae. I won't let it get you."

Rephaim stalked the boy, following him as he moved back, pushing Stevie Rae with him. Rephaim saw her eyes widen as she peered around the boy and finally truly saw him.

"No!" she cried. "No, you can't be here!"

Her words stabbed him.

"But I am here!" His anger was at the boiling point. The boy kept moving back, keeping Stevie Rae behind him. Following him, Rephaim entered the kitchen. As he did, a flickering motion caught his attention, and he glanced upward.

Darkness writhed in a sick black pool that clung to the ceiling.

Rephaim wrenched his attention back to Stevie Rae and the fledgling. He wouldn't think of Darkness now. He couldn't even consider the possibility that the white bull had returned to claim the rest of his debt.

"Stay back!" the boy cried. Unbelievably, the fledgling made a shooing motion at Rephaim, as if he were an annoying bird that had fluttered into someone's home.

"*Sssstep* aside! You are keeping me from what's mine!" Rephaim hated to hear the bestial hiss in his voice, but he couldn't help it. The damned boy was pushing him to the edge of his patience.

"Rephaim, just go. I'm fine. Dallas isn't doin' anything bad to me."

"Just go? Leave you?" the words burst from Rephaim. "How can I?"

"You're not supposed to be here!" Stevie Rae shouted, looking like she was on the verge of tears.

"How could I not be? How could you believe I wouldn't know what you were about to do?"

"Get outta here!"

"You mean run away? Like you did from me? No. I won't do that, Stevie Rae. I choose *not* to do that."

The boy had reached the wall. While he looked from Rephaim to Stevie Rae, he was feeling behind him for cords that poked from a hole that had been chiseled there.

"You know each other. You really do," the boy said.

"Of *coursssse* we do, fool!" Rephaim hissed again, hating the ungovernable beast in his voice.

"How?" The fledgling hurled the word at Stevie Rae.

"Dallas, I can explain."

"Good!" Rephaim shouted as if she'd spoke to him and not the fledgling. "I want you to explain what happened today."

"Rephaim." Stevie Rae looked around Dallas to him and shook her head like she was beyond frustrated. "This is so not the right time."

"You know each other."

Rephaim noticed the change in the boy's voice before Stevie Rae did. The fledgling's tone had hardened—gone cold and mean. The Darkness above them quivered as if in gleeful anticipation.

"Yeah, okay, we do. But I can explain. See, he—"

"You've been with him all along."

Stevie Rae frowned. "All along? No. It's just that I found him when he was real hurt; I didn't know what—"

"All this time I've been treatin' you like you was some kind of queen or somethin', like you was a *real* High Priestess," he interrupted Stevie Rae again.

Stevie Rae looked shocked and hurt. "I *am* a real High Priestess. But like I was tryin' to tell ya, I found Rephaim when he was hurt bad, and I just couldn't let him die."

Taking advantage of the fact that the boy's attention was completely focused on Stevie Rae, Rephaim inched closer.

The Darkness above them thickened.

"He was part of what almost killed you in the circle!"

"He was what saved me in the circle!" Stevie Rae shouted back at Dallas. "If he hadn't shown up, that white bull would've drained me dry."

Her words didn't faze the boy. "You've been keeping this *thing* a secret. You've been lyin' to everybody!"

"Well, heck, Dallas! I didn't know what else to do!"

"You lied to me, you whore!"

"Don't you dare talk to me like that!" Stevie Rae slapped him. Hard.

Dallas staggered back half a step. "What the fuck has he done to you?"

"You mean besides savin' my life twice? Nothin'!" she yelled.

"He's messed your head up completely!" Dallas yelled. The Darkness above them poured down from the ceiling, like it had suddenly found a weak point in a dam. It slicked around Dallas, covering his head and shoulders, swirling around his waist with a sickening familiarity that reminded Rephaim of razor-edged snakes. But Darkness didn't cut Dallas. Instead, he seemed oblivious to the glistening blackness that now coated him.

"I'm in charge of my own mind. He hasn't done anything to me," Stevie Rae said. Her eyes widened, like she finally noticed the Darkness. She took a step back from the boy, like she didn't want to be tainted by what was touching him. "Dallas, listen to me. Think. You know me. This isn't what it seems."

Rephaim could see the change come over Dallas. It was that withdrawal from him that did it—that coupled with the influence of the Darkness that encased him. Totally incensed, the fledgling screamed, "He's made you a goddamned whore and a liar! You need some sense knocked into you, girl!" Dallas lifted his hand like he was going to hit Stevie Rae.

Rephaim didn't hesitate. He leaped, closing the space between him and the boy, knocking him away from Stevie Rae and taking his place in front of her.

"Don't hurt him!" Stevie Rae was saying as she grabbed Rephaim's arm and kept him from making another strike against the boy. "He's just freaked-out. He wouldn't really hurt me."

Rephaim let her pull him back. Turning to her, he said, "I think you underestimate the boy."

"She damn sure does," Dallas said grimly.

Rephaim didn't know where the pain came from. He only knew

the bright white heat of it. His body convulsed. His back bowed in agony. Dimly, through a graying veil, he could see Dallas, eyes glowing with a scarlet hue that was impossibly bright, holding one of the wires that protruded from the wall.

"Rephaim!" Stevie Rae cried.

She started to reach for him, but then Rephaim saw her pull back. Instead, she ran to Dallas.

"Stop it! Let him go," she told the boy, pulling on his arm.

His blood red eyes skewered her. "I'm gonna fry him. And then whatever weird control he has over you is gonna be gone. You and me can be together, and I won't tell anyone shit about what happened here, long as you're my girl."

With a detached sense of understanding, Rephaim noted that Darkness was no longer present on the boy's body. It had soaked into him—it had claimed him. It augmented whatever strength the fledgling wielded.

Rephaim felt sure Dallas was going to kill him.

"Earth, come to me. I need you."

He heard Stevie Rae's words through the flickering of his consciousness, like she was candlelight trying to reach him through a gale wind. With a mighty effort, Rephaim focused his vision on her. Their eyes met, and her words came to him, suddenly clear and strong and sure.

"Protect him from Dallas because Rephaim belongs to me."

She made a motion toward Rephaim, like she was hurling something at him—and she was. A green glow slammed into his body, throwing him backward and breaking whatever it was that Dallas had been channeling into him. Breathing hard, he lay on the ground, crumpled in a heap, as he absorbed what was becoming the familiar, gentle touch of healing earth.

Dallas turned to Stevie Rae.

"You just said that thing belongs to you."

The fledgling's voice was like death. Rephaim pressed himself against the ground, opening his shocked body to the earth, willing it to enter him—to heal him enough so that he could reach Stevie Rae.

"Yeah. He does. It's hard to explain, and I get that you're pissed. But Rephaim belongs to me." Her eyes skirted Dallas and met his again. "And I guess I belong to him, weird as that sounds."

"It doesn't sound weird. It sounds fucking sick."

Before Rephaim could get to his feet, Dallas pointed a finger at her. There was a deafening crack, and Stevie Rae was suddenly standing in the middle of a glowing green circle. Her brow was furrowed, and she shook her head slowly back and forth. "You tried to shock me? You really wanted to hurt me, Dallas?"

"You chose that thing over me!" he screamed at her.

"I did what I thought was right!"

"You know what, if that's what's right, I don't want nothin' to do with it! I want the opposite!"

As soon as Dallas spoke those words, he cried out and, dropping the wire he'd been clutching in his fist, the fledgling fell to his knees and crumpled, facedown.

"Dallas? Are you okay?" Stevie Rae made a hesitant move toward him.

"Stay away from him," Rephaim rasped as he laboriously gained his feet.

Stevie Rae paused, and then instead of continuing to Dallas, she hurried over to Rephaim, pulling his arm around her shoulders. "Are you okay? You look kinda fried."

"Fried?" Despite everything, she made him want to laugh. "What does that even mean?"

"This." Stevie Rae touched one of the feathers on his chest. He was surprised to see that it looked singed. "You're a little crispy around the edges."

"You touch it. You probably fuck it, too! Damn, I'm glad it stopped me before we finished doin' it. I ain't gonna ever be sloppy seconds to a freak!"

"Dallas, that's just such a load a'—" Stevie Rae began, but when she looked at Dallas, her words stopped short.

"Yeah, that's right. I'm no stupid fledgling anymore," he said.

Brand-new red tattoos in the shape of striking whips framed Dallas's face. Rephaim thought they looked disturbingly like the tendrils of Darkness that had entrapped Stevie Rae and him within the circle. His eyes glowed an even brighter red, and his body seemed to grow larger, swelling with newly gained power.

"Ohmygood*ness,*" Stevie Rae said. "You've Changed!"

"In a bunch of different ways!"

"Dallas, you gotta listen to me. Remember Darkness? I saw it grabbin' for you. Please try to think. Please don't let it get you."

"*It* get *me*? You can say that when you're standing beside that thing? Ah, hell no! I'm never gonna listen to your lies again. And I'm gonna make sure no one else does, either!" He sneered the words at her, his voice filled with anger and hate.

As he stood up and began reaching for the wires he'd used before to channel power, Stevie Rae moved. Pulling Rephaim with her, Stevie Rae backed from the kitchen. Stepping outside the entrance, she lifted her hand, took a deep breath, and said, "Earth, close this for me, please."

"No!" Dallas yelled.

Rephaim got a brief glimpse of him grabbing the wire and pointing at them, and then with a sound like the soughing of wind through autumn boughs, the earth rained down in front of them, closing the tunnel entrance to the kitchen and shielding them from the wrath of Darkness.

"Can you walk okay?" Stevie Rae asked.

"Yes. I'm not hurt badly. Or at least I'm not anymore. Your earth made sure of that," he said, looking down at her where she stood small, but proud and powerful in the circle of his arm.

"Okay, then. We gotta get outta here." Stevie Rae stepped from his side and began hurrying down the tunnel. "There's another way outta the kitchen. He'll be out in no time, and we need to be gone from here then."

"Why don't you just seal the other exit, too?" he asked as he followed her.

The glance she gave him was visibly annoyed. "What, and kill him? Uh, no. He's not really that bad, Rephaim. He just went nuts 'cause Darkness was messin' with him, and he found out about me and you."

Me and you . . .

Rephaim wanted to hold on to the words that linked them together, but he couldn't. There was no time for such things. Rephaim shook his head. "No, Stevie Rae. Darkness wasn't just messing with him. Dallas chose to embrace it."

He thought she'd argue with him. Instead, he saw her shoulders slump. She didn't look back at him, but only said, "Yeah, I heard him."

They climbed the ladder silently and were making their way through the basement, when a sound drifted to Rephaim through the wrenched-open gate. He was just thinking that it seemed familiar when Stevie Rae gasped, "He's takin' the Bug!" and she sprinted outside with Rephaim at her heels.

They emerged in time to see the little blue car pulling out of the parking lot.

"Well, that sucks like roadkill," Stevie Rae said.

Rephaim's sharp eyes went to the eastern horizon, which was beginning to go from black to a predawn gray.

"You need to get back into the tunnels," he said.

"Can't. Lenobia and those guys'll be here crazy fast if I'm not back by dawn."

"I will leave," he said. "Return to the Gilcrease. Then you can rest underground, and your friends will find you. You'll be safe."

"What if Dallas is hotfootin' it back to the House of Night? He'll tell them about us."

Rephaim hesitated only for a moment. "Then do what you must. You know where I will be." He turned to leave.

"Take me with you."

Her words made his body freeze. He didn't look at her. "It's close to dawn."

"You're healed, aren't you?"

"I am."

"You're strong enough to fly and carry me?"

"Yes, I am."

"Then take me back to the Gilcrease with you. I'll bet that old place has a basement."

"What about your friends—the other red fledglings?" he said.

"I'll call Kramisha and tell her Dallas has lost his mind, and I'm safe, but not in the tunnels, and that I'll explain stuff tomorrow."

"When they find out about me, it will appear you're choosing me over them."

"What I'm choosing is to take some time to think before I have to deal with the shitstorm Dallas is brewin' up," she said. Then, in a much softer voice, she added, "Unless you don't want me to come with you. You could take off—get outta here—then you won't have to deal with the mess that's comin'."

"Am I or am I not your consort?" Rephaim asked the question before he could stop himself.

"Yes. You are my consort."

He hadn't known he was holding his breath until it left him in a long, relieved sigh. Rephaim opened his arms to her. "Then you should come with me. I will see you rest undisturbed today."

"Thank you," she said, and then Rephaim's High Priestess stepped into his arms. He held her tightly while his powerful wings lifted them into the sky.

Rephaim

Stevie Rae had been right. There was a basement in the old mansion. It had stone walls and a hard-packed dirt floor, but it was surprisingly dry and comfortable. With a relieved sigh, Stevie Rae settled herself, sitting cross-legged, leaning against the cement wall, and pulled out her cell phone. Rephaim stood there, not sure what he should do, while she called the fledgling named Kramisha and began a dialogue of hasty and sketchy explanations as to why she wouldn't be returning to the school: *Dallas has lost his damn mind . . . electricity must have jacked with his good sense . . . kicked me outta Z's car on the way back to the House of Night . . . no, I'm fine . . . probably be back tomorrow night . . .*

Feeling like an interloper, Rephaim left her to talk with her fledgling in privacy. He returned to the attic and paced before the open door of the closet he'd transformed into a nest.

He was tired. Even though he was fully healed, racing the sunrise carrying Stevie Rae had sapped his reserves of strength. He should retreat to the closet and rest during the daylight hours. Stevie Rae wouldn't leave the basement until sunset.

Stevie Rae *couldn't* leave the basement.

She could be hurt during daylight hours. It was true that the red fledglings were all vulnerable between dawn and dusk, so Dallas wasn't a threat to her until dark. But what if a human stumbled upon her?

Slowly, Rephaim gathered the blankets and food staples he'd accumulated and began carrying them to the basement. It was fully daylight when he made his last trip down the stairs. She'd ended the phone call and was curled up in the corner. Stevie Rae barely stirred when he covered her with a blanket. Then he made himself comfortable beside her. Not so close they were touching, but not so far away that she wouldn't see him immediately when she awoke. And he made sure he was positioned between her and the door. If someone tried to enter, they would have to get through him to reach her.

Rephaim's last thought before he fell asleep was that he finally understood the ever-present sense of rage and restlessness that surrounded his father. Had Stevie Rae truly rejected him today and cast him from her, his world would have forever been colored by the loss of her. And that understanding held more terror for him than the possibility of having to face Darkness again.

I do not want to live in a world without her. Utterly exhausted by feelings he could barely comprehend, the Raven Mocker slept.

CHAPTER TWENTY-FOUR

Stark

"I know it could kill me to enter the Otherworld, but I don't want to live in this world without her." Stark kept himself from shouting, but he couldn't keep his frustration from boiling over into his voice. "So just show me what I need to do to get to where Zoey is, and I'll take it from there."

"Why do you want Zoey back?" Sgiach asked him.

Stark ran his hand through his hair. The exhaustion that came with daylight pulled at him, fraying his nerves and jumbling his thoughts, and he blurted the only answer his tired mind could form, "Because I love her."

The queen seemed not to react at all to his declaration; instead, she was studying him with a considering expression. "I sense that Darkness has touched you."

"Yeah," Stark nodded, though her statement confused him. "But when I chose to be with Zoey, I chose Light."

"Aye, but would yie still choose it if it meant losin' what yie love most?" said Seoras.

"Wait, the whole point of Stark going to the Otherworld is so that he can protect Zoey. Then she'll be able to pull her shattered soul together and come back to her body. Right?" Aphrodite said.

"Aye, she can choose to return if her soul's whole again."

"Then I don't understand your question. If Z comes back, he doesn't lose her," she said.

"My Guardian is explaining that Zoey will be changed if she returns from the Otherworld," Sgiach said. "What if the change takes her on a path that leads away from Stark?"

"I'm her Warrior. *That* won't change, and it means I stay with her," Stark said.

"Aye, laddie, as her Warrior fer sure, but perhaps not as her love," Seoras said.

Stark felt a dagger turn in his stomach. Still, without hesitation, he said, "I'd die to get her back. No matter what."

"Our deepest emotions are sometimes separated only by the type of human beings we are at our cores," the queen said. "Lust and compassion, generosity and obsession, love and hate. They are often all very close to one another. You say you love your queen enough to die for that emotion; but if she no longer loved you in return, what color would your world be then?"

Dark. The word came instantly to Stark's mind, but he knew he shouldn't say it.

Thankfully, Aphrodite's big mouth saved him.

"If Z didn't want to be with him, as in a guy with a girl, it would suck for Stark. That's a no-brainer. That doesn't mean he'd go over to the Dark Side, and I know you know what that means 'cause your guy gets *Star Trek,* and one dork goes hand in hand with another. Anyway, isn't it the truth that what Stark would or wouldn't do in some not-happened, made-up, Zoey-dumps-him scenario is really between Stark and Zoey and Nyx? Seriously. Goddess knows I don't *mean* to sound like a bitch, but you're a queen, not a Goddess. There's some shit you just can't control."

Stark held his breath, waiting for Sgiach to use *Star Trek* or *Star Wars* or what the hell ever and blast Aphrodite into a zillion little pieces. Instead, the queen laughed, which made her look unexpectedly girlish.

"I'm glad I am *not* a Goddess, young Prophetess. The small piece of the world I control is far more than enough for me."

"Why do you care so much about what Stark might or might not do?" Aphrodite asked the queen even though Darius was giving her what Stark thought of as "Stop talking now" looks.

Sgiach and her Guardian shared a long look, and Stark saw the Warrior nod slightly, as if the two of them had just come to an agreement.

Queen Sgiach said, "The balance of Light and Darkness in the world can shift because of a single act. Though Stark is only one Warrior, his actions have the potential to affect many."

"And this world doesnae need another powerful Warrior who fights on the side of Darkness."

"I know that, and I'll never fight for Darkness again," Stark said grimly. "I watched Zoey's soul shatter because of a single act, so I understand about that, too."

"Then weigh your actions carefully," the queen told him. "In the Otherworld and in this world. And consider this—the young and naïve believe love to be the strongest force in the universe. Those of us who are more, let us say, *realistic* know that a single person's will, strengthened by integrity and purpose, can be more powerful than a score of lovestruck romantics.

"I'll remember. I promise." Stark barely heard his own words. He would have sworn to cut off his arm if that had been what Sgiach needed to hear to get the damn ball rolling and get him to the Otherworld.

As if she could read his mind, the queen shook her head sadly, and said, "Very well, then. Let your quest begin." Then she lifted her hand and commanded, "Raise the Seol ne Gigh."

There was a whooshing and a series of clicking sounds. The floor in front of the queen's dais, just beyond where Zoey rested, opened, and a slab of rust-colored stone rose from beneath the floor. It was as tall as his waist, wide and long enough for a grown vampyre to lie on its flat surface. He saw the rock was covered with intricate knotwork, and on either side of the floor surrounding it were two grooves that were curved almost like a bow. They were thicker at one end than the other, and the narrow part formed sharp points. Studying it, Stark suddenly realized two things.

The grooves looked like massive horns.

The rock wasn't really rust-colored. It was white marble. The rust color was stain. Bloodstain.

"This is the Seol ne Gigh, the Seat of the Spirit," Sgiach said. "It is an ancient place of sacrifice and worship. For longer than we have memories, it has been the conduit to Darkness and Light—to the white and black bulls that form the basis of the power of the Guardians."

"*Sacrifice* and worship," Aphrodite said, moving closer to the stone. "What kind of sacrifice do you mean?"

"Aye, well, that depends on yer quest, does it not?" Seoras said.

"That's not an answer," Aphrodite said.

"Sure and it is, lass," the Guardian said, smiling grimly at her. "And yie know it, whether yie will be of a mind tae admit it or no."

"Sacrifice is okay with me," Stark said, brushing a hand across his brow wearily. "Tell me what, or who"—he shot a sideways glance at Aphrodite, not caring that it made Darius bristle—"I need to grab and use for the sacrifice, and I'll do it."

"It'll be you that'll be the sacrifice, laddie," Seoras said.

"I think it will help that he's in a weakened state during the daylight hours. It should make it easier for his spirit to slip from his body." Sgiach spoke to her Guardian almost as if Stark weren't in the room.

"Aye, you have a point. Most Warriors fight the leavin' of the body. Bein' weak might make that part easier," Seoras agreed.

"So what do I have to do? Find a virgin or something?" He didn't look at Aphrodite then, 'cause, well, she obviously didn't fit in that category.

"It's you who's the sacrifice, Warrior. The blood of another will not do. This is your quest, from beginning to end. Are you still willing to begin, Stark?" Sgiach said.

"Yes." Stark didn't hesitate.

"Then lie on the Seol ne Gigh, young MacUallis Guardian. Your Chieftain will draw your blood, take you to a place between life and death. The stone will take your offering. The white bull has spoken, and you will be accepted. He will guide your spirit to the Otherworld gate. It is up to you to gain entry from there, and may the Goddess have mercy on your soul," the queen said.

"All right. Good. Let's get this thing done." But Stark didn't go straight to the Seol ne Gigh. Instead, he knelt beside Zoey. Ignoring the fact that everyone in the room was watching, he cupped her face in his hands and kissed her gently, whispering against her lips, "I'm coming for you. This time I won't let you down." Then he stood, drew his shoulders back, and went over to the massive stone.

Seoras had moved from his queen's side and was standing in front of the head of the stone. Meeting Stark's gaze steadily, he unsheathed a wickedly sharp dirk that had been resting in a worn leather scabbard at his waist.

"Hang on, hang on!" Unbelievably, Aphrodite was pawing around in the abnormally large metallic leather bag she'd lugged all the way from Venice.

Stark had seriously had it with her. "Aphrodite, now is not the time."

"Oh, for shit's sake, finally. I knew I couldn't lose anything this big and smelly." She pulled out a quart-sized baggie filled with brown twigs and needles, and gestured at one of the Warriors standing around the perimeter of the room, snapping her fingers and looking more regal than Stark would ever admit aloud. She had the burly-looking guy practically running to take the thing from her while she said, "Before you start what I'm sure is going to be some very unattractive bloodletting, someone needs to burn these, like incense, over here by Stark."

"What the hell?" Stark said, shaking his head at Aphrodite and wondering, not for the first time, if the girl really was mentally damaged.

She rolled her eyes at him. "Grandma Redbird told Stevie Rae, who told me, that burning cedar is some kind of big, powerful, Cherokee mojo in the spirit world."

"Cedar?" Stark said.

"Yes. Breathe it in and take it with you while you go to the Otherworld. And, please, close your mouth and get ready to bleed," Aphrodite said. She shifted her attention to Sgiach. "I think you'd consider Grandma Redbird a Shaman. She's wise and definitely hooked into the whole earth-has-a-soul thing. She said cedar would help Stark."

The Warrior she'd given the baggie to glanced at his queen. She shrugged and nodded, saying, "It cannot hurt." After a metal brazier had been lit and a few needles added, Aphrodite smiled, bowed her head slightly to Seoras, and said, "Okay, *now* let's get this thing done."

Stark bit back the words he wanted to yell at annoying Aphrodite. He needed to focus. He'd remember to breathe in cedar because Grandma Redbird knew her stuff, and the bottom line was he needed to get to Zoey and protect her. Stark wiped his hand across his forehead, wishing he could wipe away the tired fog that settled with daylight over his brain.

"Dinnae struggle against it. Yie need tae be feelin' out of sorts tae slip from yer body. It isnae a natural thing for a Warrior to be doin'." Seoras used his dirk to point at the flat surface of the huge stone. "Bare yer chest and lie here."

Stark pulled off his sweatshirt, and the T-shirt under it, and then he lay on the stone.

"I see yie have already been marked," Seoras said, pointing at the pink burn scar of a broken arrow that covered the left side of his chest.

"Yeah. For Zoey."

"Aye, well, then 'tis only right that yie are marked again for her."

Stark braced himself, lying stiff against the bloodstained stone. It should have been cold and dead, but the instant his skin touched the marble surface, the heat in it began to build beneath him. Warmth radiated rhythmically from within it, like a beating pulse.

"Ach, aye, yie can feel it," said the ancient Guardian.

"It's hot," Stark said, looking up at him.

"For those of us who are Guardians, it lives. Do yie trust me, lad?"

Stark blinked, surprised by Seoras's question, but his answer was unhesitant. "Yes."

"I'll be takin' yie to the place afore death. Yie need to be trustin' in me to take yie there."

"I trust you." Stark did. There was something about the Warrior that resonated deeply within him. Trusting him felt like the right thing to do.

"This willnae be pleasant fer either of us, but 'tis necessary. The body must release to allow the spirit the freedom to depart. Only the pain and the blood can be doin' that. Are yie ready?"

Stark nodded. Pressing his hands against the hot skin of the stone, he sucked in a deep breath that smelled of cedar.

"Wait! Before you cut him, tell him something that'll help. Don't just let his soul flail about moronically in the Otherworld. You're a Shaman, so Shaman him," Aphrodite said.

Seoras looked at Aphrodite and then glanced from her to his queen. Stark couldn't see Sgiach, but whatever passed between the two of them made her Guardian's lips curl up in the slightest hint of a smile when his eyes went back to Aphrodite.

"Well, ma wee queen. I'll be telling yer friend this: when a soul wants to truly know what it is to be good, and I do mean purely good for unselfish reasons, that is when the basest of our nature gives in to the desire fer love and peace and harmony. That surrender is a powerful force."

"That's too poetic for me, but Stark's a reader. Maybe he'll have a clue what you're talking about," Aphrodite said.

"Aphrodite, would you do me a favor?" Stark asked.

"Maybe."

"Stop. Talking." He looked up at Seoras. "Thanks for the advice. I'll remember it."

Seoras met his gaze. "You must do this on yer own, laddie. I cannae even hold yie down. If you cannae bear it, you willnae make it through the gate anyway, and best to be puttin' this tae an end now, before yie think tae begin."

"I'm not going to move," Stark said.

"The heartbeat of the Seol ne Gigh will lead you to the Otherworld. Getting back, ach, well, that'll be a path yie must be findin' fer yurself."

Stark nodded and spread his hands against the surface of the marble, trying to absorb its heat into his suddenly chilled body.

Seoras lifted the dagger and struck Stark so fast the movement of the Guardian's hand was a blur. The initial pain of the wound that slashed from his waist to the top of the right side of his rib cage was little more than a hot line in his skin.

The second cut was almost identical to the first, only it made a weeping red line across his left ribs.

And that was when the pain began. Its heat seared him. His blood felt like lava as it poured from his sides, pooling on the top of the stone. Seoras worked the razor-edged dirk methodically from one side of Stark's body to the other, until Stark's blood crested the edge of the rock as if at the corner of a giant's eyes. It hesitated there and finally poured over and down, weeping scarlet tears in the intricate knot-work and then dripping to fill the horn-shaped trenches.

Stark had never felt such pain.

Not when he'd died.

Not when he'd un-died and thought only of thirst and violence.

Not when he'd almost died from his own arrow.

The pain the Guardian made him feel was more than physical. It burned his body, but it also seared his soul. The agony was liquid and interminable. It was a wave he couldn't escape, which battered him over and over. He was drowning in it.

Stark automatically fought. He knew he couldn't move, but still he struggled to retain hold on his consciousness. *If I let go I'm dead.*

"Trust me, laddie. Let go."

Seoras was standing above him, bending again and again over his body to slice his skin, but the Guardian's voice was a distant anchor, hardly discernible.

"Trust me . . ."

Stark had already made the choice. All he had to do was to follow through with it.

"I trust you," he heard himself whisper. The world turned gray, then scarlet, then black. All Stark was aware of was the heat of the pain and the liquid of his blood. The two merged, and he was suddenly outside his body, sinking into the stone, dripping down the carved sides, and washing into the horns.

Surrounded only by pain and darkness, Stark fought against panic, but strangely, after only a moment, the terror was replaced with a numb acceptance that was kinda comforting. On second thought, this darkness wasn't so bad. At least the pain was going away. Actually, the pain seemed almost a memory . . .

"Do not fucking give up, moron! Zoey needs you!"

Aphrodite's voice? Goddess, it was irritating that even detached from his body, she could still bother him.

Detached from my body. He'd done it! The exhilaration that came with the realization was quickly followed by confusion.

He was out of his body.

He could see nothing. Feel nothing. Hear nothing. The blackness was absolute.

Stark had no idea where he was. His spirit fluttered and, like a trapped bird, it battered against nothingness.

What is it Seoras had said to him? What had been his advice?

. . . surrender is a powerful force.

Stark quit fighting and quieted his spirit, and a small memory shone through the blackness, that of his soul, pouring with his blood into two troughs shaped like horns.

Horns.

Stark focused on the only tangible idea in his mind, and he imagined himself grabbing hold of those horns.

The creature came out of the absolute darkness. He was a different kind of black than that which had engulfed Stark. He was the black of a new moon sky—deep, night-resting water—and half-forgotten midnight dreams.

I accept your blood sacrifice, Warrior. Face me and move on, if you dare.

I dare! Stark shouted, accepting the challenge.

The bull charged him. Acting purely on instinct, Stark didn't run. He didn't jump aside. Instead, he faced the bull, head-on. Screaming his anger and rage and fear, Stark ran at the bull. The creature lowered his massive head as if he would gore Stark.

No! Stark leaped at the bull, and with a motion that was dreamlike, grabbed his horns. At the same instant the creature threw up his head, and Stark vaulted over his body. He felt like he was diving from an impossibly high cliff as he hurled forward farther and farther, and somewhere, behind him in the black soullessness, he heard the bull's voice echoing three words: *Well done, Guardian . . .*

Then there was an explosion of light around him just before he tumbled onto a hard-packed piece of ground. Stark picked himself up slowly, thinking how weird it was that even though he was nothing but spirit, he still had the form and feeling of his body, and looked around.

In front of him was a grove, identical to the one that grew near Sgiach's castle. There was even a hanging tree before it, decorated with strips of cloth too numerous to count. As he watched, the cloth changed, taking on different colors and lengths and shimmering like Christmas tree tinsel.

The Otherworld—this had to be the entrance to Nyx's realm. Nothing else could look this magickal.

Before stepping forward, Stark glanced behind him, thinking it couldn't be this easy to get in and expecting the giant black bull to materialize and this time gore him for real.

All that was behind him was the black nothingness from where he'd come. If that wasn't creepy enough, the segment of ground he'd been dumped onto was a small, half circle patch of red dirt that reminded him unexpectedly of Oklahoma, and in the center of the patch a gleaming sword was stuck halfway up to the hilt. It took two hands to pull the sword free, and then, as Stark automatically wiped the otherwise spotless blade on his jeans to clean it, he realized that, like the Seol ne Gigh, the original color of the ground had been tainted by blood.

He finished wiping the blade hastily, for some reason not liking the thought of blood staining it, and then he turned his attention to what was in front of him. That was where he needed to go. His mind, heart, and spirit knew it.

"Zoey, I'm here. I'm coming to you," he said, and stepped forward, running into an invisible barrier hard as a brick wall. "What the hell?" he muttered, moving back and looking up to see that a stone archway had suddenly appeared.

There was an explosion of a cold white light that gave Stark the creepy image of a freezer door opening to expose dead flesh. Blinking, his eyes traveled down, and what he saw in front of him shocked him to his very core.

Stark was staring at himself.

At first he thought the archway must have a mirror in it, but there was no blackness reflected behind him, and his other self was grinning a familiar, cocky smile. Stark definitely wasn't smiling. Then he spoke, dispelling all thoughts of mirror images and rational explanations.

"Yeah, fucknuts, it's you. You're me. To get into this place, you're gonna have to kill me, which is not gonna happen 'cause I'm not so cool with dying. What is gonna happen is that *I'm* gonna kick your ass and kill *you* dead."

While Stark stood there, speechless and staring at himself, his mirror image lunged forward, slashing with a broadsword identical to the one Stark held, drawing a line of blood down his arm.

"Yep, this is gonna be as easy as I thought," his other self said, and lunged at Stark again.

CHAPTER TWENTY-FIVE

Aphrodite

"Yeah, light's on, but there's definitely no one home." Aphrodite waved her hand in front of Stark's open but unseeing eyes. Then she had to snatch her hand out of the way as Seoras, ignoring that he came close to cutting her, too, made another knife wound down Stark's blood-drenched side.

"He already looks like hamburger. Do you have to keep doing that?" Aphrodite asked the Guardian. There was no love lost between her and Stark, but that didn't mean she was cool with watching him get sliced to pieces.

Seoras appeared not to hear her. He was utterly focused on the boy who lay before him.

"They are bonded by this quest," Sgiach said. She'd left her throne to stand beside Aphrodite.

"But your Guardian is conscious and present in his own body," Darius said, studying Seoras.

"Yes. His consciousness is here. It is also so completely attuned with the boy that he can hear his heartbeat—feel his breathing. Seoras knows exactly how close Stark is to physical death. It is on the cusp between life and death that my Guardian must keep him. Too much one way, his soul will return to his body, and he will awaken. Too much the other, his soul will never return at all."

"How will he know when to end this?" Aphrodite asked, involuntarily flinching as Seoras's dirk sliced Stark's flesh again.

"Stark will awaken, or he will die. Either way, it will be Stark's doing and not my Guardian's. What Seoras does now enables the boy to make his own choices." Sgiach spoke to Aphrodite, but her eyes never left Seoras. "You should do the same."

"Cut him?" Aphrodite frowned at the queen, who smiled, but continued to watch her Guardian.

"You said that you're a Prophetess of Nyx, did you not?"

"I *am* her Prophetess."

"Then consider wielding your gift to help the boy, too."

"I would if I had one damn clue how to do that."

"Aphrodite, perhaps you should—" Darius began, taking Aphrodite's arm and pulling her away from Sgiach, obviously worried that she'd pushed the queen too far.

"No, Warrior. You need not draw her away. One thing you will find about being bound to a strong woman is that often her words will get her into trouble from which you cannot protect her. But they are her own words, and thus her own consequences." Sgiach finally looked at Aphrodite. "Use some of the strength that makes your words like daggers and seek your own answers. A true Prophetess gets very little guidance in this world, except through her gift; but strength, tempered by wisdom and patience, must teach you how to use it properly." The queen lifted her hand and gestured elegantly to one of the vampyres in the shadows. "Show the Prophetess and her Guardian to their chamber. Give them refreshment and privacy." Without another word, Sgiach returned to her throne, her gaze once again focused solely on her Guardian.

Aphrodite pressed her lips together and followed the ginger-haired giant whose tattoos were a series of intricate spirals that appeared to be made of tiny sapphire dots. They retraced their path back to the double staircase and then went up to a hallway where the walls were decorated with jeweled swords that glittered in the torchlight. A smaller, single staircase finally led them up to an arched wooden door, which the warrior opened and gestured for them to enter the room.

"Would you be sure someone gets me right away if Stark changes at all?" Aphrodite asked before he closed the door.

"Aye," the warrior said in a surprisingly gentle voice before leaving them alone.

Aphrodite turned to Darius. "Do you think my mouth gets me into trouble?"

Her Warrior's brows went up. "Of course I do."

She frowned at him. "Okay, look, I'm not kidding."

"Neither am I."

"Why? Because I say what I mean?"

"No, my beauty, because you do use your words like a dagger, and a drawn dagger often causes trouble."

She snorted and sat on the huge, four-poster bed. "If I sound like a dagger, then why the hell do you like me?"

Darius sat beside her and took her hand. "Have you forgotten that a throwing dagger is my favorite weapon?"

Aphrodite met his eyes, feeling suddenly vulnerable despite his gentle tone. "Seriously. I'm a bitch. You shouldn't like me. I don't think most people do."

"The people who know you like you. The real you. And what I feel for you goes beyond liking you. I love you, Aphrodite. I love your strength, your sense of humor, the depth of caring you show your friends. And I love that which was broken inside you and is only now beginning to heal."

Aphrodite kept meeting his gaze though she was blinking hard to fight back tears. "All that makes me a terrible bitch."

"All that makes you who you are." He raised her hand to his lips, kissed it gently, and then said, "It also makes you strong enough to figure out how to help Stark."

"But I don't know how!"

"You used your gift to sense Zoey's absence, as well as Kalona's. Can you not use the same road you followed before to sense Stark?"

"All I was doing with them was seeing if their souls were inside their bodies or not. We already know Stark's is gone."

"Then you shouldn't have to touch him as you did the other two."

Aphrodite sighed. "The same road, huh?"

"Yes."

She looked up at him, gripping his hand tighter. "You really think I can do it?"

"I believe there is little you cannot do once you set your mind to it, my beauty."

Aphrodite nodded, squeezed his hand before letting go. She unzipped her black leather stiletto boots and scooted back on the bed, resting against the mound of down pillows.

"Protect me while I'm gone?" she asked her Warrior.

"Always," Darius said.

He moved to stand beside the bed, reminding Aphrodite very much of the way Seoras stood beside his queen's throne. Pulling strength from the knowledge that her heart and her body would always be safe with Darius, she closed her eyes and willed herself to relax. Then she drew three deep, cleansing breaths and focused her thoughts on her goddess.

Nyx, it's me. Aphrodite. Your Prophetess. She almost added "at least that's what everyone's calling me," but stopped herself. Taking another deep breath, Aphrodite continued: *I'm asking for your help. You already know I'm not real sure how this Prophetess stuff works, so it won't surprise you to hear that I don't know how to use the gift you've given me to help Stark—but he does need my help. I mean, the guy's being sliced up in one world and flailing around trying to use poetry and an old guy's confusing words to help Z, in another. Just between us, sometimes I think Stark's more muscle and admittedly good hair than brains. Clearly, he needs help, and for Zoey's sake, I want to give it to him. So, please, Nyx, show me how to help.*

Give yourself to me, daughter.

Nyx's voice in her mind was like the fluttering of a diaphanous silk curtain, transparent, ethereal, and beautiful beyond belief.

Yes! Aphrodite's response was instantaneous. She opened herself heart, soul, and mind to her Goddess.

And suddenly she was the breeze drifting along the delicate line of Nyx's voice, soaring up and away.

Behold my realm.

Aphrodite's spirit flew over Nyx's Otherworld. It was almost indescribably lovely, with endless variations of green, brilliant flowers that swayed as if to music, and sparkling lakes. Aphrodite thought she caught sight of wild horses and the many-colored flash of peacocks in flight.

And all throughout the realm, spirits flickered in and out of view, dancing, laughing, and loving.

"This is where we go when we die?" Aphrodite asked, awestruck.

Sometimes.

"What sometimes? You mean if we're good?" Aphrodite had a sinking feeling that if being good was the criterion for getting to this place, she would probably never make it.

The goddess's laughter was like magic. *I am your Goddess, daughter, not your judge. Good is a multifaceted ideal. For instance, behold one facet of good.*

Aphrodite's spirit journey slowed, bringing her to a halt over an amazing-looking grove. She blinked in surprise as she studied it and realized it reminded her of the grove near Sgiach's castle. As she made the comparison, Aphrodite sank gently down through the canopy of tightly knit leaves to rest just above the thick carpet of moss that covered the ground.

"Listen to me, Zo! You can do it."

At the sound of Heath's voice, Aphrodite whirled around to see Zoey, looking so pale she was almost translucent, and Heath. Z was pacing around and around in a circle, looking totally creepy, while Heath stood still, watching her with an incredibly sad expression.

"Zoey! Finally! Okay, listen to me. You gotta pull yourself together and get back to your body."

Completely ignoring her, Zoey burst into tears, though she didn't stop pacing. "I can't, Heath. It's gone on too long. I can't bring my soul together. I can't remember things—I can't focus—the only thing I know for sure is that I deserve this."

"Oh, for shit's sake. ZOEY! Stop bawling and pay attention!"

"You do not deserve this!" Heath stepped close to Zoey and put his hands on her shoulders, forcing her to hold still. "And you *can* do it, Zo. You have to. If you do, we can be together."

"Great. I'm Christmas Carol-*ing like the damn ghosts of Christmas Past, Present and whatever. They can't hear a fucking word I'm saying!"*

Then perhaps, daughter, for a change, you should listen.

Aphrodite stifled her sigh of frustration and did as her Goddess advised, even though she felt like a creeper gawking through someone's bedroom window.

"You mean it, Heath?" Zoey stared at Heath, seeming for an instant more like herself than the freaky ghostly thing that couldn't hold still. "You'd really want to stay here?" She smiled tentatively at Heath, her body twitching restlessly under his hands.

He kissed her, and then said, "Babe, wherever you are is where I want to be—forever."

With a painful groan, Zoey broke out of Heath's arms. "I'm sorry. I'm sorry," she said, pacing and crying again. "I can't hold still. I can't rest."

"That's why you have to call your soul back together. You can't be with me if you don't. Zo, you can't be *anything* if you don't. You'll just keep moving and moving and losing pieces of yourself until you fade completely away."

"It was my fault you died; it's my fault you're here where you don't belong. How can you still love me?" She wiped her stringy hair from her face as she began circling around and around Heath—never still—never resting.

"It's not your fault! Kalona killed me. That's all there is to it. Anyway, what difference does it make where we are and even if we're alive or dead, as long as we're together?"

"You mean it? Really?"

"I love you, Zoey. I have since the first day I met you, and I'll love you forever. I promise. If you're whole again, we'll be together forever."

"Forever," Zoey whispered the word. "And you really do forgive me?"

"Babe, there's nothing to forgive."

With what was obviously a huge effort, Zoey stopped moving, and said, "Then for you, I'll try to do it." She spread her arms and threw her head back. Her pale body began to glow, first with a small, tentative light from within. Zoey started to call out names, and—

Aphrodite was jolted from the vision and lifted out of the grove so quickly her stomach gave a nauseating lurch. *"Oh, ugh! Too far, too fast. I may barf."*

A warm wind passed over her, calming her dizziness. When she began to move again, her nausea was gone, but not her confusion.

"Okay, I don't understand. Z pulls herself together, but she stays here with Heath instead of going back to her body?"

In this version of the future, yes.

Aphrodite hesitated and then, reluctantly, asked, *"But is she happy?"*

Yes. Zoey and Heath are content together in the Otherworld for eternity.

Aphrodite felt the sadness, heavy and thick, but she had to continue, *"Then maybe Z should stay where she is. We'll miss her. I'll miss her."* Aphrodite hesitated, quelling an unexpected urge to cry before she continued. *"It would definitely suck for Stark, but if this is where she's meant to be, then Zoey should stay.*

What is meant for each person changes with their choices. This is only one version of Zoey's future, and like many choices that are made in the Otherworld, hers has threads that change the tapestry of the future on earth. If Zoey chooses to stay, behold earth's new future:

Aphrodite was sucked down into a scene that was all too familiar. She was standing in the middle of the field she'd been in during her last vision. Just as before, she was one with people who were burning—humans, vamps, and fledglings. She reexperienced the pain of the fire, along with the abstract agony that had enveloped her during the original vision. As during the last vision, Aphrodite looked up to see Kalona standing before them all, only this time Zoey wasn't with him—making out *or* saying whatever she'd said in the second part of the vision that destroyed him. Instead, Neferet stepped into the scene. She strode past Kalona, staring at the burning people. Then she began tracing intricate patterns in the air around her, and as she did so Darkness bloomed all around her. Spreading from her, it stained the field, extinguishing the fire, but not taking away the pain.

"No, I won't kill them!" She gestured with one finger, and a cluster of tendrils wrapped around Kalona's body. "Help me make them mine."

Kalona absorbed them. Aphrodite concentrated on him and, like a mirage materializing, the tendrils of Darkness that encased the immortal's body became visible. They writhed, causing the fallen immortal's skin to twitch and shudder. Kalona gasped, and Aphrodite couldn't tell if he felt pleasure or pain, but he smiled grimly at Neferet, spread his arms wide to accept Darkness, and said, "As you wish, my Goddess."

Covered in the tendrils, Kalona moved up so that he stood in front of her, and then the fallen immortal dropped to his knees and bared his neck. Aphrodite watched Neferet bend, lick Kalona's skin, and with a greedy fierceness that was frightening, she sank her teeth into Kalona and fed from him. The tendrils of Darkness quivered, throbbed, and multiplied.

Utterly grossed out, Aphrodite looked away to see Stevie Rae enter the field.

Stevie Rae?

A dark thing moved beside her, and Aphrodite realized that Stevie Rae was standing next to a Raven Mocker, right next to him—as in so close they appeared *together.*

WTF?

The Raven Mocker's wing spread up and out, and then curled around Stevie Rae, as if holding her in an embrace. Stevie Rae sighed and moved even closer to the creature, so that his wing totally enveloped her. Aphrodite was so shocked by the sight that she didn't see where the Indian kid came from—he was just suddenly there, right in front of the Raven Mocker.

Even through the pain and shock caused by her vision, Aphrodite could appreciate how incredibly gorgeous this new kid was. His body was amazing, and he was mostly naked, so there was a lot of it showing. His hair was thick and long, and as black as the raven feathers that were braided into its length. He was tall and muscular and just super hot in general.

He ignored the Raven Mocker and held his hand out to Stevie Rae, saying, "Accept me, and he'll go away."

Stevie Rae stepped out of the creature's winged embrace, but she didn't take the kid's hand. Instead she said, "It's not that simple."

Still on his knees in front of Neferet, Kalona yelled, "Rephaim! Do not betray me again, my son!"

The immortal's words served as a goad to the Raven Mocker. He attacked the Indian kid. The two of them began to battle each other brutally while Stevie Rae stood there, doing nothing except staring at the Raven Mocker and crying brokenly. Through her sobs, Aphrodite could hear her say, "Don't leave me, Rephaim. Please, please don't leave me."

On the distant horizon behind all of them, Aphrodite saw what she thought was a blazing sun rising, but as she squinted against the brightness she realized it wasn't the sun at all but an enormous white bull climbing over the slaughtered body of a black bull as he tried, and failed, to protect the remnants of what was once the modern world.

Aphrodite was lifted from her vision. Nyx held her in a caressing breeze as her soul trembled. *"Oh, Goddess,"* she whispered. *"No, please no. A choice made by one teenage girl is able to mess up the balance of Light and Darkness in the entire world? How can that even be possible?"*

Consider that your choice for goodness opened a path for an entirely new breed of vampyre to exist.

"The red fledglings? But they already existed before I did anything."

Yes, but the path to regain their humanity was closed until your sacrifice—your choice—opened it. And are you not simply one teenage girl?

"Oh, for crap's sake. Zoey has to come back."

Then Heath must move on from my realm of the Otherworld. That is the only way Zoey will choose to return to her body if her soul becomes whole again.

"How do I make sure that happens?"

All you can do is to give them the knowledge, daughter. The choice must rest with Heath and Zoey and Stark.

With a jolt, Aphrodite was pulled back and back. Gasping, she opened her eyes and blinked through pain and the haze of red tears to see Darius bending over her.

"Have you returned to me?"

Aphrodite sat up. She was light-headed, and her head throbbed behind her eyes with a pain she knew too well. She brushed her hair from her face, surprised at how badly her hand was trembling.

"Drink this, my beauty. You must ground yourself after a spirit journey." He handed her a goblet and helped her hold it to her lips.

Aphrodite gulped the wine, and then said, "Help me get to Stark."

"But your eyes—you must rest!"

"If I rest, I take a chance that the whole fucking world goes to hell. Literally."

"Then I will get you to Stark."

Feeling weak and in way over her head, Aphrodite leaned on her Warrior as they returned to the Fianna Foil, where very little had changed. Sgiach was still watching her Guardian as he slowly and methodically continued to cut Stark.

Aphrodite didn't waste any time. She went straight to Sgiach.

"I have to talk to Stark. Now."

Sgiach looked at her, taking in her trembling body and her blood-filled eyes. "You've used your gift?"

"Yeah, and I have to tell Stark something, or it'll be bad. For everyone. Really bad."

The queen nodded and motioned for Aphrodite to follow her to the Seol ne Gigh.

"You will only have a moment. Speak quickly and clearly to Stark. If you hold him here too long, he will not be able to retrace his path to the Otherworld until he has recovered from today's journey, and you must understand that recovery could take him weeks."

"I get it. I have one chance at this. I'm ready," Aphrodite said.

Sgiach touched her Guardian's forearm. It was the lightest of caresses, but it caused a rippled reaction throughout Seoras's body. He paused in the downward stroke of another slice. His gaze remained on Stark, but with a voice like gravel, he said, "*Mo bann ri?* My queen?"

"Call him back. The Prophetess must speak to him."

Seoras's eyes closed as if her words wounded him, but when he opened them he retorted with a low growl, and said only, "Aye, wumman . . . as yie wish." He placed the hand that wasn't holding his dirk on Stark's forehead. "Hear me, boy. Yie must be returning."

CHAPTER TWENTY-SIX

Stark

Stark staggered backward, instinctively holding up his own broadsword so that it was by accident and instinct that he deflected the killing stroke from the Other, that being who was him and yet wasn't.

"Why are you doing this?" Stark shouted.

"I already told you. The only way you can get in here is to kill me, and I'm not gonna die."

The two Warriors circled each other warily. "What the fuck are you talking about? You're *me*. So if I get in there, how can you die?"

"I'm part of you. The not-so-nice part. Or you're a part of me, the good part, and I fucking hate even saying that. Don't act so damn stupid. It's not like you don't know about me. Think back to before you pussied out and swore yourself to that goody-goody bitch. We knew each other lots better then."

Stark stared, seeing the tint of red in the eyes and the harsh set of his own face. The smile was still there, but the cockiness had turned cruel, making his features familiar and alien at the same time.

"You're the bad in me."

"Bad? That's just a matter of which side you're on, isn't it? And from the side I'm on right now, I don't look so damn bad." Laughing, the Other continued, " 'Bad' is a word that doesn't come near to describing my potential. Bad is a luxury. My world is filled with things beyond your imagination."

Stark started to shake his head, wanting to deny what he was hearing, and his concentration faltered. The Other struck again, slicing a thick furrow down his right bicep.

Stark lifted the broadsword defensively, surprised there was an odd burning but no pain in either arm.

"Yeah, doesn't hurt much, huh? Yet. That's 'cause the blade's too fucking sharp to hurt. But check it out—you're bleeding. A lot. It's only a matter of time before you can't keep that sword lifted anymore. Then you're done for, and I'll get rid of you once and for all." The Other continued, "Or maybe we'll play. How 'bout I have some fun and flay you alive, piece by fucking piece, until you're nothing more than a bleeding carcass at my feet."

From his peripheral vision, Stark could see that the heat he was feeling was the warmth of the blood that was pumping steadily from the two wounds. The Other was right. He was going down.

He had to fight—and he had to fight now. If he kept hesitating, kept being purely defensive, he would die.

With an action that was completely instinctual, Stark lunged forward, striking out at his mirror image, at everything, anything that could possibly be an opening in his guard, but the red-eyed version of him blocked each move easily. And then, like a cobra, he struck back, sliding through Stark's defenses and hacking a long, deep wound in one thigh.

"You can't beat me. I know all your moves. I'm everything you're not. That goodness crap has made you weak. That's why you couldn't protect Zoey to begin with. Loving her made you weak."

"No! Loving Zoey is the best thing I've ever done."

"Yeah, well, it'll be the *last* thing you've ever done, that's for—"

Stark was wrenched back into his body. He opened his eyes to see Seoras standing over him, dirk in one hand, the other pressed against his forehead.

"No! I have to go back!" he cried. He felt like his body was on fire. The pain in his sides was unbelievable—the force of it pumped adrenaline through his system. His first instinct was to move! Get away! Fight!

"Nae, boy. Remember yie cannae be movin'," Seoras said.

Stark's breath was coming fast and hard as he forced his body to stay still—stay there.

"Get me back," he told the Guardian. "I have to get back."

"Stark, listen to me." Suddenly Aphrodite's face was there above him. "It's Heath that's the key. You have to get to him before you see Zoey. Tell him he has to move on. He has to leave Zoey in the Otherworld, or she'll never come back here."

"What? Aphrodite?"

She grabbed his arm and brought her face down close to his. He could see the blood in her eyes and was jolted by the realization that she must have just had a vision.

"Trust me. Get to Heath. Make him leave. If you don't, there's no one who'll stop Neferet and Kalona, and it's over for all of us."

"If he's to be returnin', he must be goin' the now," Seoras said.

"Take him back," Sgiach said.

The bright edges around Stark's vision began to go gray, and he struggled against being pulled under again.

"Wait! Tell me. How—how do I fight myself?" Stark managed to gasp.

"Ach, 'tis quite simple really. The Warrior within yie must die tae give birth to the Shaman."

Stark couldn't tell whether Seoras's words were a response to his question, or whether they came from his memory, and he had no time to figure it out. In less than a heartbeat, Seoras grabbed his head with a viselike grip and dragged the blade across Stark's eyelids. In a searing, blinding flash he was once more facing himself as if he'd never been gone. Although disoriented by the pain of the Guardian's last cut, Stark realized his body was reacting quicker than his mind could comprehend, and he was easily defending himself against the attack of his mirror image. It was as if the line of the last cut had revealed a geometry of strike lines into the heart of the Other that Stark had never known before, and, because he'd not known it, maybe the Other did not know, either. If that was so, he had a chance, but only a slim one.

"I can do this all day. *You* can't. Damn, my ass is easy to kick." The red-eyed Stark laughed arrogantly.

As he laughed, Stark lunged, following a strike line that pain and need had revealed, catching the outside edge of his mirror image's forearm.

"Fuck me! You actually drew blood. Didn't think you had it in you!"

"Yeah, well, that's one of your problems; you're too damn arrogant." Stark saw the hesitation that rippled through his mirror image, and a hint of understanding whispered in his mind. He followed that thought as naturally as he'd lifted the broadsword in defense and glimpsed the strike lines all across his body. "No, it's not that *you're* too damn arrogant. It's me. I'm arrogant."

His mirror image's guard wavered. Stark understood completely then, and he pressed on. "I'm selfish, too. That's how I killed my mentor. I was too selfish to let anyone beat me at anything."

"No!" the red-eyed Stark yelled. "That's not you—that's me."

Seeing the opening, Stark struck again, slicing into the Other's side. "You're wrong, and you know it. You're what's bad about me, but you're still me. The Warrior wouldn't be able to admit it, but the Shaman in me is beginning to understand it." As Stark spoke, he drove relentlessly forward, raining blows down on his mirror image. "We're arrogant. We're selfish. Sometimes we're mean. We have a bad fucking temper, and when we get pissed off, we hold a grudge."

Stark's words seemed to trigger something in the Other, and he retaliated with a speed almost beyond belief, attacking Stark with a skill and vengeance that was overwhelming. *Oh, Goddess, no. Don't let my mouth have messed this up.* As Stark barely defended himself against the onslaught, he realized he was reacting too rationally, too predictably. The only possible way to defeat himself was to do what the Other wouldn't be expecting,

I have to give him an opening to kill me.

As the Other rained the blows in to break him, Stark knew this was it. He feigned dropping his guard on his left. With unstoppable momentum the Other went for the gap, lunging forward and making himself—for an instant—even more vulnerable than Stark. Stark saw the strike line, the geometry of the true opening, and with ferocity he didn't know himself capable of, smashed the sword hilt down on the skull of the Other.

Stark's mirror image fell to his knees. Gasping for breath, he was barely able to hold the broadsword up any longer.

"So now you kill me, get into the Otherworld, and get the girl."

"No. Now I accept you because no matter how wise I am or how good I manage to become, you'll always be there inside me."

Red eyes met brown eyes once more. The Other dropped his sword, and with one swift motion hurled himself forward, driving Stark's broadsword to its hilt in his chest. In the raw intimacy of the moment the Other exhaled, so close to him that Stark breathed in the last of the Other's sweet breath.

Stark's gut clenched. Himself! He'd killed himself! Shaking his head in terrible realization, he cried, "No! I—" Even as he shouted the denial, the red-eyed Stark smiled knowingly, and through blood-stained lips whispered, "I'll see you again, Warrior, sooner than you think."

Stark lowered the Other to his knees, simultaneously drawing the great sword from his chest.

Time suspended as the divine light of Nyx's realm focused on the sword, glinting along its bloody but beautiful length and blinding Stark, exactly like Seoras's last cut had seared his vision, and miraculously, momentarily, it was as if the ancient Guardian was there beside him and the Other as the three Warriors gazed at the sword.

Seoras spoke without taking his eyes off the hilt. "Aye, it will be the Guardian's claymore for yie boy, a sword forged in hot wet blood, used only in the defense of honor, wielded by a man who has chosen tae guard an Ace, a *bann ri,* a queen. Its blade is honed tae a bonnie sharpness that cuts withoot pain, and the Guardian who bears this blade will strike withoot mercy, fear, or favor, against those who would defile our grand lineage."

Mesmerized, Stark turned the claymore, allowing the jeweled hilt to catch the light as Sgiach's Guardian continued, "The five crystals, set in as four corners, and the fifth centered with the heart stone, create a constant pulse in tune with the beating heart of its Guardian, *if* he is a chosen Warrior who guards honor afore life." Seoras paused, finally looking away from the claymore. "Are yie that Warrior, ma boy? Is it a true Guardian yie will be?"

"I want to be," Stark said, trying to will the sword to beat in time with his heart.

"Then yie must always act with honor and send the one you've defeated on to a better place. If yie can do this as a Guardian and no as a boy . . . if yie are aff the true blood soul and spirit, son, yie will find yer last horror will be the ease by which yie accept and execute this eternal duty.

"But know there is no going back, for this is the law and lot o' the Guardian pure, nae grudge, malice, prejudice, or vengeance, only yer unflinching faith in honor can be yer reward, nae guarantee of love, happiness, or gain. For after us there is nothing." In Seoras's eyes, Stark saw timeless resignation. "Yie will carry this for eternity, for who will guard a Guardian? Now yie know the truth of it. Decide, son."

Seoras's image disappeared, and time began again. The Other was on his knees in front of him, staring up at him with eyes that held fear and acceptance.

Death with honor. As Stark thought the words, the claymore's hilt warmed in his hands with a beat that mirrored the pounding of his heart. He closed his other hand on the hilt, reveling in the feeling.

Then the weight of the blade became a life force of its own, filling Stark with a terrible, wonderful strength and knowledge. Without thought, without emotion, he used the arc of a crescent moon to deal the killing blow, crashing the blade sickeningly into the Other, slicing him cleanly from skull to crotch. There was a great sighing, and the body disappeared.

The full extent of Stark's brutality slammed into him. He dropped the claymore and fell to his knees.

"Goddess! How could I do that *and* be honorable?"

Mind reeling, Stark knelt on the ground, breathing hard. He stared down at his body, expecting to find gaping wounds in his flesh and blood—lots and lots of his blood.

But he was wrong. He was completely free of any physical wound. The only blood he saw was packed into the earth beneath him. The only wound that remained was the memory of what he'd just done.

Almost with a will of its own, his hand found the hilt of the great sword. Seeing in his memory the killing blow he'd just delivered, Stark's hand trembled, but he gripped the hilt tightly, finding warmth and the echo of the beating of his heart.

"I am a Guardian," he whispered. And with the words came true acceptance of himself and, finally, understanding. It wasn't about killing the bad within him; it was never about that. It was about controlling it. That was what a true Guardian did. He didn't deny brutality; he wielded it with honor.

Stark bowed his head so that it rested on the Guardian claymore.

"Zoey, my Ace, my *bann ri shi'*, my queen—I choose to accept it all and to follow the way of honor. That's the only way I can be the Warrior you need me to be. This I swear."

With Stark's oath still hovering in the air around him, the archway that was boundary of Nyx's Otherworld disappeared, along with the Guardian claymore, leaving Stark alone, weaponless, and on his knees in front of the goddess's grove and the ethereal beauty of the hanging tree.

Stark struggled to his feet, automatically walking toward the grove. His one thought was that had to find her—his queen, his Zoey.

But as he got nearer to the grove, Stark slowed and finally stopped.

No. He was starting out wrong. Again.

It wasn't Zoey he had to find, it was Heath. As big a pain in the ass as Aphrodite could be, he knew her visions were for real. What the hell was it Aphrodite had said? Something about Heath having to move on for Zoey to come back. Stark thought about it. As much as it hurt him to admit, he could understand why what Aphrodite had seen was the truth. Zoey had been with Heath since they were kids. She'd watched him die, which had hurt her so badly her soul had shattered. If she could be whole, and be with Heath here . . .

Stark looked around, and as when he'd connected with the claymore, he was really *seeing*.

Nyx's realm was incredible. The grove was directly in front of him though he could sense the vastness of the place, and knew Nyx's realm was way bigger than this one place. But, in all honesty, the grove itself was enough—green and welcoming, it was like a shelter for his spirit. Even after what he'd been through to get there, knowing his responsibilities as Zoey's Guardian, and understanding his quest was far from finished, Stark wanted to enter the grove, breathe deeply, and let the peace of it fill him. Add Zoey's presence to all of that, and he'd be more than content to stay here for at least a slice of eternity.

So, yeah, give Heath back to Zoey, and she'd want to stay. Stark rubbed a hand over his face. He hated to admit it—it broke his heart to admit it—but Zoey loved Heath, maybe even more than she loved him.

Stark mentally shook himself. The love she felt for Heath didn't matter! Zoey had to come back—even Aphrodite's vision said so. And, sure, if Heath weren't involved, he'd probably be able to convince her to come back with him. That was the kind of girl she was—she cared about her friends more than she cared about herself.

Which was exactly why Heath would have to leave her, and not the other way around.

So he'd have to find Heath and talk him into giving up the only girl he'd ever loved. Forever.

Fuck.

Impossible.

But it should also have been impossible for him to have defeated himself and accept all that meant.

So think, damnit! Think like a Guardian and don't just act and react like a stupid kid.

He could find Zoey. He'd done it before. And once he found Zoey, Heath would be there, too.

Stark's gaze went to the hanging tree. It was bigger here than on Skye, and the pieces of cloth that were tied to its massive umbrella of branches kept changing colors and lengths as they waved gently in the warm breeze.

The hanging tree was about dreams and wishes and love.

Well, he did love Zoey.

Stark closed his eyes and concentrated on Zoey—on how much he loved her and missed her.

Time passed . . . minutes, maybe hours. Nothing. Not one fucking thing. Not even a vague inkling of where she might be. He couldn't feel her at all.

You can't give up. Think like a Guardian.

So love wouldn't lead him to Zoey. Then what would? What was stronger than love?

Stark blinked in surprise. He already had the answer. He'd been given it with the title of Guardian and the mystical claymore.

"For a Guardian, honor is stronger than love," Stark said aloud.

He'd barely finished speaking the words when a thin golden ribbon appeared directly above him in the hanging tree. It glinted with a metallic luminescence, reminding Stark of the torque of yellow gold Seoras wore around his wrist. When the ribbon unknotted and floated free of the tree and into the grove, Stark didn't hesitate. He followed his gut and this small reminder of honor, and strode after it.

CHAPTER TWENTY-SEVEN

Heath

Zoey was getting worse. It was just not fair. Like she hadn't had enough bullcrap to deal with lately? Now this had happened to her—this shattered-soul thing, and she was slipping away from him, from everything. At first it was little by little. Recently, it'd been more like humongous, cataclysmic piece by piece. As they moved farther and farther into the heart of the grove, keeping away from the edges of the trees and what was probably Kalona stalking them out there, she'd started changing faster. There didn't seem to be shit he could do about it. She wouldn't listen to him. He couldn't reason with her. She wouldn't even hold still. Literally.

He could see her in front of him. Even though he was almost jogging along the mossy bank of a musical little stream, he wasn't moving quickly enough for her. She wandered ahead of him, sometimes whispering things to the air around her, sometimes crying softly, but always restless—always in motion.

It was like he was watching her evaporate.

Heath had to do something. He realized what was happening to her was because her soul wasn't whole. That made sense. He'd tried to talk to her about it—tried to get her to call the pieces together and then go back to her body. He didn't really understand all this Otherworld stuff, though the longer he was here, the more he just *knew* things, which was probably 'cause he was dead as dirt.

Jeesh, it was totally weird to think that he was dead. Not scary weird, bizarre weird, 'cause he didn't feel dead. He felt like him, just in another place. Heath scratched his head. Damn, it was hard to figure out, but what wasn't hard to figure out was that Zo *wasn't* dead, and so she really didn't belong here.

Heath sighed. Sometimes he felt like he didn't belong here, either. Not that this wasn't a cool place. Okay, sure, Zo was a mess, and they couldn't leave the grove without Kalona or whothehellever pouncing on them and probably fucking killing him again. If that was possible. Take away that stuff, and it would be fine here.

But only fine.

It was like his spirit was searching for something else—something it couldn't find here.

"You died too soon. That's what it is."

Heath jumped in surprise. Zoey was standing in front of him, rocking back and forth, from one foot to another, staring at him with eyes that looked haunted by sadness.

"Zo, babe, you're kinda spooky when you do that pop-up-in-front-of-me thing." He made himself laugh. "It's like you're the ghost, not me."

"Sorry . . . sorry . . ." she muttered, and started walking a circle around him. "It's just that they told me that you're not happy here because you died too soon."

Heath stood still but turned with her as she paced around him. "Who's 'they'?"

Zoey waved her hand in a vague gesture at the grove. "The ones that are kinda like me."

Heath stepped closer to her so that he walked right beside her as she continued her relentless movements. "Babe, don't you remember we talked about them? They're pieces of you. It's why you're feeling so messed up right now. The next time they talk to you, I want you to ask them to come back inside you. It'll make things lots better."

Her eyes were big and lost when she looked at him. "No, I can't."

"Why not, babe?"

Zoey burst into tears. "I can't, Heath. It's gone on too long. I can't bring my soul together. I can't remember things—I can't focus—the only thing I know for sure is that I deserve this."

"You do not deserve this!" Heath stepped close to Zoey and was lifting his hands to plant them squarely on her shoulders and make her listen to him, once and for all, when a golden ribbon caught the edge of his vision, drawing his attention momentarily away from her.

A moment was all Zoey's restlessness needed, and with a miserable cry she said, "I have to go! I have to keep going, Heath. That's all I can seem to do." Before he could stop her, she went away from him with a strange, almost floating motion that carried her pale body like a feather in a strong wind, quickly, erratically, and farther into the grove.

"Well, shit. This is so not working for me." He started to follow Zoey. He had to make her hear him. He had to help her. Then he faltered, slowing to a stop. The problem was, he didn't know how to help her. "I don't know what to do!" he shouted as he slammed his fist into the side of one of the grove's moss-covered trees. "I don't know what to do!" Heath hit the tree again, ignoring the pain in his hand. "I. Do. Not. Know. What. To. Fucking. Do!" he punctuated each word with his fist until his knuckles split open, and the scent of his own blood lifted to linger around him.

That was when the shadow covered the sun. Wiping his throbbing hand on the moss, he looked up.

Darkness. Wings. Blotting out the Goddess's light.

Heart thundering, Heath crouched, fisting his bleeding hands defensively, but the attack didn't come.

What came instead was revelation in the form of whispered thoughts that seemed to seep from the shadows above and sink through the blood scent into his veins.

She would stay here with you, forever, but she must be whole.

Heath blinked in surprise. "Huh? Who's there?"

Use your mind, insignificant mortal!

"Yeah, okay," Heath said, squinting up at the hovering shadows. Was it Kalona? He couldn't get a good look at the thing.

You must make her call the pieces of her soul together, then she will be able to rest here, in the sacred grove, with you.

"I get *that*. I just don't get how to get her to do it. If that makes sense."

The answer is in your bond with her.

"My bond with her, but I don't know—" and then Heath realized he *did* know how to use their bond. All he had to do was make Zo listen to him, and he'd always been able to do that, even when he'd been acting like an asshole and drinking and messing up in school, and she'd tried to dump him. He'd always been able to bring them back together—to keep them together.

Then Heath grinned. That was it! Winged Darkness forgotten, he hurried after Zoey and the Goddess's light, unrestricted, shone down into the grove again. Their bond was the key. It was them, together, that had always worked, no matter what else had been going on in their lives. The bond was still there, too. It had brought Zo to him, even after his death. That was what he'd use. Once Zo got it that they could be together, and that it was cool with him being here and all, she'd make herself whole. And then whatever else they had to come up against, they'd face it together—forever. Hell, that shouldn't be too hard. His Zo could seriously kick some ass.

With new determination, Heath jogged after Zoey, when a whispered "Heath!" brought him up short.

"What the hell?"

"Back here!"

Heath turned around, where the golden thread had snagged in the branches of a rowan tree and blinked in total surprise when a guy stepped from behind the tree.

"Stark? What the—"

"Ssh! Do not let Zoey know I'm here."

Heath walked over to the tree. "What the hell are you doing here?" But he didn't give Stark a chance to answer. "Ah, fuck! Are you dead, too? Zo's never gonna be able to handle that!"

"Keep your damn voice down. No, I'm not dead. I'm here to protect Zoey so that she can get back to her body where she belongs." Stark paused, and then added, "You do know you're dead, right?"

"Dude, no shit? I'm dead?" Heath said sarcastically. "Glad you're here to enlighten me. Don't know what the fuck I'd do without you."

"Well how 'bout this: do you know Zoey's soul's shattered?"

Before Heath could say anything, both guys saw Zoey and Stark jumped back behind the tree, crouching in its shadow. Heath moved quickly to intercept her, blocking her view of Stark.

"You didn't come after me. You always come after me." Her body rocked back and forth as she tried to stay in one place.

"I'm coming, Zo. You know I'll never leave you. It's just that you're faster than I am right now."

"So you're not leaving me?"

Heath touched her cheek, hating that she looked so weak and unsure, and totally un-Zoey-like. "No. I'm not leaving you. Go on ahead of me. I'll catch up." When she hesitated, and it was obvious she was going to start that freaky circle pacing around him again, which would take her too damn close to Stark's hiding place, he added, "Hey, maybe it'd make you feel better to move real fast. Why don't you kinda run, or float, or whatever it is you do for a while, and then come back here. If it's okay with you, I'll hang out here for a second. I need to rest a little."

"Sorry . . . sorry . . . I forgot you need to rest . . . forgot . . ."

She started to float away, and Heath called after her, "Don't go too far, though! And don't forget to circle back here."

"I won't forget . . . can't forget *you*," she said. Without looking at him, she disappeared into the shadows.

Stark stepped away from the tree. His voice was rough with shock, "Oh, shit! It's way worse than I thought."

Heath nodded grimly. "Yeah. I know. The shattered-soul thing's totally messed her up. She can't rest, so she can't think, and that's doing something to her—something really, really bad."

Still staring after Zoey, Stark said, "The High Council said this would happen. She's turning into a Caoinic Shi'. She's not dead and not alive, and she's here in a realm of spirits without her own soul. It makes her like this, and it'll get worse. She'll never be able to rest—ever."

"Then we gotta get her to pull herself together. I think I might be able to do it, too. And, dude, I'm not trying to be an asshole, but this isn't something you can help with. If you want to give me a hand, go out there and kick the ass of the scary shit that's kept us trapped in here. You handle that. I'll handle Zo."

Heath started to walk away, following Zoey, but Stark's words halted him. "Yeah, you can get her spirit whole again by telling her you'll stay here with her, but if you do that, you'll fuck up everyone Zoey loves back in the real world."

Heath turned back to face Stark. "It's not cool for you to say shit like that. Just let her go, dude. I know you love her and all, but seriously, you've only known her a little while. I've been with her for years. I get that you'll miss her, but she'll be good here with me—she'll be happy."

"It's not about love. It's about doing the right thing. I give you my word as a Guardian that I'm telling you the truth. If Zoey doesn't return to her body, the world as she knew it—as you knew it, will be destroyed."

"What's this Guardian stuff about?"

Stark drew in a deep breath. "It's about honor."

Something about Stark's voice made Heath look at him with new eyes. The guy had changed. He looked somehow taller, older, and not his normal, cocky self. He looked sad. Very sad.

"You're telling me the truth."

Stark nodded. "Aphrodite had a vision. What she saw is that you get Zoey to pull her soul together. You do it by promising you'll stay here with her. So she doesn't turn into a Caoinic Shi'. She's herself again. And she does stay here with you—forever. But without Zoey, there's no one to stop Neferet and Kalona."

"And they take over the world," Heath finished for him.

"And they take over the world," Stark agreed.

Heath's eyes met Stark's. "I have to leave Zoey."

"I won't let her be alone," Stark told him. "I'm her Warrior, her Guardian. I give you my Oath that I'll be sure she's always protected."

Heath nodded, looking away from Stark, trying to get a handle on his emotions. He wanted to run—to find Zo and to be sure she stayed with him, here or anywhere, forever. But when his gaze went back to Stark, he knew the absolute truth: Zoey would hate it if her friends were destroyed. She'd hate it more than she loved him, more than she loved anyone. So if he *really* loved her, Heath would have to leave her.

Even though he felt like he was going to barf, Heath was glad his voice sounded calm and normal. "How are you gonna get her to pull herself together after I go?"

"Can't you tell her you're staying, get her together, and then go?"

Heath snorted, "Dude, I'm not gonna be too hard on you because you not being dead and all is totally making you moronic about this spirit stuff, but there's no fucking way I can get Zo to call together pieces of her soul by telling her a lie. I mean, come on, that doesn't even make sense."

"Yeah, okay. I guess you're right." Stark ran his hand through his hair. "Then I don't know how I'm gonna do it, but I will. I have to. If you're man enough to leave her, I'm man enough to figure out how to save her."

"Well, keep this in mind—Zo doesn't like some dude saving her. She likes to take care of herself. Mostly, you just have to stand back and let her do her thing."

Stark nodded solemnly. "I'll remember that."

"Okay. So. Let's go after her."

The two guys started walking toward the part of the grove where they'd last had a glimpse of Zoey.

"I'll keep out of it while you say goodbye. I won't let her see me till you're gone," Stark said.

Heath couldn't trust his voice, so he just nodded.

"Tell me about that other stuff you said—the scary shit that's trapping you in here."

Heath cleared his throat, and said, "At first I thought it was Kalona, but weirdness happened today that makes me think it probably isn't him. I mean, it was like that thing out there was helping me figure out how to save Zoey."

"But stay here, right?"

"Yeah, right. That was kinda the point to the whole idea."

"So Kalona told you how to be sure Zoey never leaves the

Otherworld—never makes it back to her body," Stark said. "Which is exactly what he's supposed to do."

"And he almost did that today by using me. Fucking asshole. Like it's not bad enough he killed me!" Heath looked at Stark. "So that's really why you're here? I mean, I know you had to tell me I gotta get moving, but basically you're here to kick Kalona's ass so that Zoey really does make it home with you."

"Yeah, it's looking more and more like that's what I'm here for."

Heath snorted. "Good luck with kicking an immortal's ass, dude."

"I've been thinking about it, and all I really have to do is keep him away from Z long enough for her to get whole again. Then she can get out of here and back to her body, where Kalona can't hurt her—or at least right now he can't."

"Nope. Sorry to mess up your plan, but if that was the deal, Zo wouldn't need you to protect her."

Stark gave him a question-mark look.

"It's like this—Zo's safe in the grove." Heath pointed at the grove around them. "Bad shit can't get in here. There's something special about this place. It's like everything magic about the earth down there came from this grove up here. It's a version of Super Earth, a place of total peace. Can't you feel it?"

"Yeah, Super Earth's a good way to put it," Stark said. "And I feel the peace part, too. I did from the beginning. It's why I knew she'd stay here with you."

"Yeah, she would. That's why she needs you. 'Cause as long as she stays safe in here, she won't go back to the real world. So, again, I say good luck with protecting her against Kalona. The asswipe killed me. Hope you do better than me. And if you do, kick his ass for me, and for Zo, too."

"Will do. Hey, Heath, I want you to know something," Stark said. "I wouldn't be brave enough to do what you're doing. I wouldn't be able to leave her."

Heath glanced at him and shrugged. "Yeah, well, I love her more than you do."

"You're doing the right thing, though. The honorable thing," Stark said.

"You know, from where I'm standing right now, honor doesn't mean shit. Love's what works for me and Zo. It always has. It always will."

They walked on silently, both lost in their own thoughts, and as they followed Zoey, Heath's words replayed in Stark's head, over and over, *"Love's what works for me and Zo. It always has. It always will,"* until with jolt of surprise he got it—he really got it. It didn't make what he was about to do any easier, but it did make it bearable.

They found her in a little clearing deep within the grove. She was walking around and around a tall evergreen that looked magnificent, but weirdly out of place among the rowans, hawthorns, and moss. The scent of the tree filled the area. They crept in, being careful to keep shrubs between them and Zoey's line of vision. When Stark nodded and motioned to a man-sized clump of moss-covered rocks that was close enough to Zoey, but still under cover, Heath stopped there with him and took a deep breath, testing the air.

"That's bizarre." Heath kept his voice low so she wouldn't hear him. "Wonder what a cedar tree is doing out here."

"Cedar? That's what that is?" Stark said.

"Yep. There's a huge one between Zo's old house and mine that looks almost exactly like that—smells totally the same, too."

"It's what Zoey's grandma said to burn near me while I was here, in the Otherworld. Aphrodite brought a big bag of it. They lit it just before I left my body." He looked at Heath. "The tree's a good sign. It means we're following the right path."

Heath met Stark's gaze a long time before he said, "I hope it is a good sign, but you gotta know that doesn't make this any easier for me."

"Yeah, I get that."

"Do you? 'Cause I'm getting ready to leave the only girl I've ever loved to you even though I know she needs me bad."

"What do you want me to say to you, Heath? That I wish it didn't have to be this way? I do. That I wish you weren't dead and Zoey's soul wasn't shattered, and the worst thing I had to worry about was being jealous of you and that asshole, Erik? I do."

"You don't have to be jealous of Erik. Zo will never be with any guy very long who's a possessive turd. Don't let those kind of guys stress you."

"If I get her back, whole and in her body, I'm not gonna ever let any other guy stress me again," Stark said.

"When," he said solemnly. Stark's brow furrowed. Heath sighed and explained. "*When* you get her back, not if. I'm not gonna leave her if you can't be sure about what you're doing."

Stark nodded. "Okay, you're right. *When* I get her back. I am sure I'm doing the right thing; *we're* doing the right thing. It's just that I know no matter what, it's gonna end up hurting Zoey."

"Yeah, I know." Heath's chin jerked in Zoey's direction. "But nothing's as bad as what's happening to her right now." Heath bowed his head for a moment and then slapped each of his shoulders, like he was banging against his football uniform's shoulder pads. He shook himself, blew out a long breath, and then raised his head to meet Stark's eyes one last time. "Make sure she knows I don't want her to be all snot crying and freaked about me. Remind her for me that she's seriously unattractive when she's like that."

"I will."

"Oh, speaking of, you'd better get used to carrying around Kleenex in your pockets, 'cause I'm not even exaggerating. Zo's snot cry is nasty."

"Okay, yeah, I'll do it."

Heath held out his hand to Stark. "Take care of her for me."

Stark grasped his forearm. "Warrior to Warrior, I give you my Oath on it."

"Good, 'cause I'm gonna hold you to your Oath next time I see you."

Heath dropped Stark's arm, drew another deep breath, and stepped away from their concealment. He tried not to think about what was going to happen.

Instead, he looked at Zoey and saw beyond the shadowlike thing she was becoming, and thought about the girl he'd loved since he was a kid. He could see the uneven bangs she'd cut for herself in fourth grade. He smiled, thinking of her tomboy time in middle school, when her knees had stayed bruised and scabby for months and months. Then there was the summer before her freshman year when he'd gone on vacation with his family for a month and left her gangly and awkward, but had come back to discover she'd turned into a young goddess. His young goddess.

"Hey, Zo," he said as he caught up and fell into step with her restless, circular pacing.

"Heath! I was just wondering where you were. I, uh, stopped here so you could catch up with me. I missed you."

"You're fast, Zo. I caught you soon as I could." He looped her arm though his. Her skin felt scarily cold. "How ya doin', babe?"

"I don't know. I feel kinda weird. Dizzy but heavy, too. Do you know what's wrong with me, Heath?"

"Yeah, babe, I do." He stopped walking, but kept her arm linked with his, so that she was forced to stop, too. "Your soul's shattered, Zo. We're in the Otherworld, remember?"

Her big dark eyes met his, and for an instant, she almost seemed like her old self. "Yeah, I remember now, and I'm telling you, it's a big bunch of bullpoopie!"

Tears made his vision of her swim, but he blinked hard and smiled. "Damn right it is, but I know how to fix things."

"You do? That's great, but, uh, can you fix things while I walk 'cause this standing still stuff is just not working for me."

Instead of letting her go, Heath put his hands firmly on her shoulders and forced her to stay there and look into his eyes.

"You gotta pull the pieces of your soul together and then get to your body back there in the real world. You gotta do it for your friends—for Stark—for your grandma. Zo, you even gotta do it for me."

Zoey's body twitched, but he could see she was making an effort to hold herself still.

"Not without you, Heath. I don't want to go back to the real world without you."

"I know, babe," he said softly. "But sometimes you gotta do stuff you don't want to do. Like me right now—I don't want to leave you, but it's time for me to move on."

Her eyes widened, and her hands went up to cover his gripping her shoulders. "You can't leave me, Heath! I'll die if you leave me."

"No, babe. You'll do the opposite. You'll pull yourself together, and you'll live."

"No, no, no! You can't leave me." Zoey started crying. "I can't be here without you!"

"That's what I'm trying to get you to see, Zo. If I'm not here, you'll go back where you belong and stop being this pathetic, ghost thing you're turning into."

"Okay, no. No. I'll pull myself together. Just stay here. Stay with me. It'll be fine, you'll see. I promise, Heath."

He'd known she'd say something like that, so he was ready with his answer, but that didn't make it break his heart any less. "It's not just about you, Zo. It's also about what's right for me. It's time I move on to another realm."

"What do you mean? Heath, I don't understand," she sobbed.

"I know you don't, babe. I don't really understand it, but I can feel it," he said truthfully. As he spoke, the right words came to him, and as they did, peace filled Heath, soothing his heartache and making him know beyond all else he really was doing the right thing. "I did die too soon. I want my life, Zo. I want my chance."

"I-I'm sorry, Heath. It's my fault, and I can't give your life back to you."

"No one can, Zo. But I can have another shot at life. Not if I stay here with you, though. If I stay here, I'll never have lived, and neither will you."

Zoey had stopped sobbing, but tears still leaked from her eyes, flooding her cheeks and dripping down her face as if she were standing outside during a rainy summer day.

"I can't. I can't go on without you."

Heath shook her gently and made himself smile. "Yeah, you can. If I can do it, you can, too. 'Cause you know you're smarter and stronger than I am, Zo. You always have been."

"No, Heath," Zoey whispered.

"I want you to remember something, Zo. It's important, and it'll make more sense when you have yourself together again. I'm gonna leave here and get another chance at life. You're gonna be a big, famous vamp High Priestess. That means you're gonna live like a gazillion years. *I'll find you again.* Even if it takes a hundred of those years. I promise you, Zoey Redbird, we'll be together again." Heath pulled her into his arms and kissed her, trying through touch to show her that his love was never-ending. When he finally forced himself to let her go, he thought he saw understanding in her haunted, shocked gaze. "I'll love you forever, Zo."

Then Heath turned and walked away from his true love. The air before him opened, curtainlike, and he stepped from one realm to another and disappeared completely.

Utterly broken, Zoey staggered back to the cedar tree. Silent as a corpse, with tears leaking steadily down her face, she resumed her circular pacing.

CHAPTER TWENTY-EIGHT

Kalona

Kalona couldn't tell how long he'd been in Nyx's realm.

At first it'd been such a jolt to be wrenched from his body by the Darkness Neferet harnessed that, physically and spiritually, he'd been unaware of anything except the awe and fear of having returned to Her realm.

He hadn't forgotten the beauty of the place—the pure wonder of the Otherworld and the magic it held for him. Especially for him.

He'd been different when he'd belonged there.

He'd been a force for Light, protecting Nyx against anything Darkness could conjure to attempt to sway the balance of the world toward the evil and pain and selfishness and despair on which it thrived.

For centuries uncountable, Kalona had protected his Goddess against everything except himself.

Ironic that it had been love that Darkness had used to bring him down.

Still more ironic that, after he'd fallen, Light had also used love to entrap him.

He wondered briefly if love could possibly do anything worse to him than it already had. Was he even capable of it anymore?

He didn't love Neferet. He'd used her to free himself of the earth's imprisonment, and then, in turn, she'd used him for her own means.

Did he love Zoey?

He didn't want to be the cause of her destruction, but guilt wasn't love. Regret wasn't love, either. They also weren't strong enough emotions to make him want to sacrifice the freedom of his body to save her.

Moving through the Goddess's realm, the fallen immortal had put all questions of love and its painful trappings from his mind and focused on the task at hand.

The first step was to find Zoey.

The second was to be certain she could not return to the earthly realm, so that he could reclaim his body and fulfill the oath he'd sworn to Neferet.

Finding Zoey hadn't been difficult. He'd only had to concentrate his will on her, and his spirit had ridden the tide of Darkness directly to her—to the fragmented pieces of her soul.

The human boy he'd killed was there with her, or rather he was with the part of her that was most purely Zoey in this lifetime.

It was odd to see him comforting her—reassuring her—and then, somehow, instinctively, guiding her to the Goddess's sacred grove. A place so purely made of Nyx's essence that, as long as the balance of Light and Dark remained in place in the world, no evil could ever enter it.

Kalona remembered the grove well. It was within it that he had first realized his love for Nyx. In that terrible time before he chose to fall from Her, it was the only place he could go to find even a small measure of peace.

He'd tried to enter again. To follow Zoey and Heath and be finished with this burden Neferet's machinations had laid upon him, but Kalona had been unable to breach the barrier of the sacred grove. The attempt had left him weak and breathless, reminding him all too well of the way he felt whenever he was entrapped by the earth.

This time it was the peace and magic of the Goddess's earth that had rejected him, and not imprisoned him.

He had been too much a part of Darkness for Nyx's grove to accept him.

Kalona half-expected Nyx to appear before him at any moment—accuse him of being the interloper he so obviously was—and, again, cast him from her realm.

But the Goddess did not appear. It seemed Neferet was correct. Had it been his body *and* soul that Nyx had banished, Erebus himself would have met him to do his Goddess's bidding and, with the all the powers of a divine consort, driven his spirit from the Otherworld.

So Kalona was allowed this *freedom,* this Goddess-be-damned *choice* to return and glimpse what he most desired but could never have.

Anger, familiar and safe, boiled within the immortal.

He stalked Zoey and the boy. It didn't take Kalona long to realize that by simply forcing them to stay within the grove, he would eventually accomplish his task.

Zoey was fading away from herself. She was becoming an unresting Caoinic Shi', and as such, she would never return to her body.

The thought of Zoey turning into a being not living and not dead, eternally unable to rest, gave Kalona a curiously painful feeling.

Feeling again! Would he ever be rid of it? Yes. There must be a way. Perhaps Neferet had been right. Perhaps it would be as easy as ridding himself of Zoey. Then he would be free of the guilt and desire and loss she evoked in him.

Even as the thought came to him, Kalona knew he would not be free of her if he left her here to become a wraith, a mere shade of herself. The knowledge of that would haunt him for eternity.

Kalona reconsidered as, from outside the grove, he watched Heath by Zoey's side, attempting to comfort her when comfort was impossible.

He does love her, and she him. It surprised Kalona that he felt no anger or jealousy at the thought. It was simple fact. Had the world not turned upside down for Zoey, she might have spent an innocent, mundane, happy lifetime with this human boy.

And with sudden clarity, Kalona understood how he could rid himself of Zoey and fulfill Neferet's oath.

She would be content here with the boy, and her contentment was enough to soothe the guilt he felt at being the impetus behind her death. She would be here, in Nyx's grove, with her childhood love, and Kalona would return to the earthly realm free of his entanglement with her. *It would be an action for good if she remained,* Kalona rationalized. *She would never know earthly worries and pain again.* It seemed a satisfying solution.

Kalona put out of his mind the thought of what it would be like to be bereft of the only person who, in two lifetimes, had reminded him of his lost Goddess and truly made him *feel.*

Instead, he concentrated on the boy. Heath was the key. It was his death that had caused her soul to shatter, and it was guilt over his death that kept her from being whole again. *Foolish human! Does he not know only he can assuage her guilt and allow the healing of her soul?*

No, of course he didn't. He was only a boy, and not a very insightful one at that. He'd have to be led to the realization.

But the boy was in the grove, and Kalona was denied entrance there. So Kalona hovered and observed, and when the boy's anger spilled over to rage and blood, he used that sliver of base emotion to whisper to him, guide him, send him on his way.

Nearly content, Kalona withdrew to the edge of the grove to wait. The boy would help Zoey mend her soul, but she wouldn't leave him—not if he was the vehicle through which she was made whole again. So it was only a matter of time, and a very little amount of time at that, before her earthly body perished without her spirit.

Then he could return to his own body, and his oath to Neferet would be fulfilled. *Then,* Kalona thought grimly, *I will be sure the Tsi Sgili never gains control over me.*

Smug in his rationalizations and internal deception, the immortal didn't see Stark enter the grove, so he didn't witness Zoey's world turning upside down again.

Stark

Stark watched Heath step through the curtain from one realm to the next. For a moment, he couldn't make himself move, not even to go to Zoey.

He'd been right. Heath was braver than he was. Stark bowed his head, and whispered, "Be with Heath, Nyx, and somehow let him find

Zoey again in this lifetime." Stark's lips curled up, and he added, "Even if it will cause me a pretty big pain in the ass later on."

Then Stark lifted his chin, wiped his eyes, and left the concealing rock, going quickly and silently to Zoey.

She looked scary bad. Her matted hair lifted in a strange breeze that seemed to whisper around her as she paced, as if moving in time to a ghostly wind. Just before she saw Stark, she raised her hand to brush back some of it from her face, and he saw that her hand and even her arm suddenly looked transparent.

She was literally fading away.

"Zoey, hey, it's me."

The sound of his voice acted on her like an electric shock. Her body jerked, and Zoey whirled around to face him. "Heath!"

"No. It's Stark. I-I'm sorry about Heath," he blurted, feeling stupid but not knowing what else to say.

"He's gone." She looked blankly at the place Heath had stood before he disappeared, and then her pacing took her around the circle again, and her anguished gaze moved to Stark's face.

He knew when she recognized him because she staggered to a stop, wrapping her arms around herself as if in protection from a blow.

"Stark!" She shook her head from side to side, over and over. "No, not you, too!"

He knew what she must be thinking and went to her instantly, pulling her stiff, cold body into his arms and holding her close. "I'm not dead." He said the words slowly and carefully, looking into her face. "Do you understand, Zoey? I'm here, but my body is just fine. It's back in the real world with yours. Neither one of us is dead."

For a moment she almost smiled. She did, briefly, step fully into his embrace and allow him to hold her.

"I've missed you so much," he murmured.

She pulled away from him, studying his face carefully. "You're my Warrior."

"Yeah. I'm your Warrior. I'll always be your Warrior."

With a small sigh, she started pacing her circular path again. "Always is done now."

He kept pace with her, not sure how to reach this strange, ghostlike version of his Zoey. He remembered that Heath had talked to her pretty much like he normally did, so ignoring her confusing words and the fact that she couldn't stop moving, he took her hand, acting like they were just walking through the grove together. "This is a pretty cool place."

"It's supposed to be peaceful."

"I think it is."

"No. Not for me. Nothing will ever be peaceful for me again. I lost that part of me."

He squeezed her hand. "That's why I'm here. I'm going to protect you so that you can pull the pieces of your soul together, and then we'll go home."

She didn't even glance at him. "I can't. Go back without me. I have to stay here and wait for Heath."

"Zoey, Heath's not coming back here. He went on to another lifetime. He'll be reborn. Back in the real world *is* where he'll be."

"He can't be there. He's dead."

"Okay, I'm not so good at understanding this Otherworld stuff myself, but from what I can figure, Heath left here so that he can be reborn and live another lifetime. That's how he'll see you again, Z."

Zoey paused, stared blankly at him, shook her head, and then resumed her endless pacing.

Stark pressed his lips together hard to keep from saying what was tearing him apart inside—that she would've pulled herself together because of how much she loved Heath, but not for him. She didn't love him enough.

Stark shook himself mentally. This wasn't just about love. He'd known it when Seoras had first confronted him, asking whether he'd risk his life for Zoey, even if he lost her. "*I stay with her,*" Stark had told him. "*Aye, laddie, as her Warrior fer sure, but perhaps not as her love.*"

Perhaps not as her love.

Stark looked at Zoey and really saw her. She was completely broken.

Her tattoos were gone. Her spirit was shredded. She was losing herself. Yet still he saw the goodness and strength within her, and Stark was drawn to her. She wasn't what she'd been before—she wasn't what she could be—but even shattered, she was his Ace, his *bann ri shi'*, his queen.

. . . Know there is no going back, for this is the law and lot o' the Guardian pure, nae grudge, malice, prejudice, or vengeance, only yer unflinching faith in honor can be yer reward, nae guarantee of love, happiness, or gain.

Stark was Zoey's Guardian, no matter what. He was bound to her by something stronger than love: honor.

"Zoey, you have to come back. Not because of you and Heath, and not even because of you and me. You gotta come back because it's the right thing, the honorable thing to do."

"I can't. There's not enough of me left."

"There is now that you've got help. Your Guardian's here." Stark lifted her hand to his lips, kissed it, and then smiled down at her as he remembered. "Aphrodite made me memorize a poem for you. It's one of Kramisha's. She and Stevie Rae think it's like some kind of map you might be able to follow to get yourself whole again."

"Aphrodite . . . Kramisha . . . Stevie Rae . . ." Zoey whispered hesitantly, as if relearning the words. "They're my friends."

"Yeah, that's what they are," Stark squeezed her hand again. Since he seemed to be getting through to her, he kept going. "So, check out the poem. Here goes:

A double-edged sword
One side destroys
One releases
I am your Gordian knot
Will you release or destroy me?
Follow truth and you shall:
Find me on water

Purify me through fire
Trapped by earth nevermore

Air will whisper to you
What spirit already knows:
That even shattered
anything is possible

If you believe
Then we shall both be free

When he'd finished reciting the poem, Zoey stopped moving long enough to meet his gaze, and say, "It doesn't mean anything."

She started walking again, but she had a tight hold on his hand, keeping him with her.

"Yeah, it does. It's about you and Kalona. He has something to do with you getting free of here." Stark paused, and then added, "You remember you two are linked together, right?"

"Not anymore we're not," she said quickly. "He broke that link when he broke Heath's neck."

I sure as hell hope so, Stark thought, but what he said was, "Yeah, still, part of it's already come true. You followed what you thought was the truth about him to find him on water. So the next line says: *Purify me through fire.* What do you think that could mean?"

"I don't know!" Zoey shouted at him. Even though she was obviously getting pissed, Stark was glad to see the animation in her face that had been so blank and dead-looking. "Kalona isn't here. Fire isn't here. I don't know!"

Stark kept a tight hold on her hand and let her settle down before he told her, "Kalona is here. He's come after you. He just can't get into the grove." Then, without rational thought, he spoke the next words as if they came from his heart and not his mind. "And fire got me here. Or at least it felt like fire."

Zoey glanced at him, and in a very matter-of-fact voice, changed the course of his life by saying, "Then it sounds like that poem's for Kalona and you, not Kalona and me."

Her words settled over Stark like a mesh of steel. "What do you mean, Kalona and me?"

"You went with me to Venice, and you knew the real truth of how much of a monster Kalona is before I did. Fire brought you here. The rest probably means something to you if you think about it enough."

"A double-edged sword . . ." Stark spoke the words softly. The claymore was double-edged. And he'd destroyed as well as released with it. He did know the truth about Kalona being dangerous when he followed him with Zoey to Venice . . . the fire of pain from Seoras's cuts had brought him to here, a place that reminded him of earth, even though it was in the Otherworld. And Zoey was trapped here, needing to be released. And now he had to follow what his spirit knew about honor to bring this whole thing to an end. "Oh, shit!" He looked at Zoey, ever-moving beside him, and the pieces of the puzzle fell into place. "You're right. The poem is for me."

"Good, then it shows you how to be free," Zoey said.

"No, Z. It shows me how to make both of us free," he said. "Kalona and me."

Her troubled, restless eyes lit on his face before looking hastily away. "Free Kalona? I don't understand."

"I do," he said grimly, remembering the killing blow that had freed the Other. "There are a lot of different ways to be free." He tugged on her hand, making her slow down and look at him. "And I do believe in you, Zoey. Even shattered, you still hold my Oath. I will protect you, and as long as I remember honor and don't ever let you down again, I think anything is possible. That's what being your Guardian's all about: honor."

He lifted her hand and kissed it again before he began walking. He didn't let her circular pacing control him. This time Stark led her in a straight line directly for the edge of the grove.

"No. No. We can't go over there," Zoey said,

"Over there is where we have to go, Z. It'll be okay. I trust you." Stark kept walking toward the widening bright spots between the green that marked the grove's edge.

"Trust me? No. It doesn't have anything to do with trust. Stark, we can't leave this place. Ever. There are bad things out there. *He's* out there." Zoey was pulling at his hand hard, trying to get him to change direction.

"Zoey, I'm gonna say some things to you really fast, and I know your concentration is messed up right now, but you gotta hear me." Stark was almost dragging Zoey with him, but he kept relentlessly moving them ahead, to the boundary of the grove. "I'm not just your Warrior anymore. I'm your Guardian. And that means a major change for me *and* for you. The biggest change is that I'm bound to you by honor even more than I am by love. I'm not ever gonna let you down again. I can't tell you what your change is gonna be." The end of the grove shimmered in front of them. Stark stopped and, following a gut impulse, he dropped to one knee in front of his shattered queen. "But I do believe one hundred percent that you're gonna be up to it. Zoey, you're my Ace, *mo bann ri,* my queen, and you have to pull yourself together, or none of us are getting out of here."

"Stark, you're scaring me."

He got to his feet. Stark kissed both of her hands, and then her forehead before saying, "Well, Z, stay tuned, 'cause I've only just started." He gave her his old, cocky grin. "No matter what happens, at least I made it here. If we get back, we'll be able to tell the sticks-up-their-asses Vampyre High Council 'told ya so!'" Then he parted the leaves of two rowan trees and stepped over the rocky boundary of the grove.

Zoey stayed within the grove but held the branches open so she could stare out at Stark as she rocked back and forth, causing the leaves to rustle like a murmuring audience.

"Stark, come back!"

"Can't do that, Z. I got something to take care of."

"What? I don't understand!"

"I'm gonna kick some immortal ass. For you, for me, and for Heath."

"But you can't! You can't beat Kalona."

"You're probably right, Z. I can't. But *you can.*" Stark threw wide his arms and yelled into Nyx's sky. "Come on, Kalona! I know you're here! Come get me. It's the only way you're going to be sure Zoey won't get back, 'cause as long as I'm alive I'm gonna fight to save her!"

The sky above Stark rippled, and the pristine blue began to gray. Tendrils of Darkness, like smoke from a toxic fire, spread, thickened, and took form. His wings appeared first. Massive, black, and unfurled, they blotted out the golden light of the Goddess's sun. Then Kalona's body formed—bigger, stronger, more dangerous-looking than Stark had remembered.

Still hovering above Stark, Kalona smiled. "So, it is you, boy. You sacrificed yourself to follow her here. My work is done. Your death traps her here more easily than I ever could have."

"Wrong, asshole. I'm not dead. I'm alive, and I'm gonna stay that way. So is Zoey."

Kalona's eyes narrowed. "Zoey will not leave the Otherworld."

"Yeah, well, I'm here to make sure you're wrong again."

"Stark! Get back in here!" Zoey shouted from just inside the boundary of the grove.

Kalona's gaze went to her. He sounded sad, almost heartsick when he spoke. "It would have been an easier thing for her had you let the human boy do my will."

"That's the problem with you, Kalona. You have that god-complex thing going on. Or, no, I guess I should call it a God*dess* complex you got. See, just because you're immortal, it doesn't make you in charge. Actually in your case, it just makes you wrong for a really, really long time."

Slowly, Kalona shifted his gaze from Zoey to Stark. The immortal's amber-colored eyes had gone flat and cold with anger. "You are making a mistake, boy."

"I'm not a boy anymore." Stark's tone matched Kalona's.

"You'll always be a boy to me. Insignificant, weak, *mortal.*"

"Which makes you wrong three times in a row, mortal doesn't mean weak. Come on down here and let me prove that to you."

"Very well, boy. Let the pain this causes Zoey be on your soul, not mine."

"Yeah, 'cause I'd hate for you to fucking take responsibility for any of the messed-up shit you've done!"

As Stark knew it would, his taunt pushed Kalona's simmering rage to boiling. He roared at Stark, "Do not dare speak to me of my past!"

The immortal stretched out his arm, and from the Darkness writhing in the air around him, plucked a spear, tipped by metal that glistened wickedly, black as a moonless sky. Then Kalona dropped from the sky.

Instead of landing in front of Stark, his massive wings swept down and forward, slicing the ground in a perfect circle around Stark. Under his feet, the earth shuddered and then disintegrated, and like hell opening beneath him, Stark was falling down . . . down.

He hit bottom with such force his breath was knocked from him, and his vision grayed. He struggled to stand as he heard mocking laughter all around him.

"Just a small, weak boy trying to play with me. This won't even be amusing," Kalona said.

Arrogant. He's more arrogant than I ever was.

And with the thought of what he had been, and what he'd already defeated, Stark's chest loosened. He was able to draw breath. His vision cleared in time to see a flash of brilliant light pierce the darkness between him and Kalona, and the Guardian claymore was there, blade driven in the earth at his feet.

Stark grasped the hilt and felt it instantly, the warmth and the pulse of his heartbeat as the claymore, *his* claymore, sang in tune with his blood.

He looked at Kalona and saw surprise in the immortal's amber eyes.

"I told you I wasn't a boy anymore." Without hesitation, Stark strode forward, holding the claymore with both hands, perfectly centered on the geometrical strike lines that coalesced over Kalona's body.

CHAPTER TWENTY-NINE

Zoey

The shock I felt when Kalona materialized above Stark was terrible. The sight of him brought back everything that had happened in that last moment on that last day, before my world exploded in death and despair and guilt. Fully formed, his amber gaze met mine, and I was frozen by the sadness I saw there, and by the memory of how I'd looked into his eyes before and believed I'd glimpsed humanity, kindness, even love.

I'd been so, so wrong.

Heath had died because of how wrong I'd been.

Then Kalona's gaze moved from me back to Stark, as my Warrior taunted him.

No! Oh, Goddess! Please make him be quiet. Please make him run back to me.

But Stark seemed to like taunting Kalona. He wouldn't shut up; he didn't run. Horror filled me as Kalona plucked the spear from the sky. His wings cut a hole in the ground and then he and Stark disappeared into its blackness.

It was then I realized that Stark was also going to die because of me.

"*No!*" The soundless scream tore from deep inside me, where everything felt empty and hopeless and restless. I needed to run—to keep moving—to escape from what was happening here.

I couldn't handle it. There wasn't enough of me left to handle it.

But if I didn't handle it, Stark would die.

"No." This time the word wasn't a ghostly, soundless scream. It was my voice—*my* voice, and not that awful not-here crap that had been babbling out of my mouth.

"Stark. Can. Not. Die." I tasted the words and followed their form and familiarity, listening for myself, as I stepped from the grove and headed to the black hole in the ground inside of which my Warrior had disappeared.

When the hole opened at my feet, I looked down to see Stark and Kalona facing each other in the middle of it. Stark was holding a gleaming sword in both of his hands against Kalona's dark spear.

I realized then that it wasn't just a hole in the ground. It was an arena. Kalona had created an arena with high walls, unbroken and slick. Walls that couldn't be climbed.

Kalona had Stark trapped. Now he couldn't run, even if he would listen to me. He couldn't escape. He also couldn't possibly win. And Kalona wouldn't be happy with beating Stark up a little—or even a lot. Kalona meant to kill Stark.

The restless numbness started to smother me again as Stark faced Kalona. I let my feet move but forced myself to stay where I could see the adversaries, walking the circumference of the arena as, unbelievably, Stark attacked the fallen immortal.

Laughing cruelly, Kalona deflected the sword with a flick of the spear, and with a movement so blindingly fast there was no way Stark could have seen it coming, Kalona smashed his open hand into Stark's face with ferocious, sneering disdain. Stark's forward momentum carried him awkwardly past the immortal, and he fell to the ground, holding his hands over his ears like he was trying to ease the pain in his head.

"A Guardian claymore—that's amusing. So you think you can stand with them?" Kalona spoke while Stark regained his balance and turned to face him again, his sword held up before him.

Blood trickled from Stark's ears, nose, and lips, making thin scarlet threads down his chin and neck. "I don't *think* I'm a Guardian. I *am* a Guardian."

"You can't be. I know your past, boy. I've seen you embrace Darkness. Tell the Guardians about that and then see if they still want you."

"The only other person who can make, or unmake, me a Guardian is my queen, and she knows about me *and my past*."

I watched Stark lunge again. With a disdainful sneer, Kalona used the spear to brush aside the blade. This time when he hit Stark, it was with his closed fist, and the force of it broke his nose and bloodied his cheekbones, knocking my Warrior to his back.

I held my breath, watching helplessly for what I knew would be Kalona's killing blow.

But the immortal didn't do anything except laugh while Stark struggled painfully to his feet. "Zoey isn't a queen. She isn't strong enough. She's just a weak girl who let herself be shattered by the death of one human boy," Kalona said.

"You're wrong. Zoey isn't weak; she cares! And about that human boy? That's part of the reason I'm here. I need to collect the life debt you owe for killing him."

"Fool! It's only Zoey who can collect that debt!"

With those words, it was as if Kalona had taken his spear and sliced through the fog of guilt that had been blanketing me since I'd watched him twist Heath's neck, allowing everything to become very clear to me.

I might not see myself as a queen—or as much of anything sometimes—but Stark believed in me. Heath believed in me. Stevie Rae believed in me. Even Aphrodite believed in me.

And, as Stevie Rae would have said, Kalona was as wrong as manboobs.

Caring about others didn't make me weak. It was the choices that I'd made because of that caring that defined me.

I'd let love shatter me once, and as I watched Kalona play with my Warrior, my Guardian, I chose to let honor heal me.

And that, finally, made my decision.

I turned my back on the arena and moved quickly to the edge of the Goddess's grove. Blocking out the sense of restlessness that threatened to pull me ever forward without really taking me anywhere, I made myself stand still. Spreading my arms wide I focused first on the last spirit who had spoken to me.

"Brighid! I need my strength back!"

The redhead materialized before me. She looked like a Goddess herself, all fiery and tall, full of power and confidence that I didn't have.

"No," I corrected myself out loud. "The power and confidence are mine. I just lost them for a while."

"Ready to accept them back?" she said, familiar eyes meeting mine.

"I am."

"Well, it's about time." She stepped forward and put her arms around me, pulling me close to her in an embrace that was as strong as it was intimate. My arms closed around her, and with that acceptance she dissolved against my skin, and I was filled with a surge of heat that was power—pure power.

"One down," I muttered. "Get your butt in gear, girl."

I spread my arms again. This time my feet stayed planted firmly on the earth and the desire to move, search, flee, flowed over and past me, harmless as spring rain.

"I need my joy back!"

My nine-year-old self didn't materialize. She bounded from the grove. Giggling, she hurled herself into my arms. I caught her, and, as she yelled, "Yippee!" she soaked into my soul.

Laughing, I spread my arms again. Joy and strength allowed me to accept the last of my missing soul—compassion.

"A-ya, I need you back, too," I called into the grove.

The Cherokee maid stepped gracefully from the tree line. "*A-de-lv*, sister, I am glad to hear you call my name.

"Yeah, well, I can honestly say I'm glad to have you as part of me. I accept you, A-ya. Totally. Will you come back?"

"I've been here all along. All you had to do was ask."

I met her halfway and hugged her hard, bringing her back to me, and in turn, bringing myself back.

"Now, let's see who's a weak little girl," I said, hurrying back to Kalona's arena.

I stepped to the edge and looked down. Stark was on his knees again. The sight of him squeezed my heart. My Guardian looked awful. His lips were swollen and split wide in a bunch of places. His nose had been smashed crooked and was oozing blood. His left shoulder was a shapeless, dislocated mess, leaving his arm dangling limply at his side. The beautiful sword was lying on the ground, just out of his reach. I could see that the bones of one foot and a kneecap had been shattered, but still Stark struggled along on the ground at Kalona's feet, hopelessly trying to move closer toward his claymore.

Kalona was hefting his spear as if he was testing the balance of it and studied Stark. "A broken Guardian for a shattered girl. It seems you two fit better together now," he said.

And that seriously pissed me off.

"You have no idea how tired I am of your crap, Kalona," I said.

Both of their heads snapped up. I didn't look away from Kalona, but I could feel Stark's grin.

"Go back to the grove, Zoey," Kalona said. "It is better for you there."

"You know what I really hate? Guys trying to tell me what to do."

"Yep, my queen, that's what Heath said." The grin was in Stark's voice now, and I had to look at him.

I met his battered gaze, and the pride in me I saw reflected there made my eyes fill with tears. "My Warrior . . ." I whispered to him.

That one instant—my one small mistake—was enough for Kalona. I heard him say, "You should have chosen to return to the grove." I saw Stark's eyes widen, and as my gaze flew back to the immortal, Kalona spun around, his right arm stretched back like an ancient warrior god. He released the spear with a burst of strength and speed that I knew I couldn't—

"No!" I screamed. "Come to me, air!" I leaped into the arena, trusting the element to cushion me, but even as I felt the current catch me, I saw it was too late.

Kalona's spear struck Stark in the middle of his chest. It traveled through his body, the barbs in the spear shank catching his rib cage and hurling him backward with such momentum that he was impaled against the far wall of the arena with sickening force.

My feet touched the ground, and I was already running to Stark. I reached him, and his gaze met mine. He was still alive!

"Don't die! Don't die! I can fix this. I have to be able to fix this."

Unbelievably, he smiled. "That's right. My queen won't let anything shatter her again. Collect your debt, and let's go home."

Stark closed his eyes and, with a smile on his broken lips, I watched his body convulse once. Bloody air bubbles foamed around the spear in his chest, and suddenly there was no movement, no sound from him at all. My Warrior was dead.

This time when I faced the being who had just killed someone I loved, I didn't give in to horror and pain. This time I kept spirit close to me instead of hurling it away, and from it I drew the power of knowledge and let instincts, and not guilt and despair, guide me.

Kalona shook his head. "I wish this could have ended differently. Had you listened to me, accepted me, it would have," he said.

"Glad to hear you agree with me, 'cause this *is* going to end differently," I said. Before I started toward him I picked up Stark's sword. It was heavier than I thought it was going to be, but it was still warm from Stark's hand, and that warmth helped me find the strength to lift it.

Kalona's smile was almost kind. "I won't fight you. That is my gift to you." He unfurled his great wings. "Goodbye, Zoey. I will miss you and think of you often."

"Air, don't let him leave." I flung the element at him. His fully spread wings were easily caught, and a mighty gust of wind pinned them against the wall of the arena, eerily mirroring Stark's final pose.

I walked up to him and, with no hesitation, drove the claymore through his chest.

"That's for Stark. I know this won't kill you, but it sure as hell feels good to do it," I said. "And I know he'll appreciate it."

Kalona's eyes glinted dangerously. "You cannot hold me here forever. And when you finally release me, I will make you pay for this."

"Okay, see, just like Stark said—you're wrong. Again. There are different rules in the Otherworld, so I probably could keep you here forever, if I wanted to stay and turn into Crazy Vengeance Girl, but here's the deal: I already almost turned into one kind of crazy girl. I'm not so much interested in doing that again. Plus, I want to go home. So, here's what you're gonna do. You're gonna pay me the life debt you owe me for killing my consort, Heath Luck, by bringing Stark back to me. Then Stark and me, we're going home. Oh, and by the way, I don't care where you'll be going."

"You've gone mad. I cannot bring the dead back to life."

"In this case, I think you can. Stark's body is safe back in the real world, along with mine. We're in the Otherworld, and it's all about spirit here. You're an immortal, which means you're all about spirit. So you're gonna take some of your immortal spirit and share it with my Guardian. And bring him back to me. Now. Because you owe it to me. Do you get it? I claim the debt, and it's time you paid up."

"You don't have the power to make me," Kalona said.

She does not, but I do.

The disembodied words settled down into the arena. I recognized the sound of Nyx's voice immediately and looked around expectantly, trying to see her. It was Kalona who found her, though. He was staring over my shoulder with an expression that utterly changed his face. It took me a second to recognize it. He'd looked at me with lust, with possessiveness, and even with what he'd called love. But he'd been wrong. He didn't love me. Kalona loved Nyx.

I followed his gaze and turned to see the Goddess standing beside Stark's body. One of her hands rested tenderly on his head.

"Nyx!" the immortal's voice sounded broken and surprisingly young. "My Goddess!"

Nyx's eyes lifted from Stark's body, but she didn't look at Kalona. The Goddess looked at me. She smiled, and everything within me was suffused in joy.

"Merry meet, Zoey."

I grinned, and bowed my head. "Merry meet, Nyx."

"You've done well, daughter. You've made me proud of you again."

"It took me too long," I said. "I'm sorry about that."

Her gaze was unwaveringly kind. "As always with you, as with many of my strongest daughters, it is yourselves you should be forgiving. There is no need to ask it of me."

"And what of me?" Kalona rasped. "Will you ever forgive me?"

The Goddess looked at him. Her eyes were sad, but the set of her mouth was grim, her words clipped and emotionless. "If you are ever worthy of forgiving, you may ask it of me. Not until then." Nyx lifted her hand from Stark's head and flicked her fingers at Kalona. The claymore disappeared from his chest. Wind abated, and he dropped from the wall of the arena. "You will pay my daughter the debt you owe her, and then you will return to the world and the consequences awaiting you there, knowing this, my fallen Warrior, your spirit, as well as your body, is forbidden entrance to my realm." Without another glance at Kalona, Nyx turned her back to him. She bent to kiss Stark's bloody lips gently, and then the air around her rippled, glistened, and she faded away.

When Kalona got to his feet I backed away from him fast, lifting my hands and getting ready to throw air at him again. Then his eyes met mine, and I saw that he was weeping silently.

"I will do as she commands. Except for one time, one single time, I always did as she commanded," he said.

I followed him as he walked to Stark's body. "I return to you that last sweet breath of life. With it live again, and accept a small piece of my immortality for the human life I have taken." Then, totally shocking me, Kalona bent and, mimicking Nyx, he kissed Stark.

Stark's body jerked. He gasped and inhaled a long breath.

Before I could stop him, Kalona put one hand on Stark's shoulder, and with the other he wrenched the spear from his body. With an agonized cry, Stark collapsed.

"You jerk!" I ran to Stark and cradled his head on my lap. He was breathing hard, in panting gasps, but he was breathing. I looked up at Kalona. "No wonder she won't forgive you. You're cruel and heartless and just plain wrong."

"When you get back to the world, stay away from me. You'll be out of her realm then, and Nyx won't come running to save you," he said.

"The farther I am from you, the better."

Kalona stretched open his wings, but before he could take to the sky, tendrils of Darkness, sticky and sharp, oozed from the black sides of the arena and the pitch-colored dirt beneath his feet. While he stared at me, they wrapped around his body, slicing his flesh. Segment by segment they cut him, covered him, until he was nothing but writhing darkness, blood, and amber eyes. Then the tendrils reached his eyes, plunging into them. I cried out in horror as they ripped something that was so bright and shining from inside him that I had to close my eyes against its brilliance. When I opened them again Kalona's body had disappeared along with the arena, and Stark and I were inside the grove.

CHAPTER THIRTY

Zoey

"Zoey! What is it? What's happened?" Stark struggled, trying to make his broken body work.

"Ssh, it's okay. Everything's okay. Kalona's gone. We're safe."

His gaze found mine, and all the tension went out of him. He slumped in my arms and let me cradle his head in my lap. "It's you again. You're not shattered anymore."

"It's me again." I touched his cheek in one of the few places on his face that wasn't bloody, broken, or bruised. "This time you're the one who looks shattered."

"No, Z. As long as you're whole, I'll be fine." He coughed then. Blood poured from the gaping wound in his chest. His eyes closed, and his face contorted in agony.

Oh, Goddess! He's hurt so badly! I tried to speak calmly. "Okay, good, but you don't really look fine. So how about you and me get back to our bodies. They are both waiting for us, right?"

Another shudder of pain went through him. He was breathing in shallow, panting breaths, but he opened his eyes to meet mine. "You should go back. I'll follow you after I rest a little while."

Panic fluttered around inside me. "Oh, no. I'm so not leaving you here. Just tell me what you need to get back."

He blinked a few times and then his broken lips curled in a hint of his cocky smile. "I don't exactly know how to get back."

"You don't what? Stark, seriously."

"Seriously. I don't really have a clue."

"How'd you get here?"

His lips curled again. "Through pain."

I snorted. "Well, then getting you back should be easy 'cause you have some pain going on here."

"Yeah, but back there I have an ancient Guardian in charge of keeping me on the line between life and death. I don't exactly know how to tell him it's time for me to wake up. How are you getting back?"

I didn't even need to think about it. The answer was as natural as breathing. "I'm going to follow spirit to my body. It's where I belong, back there, in the real world."

"Do that." He had to pause as another wave of pain engulfed him. "And after I rest, I'll do the same thing."

"No, you don't have an affinity for spirit like I do. It won't work for you."

"It's good that you still have your elements. I wondered about that, what with your tattoos being gone."

"Gone?" I turned my hand over and, sure enough, there were no tattoos filling my palms with sapphire filigree. Then I glanced down at my chest. The long pink scar was there, but it, too, was tattoo free. "Are they all gone? Even the ones on my face?"

"All that's left is the crescent," he said. Then he grimaced in pain again. Clearly beyond his exhaustion level, he closed his eyes, and said, "Go ahead and follow spirit home. I'll figure something out. When I'm not so tired. Don't worry. I won't leave you—not really."

"Oh, hell no. I'm not losing another boy with some kind of abstract I'll-see-you-again Zoey thing. That's not working for me ever, *ever* again."

He opened his eyes. "Then tell me what to do, my queen. And I'll do it."

I ignored the "my queen" stuff. I mean, I'd heard him call me that earlier, and then again to Kalona. I wondered briefly if that had been before or after the immortal had started smacking him in the head, then I focused on the "I'll do it" part of what he'd said. So, he'd do what I told him . . . but what the heck did I need to tell him to do?

I looked down at him. He was so messed up—even worse than he had been when he'd taken the arrow meant to kill me and burned the crap out of his chest, almost dying. Again.

But then he'd gotten better pretty much on his own. He'd had to. I'd been messed up, too.

I drew a deep breath, remembering the whole Mother Hen lecture Darius had given me when I'd wanted Stark to feed from me so he could heal quicker. He'd explained that between a Warrior and his High Priestess, the bond was so strong that Warriors could sometimes sense emotions from their High Priestesses. I glanced down at Stark's bruised face. He'd definitely been able to do that. When that happened, they could also absorb more from their High Priestesses than their blood—they could absorb energy.

Which was exactly what Stark needed—energy to heal—energy to return to his body.

This time he wouldn't get better on his own and, thank the Goddess, I wasn't messed up anymore.

"Hey," I said. "I know what I want you to do."

His eyes fluttered open, and I hated the pain that I saw reflected within them. "Tell me. If I can do it, I will."

I smiled at him. "I want you to bite me."

He looked surprised and then, even though it obviously hurt him, his cocky smile was back. "*Now* you ask me? When my body's totally messed up. Great."

"Don't be such a guy," I told him. "It's because you're body's totally messed up that I'm asking you.

"I'd make you think differently if I was well."

I shook my head at him and rolled my eyes. "If you were well, I'd smack you right now." And then, moving carefully, trying to be as gentle as I could, I slid him off my lap. He tried to stifle a groan. "Sorry! I'm so sorry I'm hurting you." I lay down beside him and started to pull him into my arms, wanting to hold him close to me as if I could absorb his pain.

"It's okay," he gasped. "Just help me onto my good side."

Good side? I wasn't sure whether I should laugh or burst into tears, but I helped him turn on his side, the one that didn't have the shattered shoulder, so that we could face each other. Tentatively, I moved closer to him, thinking that I should maybe slice down my arm so he could drink from me more easily without moving too much.

"No." His hand twitched, trying to reach out to me. "Not like that. Come closer to me, Z. The pain doesn't matter." He paused, then added, "Unless you can't because of my blood. Does this make you need it?"

"The blood?" I realized what he was saying and blinked in surprise. "I haven't even noticed it." Seeing his wry expression, I went on, "I mean I *noticed* that you're bleeding all over. I didn't smell it." Wonderingly, I touched the blood on his lip with my fingertip. "It doesn't make my bloodlust happen."

"We're spirit here, that must be why," he said.

"Then will this work? You feeding from me?"

His eyes met mine. "It'll work, Z. Between us there's more than physical stuff. We're bound by spirit."

"Okay, good. I hope so," I said, feeling suddenly nervous. The only other guy I'd let feed from me had been Heath—my Heath. My mind skittered away from thoughts of him and comparisons with Stark, but I couldn't deny one aspect of what was about to happen. Letting a guy drink my blood was sexual. It felt good. Really good. That was how we'd been made. It was normal, natural, and right.

It was also making my stomach hurt.

"Hey, just relax and bring your neck over here."

My wide eyes took in Stark's battered face and his broken body.

"Yeah, I know you're nervous, but as messed up as I am, you don't need to be." His expression changed. "Or is it more than being nervous? Are you changing your mind about wanting to?"

"No," I said quickly. "I'm not changing my mind. I won't change my mind about you, Stark. Ever."

Trying to be as careful as I could, I moved closer to him. Scooting up so that the curve of my neck was near his mouth, I swept back my hair and leaned over him, holding myself tense, ready for his bite.

But he surprised me. Instead of his teeth I felt the warmth of his lips as he kissed my neck gently. "Relax, my queen."

His breath made shivers go down my skin. I trembled. How long had it been since anyone had really touched me? It must only be days back in the real world, but here, in the Otherworld, it felt like I'd been untouched and untouchable for centuries.

Stark kissed me again. His tongue touched my neck and he moaned. This time I didn't think it was from pain. He didn't hesitate any longer. His teeth nicked my neck. It stung, but as soon as his lips closed on the small cut, pain was replaced by pleasure so intense that it was my turn to moan.

I wanted to wrap my arms around him and lock my body with his, but I held myself very still, trying my best not to cause him any more pain.

Too soon his mouth left my skin. His voice already sounded stronger when he said, "Do you know when I first knew I belonged to you?" His breath whispered warm against my neck, making me shiver again.

"When?" I sounded breathless.

"It was when you faced me down in the infirmary back at the House of Night, before I'd Changed. Do you remember?"

"I remember." Of course I remembered—I'd been naked and threatened to kick his butt with the elements as I stood between him and Darius.

I could feel his lips tilt up against my skin. "You looked like a Warrior queen, filled with the Goddess's anger. I think that was when I knew I would always belong to you, because you reached me even through all that darkness."

"Stark." I whispered his name, utterly overwhelmed by what I was feeling for him. "This time you reached me. Thank you. Thank you for coming after me."

With a wordless sound, his mouth was on my neck again, and this time he bit harder, and really drank from me.

Again, pleasure quickly replaced the sting of pain. I closed my eyes and concentrated on the exquisite heat that was rushing through my body. I couldn't stop myself from touching him, and slid one hand around his waist so that I could feel the tight muscles just underneath the skin of his back. I wanted more of him. I wanted him closer to me.

He took his lips from my neck, and he actually held himself up. His eyes were dark with passion, and he was breathing hard. "Now, Zoey, will you give me more than just your blood? Will you accept me as your Guardian?"

I stared at him. In his eyes there was something that I'd never seen within him before. The boy who had walked away from me in Venice, jealous and pissed, was gone. The man who had grown in his place was more than a vampyre, more than a Warrior. Even as he lay there broken in my arms, I could feel the strength in him: solid, dependable, honorable.

"Guardian?" I said wonderingly, touching his face. "So that's what you've Changed into?"

His gaze never left mine. "Yes, if you accept me. Without his queen's acceptance a Guardian isn't anything."

"But I'm not really a queen."

His torn lips didn't stop Stark's cocky smile. "You're *my* queen, and anyone who says different can fuck off."

I smiled at him. "I already accepted your Oath as my Warrior."

Stark's cockiness was instantly gone. "This is different, Zoey. It's more. It might change things between us."

I touched his face again. I didn't really understand what he was asking, but I knew that he needed something more from me, and I knew that whatever I said and did now would affect us for the rest of our lives. *Goddess, give me the right words,* I prayed silently.

"James Stark, from here on out I accept you as my Guardian, and I also accept all that goes with it."

He turned his head and kissed my palm. "Then I will serve you with my honor and my life, forever Zoey. My Ace, *mo bann ri,* my queen."

His oath rippled through me like a physical thing. Stark was right. It was different than what had happened between us when he'd sworn his Oath to me as a Warrior. This time it was as if he'd given me a piece of himself, and I knew that without me, he could never truly be whole again. The responsibility of it scared me almost as much as it strengthened me, and I pulled his mouth down to my neck again.

"Take more from me, Stark. Let me heal you."

With a moan, his mouth met my neck. His bite deepened, and something completely amazing happened. First, the unique power that accompanied the element air surged into me and flowed from me to Stark. He shivered and I knew it was from the intense pleasure that was filling him as the element gifted him with a swirling rush of energy. At the same instant a sweet, familiar pain swept over my forehead and cheekbones, and against my closed eyelids I got the flash of an image of Damien, shouting with joy. I gasped in amazement. I didn't have to ask. I didn't need a mirror to see. I knew the first of my tattoos had returned.

Following closely behind air came fire. It heated me and then spread throughout Stark, filling him, strengthening him, so that he was able to lift his arm and pull me closer, drinking even more deeply. Sensation burned down my back as my second tattoo returned, and I saw Shaunee laughing and doing her victory bump and grind.

Water washed through us then, bathing us, filling us, continuing to carry us around the circle we'd begun. I kept my eyes tightly closed, taking in every moment of the miracle Stark and I were experiencing together, and trembled with pleasure as my third tattoo, the one that wrapped around my waist, returned, while Erin laughed and yelled, "Hell, yes! Z's coming back!"

Earth came next, and it was like Stark and I became a part of the grove. We knew the rich pleasure of it and the power that rested there in the roots and ground and moss. Stark's hold on me got stronger. He shifted me in his arms so that he was over me. His arms cradled me to him, and I knew his wounds no longer pained him because I could feel what he felt. I shared his joy and pleasure and wonder. My palms were seared by the Goddess's touch again, as my fourth tattoo returned. Strangely, I didn't get a visual image of Stevie Rae as her element filled me, only a sense of her and a distant joy, as if she had somehow moved beyond my reach.

Spirit sizzled through us last, and suddenly I didn't simply feel what Stark felt—it was like we were joined. Not in body, but in soul. And our souls blazed together with a brilliance that was brighter than any physical passion could ever be as my final tattoo returned.

With a gasp, Stark pulled his lips from my skin and buried his face in my neck. His body was trembling, and his breath was coming fast, like he'd just sprinted a marathon. His tongue touched the wound he'd made on my neck, and I knew he was closing and healing it. I raised my hand to caress his hair, and was shocked to feel that the sweat and blood was gone from him.

He lifted himself up then and, struggling to get his breathing under control, stared down at me.

Goddess, he was gorgeous! Just moments before he'd been mortally wounded, beaten, bloody, and so broken he could hardly move. Now he radiated energy and health and strength.

"That was the most amazing thing that's ever happened to me," he said. Then his eyes widened. "Your tattoos!" He touched my face reverently. I turned my head so that his fingers could trace the filigree markings that, once again, covered my back and shoulders. Then I lifted my hand so he could press his palm against mine and the sapphire symbols there.

"They're all back," I said. "The elements brought them."

Stark shook his head in wonder. "I felt it. I didn't know what was happening, but I felt it with you." He pulled me into his arms again. "I felt everything with you, my queen."

Before I kissed him, I said, "And I'm a part of you now, my Guardian."

Stark kissed me for a long time, and then he just held me close to him, touching me gently as if he was trying to convince himself I wasn't going to evaporate from his arms.

He kept holding me when I cried for Heath, and he told me about how Heath had made the choice to move on, and how brave he'd been.

Stark hadn't really had to tell me that part, though. I knew how brave Heath really was, just like I knew his bravery was part of how I'd recognize him again. That, and his love. Always his love for me.

After I was done crying and mourning and remembering, I wiped my eyes and let Stark help me to my feet.

"Are you ready to go home now?" I asked him.

"Oh, yeah. Home sounds good. But, uh, Z, how am I getting there?"

I grinned at him. "By trusting me."

"Ach, well, it'll be a wee easy trip then, won't it?"

"Where the heck did you get that Irish accent?"

"Irish! Are yie deaf, wumman?" he growled the words at me while I frowned at him. Then Stark's laughter filled the grove. He hugged me, and said, "Scottish, Z, not Irish. And you'll see where I got it real soon."

CHAPTER THIRTY-ONE

Stevie Rae

As the sun set, Stevie Rae's eyes opened. For a second she was super confused. It was dark, but that didn't disorient her—that was cool. She could feel the earth around her, cradling and shielding her—that was cool, too. There was a slight movement off to her side, and she turned her head. Her keen night vision was able to differentiate one depth of blackness from another, and the huge wing took form, followed by a body.

Rephaim.

Everything came back to her then: the red fledglings, Dallas, and Rephaim. Always Rephaim.

"You stayed down here with me?"

His eyes opened, and she felt her own widen in surprise. The blazing scarlet within them had calmed to a rusty color that was more amber than red.

"I did. You're vulnerable when the sun is in the sky."

She thought he sounded nervous, almost apologetic, so she grinned at him. "Thanks, even though it's kinda stalkerlike of you to watch me sleep."

"I did not watch you sleep!"

He said it so quickly that it was obvious he was lying. She opened her mouth to tell him it was okay—that he didn't need to do it all the time, but that it was real nice of him to be sure she stayed safe, especially after the day she'd had—and her phone chose then to chirp its "You have voice mail" sound.

"It has been making noise. A lot of noise," Rephaim told her.

"Crap. I can't hear nothing when I'm 'sleep like that." She sighed and reluctantly picked up the iPhone from where she'd set it beside her. "I guess I'd better face the dang music." Stevie Rae opened the screen, saw the battery was almost dead, and sighed again. She tapped to the missed-call screen. "Ah, crap. Six missed calls. One from Lenobia and five from Aphrodite." Heart pounding, she clicked into Lenobia's first. Putting it on speaker she glanced at Rephaim. "You might as well hear what's goin' on. They're probably gonna be talkin' 'bout you."

But Lenobia's voice didn't sound all "Holy crap you're with a Raven Mocker and I'm gonna have to come hunt you down!" She seemed totally normal. *"Stevie Rae, call me when you awaken. Kramisha said she wasn't sure where you were, but that you're safe even though Dallas ran off. I'll come get you right away."* She hesitated, lowered her voice, and added, *"She also told me what happened with the other red fledglings. I've sent prayers to Nyx for their spirits. Blessed be, Stevie Rae."*

She smiled up at Rephaim. "Aw, that was nice of her."

"Dallas hasn't reached her yet."

"No," she said, her smile going out. "Definitely not." She turned her attention back to the phone. "Four missed calls from Aphrodite, but she only left one message. Here's hoping it's not scary bad news." She clicked the PLAY button. Aphrodite's voice sounded tinny and distant, but no less bitchy.

"Oh for shit's sake, answer your fucking phone! Or are you in your casket? Goddess! Time zones are annoying. Anyway, update: Z's still an eggplant, and Stark's still checked out and being sliced up. That's the good news. The bad news is my newest vision stars you, a hottie Indian kid, and the biggest baddie of all the Raven Mockers, Rephaim. We need to talk 'cause I have one of my feelings about this, which means Not Good. So hurry the hell up and call me. If I'm sleeping, I'll actually wake up and answer you."

"Big surprise that she hung up without saying bye," Stevie Rae said. Not wanting to stay in the same room with the words *and the biggest baddie of all the Raven Mockers, Rephaim,* hovering around, she shoved her phone in her pocket and started up the basement stairs. She didn't have to look behind her to make sure he was following. She knew he would.

The night was cool, but not cold, right on the edge of that freezing/slushy line. Stevie Rae felt sorry for the poor people in the houses surrounding the Gilcrease and was glad to see a bunch of the lights were back on. But at the same time, it gave her an eerie "we're being watched" feeling, and she hesitated on the front porch of the mansion.

"No one is about. They're putting their focus on fixing the power to the people first. This will be one of the last places they come, especially at night."

Relieved, Stevie Rae nodded and left the porch, walking aimlessly toward the fountain that sat silent and cold in the middle of the yard.

"Your people are going to find out about me," Rephaim said.

"Some of them already have." Stevie Rae reached down and touched the top edge of the fountain, breaking off an icicle that was suspended there and letting it fall into the water in the basin below.

"What will you do?" Rephaim stood beside her. They both stared down at the dark fountain water as if they could discover the answer there.

Finally, Stevie Rae said, "I think the question is more like, what will you do?"

"What would you have me do?"

"Rephaim, you can't answer my question with a question."

He made a derisive noise. "You did mine."

"Rephaim, stop. Tell me what you want to do about, well, *us*."

She stared at his changed eyes, wishing his features were easier to read. He took so long to answer that she thought he wasn't going to, and frustration gnawed at her. She had to get back to the House of Night. She had to do damage control there before Dallas messed everything up.

"What I would do is stay with you."

His words, simple, honest, and said in one rush didn't sink in at first. At first she just looked at him questioningly, unable to fully grasp what he'd said. And then she truly heard him, and understood, and she felt an unexpected, unwanted, rush of joy.

"It's going to be bad," she said. "But I want you to stay with me, too."

"They'll try to kill me. You must know that."

"I won't let them!" Stevie Rae reached out and took his hand. Slowly, very slowly, his fingers twined with hers, and he gave a little tug, pulling her closer to his side. "I won't let them," she repeated. She didn't look at him. Instead, she held his hand and stole one small moment together. She tried not to think too much. She tried not to question everything. She stared down into the still, black water of the fountain, and the cloud that was blanketing the moon lifted, revealing their reflection. *I'm a girl who's somehow been bound to the humanity of a guy who is a beast.* Aloud, she said, "I'm bound to you, Rephaim."

Without any hesitation he said, "And I you, Stevie Rae."

As he spoke, the water rippled, as if Nyx herself had breathed across its surface, and their reflection changed. The image revealed in the water was Stevie Rae holding the hand of a tall, muscular Native American boy. His hair was thick and long, and as black as the raven feathers that were braided into its length. His chest was bare, and he was hotter than an Oklahoma blacktop in the middle of the summer.

Stevie Rae stayed very still, afraid if she moved the reflection would change. But she couldn't help smiling and, softly she said, "Wow, you're really pretty."

The guy in the reflection blinked a bunch of times, like he wasn't sure he was seeing clearly, then in Rephaim's voice, he said, "Yes, but I don't have wings."

Stevie Rae's heart fluttered, and her stomach tightened. She wanted to say something profound and really smart, or at least a little romantic. Instead, she heard herself say, "Sure, that's true, but you are tall and you got those cool feathers braided into your hair."

In the reflection, the boy lifted the hand that wasn't holding hers and touched his hair. "They're not much if you compare them to wings," he said, but he smiled at Stevie Rae.

"Well, yeah, but I'll bet they're easier to fit into shirts."

He laughed, and with an obvious sense of wonder, let his hand touch his face. "Soft," Rephaim said. "The human face is so soft."

"Yeah, it is," Stevie Rae said, totally mesmerized by what was happening in their reflection.

As slowly as he'd woven their fingers together, without taking his gaze from their reflection, Rephaim reached from his face to hers. His hand touched her skin lightly, gently. He stroked her cheek and let his fingers brush her lips. She smiled, then, and couldn't help an awkward giggle. "It's just that you're so pretty!"

Rephaim's human reflection smiled, too. "*You're* pretty," he said so softly she almost didn't hear him.

Heart hammering, she said, "You think so? Really?"

"Really. I just can't ever tell you. I can't ever let you know how I really feel."

"You are now," she said.

"I know. For the first time I feel—"

Rephaim's words cut off midsentence. The reflection of the boy wavered and then disappeared. In its place Darkness lifted from the still water, forming the shape of a raven's wings and the body of a powerful immortal.

"Father!"

Rephaim didn't need to speak the name. Stevie Rae knew what had come between them the moment it had happened. She pulled her hand from his. He resisted for only an instant before letting her go. Then he turned to face her, bringing one dark wing forward to blot out her view of their reflection in the fountain.

"He's returned to his body. I can feel it."

Stevie Rae didn't trust herself to speak. She could only nod.

"He's not here, though. He's far away from me. Must still be in Italy." Rephaim was speaking rapidly. Stevie Rae took a step away from him, still unable to say anything at all. "He feels different. Something has changed." Then it was like his thoughts were catching up to him, and Rephaim's eyes met hers. "Stevie Rae? What are we going to—"

Stevie Rae gasped, cutting off his words. Earth swirled around her, filling her senses with a joyous dance of homecoming. The cold Tulsa landscape shimmered, shifted, and suddenly she was surrounded by amazing trees, all green and shiny-leafed, and a bed made of thick, soft moss. Then the image focused, and Zoey was there, in Stark's arms, laughing and whole again.

"Zoey!" Stevie Rae shouted, and the image disappeared, leaving only the joy of it and the certainty that her BFF was whole again and most definitely alive. Grinning, she went to Rephaim and threw her arms around him. "Zoey's alive!"

His arms tightened around her, but only for the space of a breath, and then they both remembered the truth, and at the same time, stepped away from each other.

"My father returns."

"So does Zoey."

"And for us that means we cannot be together," he said.

Stevie Rae felt sick and sad. She shook her head. "No, Rephaim. It only means that if you let it."

"Look at me!" he cried. "I'm not the boy in the reflection. I'm a beast. I don't belong with you."

"That's not what your heart says!" she shouted back at him.

His shoulders slumped, and he looked away from her. "But, Stevie Rae, my heart has never mattered."

She stepped close to him. Automatically, he faced her. Their gazes met, and with a terrible despair she saw that the scarlet was, once again, blazing in his eyes. "Well, when you decide your heart matters as much to you as it does to me, come find me again. It should be easy. Just follow your heart." Without any hesitation, she put her arms around him and held him tightly. Stevie Rae ignored the fact that he didn't return her embrace. Instead, she whispered, "I'll miss you," before she left him.

As she started walking down Gilcrease Road, the night wind brought to her Rephaim's whispered, *I'll miss you, too . . .*

Zoey

"It's really beautiful," I said, looking up at the tree and the zillions of dangling strips of cloth tied there. "What do you call it again?"

"A hanging tree," Stark said.

"Doesn't seem a very romantic name for something so cool," I said.

"Yeah, that's what I thought at first, too, but it's kinda grown on me."

"Ooh! Look at that piece. It's so sparkly." I pointed up at a thin ribbon of gold that had suddenly appeared. Unlike the rest of the strips of cloth, it wasn't tied to another. Instead, it floated free down and down until it wafted just above us.

Stark reached up and snagged it. He held it out to me so that I could touch its bright softness. "It's what I followed to find you."

"Really? It's like a thread of gold."

"Yep, gold's what it reminded me of, too."

"And you followed this to find me?"

"Yep."

"Okay, well, then. Let's see if it'll work twice," I said.

"Just tell me what to do. I'm yours to command." Eyes flashing with humor, Stark bowed to me.

"Stop messing around. This is serious."

"Oh, Z, don't you see? It isn't that I don't think this is serious. It's just that I totally trust you. I know you'll get me back with you. I believe in you, *mo bann ri*."

"You have picked up some weird words while I've been gone."

He grinned at me. "Just you wait. You haven't heard nothin' yet."

"You know what, boy? I'm tired of waiting." I wrapped one end of the golden thread around his wrist. I kept the other end tightly fisted in my hand. "Close your eyes," I said. Without questioning me, he did as I said. I tiptoed and kissed him. "See you soon, Guardian."

Then I turned away from the hanging tree and the grove and all the magic and mysteries of Nyx's realm. I faced the yawning blackness that seemed to stretch into forever. Spreading my arms wide, I said, "Spirit, come to me." The last of the five elements, and the one I'd always felt closest to, filled me, making my healed soul thrum with joy and compassion, strength and—finally—hope. "Now, please take me home!" As I spoke, I ran forward and, completely unafraid, leaped into the darkness.

I thought it would be like diving off a cliff, but I was wrong. It was gentler, softer. More like riding an elevator down from the top of a skyscraper. I felt myself settle, and I *knew* I was back.

I didn't open my eyes right away. First I wanted to concentrate—to savor each returning sensation. I felt that I was lying on something hard and cool. I drew in a deep breath and was surprised to smell the cedar tree that used to be on the corner down from my mom's house in Broken Arrow. I only heard the soft murmuring of whispered voices at first, but after just a few breaths that changed with Aphrodite's shout of "Oh, for shit's sake, open your eyes! I know you're in there!"

I did open my eyes then. "Jeesh, are you from a trailer? Do you have to be so loud?"

"Trailer? Look, you're not supposed to be cussing, and that's definitely a nasty word to me," Aphrodite said. Then she smiled and laughed and pulled me into a super hard hug that I was sure she'd deny ever doing later. "You're really back? And you're not, like, brain-damaged or anything?"

"I am!" I laughed. "And I'm no more brain-damaged than I was when I left."

Over her shoulder Darius appeared. His eyes were suspiciously shiny as he fisted a hand over his heart and bowed to me. "Welcome back, High Priestess."

"Thanks, Darius." I grinned at him and held out my hand so he could help me stand. I had weird jelly legs, so I kept hold of him as the room rolled and pitched around me.

"She needs food and drink," said a super in-charge-like voice.

"Right away, Majesty," came the immediate response.

I finally blinked the dizziness clear, so that I could see. "Wow, a throne! Seriously?"

The beautiful woman sitting on the carved marble throne smiled at me. "Welcome back, young queen," she said.

"Young queen," I repeated, half-laughing. But as my eyes traveled around the room, my laughter dissolved, and the throne, the cool room, and questions of queendom utterly evaporated.

Stark was there. He was lying on a huge stone. There was a vampyre Warrior standing at his head, and the guy was holding a razor-sharp dagger above Stark's chest, which was already bloody and covered with knife slashes.

"No! Stop it!" I cried. I pulled away from Darius and started to lunge toward the vamp.

More quickly than she should have been able to move, the queen was suddenly standing between the Warrior and me. She put a hand on my shoulder and spoke one question softly to me. "What did Stark tell you?"

I shook myself mentally, trying to think beyond the bloody sight of my Warrior, my Guardian.

My Guardian . . .

I looked at the queen. "That's how Stark got to the Otherworld. That Warrior. He's really helping him."

"My Guardian," the queen corrected me. "Yes, he is helping Stark. But now his quest is complete. It is your responsibility as his queen to bring him back."

I opened my mouth to ask her how, but closed it before I spoke. I didn't have to ask her. I knew. And it was my responsibility to help my Guardian return.

She must have seen it in my eyes, because the queen bowed her head, ever so slightly, and then stepped aside.

I walked over to the man she'd called her Guardian. Sweat slicked his muscular chest. He was completely focused on Stark. It seemed he didn't see or hear anyone else in the room. As he lifted the knife, obviously getting ready to make another cut, the torchlight glinted off a golden bracelet that was fashioned to twist around his wrist. I understood then where the golden thread that had led Stark to me had come from, and I felt a rush of warmth for the queen's Guardian. I touched his wrist gently, beside the piece of gold, and said, "Guardian, you can stop now. It's time for him to come back."

His hand stopped instantly. A tremor went through the Guardian's body. When he looked at me, I saw that the pupils of his blue eyes were fully dilated.

"You can stop now," I repeated gently. "And thank you for helping Stark get to me."

He blinked, and his eyes cleared. His voice was gravelly, and I almost smiled when I recognized the Scottish accent Stark had mimicked for me. "Aye, wumman . . . as yie wish." He staggered back. I knew that the queen had taken him in her arms, and I could hear her murmuring things to him. I knew other Warriors were in the room, too, and I could feel Aphrodite and Darius watching me—but I ignored them all.

To me, Stark was the only person in the room. The only thing that mattered.

I went to him where he was lying on the stone in his pooling blood. This time the scent of it came to me, and it did affect me. Sweet and heady, it made my mouth water. But it had to stop. Now was not the time for my head to be messed up by Stark's blood and the desire that lingered in me for it.

I lifted my hand. "Water, come to me." When the soft dampness of the element surrounded me, I waved my hand over Stark's bloody body. "Wash this from him." The element did as I asked, raining gently on him. I watched it clean the blood from his chest, pour over the stone, follow the intricate knotwork all down the sides of the huge boulder and fill the two grooves that cut into the floor on either side of it. *Horns,* I realized. *They remind me of super big horns.*

Weirdly enough, when the blood was all washed away, the grooves weren't white like the rest of the floor. Instead, they shimmered a beautiful, mystical black, reminding me of the night sky.

But I didn't take time to wonder at the magic I felt there. I went to Stark. His body was clean now. The wounds weren't bleeding anymore, but they were raw and red. And then I realized what I was seeing and I drew in a deep breath. On each side of Stark's chest the slash work formed arrows, complete with feathers and pointed, triangular tips. They made a perfect balance to the burned broken arrow over his heart.

I put my hand out then and rested it on top of that scar, the one from the time he'd saved my life—the first time he'd saved my life. I was surprised to find that I still clutched the golden thread. Gently, I lifted Stark's wrist and wrapped the thread of gold around there. The silky length hardened, twisted, and closed, looking much like the old Guardian's, except on Stark's bracelet I could see caved images of three arrows—one of them broken.

"Thank you, Goddess," I whispered. "Thank you for everything."

Then I placed my hand over Stark's heart and leaned down. Just before I pressed my lips to his, I said, "Come back to your queen, Guardian. It's all over now." Then I kissed him.

As his eyelids fluttered and opened, I heard Nyx's musical laughter fill my mind, and her voice saying:

No, daughter, it's not all over. It's just beginning . . .

The end for now

Stay tuned for more in the next instalment of the House of Night